A Six Pack Of Brewpub Mysteries

Numbers 7 through 12

Written by

Fredric G. Bender

Cover design
by
Alex Yarborough

All rights reserved: no part of this publication may be reproduced or transmitted by any means without the prior permission of the author.

A Six Pack of Brewpub Mysteries is a work of fiction. Any resemblance to actual persons, living or dead, is purely coincidental. Any resemblance to actual brewpubs, breweries or bars is purely coincidental.

Content

Jim and Laura Verraten are a young married couple living on the Southside Flats of Pittsburgh. Jim is a cyber security expert who knows how to keep hackers out and let himself in. Laura works for a travel magazine writing articles of interest on various localities she visits. Often the two are together in their professional travels around America. They have a hobby of trying to visit brewpubs in any town that they happen to be in and always enjoy a good brew or two. It just seems that whenever they do, they get more than they bargain for, usually a corpse or two. The game is afoot!

7 *A Trout in the Milk Stout* 7

After a week of business, the weekend at Carmel, Ca is being enjoyed by Jim and Laura Verraten and they have settled into a brewpub – Oliver's Organic Lagers and Ales. What they were hoping for was a quiet, relaxing time by the Pacific seaside. What they received was not only a dead body but a hard to crack clue.

8 *A Shot and a Stout* 57

Deep in West Virginia coal country is the Bituminous Brewpub in an old company store. Jim and Laura Verraten decide it will make for an interesting evening after work. They learn of some famous coal mining songs and also discover the bonding one coal miner has for the other. Hunting accident or murder – You be the judge.

9 The Maibock Medium Mystery 117

Jim and Laura Verraten are in New England where Laura is working on an article. They decided to stay in a B&B in the quaint touristy town of Mystic with its ties to the days of whaling, a harbor and a brewpub named the Bowsprit. How can Moby Dick and Herman Melville help solve a most mysterious murder?

10 Horror in the Hop Yard 191

The Verratens are in the State of Washington and decide to visit a farmhouse brewpub, the 484, in the heart of the Nation's largest hop growing area – the Yakima Valley. They have signed up for a course on hops but they get much more than they have signed up for when a mutilated corpse is found in the hop yard?

11 The Banker and the Berliner Weisse ...267

Jim and Laura Verraten are in Columbus, Ohio where Jim is presenting a solution to ransomware to State officials. They find a brewpub named after a famous German painter, Albrecht Durer, and meet an interesting banker at the bar only to find that the still waters on the Scioto River run deep, very deep!

12 The Patsy and the Porter **331**

A Murder Mystery play, set on an old time train ride through the Ozarks, catches the interest of Jim and Laura Verraten. The step back in time includes a step in another direction entirely where Jim has no access to his always helpful computer.

Bonus: The Verratens Call *395*

Appearing to be in authority, the Verratens enter a brewpub whose owner has goals higher than making beer. Confronted with reality those dreams crumble to dust, yet the owner was not guilty of any crime let alone a murder.

Also by the author:

Available on Amazon and Kindle

Brewpub Mystery Series:

Jim and Laura Verraten enjoy brewpubs almost as much as they like solving murders. Travel with them across the United States where their jobs as cyber security expert and travel writer take them and where they always seem to find the best brewpub in town - - - and Oh! a murder or two.

Prelude to a Waterfall:

Civil War historical fiction about two young men, one from Lenoir, North Carolina and one from Troy, New York, caught up in the flow of their time. Heavy on the Prelude and light on the Generals, this work adds dimension to anyone interested in the Civil War and those young men who fought it.

The Barn Find:

Fiction. An Isotta Fraschini limousine from the Roaring Twenties comes on the market in need of restoration. A small town mechanic and car restorer goes way out on the limb to purchase and restore a once in a lifetime classic not knowing what all he is getting himself into. If only cars could talk.

A Trout in the Milk Stout

7 from the Series

A Brewpub Mystery

by

Fredric G. Bender

All rights reserved: no part of this publication may be reproduced or transmitted by any means without the prior permission of the author.

A Trout in the Milk Stout is a work of fiction. Any resemblance to actual persons, living or dead, is purely coincidental. Any resemblance to actual brewpubs, breweries or bars is purely coincidental

Milk Stout

An English style of stout using lactose, milk sugar, as a sweetener. Derived in the latter 1800's from 'Stout Porters' signifying a very strong Porter, but now brewed to be less alcohol than a Porter. The historical name 'Milk Stout' is no longer used in England but often may be found elsewhere.

Malt Bill: Pale malt base; roasted barley, black malt, Victory

Yeast: Top fermenting

Hops: East Kent Goldings, Fuggles, Northdown, Challenger

Adjuncts: Lactose (unfermentable by yeast) required, optional corn and treacle.

IBU (International Bitterness Units): 20-40

ABV (Alcohol By Volume): 4% to 6%

SRM (Standard Reference Method Color): 30-40 Dark Brown to Black

Taste: Medium to high sweetness offers a counter distinction from the chocolate coffee bitterness of the highly roasted malts. Low to no hop aroma with medium hop bitterness. Slight fruity esters with Rich creamlike silky smoothness.

Carbonation: Low to moderate.

Variations: From low carbonation sweetened expresso to high alcohol slightly sweet moderately roasted styles with a persistent brown head.

A Trout in the Milk Stout

A red mustang cruised along State Route 1 leading to Carmel-by-the-Sea, California and inside was a tall, cleanly shaven young man at the wheel. His hair was of medium brown color and of medium length. He wore sunglasses as he drove westward into the early evening sun above in the cloudless sky. Next to him was a slightly younger woman of slightly lesser years with slightly lighter and slightly longer hair. She also wore sunglasses and had just finished typing and closed her I Pad. The couple was Jim and Laura Verraten from Pittsburgh, Pennsylvania and they were taking a weekend in Carmel after spending the week in Silicon Valley where Jim had attended a cyber security conference. Laura had filled in her time productively by writing an article 'Silicon Valley for the Rest of Us', an assignment from her manager for a travel magazine. Her manager appreciated that she only had to pay for airfare and meals, not hotels or rental cars, when she traveled with her husband. She would also do a smaller piece over the weekend focusing on the small town of Carmel, California where they would holiday before heading home late Sunday evening on the red-eye.

What lay ahead for them was a small town, or idyllic village as some would say, with a population of 3,700 and nestled on the Monterey Peninsula next to Pacific Ocean. The median cost of a home was over a million and a third dollars putting it well out of reach of all except the rather wealthy and strict building codes prevented its quaint, laid back character from changing. To call it a resort would be as much of a mistake as calling it a utopia yet it resembled in many ways each as witnessed by many famous Carmelites who had either retired there from the film and music industry or had second homes there. It was artsy, exceedingly so, and many California trends and movements found a place within its limits. Restaurants and bars abounded along with health spas. The couple in the red rental car always headed for local brewpubs when available, and increasingly over the years they were not hard to find. In fact, Carmel had several and one type appealed to both of them as something out of the ordinary, namely a brewpub specializing in organic brews and foods. There was a couple to pick from in this trendy, health conscious hamlet. Driving around town they noticed the beach in the small cove, about a mile long. It had its own small public parking lot. The homes of Carmel-by-the Sea had a variety of styles, a lot of red tiled roofs, and seemed to be on rather small lots. They were one and two story only, even in the business district the buildings were low. There was nothing one could call a high rise anywhere in the village that they drove.

They stopped at the parking lot of the Sun and Driftwood Motel and after check-in took their luggage to the room.

"Time for a beer?" asked Laura.

"Past time. Let's go" Replied Jim as they headed over to a brewpub they has spotted before.

At a corner of the block they saw a sign hanging out over the sidewalk on the diagonal, visible from either direction. Deeply carved into wood were four large gilded letters 'OOLA' and below them smaller letters spelled out 'Oliver's Organic Lagers and Ales'. The external tiled façade was modern yet not industrial in appearance while the double door was fastened open presenting a welcoming invitation to passersby who could see on the sandwich board on the sidewalk the specials of the day. The parked the rental in the brewpub's lot next to an assortment of BMWs, Audis, a few Porches, a classic Jaguar XK 120 Roadster in British Racing Green with tan interior, a late model silver Bentley and just pulling up was a jet black Ferrari California 2 Plus, a front engine V-8 grand tourer.

The couple glanced at them, entered the brewpub and sat down at the redwood bar. Behind the row of taps were Oliver's offerings:

Oliver's Organic Lagers and Ales

SEASONAL

Ollie's Organic Saison   5.1% ABV   30 IBU

Ollie's Organic Scotch Ale   4.3% ABV   16 IBU

Ollie's Organic Red Ale   5.8% ABV   25 IBU

STANDARD

Ollie's Organic Pilsner   5.2% ABV   28 IBU

Ollie's Organic Berliner Weiss   3.8% ABV   4 IBU

Ollie's Organic Vienna Lager   5.5% ABV   26 IBU

Ollie's Organic Eternal Octoberfest   4.9% ABV   22 IBU

Ollie's Organic Hefeweizen   5.1% ABV   8 IBU

Ollie's Organic Oatmeal Stout   5.8% ABV   39 IBU

Ollie's Organic Milk Stout   4.1% ABV   20 IBU

Ollie's Organic IPA   6.2% ABV   55 IBU

Ollie's Organic Double IPA   8.1% ABV   85 IBU

The bartender walked over to the Verratens and asked "Here for dinner or just our organic beer?"

"Just beer now" answered Laura but we might stay for dinner or get some snacks. Can we get food at the bar?"

"You certainly can, have you decided on your brews yet?"

"I need a few minutes, you have quite a nice selection and all organic I see" Laura responded.

"All our meals are all organic too" said the bartender then looking at Jim added "Have you decided yet, Sir?"

"Jim's the name and yes I have. A pint of Ollie's Red Ale" he said.

Laura quickly added "and a pint of Ollie's Organic Milk Stout also. Oh, and a menu too."

"Great. Be right back with those."

Laura looked in the mirror behind the bar and focused on some of the people at the tables. She whispered to Jim "The beautiful people, very well dressed, classy."

"Us?" Jim asked with a grin. Laura just shook her head and pursed her lips. The bartender walked over with the two pints and placed them on the bar.

"Jim, the Organic Red Ale, and the Organic Milk Stout for . . ." said the barkeeper waiting for a response.

"For Laura, and you are?" asked Laura.

"Kristen, Kristen Glas but call me Cat, enjoy your beers. What brings you to Carmel?"

"Just a second weekend getaway, flew out a few days early for the first one last weekend, then a week of business to attend to before we head back east Sunday. We're from Pittsburgh."

"First time in California?" Cat asked.

"No, we've been here a few times but first time to Carmel. Such a nice town."

"Usually, but we get our problems now and then."

"I think all towns do" added Jim.

"Well, here's the menu. If you see anything you want just let me know."

The couple sipped their beers and scanned the menu. On it were all organic trendy items popular in West Coast and Californian culture. Since Jim had overeaten at the conference all week, they decided on just some appetizers for their evening meal, and another beer or course. Cat came over "Decided on food?" she asked.

"That we have, but just appetizers tonight" answered Laura "Jim is having the grilled octopus with pearl pasta and I'm having baby red beet salad with arugula, and were going to share an order of potato skins topped with the mix of wild mushrooms, avocado and capers."

"Would you want that all served at the same time?" Cat asked.

"Yes we would" answered Laura.

"How's your Milk Stout?" Jim asked his wife.

"Very good. How's yours?"

"Excellent, but I don't think being organic makes a difference" he responded.

"Probably not, but some people swear by it" Laura replied.

"True. I wonder if we can get a tour when were done eating" Jim added. The couple looked around the brewpub and took in the atmosphere. There was a cathedral ceiling with stringers of yellow lights on each beam. From its center ridge beam two large Spanish colonial style chandeliers hung down, each with a dozen or more lights arranged on two tiers. On the walls were paintings of the beach, the sea and the hills of the area interspersed with several still life paintings of the local produce. Near each grouping hung a small wooden box holding business cards, presumably of the artist who painted each group and presumably they were for sale although neither Laura nor Jim could make out the small price tag on each. Laura had mentioned while they were driving around town seeing art gallery after art gallery that the hamlet had always been considered somewhat of an artist's colony, especially in the decades immediately after it was founded early in the 1900's.

"If we see something we really like, we could have it shipped back home" Laura commented.

"True, we have all day tomorrow to enjoy the beach and shop around." Cat arrived with their light meals.

"Can I get you anything else to drink?" she asked seeing that their beers were almost empty.

"I believe so. I'll have an Organic Saison" said Laura.

"The double IPA please" spoke Jim. "By the way, were fans of brewpubs. Is there any way to get a quick tour of the brewery?"

" I can arrange that for you, we do it all the time. Jason's brewing tonight, another batch of milk stout I think" Cat replied. Jim smiled; it was one of the parts of his travel he enjoyed the most. Each brewpub brewery was similar in basic ways, yet each distinctively different in many areas of detail. This would be his first one specializing in organic beers although some others had made one or two for their offering. Cat returned with the Saison and Double IPA.

Laura asked "Does having all organic beer and food really draw in the customers, your quite busy here?"

"It really does. There's a lot of food and drink choices here in Carmel, a lot have a few or some organics available. I know a lot of our customers personally and don't think we would have half the business without being all organic. It's what we're known for" Cat concluded before spotting another customer who needed a refill. Laura and Jim finished their light meal of octopus, baby beets and shared potato skins.

"I could get used to this food" Laura remarked.

"It's good for a change, but I still like something less fancy" Jim added. The restaurant was now very busy and as the silver Bentley drove away, its spot was immediately filled by a Tesla. The black Ferrari was replaced by a Lexus. When they were finished with their meal and second pints Cat came over and said "I have a minute now. Let me introduce you to Jason back in the brewery, he will show you around and answer any questions."

Jim smiled "Sounds like a plan." The Pittsburghers followed Cat down to the end of the bar by the kitchen, then around to the side and through a door into the brewery. The first thing they noticed were bags and bags of various malts, hops and adjuncts such as lactose, made from leftover whey, a byproduct of cheese making. Next to the ingredient storage area were empty kegs, clean and ready to be refilled. Jim could see the tops of the stainless steel fermentation tanks as they walked on.

Cat spoke out "Jason ought to be around here somewhere. I'll take you over to the mash tun, he's probably there or in the brewery office." "Jason . . . Jason . . . Where are you hiding?' she said loudly, then turning a corner she stopped, looked at the floor and cried out "AHHHH! No. No!"

Jim looked down and saw a man sprawled out on the floor amidst spilled bags of malt. There was no sign of life in him. "Jason?" Jim asked. Cat responded affirmatively as Jim bent down on a knee to examine him more closely, feeling for a pulse. Jason's eyes were fixed, glassed over "Laura call 911. I think he's dead" Jim ordered.

Within a few minutes the emergency medic squad arrived but nothing could be done for Jason. In the meantime, a shaken, red eyed Cat had informed the restaurant manager and the situation was kept quiet at that level. Also, in the meantime both Jim and Laura had taken pictures before any disturbance in the area by medics or investigators had happened. About fifteen minutes later, while the Verratens – one at a time - were being interviewed by the police in the brewery office, the owner of OOLA, Oliver Gould arrived in the brewery proper with his wife Jennifer. He had been called by the restaurant manager. The Verratens told all they knew, which was not much, then they were dismissed and went to the bar. There Cat came over, for she had given her statement before the Verratens. Cat had composed herself, "Maybe it was a heart attack or some rare aneurism" she suggested.

"Maybe" said Laura, "Sometimes something's wrong and breaks in youth or young adulthood. How old was Jason anyway, around twenty five, thirty?"

"I think just under thirty. Started here a year ago. Came from another brewpub up in San Fran."

"Looks like a stack of malt bags fell on him. Might have killed him outright or triggered a hidden medical issue. We'll have to wait for the coroner's report to know for certain. I think we'll each have a pint of pilsner before we go" Jim concluded. Cat brought three pints over, one each for Laura and Jim and one for herself.

"On the house, to better days" she toasted.

"To better days" Laura and Jim each repeated.

"Did you know Jason well?" inquired Laura.

"Only professionally, but I used to join him for a house meal here once in a while. He seemed like a great guy."

"Did he ever mention what brought him to Carmel a year ago?" Laura asked.

"He said he needed a less stressful environment than the city, said he felt much more at ease here especially as part of the Organic movement."

"Do you think he was talking general stress? Did he mention any specific details?" Laura added.

"Hmmm, let me think a second. . . Well, he did mention headaches and some occasional pain above his right eye. He was a forgetful fellow, often having to repeatedly have to recheck the malt bill to get the brew right, but never a mistake, very conscientious. You know, now that I think of it, I've seen him stumble a few times and bump into things, maybe he stumbled or fell into the stack of malt bags. I've told Oliver they shouldn't be stacked so high. OSHA would never approve."

"Interesting" Laura said "Anything else?"

"He had a girlfriend up in San Fran, they broke up. He rented a two room apartment just outside of town here. Sometimes he had trouble getting his words out when he wanted to speak quickly. Oh, and he used to joke he didn't need to get drunk to have double vision."

"Double vision? That's an interesting comment" said Laura. Cat added a few more details about Jason, his food preferences and such, and how he liked to relax on the beach when off work. She indicated the owner, Oliver Gould, had been the original brewer but the success of the organic brewpub gave rise to way too many other responsibilities so he had hired two assistant brewers to make his original recipes.

"There was another assistant brewer?" Laura pressed.

"Yes" replied Cat now realizing the couple's line of questioning was more than just bar chat, they seemed more focused on details. "Say, are you two with the police back in Pittsburgh?" she asked.

"No" Laura replied "But we have consulted with the police before a few times. Who was the other brewer and did you ever notice any problems between them?"

Cat opened up to Laura. "I really liked Jason, thought we were getting closer over time. The other brewer is Bruce Weber, been here a long time. Never heard of any trouble between the two, but Bruce has his faults. A quick temper is one and a bit of paranoia is the other."

"Did you mention this to the police?" Laura asked.

"They didn't ask" Cat responded. The three had a second round of pilsner and talked for about an hour more while Cat kept an eye on the customers at the redwood bar, refilling pints when needed. Jim was preoccupied with his emails but had time to notice that there was no hard liquor or wine, odd he thought for a California establishment. Cat explained that wine bars were was so common in Carmel that they were seen as ordinary. OOLA was special. Before the Verratens left for their hotel they asked Cat for her number and if she was working tomorrow. She was. The couple parted ways from the sad bartender.

Walking to their rental car, the parking lot had begun to empty out from the dinner crowd and Jim noticed the black Ferrari California still there along with two police cars, the medics van having departed with the body to the coroner's office as Jason McLaughlin had been officially pronounced dead at the scene. Back at the hotel the couple lay in bed discussing their day and the experience at OOLA. Jim was looking at the pictures they each had taken of

Jason laying on the floor. Laura was using her I Pad to look at medical conditions.

Jim starred at the body on the floor. It was covered in malt sacks that had fallen form an over stacked pallet. Why was the pallet stacked so high, higher than usual for shipping? Several bags had burst open when they had hit the floor. Malted barley and powdered lactose had spread out over Jason and the floor. The unfortunate assistant brewer was face down, on his stomach, his right arm outstretched and his left arm tucked in under his chest. Jim spotted something in the powdered lactose, but he wasn't sure so he checked Laura's pictures also. He set up a special file with all the pictures and began to post process them. He highlighted, adjusted contrast levels, adjusted lightness and from several pictures taken of the body at differing angles he pieced together five letters in a row. They were T R O U T. The deceased index finger with white powder on its tip was stretched out near the last T, and his others tucked back into his palm. They were very lightly drawn, somewhat irregular perhaps slowly, perhaps with difficulty, certainly not as well as could have been done by a man with full facilities and abilities. The faintness and irregular size in a background of spilled white power that had been subjected to the trails of right arm and hand movements would hide them from easy visual recognition. On the contrary, on the left side of Jason, the spilled powder seemed as smooth and unblemished as a wave from a choppy ocean that washed way up on the beach losing its random, rough character and, after sinking into the sand, leaving it as uninterrupted and fresh as could be, uninterrupted except for one pattern at the high water mark, or in this case the high lactose mark, a shoeprint.

With that, Jim decided to turn in for the night as did Laura at the end of her search for medical conditions. She had found enough to give a doctor she knew back in Pittsburgh a call at home on Saturday.

Before a breakfast of Huevos Rancheros and coffee the couple had walked the beach at the western side of Carmel. Although big cities offered certain advantages there seemed to them that nothing could be more pleasant than living in such a town as Carmel. Late morning found them visiting several art galleries and outside one specializing in upcoming local artists Laura, aware of the three hour time difference to Pittsburgh, called a doctor she knew. She luckily found him at home and discussed all the symptoms that Cat had mentioned to her the previous evening. Pain around the eye, perhaps occasional double vision, perhaps occasional difficulty speaking, some loss of balance, some difficulty concentrating and some short term memory loss added up to one possibility, a brain aneurysm the doctor told her. It was on Laura's suspect list and her call confirmed it. "Ok then, and thanks for your help" she concluded as she disconnected. "Jim" she said turning toward her husband "He thinks it might have been a major stroke of some sort from a cerebral aneurysm, usually there since birth. They get worse and worse until they either rupture on their own or a stressor causes them to break in early adulthood. He said the coroner will easily find it if that's what ended his life."

"Interesting. I guess it's kinda like in youth football where once in a while one bursts during the game and there were no signs beforehand. But it took the stress of the exercise and a hard hit to find it" replied Jim.

"I think so" added Laura "The bags falling on him would then be the immediate causal event that precipitated it."

"But we have to ask - Why did the event occur at all?" Jim suggested. "Why did he appear to have scratched out the letters T R O U T in the lactose? If simply an unfortunate event caused by loss of balance, why write anything at all? What has a trout got to do with anything? They live in mountain streams not the sea, and why is there a shoe print at the edge of the spilled powder?"

"Let's walk over to the police station before lunch, see if the coroner has found out anything" Laura suggested. The couple knew that although they had given statements, they had no standing in the death and any information they received would be a mere courtesy. At the station they spoke to Detective Larson who thanked them for their cooperation the evening before and indicated that although the coroner's report was not yet concluded as it would take some time yet to get the standard blood tests for drugs and poisons back, it did show a very large ruptured aneurysm in the brain that would have caused almost instantaneous death. He said it was looking like natural causes would be ruled pending the blood work. The Verratens thanked him for the information and headed over to the OOLA for lunch.

Entering OOLA they saw the black Ferrari California again parked the parking lot and after ordering two Vienna Lagers from assistant bartender Joyce Guenette they asked where Cat was. "She starts in a half hour, then I switch to tables" responded Joyce.

"Just a menu to look at for now" Laura said. In a while the couple saw Kristen Glas arrive, talk briefly with another woman, and soon after take her place behind the redwood bar. She saw the Verratens and walked over to them.

"Afternoon" she said, "Jennifer, the owner's wife, says it is looking like it was natural causes."

"That's what we heard too. A shame" responded Laura.

"Are you too having lunch today?" Cat asked. The couple responded with an order for two California burgers topped with onion bacon jam, avocado, lettuce and white cheddar. Cat had a few minutes to chat before the afternoon crowd filled the bar. She spent them talking with Laura.

At one point Jim interrupted and asked Cat "I've noticed a nice black Ferrari in your lot a few times. Do you know who it belongs to?"

"That's owner's ride, Oliver and Jennifer Gould. Really nice, huh?"

"Yes it is, I bet expensive too" Jim added.

"I think they paid a couple hundred for it new" the bartender responded.

"OOLA's been good to them" Laura chimed in.

"Very good. Allowed them to move into town" and with that Cat got busy and had to serve others at the redwood bar. The Verratens finished their lunch and decided to browse around the art filled town some more and after another art gallery, this one of modern art, they saw a bookstore specializing in classic literature and old first edition books. Intrigued, they entered.

"Welcome, can I help you" asked a bearded older gentleman in a beret putting down a book as his wife looked over her reading glasses from her desk.

"Just looking" Jim replied while Laura headed over to the English literature section and he spotted the American literature aisle. After a quarter hour Laura joined him with a Virginia Woolf first edition of 'Three Guineas', unsigned and therefore within her price range.

"Find something?" Jim asked his wife.

"Yep, always liked her and we don't have to pay for shipping. You find anything?" Laura concluded.

"Not really. Let's check out and go to the beach" Jim said as he took the book from Laura and walked over to the checkout.

"Virginia Woolf? Must be for your wife?" the gray bearded gentleman inquired.

"Very perceptive" Jim responded "How did you guess?"

"After nearly half a century in the business you get a feeling of who buys what. Will that be cash or credit?"

"Credit" Jim responded as he reached for his wallet.

"Very good. Had a trout in the milk a month ago, cost me a hundred."

"A what? I don't understand" Jim followed.

"A trout in the milk, a counterfeit $100 bill, had to eat it" the elderly owner responded.

"A trout in the milk? I don't understand, what's that?" Jim queried.

"Oh, just an old expression for a counterfeit of anything" he said while running the credit card. Jim remembered the letters in the spilled lactose spelling out 'trout'.

"Interesting, never heard of that before. Can you tell me more about the trout reference like where did it come from and how did it get that meaning?"

"In the Journal of Henry David Thoreau, November11, 1850. He penned 'Some circumstantial evidence is very strong, as when you find a trout in the milk' "the elderly gentleman said, then continued "In New England dairy farms of the time it was not unheard of to add water from a brook to the milk

29

before taking it to the city for sale. And legend has it that once a small trout was found in the milk, strong circumstantial evidence that the milk had been diluted with brook water. Now the expression stands for anything adulterated or counterfeit." Jim just starred off past the hand returning his credit card.

"Oh, sorry. I was just thinking" Jim said as he took the card and the book in its paper bag, "Thanks for the history lesson."

"Anytime, and thanks for your purchase."

Outside the bookshop Jim told Laura he had something interesting to tell her when they found a bench to sit down on. A block later they found one next to a planting of summer annuals. "Laura, remember the first ale you had at OOLA? The very first one?" he asked.

Laura thought back and replied "Yes, I had an Organic Milk Stout, very sweet, silky and coffee like. Why?"

"Remember why it's called 'milk stout'?" he asked.

Laura thought over the beer styles for a moment then replied "It's because they put milk sugar in it that yeast can't ferment, so it stays sweet. . . And that milk sugar is called lactose! It's what killed Jason when it fell on him."

"Yes, that and several other bags of malt" Jim added. "We didn't see it at the time, and I'm sure neither did the police, but post processing of the pictures we took showed some letters spelling out the word 'trout' in the lactose milk sugar, in other words there was a trout in the milk."

"Say, that sounds oddly familiar now that you mention it, but I can't place it" Laura commented.

"The fellow at the bookshop explained it to me, it's from Thoreau in 1850, when farmers diluted milk with creek water before selling it, and has come down to mean counterfeit or adulterated. Supposedly someone found a small trout minnow in their morning milk, something like that. The coincidence was unexplainable except by intentional dilution with creek water" Jim said.

"Are you thinking what I'm thinking" Laura asked.

"Indeed, I am" replied her husband "Let's go talk with Cat."

After taking Virginia Woolf to their hotel room, the couple headed back to OOLA and sat at the end of the redwood bar where there was some late afternoon privacy. Cat came over "Hi. We have growlers and red solo cups if you'd like to take something to the beach" she said.

"Just two pils" Laura replied and "Do you have a few minutes to talk again?"

"Certainly, be right back with the beers."

Laura then explained to Cat that their suspicion was raised that the death of Jason might not be accidental. She asked how long Cat had worked at OOLA and what the hiring procedure was like, she asked if the owners were wealthy before opening the brewpub, she asked if there was ever any trouble between Jason, Bruce and the owners Oliver and Jennifer. What Laura found out was that Cat had been employed at OOLA for about three years and an electronic resume of her previous five years employment and that it was kept on the OOLA computer in the office. She indicated that to the best of her knowledge based on what she had heard about the owners from other employees and some customers, the owners had borrowed heavily to open OOLA after working at another brewpub in LA. She believed they were not from wealth but had worked their way up into ownership of their own business. She also said that from time to time she had heard arguments behind the closed office door when she was punching in her time card, but only sometimes could identify the people involved, sometimes Jason and sometimes Bruce, but could not make out what the heated arguments were about.

Jim had not seen the black Ferrari in the parking lot. "Cat, is Bruce brewing today?" he asked.

"No, not usually on Saturdays" Cat responded.

"Do you think we might be able to have another look at the brewery then?" he pressed.

Cat sensed that they were definitely more involved than the police investigator, and decided to support them fully. "I don't see why a brewpub fan from back East would not be allowed to finish his interrupted tour, on his own. I can wait out here with an eye on the parking lot while you look around some more, I can spot that Ferrari a mile away. Be quick."

The Verratens entered the brewery. All had been cleaned up. Their self guided tour was not so much about the equipment that Jim would normally focus on, but instead on the ingredients. Bag after bag was stacked on top of pallets from various suppliers, in the corner was a fork lift used in pallet unloading. Jim and Laura divided up the workload and began quickly taking pictures of the labels on the malts and adjuncts especially the powdered lactose. Keeping an ear open for Cat, they finished the work in about twenty minutes without any problem. They returned to the redwood bar. Cat smiled.

"Cat" Laura asked "How do the beer ingredients arrive? I see everything is on pallets, so I assume they're not unloaded bag by bag by hand."

"Oliver has a small box truck he keeps on a lot outside town. He uses it to call on various vendors to make up a load" she responded.

"Hmmm, you have WiFi here, I wonder if you you have a password or connection into the establishment's computer" Jim asked.

"I do. I use it for my tax preparation and checking my tips payout and hours. We all do. But some files are locked to us." she said.

Jim just smiled. "If you would log into your account on my computer, I can take it from there" Jim replied, "And don't worry, anything I do will be untraceable to you, it's just like you opening a door, easier and quicker than if I have to do it myself. I'm a professional cyber security expert."

Cat agreed and Jim began to look around OOLA's files. It was child's play to him, something he learned to do way back in high school. First on his agenda was Jason's resume. It listed the brewpub in San Fran where he had worked previously and some unrelated retail jobs at a national coffeehouse. Laura wrote down the names and related information. Next were the ingredient purchase files. They were organized by vendor. Jim scanned the malts and adjuncts, interestingly none were marked 'Organic'. Jim wrote down the names of the vendors. He also looked back in the purchase records and found that in the first years of OOLA, all the malts and adjuncts were Organic, and priced much higher pound for pound, but in time items labeled Organic in the product name, description or specification were fewer and fewer until a few years ago, there were none at all. Jim estimated the cost savings to be enormous looking at the volume of Ales and Lagers sold, easily enough to provide for a black Ferrari California. Yet, he remembered all the bags in the brewery were stamped 'Organic'. He logged off and returned to his and Laura's recent pictures of the pallets in the brewery. Laura called up one of the vendors and a photo of a bag of their Organic malt. The Verratens compared the two images. The word 'Organic' did not appear on the vendor's bag. They began to repeat this with as many vendors and malts as they had and could find online. Each time a bag of malt was seen on a vendor site, the same malt in OOLA's pallets was different with the term 'Organic' stamp applied on the bag. The size, the font, and the location were all different, but to any casual observer on a brew tour they would easily pass as authentic.

Laura told Cat what they had found out. OOLA's beers were not organic but priced as such at quite a premium over non-organic beer. True Organic beers can cost up to double in their malt bill, often adding over two or three dollars to each pint and then selling at a premium price over non-organic beer. "The Goulds are running a scam; at least one of them was anyway" Laura concluded.

"Amazing" Cat said, "I have to believe they both were in on it. Obviously Ollie was, as he always had to be the one to go and get the supplies; but Jennifer thought of nothing but money and status. She treated us girls like dirt, cold as an iceberg around here and never a donation to a charity. Heard a few rumors about her, seems like she might have been a source of coke when she was younger. It wouldn't surprise me that she was the mastermind of switching to cheaper malts. So are you two going to the police on this?"

"Good question" Laura said, "I think there is proof enough to convict OOLA on mislabeling and outright fraud, but it's a big leap to prove Mr. Gould intentionally killed Jason by pushing the malt bill stack over on him."

"Gould did know of his condition, or suspected it. There was enough to observe and piece together, and the two had worked closer together than you and Jason for the last year. He saw what you saw. He could have just taken a chance the falling bags would break open the aneurysm and had a backup plan if it didn't. And I know he was here Friday night in the brewery when Jason was working" Jim said.

"How?" asked Cat.

"I saw the black Ferrari in the parking lot last night; it left right before our tour when we found the still warm body. When I felt for a pulse, Jason's head moved easily on his neck. The inevitable immobility of rigor mortise had not yet begun. He had not been dead long, perhaps thirty minutes at most" Jim remarked.

"He had motive and opportunity" Laura added.

"Or they did" added Cat "So what are you going to do?"

"It is all very circumstantial, not enough to ever convict anyone of murder in court. . . unless. . .? I think it's time Laura and I pay a visit to the police."

Arriving at the station a quarter of an hour later, Jim asked if the Chief was around and available to talk.

"What's this all about?" the officer at the desk inquired.

"It's about the death of Jason McLaughlin last night."

"What about it?"

"We have some information the Chief or Detective Larson may find interesting and highly relevant."

"Your names?"

"Jim and Laura Verraten, we discovered the body and were interviewed last night."

"And you are working for who?" the officer asked after writing the names down.

"We're not with any agency in the matter, just citizens with relevant information" Jim responded.

"Wait here" said the officer before going into the Chief's office. Jim and Laura looked at each other and waited. The officer returned and said "Chief Brown will see you now."

"Please have a seat" Chief Brown said as they entered his office, "I understand you were interviewed by Detective Larson last night regarding the McLaughlin death. You want to change your story or have something to add?"

"We don't want to change our 'story' at all" said Laura with emphasis on the word story, "But we have uncovered some additional information."

"The Carmel force is on top of the case, we're waiting on the final coroner's report. If we need assistance, we can call upon the County detectives for help, but I doubt that will be needed" Chief Brown responded, then thought and added "What type of 'information?"

Jim began "Chief, Laura and I are not inexperienced in these matters. Here is a list of police contacts that you may call who will vouch for our seriousness and help provided to them in murder cases in the past." Chief Brown took the list and looked at it, setting it down on his desk next to his phone. Jim continued "After we went back to the hotel last night, we talked it all over. Laura made a call earlier today to her doctor friend today and we do not disagree that an aneurysm will be ruled the proximate cause of death, our concern is whether it was a chance event or a deliberate attempt by someone, the owner Oliver Gould and his wife Jennifer."

"Go on" the chief ordered.

"You see last night before bed I was looking at the pictures we took of Jason on the floor. I forwarded them all to Detective Larson already. I did a fair amount of post processing of them to pull out details not initially obvious, adjustments of contrast and shadowing, of light and dark scaling. What I found were the letters T R O U T spelled out in the lactose sugar powder, essentially a form of milk powder, then when I knew what I was looking for, I could also see them vaguely in many of the pictures. A short while ago at a bookshop I learned the significance of those letters and the substance they were written in. It comes from a very old expression, 'A trout in the milk', for an adulterated or counterfeit product, in short from adding stream water to milk on dairy farms before being sold in the city, thereby getting milk prices for mere water. What we call today adulterated products. I checked the storage area at OOLA when on a self guided brewery tour today and found that the bags of organic ingredients for their beer are not Organic at all; they are the cheaper ordinary malts and adjuncts."

"That's motive" spoke out Laura "The additional profit at Organic beer prices with no Organics used would increase their income substantially, perhaps enough for the black Ferrari they bought." The Chief nodded.

Jim continued "Last night as I sat at the bar before we found the body, I noticed a black Ferrari California model pull into OOLA's parking lot, it's distinctive if you know your Ferraris, but no one entered the bar or restaurant. It must have been the owner using the brewery door around the back. Then a while later I saw the Ferrari was gone. It was then we began our tour and discovered the body. At the time we were interviewed I had thought nothing at all about that car, but now I consider it significant, now I think that was when Oliver Gould, with or without his wife, killed Jason McLaughlin."

"That's opportunity" concluded Laura, "We suspect that Jason had found out that the malt bags were bogus, just stamped by the owner as Organic as only the owner ever made the runs to get the beer supplies. So Jason, probably refusing a bribe or possibly trying to blackmail the owner, was done away with. One of the two owners had put two and two together and knew of Jason's condition. If he couldn't be bribed then he had to be done away with. A stack of fifty pound bags falling on him from twelve feet up would probably trigger the burst."

"It's all very circumstantial" replied the Chief "One possible explanation of many."

"I agree it's highly circumstantial" Laura agreed.

"No jury would convict on it" Jim added "Were there any hidden security cameras in the brewery?"

"None" concluded Chief Brown.

"But there might be a way" Jim said.

"What do you mean, he never would admit it to us" the Chief replied.

"I have enough proof of Organic adulteration on my I Pad to destroy his business reputation, or give it to you and you could bring charges for adulteration or mislabeling, but then he gets away with murder. Now, if you would agree I could go in undercover and threaten to blackmail him, and in the process lead him into admitting his crime against Jason. I would certainly be able to get his attention and go from there, and I would be working for you with a wire on me" Jim proposed.

The Chief thought it over then spoke "If I remember correctly, Larson said you two were from out East, here on vacation. What's your schedule?"

"We fly out tomorrow night from San Fran on a red eye, but we could stay over" Laura answered, "but that might not be necessary." Laura called Cat over at OOLAs. Cat indicated that Oliver usually came in Sundays around noon for several hours to prepare checks for the staff for the past week's work. If the weather was good, and it usually was, his wife would be along and take the afternoon at the beach while he worked. With all that in mind, the three developed a plan in the Chief's office, a plan that was the only chance to sway a jury and get justice for Jason.

Sunday around noon Cat saw Laura walk into OOLA with Jim behind her; the couple took their seats at the redwood bar that offered a view of the parking lot. After ordering two Milk Stouts Laura told

Cat they had a plan and were waiting for Oliver to show up, Jim was going to meet with him and no one else was to be involved. They slowly sipped their pints and ate an avocado and pine nut salad, Jim's topped with bacon. Within an hour the black Ferrari pulled into the parking lot and the two owners got out. Oliver headed for the office door into the brewery while Jennifer, wearing beach wear, came into the bar and ordered an arugula salad with mixed mushrooms and capers to go. Jim watched for her to take her lunch with her and head for the beach. It was now time for him to act. He left his seat and went into the brewery causing Cat to remark to Laura "I'm worried. I don't know what to expect." Laura told Cat not to worry, that her husband was going to the brewery office for a meeting with the owner and that everything was under control.

In the silent brewery Jim walked past the stacks of malts and containers of hops. Oliver was nowhere to be seen, 'Good', he thought, probably in his office writing payroll checks. Jim walked past the fermentation vats and the mill and toward the office. He saw the door was open and approached. Oliver, busy with his numbers, did not hear the approach and only looked up when he heard a knock on the doorframe. Puzzled at the sight of Jim he asked sternly "What are you doing here? Can I help you?"

"I think so, in fact I'm sure you can" responded Jim "May I come in?" as he walked in and sat down putting his feet up on the coffee table.

"If it's a brewery tour you're after, we offer those on a loose schedule. I don't do them. Who let you in back here?"

"I'm not after a brewery tour, I had one and I let myself in. You didn't answer my question. May I come in? or should I just go to the newspaper?" Jim responded with a veiled threat.

"Newspaper? What the hell are you doing here? What are you talking about?" Oliver queried.

Jim noticed Oliver did not threaten do call the police, something a totally innocent man might just have done to the uninvited interloper. He pressed on. "Mr. Gould, Oliver if I may, Ollie you see I've got some business to discuss with you" Jim said aggressively taking control of the conversation dynamic from the surprised owner.

"Whatever you're selling, I'm not interested" Oliver said.

"Oh, I understand, but I think you will be in a minute. You see, I am an insurance salesman... of a sort, but I sell other things too." The owner knew he wasn't selling real insurance and began to quickly think it might be a shake down for protection money, so let him go on. Jim continued "You see Pal, I had some of your beers a while back and was very impressed, most excellent, I must say. I liked that they were Organic too as I'm sure most of your customers do also. Then I had a brewery tour, very impressive top line equipment by the way, real quality, and I saw your pallets of organic malts, but you know I'm kinda an obsessive compulsive guy. When I bought a new car the other year, the first thing I did was check the speedometer, I hate getting tickets you understand. The second was check my mileage against the MPG statement on the sticker, I just don't like to be cheated you see. If I didn't get that mileage when I drove carefully, then I'm gonna be real mad and demand a price adjustment or begin to give the dealer some. . . let us say 'problems', problems he wished he never had. You'd probably be surprised at how many times things are not what they say they are."

The owner had a thought, was this nut leading up to his Organic beer?

Jim continued on, he had full control now of the conversation. "Take here for instance. The fine people of Carmel-by-the-Sea come in for an Organic pint, not just any pint mind you, but a pint from a brewpub that specializes in such. A real draw. Those rich Organic types, and there are many of them around here, feel at home at your brewpub. How do you think they'd feel if they knew they were drinking ordinary beer at Organic prices, or at any price? I think they might stay away. Don't you?"

The owner Oliver interrupted "Say here, what are you implying anyway? All our beer and food is organic."

"See here Pal, I wish it were, I really do, then I would not be here. On my tour I took some pictures and did some checking around. Your Organic labels are a fraud. A lot of those malts are not even produced as Organic and for the ones that are, that labeling is totally different. What did you do, make your own label stamps up and print them on the bags when you did your pick-ups in San Fran?"

"How do you know I pick them up? Have you been staking me out?" Oliver said.

"Jason told me."

"Jason?"

"Yea, Jason. I plan my business carefully, Ollie. Now for the sales pitch, I've got a great one for you" added Jim.

"What business are you in, extortion?" demanded Oliver.

"No. Partnerships and sometimes various insurances, but the two go hand in hand" Jim said "and nobody uses the word extortion anymore. See Pal, it's like this. I like your brewpub here. You're onto a good thing. I like good things. I'd hate to see it ruined. At first, I thought just a nice insurance policy might be right for you, you know, pay the monthly premium and everything is Hush-Hush but since Friday everything changed. Now I think a partnership is in order, and by the way, a partnership deal includes trouble at any future competitor who tries to move strongly into the Organic beer market here in Carmel. A partnership with us has strong benefits." The unfamiliar words and behavior came to Jim ad hoc; he had watched his share of Godfather movies and a few gangster films out of the 30's so could easily improvise the part, perhaps not well enough for an Oscar but good enough, he was sure, to convince Oliver of his authenticity in the matter at hand. Oliver Gould just sat and starred with his eyes wide open.

"With us? And what about Friday?" Oliver asked.

"I'm a front man for a group of friends you see, we cover for each other. Friday you ask? You murdered Jason McLaughlin Friday evening. That changed my plan."

"Preposterous! Are you out of your mind? He had an accident with the malt bags and it looks like a genetic problem burst an artery in his brain. At least that's what I've been told."

"Well, I agree from my snooping around that the autopsy will show an aneurysm of the brain killing him, but you are a smart man Ollie, I can tell. You recognized his symptoms and looked them up I would say. A police check of your computer will show that. And my hidden camera recorded you pushing the sacks over on poor Jason." Jim waited for effect; he had played two cards he didn't have.

Oliver responded "So what if I looked up Jason's symptoms on my computer, I had compassion for the man. And why would you have hidden a camera and taken pictures of a brewer just doing his job. I think your bluffing."

"I take a lot of movies. Goes along with my business. Sometimes I get nothing at all, just like fly fishing for trout. Sometimes I get something embarrassing, sometimes an affair going on. But I have to say this is the first time I caught a murder being committed. I have a real small fisheye camera, bought it at one of those spy stores up in San Fran, hide it almost anywhere. This time I caught a record fish – for me anyway. My partners were surprised, bought me a big steak dinner."

"Partners?"

"You don't think I work alone do you in my kind of business? Or that I'd be stupid enough to come in here today without my partners knowing what I was doing, and they do expect to hear from me as soon as I walk out of here" Jim saw that Oliver had closed his eyes and was thinking.

"What now?" Oliver responded? "What are you really after?"

"I think a partnership is warranted by murder" Jim responded.

"I will have to see the tape" Oliver said. "You got me on the Organic label, I could pay a monthly fee or insurance as you say for that, if it was reasonable; but a partnership in the business is way more serious. Jason was going to go to the authorities once he found out about the illegal Organic stamp I used on the malt. He wouldn't take a cut like Bruce would. He was too honest, too idealistic to bargain with. I didn't know how else to save my business than to take the chance that when I pushed the bags over on him, they would kill him. If they hadn't, then I would have suffocated him right there on the floor. I guess you and I are not too far apart, really."

"I was having some pub grub at your bar when I saw the Ferrari arrive, I was going to retrieve my camera after I was done eating. A while later I saw your Ferrari leave, then I went in for my camera and found Jason on the floor. Dead. And a footprint crushed in the malt."

"Yes. Dead of course. I tried not to step in the broken bags, thought I had avoided it, but I felt his neck and there was no pulse. So I left. Killing him was easier than I thought when I was planning it for weeks, but I guess you and your partners know that. How many have you killed?"

"That's my business, Pal, not yours."

"What do you and your partners want now? What percent of the business? What kind of deal?" Oliver asked.

"Depends. How is OOLA structured? Do you own all of it?" Jim asked the admitted murderer.

"Half, and my wife the other half" Oliver said then added "But whatever share you take comes out of both our shares. I'm not getting screwed out of everything by you and her too."

"How do you mean?" asked Jim.

Oliver explained "Well, if your share comes out of only mine, my wife Jennifer keeps her half if we get divorced and we are probably headed in that direction. Then I'll be left with less than her and it was all her idea anyway, not fair."

"What was all her idea?" Jim asked.

"The counterfeit Organic beer. Killing Jason. Whatever partnership we settle on comes out of both ours, not just mine. She was always the money hungry one. I would have been fine with an ordinary brewpub or an Organic one with less profit, by she always kept pushing for more and more. No matter what I made, it was never enough. And all she does is socialize, go to the beach and spend money on herself. I wish I had never met her. I think I ought to call her and get her in here, she's going to have to sign the paperwork anyway."

"Oh, there will be no paperwork to sign. My name won't be anywhere."

"I understand. But as half owner she ought to be here anyway, I'll call her" said Oliver Gould, currently half owner of OOLA.

Jim Verraten and Oliver Gould discussed details and percentages of the ownership; the partnership would be based on a split of the monthly profit. It would then be in the interest of the new partner to enforce his part of inhibiting and significant competitor from opening up in Carmel.

Clad in her blue crochet tunic top, Jim could see a black bikini underneath Jennifer's beach wear as she angrily stormed into the brewery office. "What is so important I had to come up here?" she asked her husband behind the desk.

"Pull up a chair" Oliver said, "We have a lot to discuss." In the next fifteen minutes Jennifer's expressions ranged from surprise to puzzlement to downright hate as she heard Jim's position and glared at him through cold, calculating eyes.

"So why don't we just kill you right here and now? Ollie has a gun in his desk" she pondered aloud.

"We could do that, Dear" Oliver said sarcastically, "But Jim here has a lot of friends and he has assured me then you and I would not survive long if he fails to report back."

"You idiot" she said looking at her husband. "Why did you admit that we killed Jason? I should have known better than trust you. I should have done it myself; after all it was my idea anyway. Or I should have found someone to do it outside here, make it look like a robbery gone wrong where he lives. I bet you even searched Jason's symptoms on the office computer instead of up in San Fran at a public library like I told you to do."

"What's done is done, Dear. We now have a new partner." The three continued to work out the partnership details and finally when a deal was reached Jim left the two of them alone in the office.

He rejoined Laura at the redwood bar and watched as a plain clothed officer from the police department entered the brewery office and two police cars with uniformed officers arrived at OOLA's parking lot and made the arrest of Oliver and Jennifer Gould. Cat, Jennifer and Jim all watched as the owners were taken out in handcuffs.

"They admitted it all, the wife planned it and the husband did it" Jim told the two women.

"I guess I'm out a job" said Kat.

"Maybe, maybe not. The Goulds are going to need a lot of cash for their defense. Maybe a White Knight buyer will buy the business and brew real organic beer, have it certified by the town of Carmel itself to rebuild confidence. It would still make money, just not quite as much; it's a great concept for Carmel anyway" Jim concluded.

"You know, I think your right. I might even know some people and some of the staff here that might get together to buy it" Kat said.

"Now you're thinking" added Laura. The three parted friends and promised to stay in touch.

On the way to their Sunday night red eye back to Pittsburgh Laura said "Well Jim, I still don't know how you did it."

In a voice composed of Cagney, Bogart and Brando her husband answered "See here you dame, never give a sucker an even break. They were both rats and I made one into a stool pigeon. It was just business, nothing personal. I made him an offer he couldn't refuse."

"Well, you took a big chance alone in there, he could have killed you if he had a gun which I suspect he did; he could have gotten tough with you" Laura interjected.

Jim continued "Tough? He wasn't tough. He wasn't tough. He wasn't nothin! He was a lousy double crossing rat fink hiding behind a skirt. You shoulda seen me in dere. Why I coulda mopped the floor with him. Beside I was a front for the mob, he knew better than mess with me and my friends."

"Hah! Your friends?"

"He believed I had friends that would rub him out if he messed with me. See here now, he was afraid he would go to sleep with the fishes" Jim added.

"You did mop the floor with them. I'm proud of you. Probably Jason's only chance to get justice. Did you take an acting class in college or something?" Laura asked.

"Nah, why would a mug like me take a class like that? Huh? So you dolls think we guys are soft on the inside, do you?" Jim said to his wife then added "I simply watched a lot of gangster movies in my life."

END

A Stout and a Shot

8 from the Series

A Brewpub Mystery

by

Fredric G. Bender

All rights reserved: no part of this publication may be reproduced or transmitted by any means without the prior written permission of the author.

A Stout and a Shot is a work of fiction. Any resemblance to actual persons, living or dead, is purely coincidental. Any resemblance to actual brewpubs, breweries or bars is purely coincidental.

Stout

A black beer with pronounced roasted flavor. Evolved over the last two centuries as a 'stouter' version of London porters. Balanced versions have some malty sweetness while bitter versions are very dry.

Malt Bill: Roasted Barley, Flaked Barley

Yeast: Top fermenting

Hops: Any Goldings, Williamette

Adjuncts: Some with oatmeal, lactose, cacao nibs, coffee

IBU (International Bitterness Units): 25-45

ABV (Alcohol By Volume): 4.0% to 4.5%

SRM (Standard Reference Method Color): 25-40 Jet Black

Taste: No esters or hop aroma. Moderate to high roasted flavor. Bittersweet cocoa and or coffee like flavor. Medium to high hop bitterness. Medium to full body smooth mouthfeel.

Carbonation: Thick, creamy, long lasting tan head

Variations: Irish stout such as Guiness or Murphys, Extra Stout is hoppier and much higher alcohol at up to 6.5% for export to hot climes. British sweet stouts once known as 'milk' stout from the addition of lactose. Oatmeal stout originally with a high oatmeal component for health. American stout uses a high level of American hops. Russian Imperial stout once brewed for the Russian Court up to 12% ABV and 90 IBUs is revived by the craft brew movement.

A Stout and a Shot

West Virginia State Highway 3, the Old Daniel Boone Parkway, although with only one curvy lanes in each direction, was not much of what one would expect of a true parkway in modern times. In mid-morning the light grey mist was just starting to thin as the first direct sunlight luminated the top third of the tree covered eastern mountainsides of the valley road.

The outline of the uppermost trees on the western ridges began to appear above them, yet not in even the faintest green but in a drab mist induced daubs of various shades of downy grey emanating from upright charcoal colored trunks anchored into the hillsides. On the shady west facing slopes not a distinctive form could be seen much past the roadway except for a small stream and frequent road cuts through eroding thin dark grey shales with layers of brown sandy muds that were laid down horizontally hundreds of millions of years ago and now resembling a book laying sideways on a table with its dirty pages seen edge on. A house or two and a trailer or three and a garage or two was barely seen through the mist but a field and barn only once in a great was observed for this was not farmland but mountainous coal country and underneath the road and homes, at various depths in the sedimentary rock layers of the Carboniferous Period were various seams of coal, some full and waiting, some mined out and abandoned back to nature. The few scattered homes interspersed among the many trailers along the road were closed tight, not a light on, and in various stages of disrepair. The trailers matched and bettered the neglect of the homes and some showed flood or fire damage, mostly unrepaired. Some had been abandoned recently, some long ago as witnessed by their exposed fragile steel skeletons. Some which should be abandoned as their condition warranted still housed an occupant or more as the presence of an older pickup in the driveway bespoke of its owner still living inside as did the rare horse in the field, the occasional dog lying on the porch, and the mostly feral cats sitting on the steps looking and waiting patiently for a breakfast.

In time the Toyota Highlander hybrid of Jim and Laura Verraten left the stream beside as the road began to climb up on the side of a ridge. Gone below were the traces of civilization replaced by steep switchbacks; gone also were the majestic hardwood trees of the past, logged and yielding to steep second growth forested terrain. Finally the road leveled out and in the increasing lightness the greys of the mist and leaves exhibited various shades of grey green hues; their trunks showed some dark browns interrupted by the occasional white sycamore. The rough and threatening switchbacks in the past for now, the Daniel Boone Parkway resumed a more orderly course at a slightly higher elevation where homes and even a small community with church, school and post office appeared hugging the road. A while later a coal operation was passed by the couple. Jim drove under a conveyor needed to transport the raw coal from the various mine tunnels out into the open and over the road to a cleaning and loading station in the middle of nowhere. At the horseshoe bend of the Big Coal River, which most people would call a stream or small creek, was the village of Racine with its two hundred and fifty six inhabitants. The Highlander turned left onto State Route 94 and soon left civilization behind for the second time as it traveled mostly north through forested, mountainous terrain. In a while the usual evidence of civilization began to emerge at the sides of the road and soon the Highlander was following behind a large coal truck for the last mile into the small city of Marmet on the Kanawha River. There in the wide open valley carved by that West Virginian river, Jim and Laura Verraten in their Highlander Hybrid entered the Interstate and followed the Kanawha to their destination of the State Capital of West Virginia, Charleston, only a quick 12 miles away.

Laura Verraten worked for a public relations company that had her on assignment down to the border area of southern West Virginia and eastern Kentucky along the Tug River for background information and photographs for a piece on the Hatfield and McCoy Feud. The tourism board of the area wanted to attract more visitors from western Pennsylvania and the public relations company in Pittsburgh was a perfect match. Her slant would be to highlight not only the Hatfield McCoy area but other points of interest through southern West Virginia that might draw a visitor from Pittsburgh and surrounding areas. Her article would be printed in several travel brochures and magazines. "Well, that route was a waste of time" she said to her husband driving the hybrid.

"I don't think so" he replied, "You get to know an area better once you leave the main highways."

"I see why they call West Virginia Wild but I don't see the Wonderful in it. Looks pretty depressing to me" Laura said looking at a coal train moving slowly over the railroad tracks.

"I'm sure you will have found a lot of wonderful things to do in your article" Jim responded.

"How long will your meeting take this afternoon?" she asked her husband, a cyber security expert.

"Probably all afternoon, you'll have plenty of time to work" he responded.

The couple checked into their hotel in Charleston at the point the Elk River joined the Kanawha and had a quick hotel lunch before driving the mile south to the State Capitol Complex. There Laura dropped Jim off for his computer security meeting where he was a speaker presenting an update on the latest in software measures to prevent password code theft. Laura continued a few minutes south to the historic Craik-Patton House, built 1834 and named Elm Grove by James Craik. During the tour there she learned of the Patton family buying the home for a time before moving onto California where General George S.

Patton of the Second World War fame was born. She also learned the house had originally been in Charleston itself and was slated for demolition but saved and moved to its current location by the efforts of several organizations since it was one of the first Greek Revival homes of the area. She thought this would be a good point of interest to highlight in her article especially due to its connection to General Patton whose grandfather, a Confederate Colonel, had bought the home before the Civil War. The house tour was interesting, but it was not what one would think of as a grand mansion of the Old South for no extreme fortunes had been made in this mountainous part of Virginia in antebellum times, only modest ones.

Driving back to the West Virginia State History Museum where she was to meet up with her husband after his meeting concluded, she learned that any really serious money came much later after West Virginia succeeded from Virginia after mother Virginia succeeded from the United States and joined the Confederacy. Mountainous West Virginia had no large tobacco plantations as in tidewater Virginia that depended on the warm and relatively flat terrain Piedmont Plateau, no rice as in the Old Rice Kingdom of the southeastern tidewater coast of North Carolina to Florida and no cotton plantations of the Deep South. What it did have was seam after seam of coal waiting to be mined covered by a magnificent hardwood forest waiting to be cut. These two natural resources, after the Civil War, would provide the nascent State with great wealth by great exploiters of natural resources once the relatively new technology of railroading penetrated its interior. In the 1840's the Baltimore and Ohio traversed the northern part of the state with a terminus in Wheeling. In the southern part the Central Virginia began to inch its way along interrupted by the Civil War, but after Appomattox it became part of the Chesapeake and Ohio and soon a great many coal mines opened along its route. In the 1880's the Norfolk and Western laid track into the twenty year old State to compete with the C&O. Many short lines were developed to feed these trunk lines. The stage was laid down for the State to export vast quantities of coal and lumber to all who needed it and make coal and lumber barons of those who supplied it.

All this information was coming together as Laura absorbed and digested it for her article featuring the Hatfield -McCoy Feud. Whether it had started over the 1865 killing of Asa Harmon McCoy, a Union infantry private of Company E, 45th Kentucky regiment, upon his return from the Civil War by Confederate sympathizer 'Bad Jim' Vance, a Hatfield nephew, of the Confederate guerrilla group named the Logan Wildcats , or in 1878 over a stray Hatfield pig with uncertain earmarks by a McCoy, or by claims and counter claims over large tracts of virgin timber along the Tug River, one thing was certain – the repeated killings of not only men on both sides over decades became notorious across America as the McCoy's lumbering operation failed while 'Devil Anse' Hatfield's became a success. Class resentment probably played as large a part in the feud as the death of a private from the 45[Th] Kentucky where such actions of one side against the other were common enough in the politically divided southern Appalachians both during and after the Civil War. The constant dividing of farms among many children into smaller and smaller plots, the loss of marginal farms unable to survive as America developed the Midwest ground local ambition down and let resentment bloom as the poor became yet poorer and as always, the rich richer.

Laura thought the story of the Feud to be a microcosm of West Virginia. Once independent families living on farmland they had claimed from Native Americans and virgin forest had been reduced over time to menial labor for others who managed to acquire the natural resources of the State, be it above ground in the forestry industry or below ground in the coal mining industry. At the State Museum Laura learned of the West Virginia Coal War and the Battle of Blair Mountain in the fall of 1921 when over ten thousand armed coal miners confronted a third their number of lawmen and strikebreakers controlled by mine owners. After a million rounds were fired and a hundred lay dead the battle was stopped by Federal intervention. Laura's phone rang. She looked at it. Jim was calling.

"Hey Jim, done yet?" she asked her husband.

"No. That's why I'm calling. I'll be a little late. They want a demo. How long is the museum open today?" he replied.

"About another hour."

"Good. That's enough time. I'll see you then. How's your afternoon going?" he asked.

"Fine. I've learned a lot and not all of it good. I'll tell you more later. Got any leads for dinner tonight?"

"The Bituminous Brewpub sounds interesting, about a half hour drive into a small town in the coal fields. Charleston here has the chains and a few others but this brewpub sounds interesting" he said.

"What is Bituminous? What kind of brewpub is that?" Laura inquired.

"I'll tell you later, see if you can find out at the museum" Jim concluded.

At his cyber security meeting the assembled group of state officials expressed disbelief that their governmental computer system could be hacked. Jim had agreed to provide a demonstration of how easy it was for someone like him to get into their system. He offered to use his own laptop for the test as it would not have any of their passwords stored on it. First he started with some of their names and addresses, both public information, and soon had their phone numbers, dates of birth, social security numbers and where they did their banking. Next he secured several of their email account passwords. Ten minutes later he was in the public section of the government's computer and from there was able to insert a program of his to get past their firewall. Once inside he simply matched up some of the data he had hacked from outside sources to internal data and retrieve user names and passwords of six of the officials. Now he could read whatever each official had clearance to access, but that was not enough. Again he inserted a personally written program and gained access to the Administrator's account gaining all the codes. Now he had control to add or delete anything he wanted to. He went to the State's Treasury Department and inserted into the tax returns for the month the phrase 'Jim was here' before logging off. Next he asked an official who had access to the accounting database to have a look at the quarterly tax income, bottom line.

"My God!" the accounting official exclaimed "Jim was here!"

"What do you mean" asked another, "What did he do?"

"Well, he didn't do any damage but he could have. All he did was leave a message, proof if you will, that said 'Jim was here'."

"That's right" added Jim Verraten, computer security expert. "I could have done anything. I could have entered a tax receipt for someone who paid no taxes. I could have issued a tax refund to myself, I could have deleted all records from a town or a county – just for the fun of causing havoc - and believe me Gentlemen, someday someone will do something just like that or worse. Our company can help you prevent these types of attacks now and in the future.

Stunned, one official commented "And you did this in just a half an hour, no special preparation ahead of time?"

"None whatsoever"

"Well, we had no idea. It's a big world outside West Virginia so we learned something today. We'll meet next week with the Governor and see what we can put together to fund an emergency security project. We just can't be this vulnerable" the head of the meeting commented.

Jim met up with Laura in the parking lot that served both the governmental offices and the museum. "How'd you do?" she asked.

"Nailed it. Seems their entire computer system has been installed only by State residents, kind of a keep the money at home philosophy, they were OK against low level threats but lacked real security expertise. I think they'll be fine now once we get a contract" he responded.

"That's good. I know this State needs all the help it can get" Laura responded. The couple drove back to their hotel to relax a while and change clothes before dinner. They had a view of the Kanawha and Elk Rivers and sat looking at their confluence.

"I guess that's why Charleston is here, that junction of the two rivers. In the old days this must have been a great spot as far as transportation went, before railroads and modern roads. I imagine all the steamboats that have passed where they joined here" remarked Jim.

"It is. They built a Fort here in 1788 and in 1794 became recognized as an official town. So where are we going for dinner?" Laura asked.

"The Bituminous Brewpub. Did you find out what it means at the museum?" he asked in return.

"I did. It means soft coal, the kind we have out here. I think I knew that back in elementary school but forgot. It came back to me as soon as someone started explaining it to me. So where is this brewpub, in walking distance?" Laura inquired.

"No no, but an easy drive down the Interstate to Teays Valley, ought to take about thirty minutes. I'm going to take a shower first, put on the news."

An hour later the couple had relaxed from their day and changed into their evening clothes, Jim was glad to shed his suit and tie for something comfortable. As they drove west on I-64, Laura asked Jim if he knew the significance of the name Teays. "I can't say I do" he replied.

"Then we are even on me forgetting what Bituminous was and how far a drive it was to the brewpub" Laura responded.

"That we are. So are you going to tell me or do I have to guess?"

"You'd never guess, I'll just tell you. Teays is the name of an extinct River that was as big as the Ohio long before the last Ice Age. It flowed from the mountains here all the way into northern Ohio,

Indiana and Illinois before joining the upper Mississippi."

"What about the Ohio?" Jim asked.

"It didn't exist. Not until the Ice Age anyway. The glaciers dammed up the Teays and all that water finally cut a new channel at the edge of the ice. That's todays Ohio River. The old Teays got backfilled in with glacier rubble above the Ohio, but you can still find spots where you can see its old valleys. We ought to take a weekend sometime and look for that" Laura suggested.

"Hmmm. River archeologists of a sort then."

"River Hunters. Now there's a title for a future article" Laura concluded. Laura explained how the Kanawha down to Teays Valley was part of the ancestral river but during glaciation cut a new channel leaving Teays Valley dry. Before they knew it Laura's history lesson was over and they were in the Teays Valley, a few minutes later they were pulling into the parking lot of the Bituminous Brewpub.

The brewpub had parking on both sides and in front. It stood alone, dominating, on its ample site and was located at the edge of town bordered on its right side by a small strip mall; the other side was a gas station. Across the road on a small knoll occupied by a few houses and fields interspersed among forested areas. The brewpub was in an older brick building probably a company store, a relic of a century or more ago. Although old, it had been solidly built and had survived the ravages of time quite well. Sitting on a foundation of sandstone the entrance was reached by going up six wide steps made of stone with simple handrails made of simple pipe on the sides. Once up onto the concrete porch the double door was centered in the building and flanked by a large picture widow on each side, once most probably for showcasing goods for sale. Above this first floor was a second floor with three smaller double windows on the front. The third level contained the sloped roof with a single window at the center.

The couple went through the double door and into the large first floor single room. Their view of the inside was broken only by some support columns. Across the entire back wall was a new bar. Just off the bar was an area for small tables for two or even a crowded four that extended over a quarter of the area of the first floor and in with the small tables against a wall was small dance floor with both a jukebox and small stage for live music or karaoke. The rest of the interior first floor room up to the front was set up with larger tables for family or group dining. Restrooms had been added on at the back corner. Next to one of the brick support columns was a dumbwaiter to the second floor kitchen and also a waitress station. Checkout register was near the front door. It was a layout that bespoke the previous version of the brewpub before it had become a brewpub a dozen years earlier. Then it was a roadhouse just over the city limit since the late 1940's. Before that it had been a company store until after World War Two. The new owners had added a small new building for the brewery in the back that was accessed through a door at the end of the bar and also from the outside, but they had not changed the original interior structure and layout much at all except to update and expand the beer draft system that the new business was based on and also change the décor from Honkey Tonk to reflect the areas mining tradition.

"Good evening, will you be having dinner tonight?" the greeter asked.

"Perhaps later, for now we just want to go to the bar" Laura replied.

"Straight ahead then to the back. If you want one of the large tables just let me know. The smaller pub tables are seat yourself. Enjoy."

The couple made their way to the bar. The spirit of the old company store seemed to emerge as they walked under the collection of miner's antique lunch buckets and dinner pails hung from the ceiling, from the many styles of carbide lamps mounted on shelves attached to the support columns, and on the walls from several photos of the building taken a century ago with lines of blackened faced coal miners waiting in a long line for their pay in company script spendable only at the company store. On the walls along with the old photos of the insides of coal mines and above ground works were mounted antique hardhats, some dented, all dirty and well beyond washing.

Jim and Laura took their seats towards the right side of the bar and looked around while waiting on the bartender. At this end of the old company store the décor featured photos and old posters from various coal hauling railroads such as the Norfolk Southern pulling a mile long string of hopper cars filled above their rims with black gold. Carefully mounted in frames on the walls were black fossils from the mines. There were small black ferns on grey shale; there were white ferns on black shale. There was a four foot long Lepidodendron tree branch with a bark that resembled a pineapple. Another fossil, standing upright in the corner was a six foot tall section of the spore tree Sigillaria with a bark somewhat resembling the skin of a crocodile; this sample had a diameter of two feet and was taken from a mine twenty miles away. Laura heard a bird chirp and looked around. Behind the bar she spotted a canary in a large cage. Inside were several perches, a mirror, a couple bird toys, a water feeder, a bowl of seeds and the half eaten leafy top of a stalk of celery. She immediately recognized it as the proverbial canary in a coal mine, although those safety birds would not have had such a large luxurious cage as they awaited their fate. The bartender came over with two beer lists. "Hello. Welcome to the Bituminous, my name's Dan" he said, "Do you know what you're drinking or would you like a few minutes to decide?"

"A few minutes, Dan" responded Jim. "This place has gone all out invoking the coal mines. It'll be interesting seeing what they've done with their beers" he said to his wife looking at the beer list.

Bituminous Brewpub
Beer List

Carbide Light – A sessionable brew that won't fill you up, with a bitter El Dorado hop bite at 4.2%

Canary Helles - Colored like our own canary, this refreshing Ale is brewed at 4.5% ABV

Coal Seam Saison – Very dry with high carbonation, complex but not malty at 4.7%

Backfill Brown Ale – Slight malty sweetness at a mild 4.7% ABV

Coke Black Stout – Pitch black from heavily roasted malts with a hint of expresso at 5.2% ABV

Black Damp Porter – Toasted malt aroma with a chocolate caramel taste at 5.6% ABV

Red Dog Ale – Amber malts balanced with Centennial hops at 6.2% ABV

Slate IPA – Full hop aroma and bitterness at 6.5% ABV

16 Tons IPA - Our Double IPA extra strong at 7.0% ABV

WV Tipple Tripel – Based on Belgium triple strength ales this golden colored ale is brewed at 8.7%

The bartender returned. "Made up your minds or need some help?"

"I think we're OK Dan, been to a few brewpubs before" responded Jim with a smile. "I'll have a Coke Black Stout and I hope you don't mean the pop."

"We do not. It's our version of Jet Black Stout. As dark as a lump of coke yet very drinkable. And for you Ma'am?"

"I'll have a pint of Black Damp Porter if you can tell me what Black Damp is" Laura said.

"Black Damp was when the mine lost its fresh air circulation, and especially after a fire, when there was no oxygen to breathe, only nitrogen and carbon dioxide or monoxide. Very dangerous. It would collect in pockets. Still want one?"

"Yes. I keep my word although it doesn't sound appetizing. That was interesting" said Laura. The bartender went to fetch the two pints. Laura looked around and saw on a wall over at the small stage a picture labeled Tennessee Ernie Ford surrounded by memorabilia. "Be right back, I'm curious" she told Jim.

Looking at the picture of the man wearing a white cowboy hat and dressed in a maroon jacket that sported white pin stripping by the shoulders to the neck she noticed he had a full head of slightly wavy coal black hair combed up and back without any part on either side. Above his nice smile was a thin pencil moustache with about a half inch shaved from the middle. Next to the picture on the right was a framed album by Capitol Records named "16 Tons". It was done in blue and had the image of the same man, Tennessee Ernie, on the cover next to the entrance of a coal mine but this time he was wearing a snog miners helmet and his black hair underneath could not be seen. On the left of the picture, again framed behind glass were the lyrics to the 1955 song 16 Tons. Laura read the lyrics to a song she had never heard:

Some people say a man is made out of mud
A poor man's made out of muscle and blood
Muscle and blood and skin and bones
A mind that's a-weak and a back that's strong

You load sixteen tons, what do you get
Another day older and deeper in debt
Saint Peter don't you call me 'cause I can't go
I owe my soul to the company store

I was born one mornin' when the sun didn't shine
I picked up my shovel and I walked to the mine
I loaded sixteen tons of number nine coal
And the straw boss said "Well, a-bless my soul"

You load 16 tons . . . .

Beside Tennessee Ernie was another similar tribute, this one for Jimmy Dean. Laura recognized the name from the meat section of the grocery store but didn't know he was a singer too. The featured song this time was 1961's Big Bad John, and the lyrics described a 6'5" man of 245 pounds of muscle that no one gave any lip to. The song describes a mine accident and how he held a massive beam up allowing twenty miners to escape knowing that he would then not be able to get himself out. Sad, she thought. The third of many tributes was to Loretta Lynn and her Coal Miner's Daughter song of 1970 about the hardships of growing up in a coal patch and returning as an older adult to her abandoned, falling down home of her youth. Laura saw her pint next to Jim and went back leaving unread several other tributes and with her she brought a touch of melancholy.

"You ought to have a look at their tribute wall; it's so depressing like this whole trip. Going to be tough putting a positive spin on the area to attract tourists" she said sitting down before sipping her Black Damp Porter and wondering why she ordered ale with such a foreboding name.

"We both have coal miners in our ancestry" Jim reminded her, "as do many of your readers. That ought to count for something."

"Oh, don't get me wrong, it will; but somewhat depressing to see what they went through" Laura said.

"Ten to twelve hour work days six days a week? Having to lay rails and roof support timber for free for the company? Piecework pay based on the tonnage you loaded? Almost certainty of black lung or death by cave in or mine explosion? Sounds like a great job, yet there was nothing else for them here" Jim added sarcastically.

"You do know more about it than I thought" Laura added.

"I do, I just haven't had reason to talk about it much. Before she died my Great Grandma made me promise I'd never go to work in the mines. Told me how my Great Grandad I never knew didn't see the sun all winter except Sundays; went to work before daybreak and came home after sunset. Had to hide from the company's Coal and Iron Police who were out after him for Union activities."

"You never told me about him" Laura said.

"I repress it. He died in a roof cave in, along with over 800 other miners that year in various mining accidents. I don't know much about him except he liked to plant a big garden in the spring; raised a lot of vegetables for his family. I think his garden must have been his grip on sanity, his own little Eden after a long dark, damp day of working bent over and seeing only by carbide lamps and candles, breathing coal dust and noxious fumes in a poorly ventilated shaft. It was a hard life for little script to spend in a company store just like this." Jim concluded.

"Jim, you've come a long way, most of us have. It's just a bit hard to understand why some stay in the mines today" Laura said while taking a sip of her Black Damp Porter.

"Did you learn why at the museum this afternoon?" Jim asked.

"I think so. There's not many coal miners left, maybe one or two for every ten a hundred years ago. Wages are very good for the few who work, when they work, as machines replaced the pick, shovel and mule. But they get out much more coal than the old days. Production is near record highs. So for those who get a job, it's a very good living with better working conditions than your Great Grandfather."

"Until a closing, accident, explosion or disease."

"Until a closing, accident, explosion or disease" Laura repeated.

Jim took a long drink of his Coke Black Stout, a stout as black as a Guinness, if possible. Even when he held it up to the light it was black, not brown and no refraction of ruby colored light getting through. It was the blackest ale he had ever had, and quite tasty too with a subtle touch of caramel over a not too subtle roasted chocolate coffee. "Let's look at the menu" Jim said "And change the subject." More and more people arrived and soon most of the barstools were full. Many families occupied tables in the dining section. It seemed the locals did not feel heavy hearted but quite happy to be out on a Friday evening. It was understandable and acceptable; they had been raised in the region and the brewpub's décor was a reflection of their ancestral pride.

Laura ordered a burger and skins while Jim ordered the Salisbury steak with mashed potatoes. They talked small talk with each other as all at the bar did, all except for one lone fellow sitting by himself at a small table at the end of the bar against the wall. He had arrived shortly after the couple did. While Laura was looking at the singer tributes, Jim saw him in the mirror walk over and sit at the table when the bar itself had many seats available, odd, he thought. As he was brought his drinks by the waitress without ordering, Jim assumed he must be a regular, probably waiting for some friends. The man, somewhere in his forties, sat looking through the window with his face away from the growing crowd. Now and then he turned to gain the attention of the waitress who brought him his pints and occasional shot of Old Crow whiskey.

Throughout their meal Jim noticed the lone man changed his ratio of pints of ale to shots of Old Crow in the direction that favored Old Crow whiskey, but as he was well over 6 foot tall and around 250 pounds Jim did not think much of it other than it must be his typical Friday night bender. Jim saw in the back bar mirror that the lone fellow had checked his watch repeatedly; his friends must be running late. Jim turned and saw a black patch with four large yellow letters on the fellow's sleeve by the shoulder. Jim read the letters: U M W A and above them he could see United Mine Workers of America. Jim could not see it but on his other sleeve was a second patch with his Union's Local and Number on it. The man wore what appeared to be work pants and work boots, both having residual black oily stains although appearing recently laundered and washed.

When Jim finished his Salisbury Steak he asked Dan if he could anonymously buy the lone fellow a drink or pick up his tab.

"That won't be necessary" Dan replied, "That's John Rizzo. Known as Big John around here. The owner covers his drinks on Friday night since he lost his job."

"He was a miner?" asked Jim trying to confirm the presence of Big John's miner union patches.

"Right, and a damn good one they say" but his mine shut down about two years ago. Companies want new, young men. Cost less you know. He'll never see the inside of a mine again, poor fellow."

"I see."

"He used to come in here on Friday nights with two of his friends that were let go the same time as John. On his work crew I believe. But they're gone now" the bartender said.

"Moved away?"

"No. Earlier this year Gary Falconi was killed when jogging, a hit and run. Police never did track it down. Then a few months later Tony Calabrase was shot and killed during a mugging over in Charleston. Wallet gone, a few suspects but no arrests. No match on the ballistics. So now Big John drinks alone. Nobody ever moves away, most can't afford to, many only know this area and can't imagine living elsewhere; they just get by day to day on assistance."

Jim ordered another Coke Black Stout for himself and knowing Laura was not so happy with the Black Damp Porter he said "Laura, what are you changing to?"

"The Coal Seam Saison" Laura ordered looking at the bartender. A few minutes later the two fresh pints arrived and Laura said "The Porter was good, but I didn't like the name." She noticed the brewpub filling up. "They have a good business here on a Friday evening. Some people must have some money to spend" she commented in reference to Big John.

"For now they do" replied Jim, looking in the bar mirror and seeing the unemployed coal miner check his watch again. Jim looked at his own watch; it was a quarter past nine. "How about a taste?" he asked his wife who then handed her pint to him. He sipped and returned it.

"Really dry" she said, "I bet it has some Brett in it."

"I think you're right. Like it?" Jim responded

"I do, but just for one, it's so dry" she answered.

"I know what you mean, like some of the double IPA's which really are much more than double the hops. Good for one only." As he turned back Jim noticed in the bar mirror that Big John was checking his watch yet again. He checked his, it was nine thirty five. Again, about five minutes later, Big John checked his watch and then immediately finished his remaining half pint and downed a double shot in one swallow that had sat untouched for over a half hour. Big John then stood up and quickly left the brewpub.

There was an unusual quietness that overcame the dining room as Laura and Jim were debating if to return to the hotel or try another beer when a uniformed policeman entered the brewpub at ten after ten. Then they saw the bartender looking out the window and reflections of flashing blue and red lights in the glass as the policeman spoke to the manager on duty. When the officer had left, the bartender went over to the manager and inquired as to what all was about. Laura and Jim suspected a parking lot crash or something of the sort, but when the bartender returned to his station they were in for a shock.

"What was that all about, Dan?" Jim inquired of the bartender, expecting a simple response. The response was simple, but simplicity alone is no guarantee of insignificance.

"Big John's dead" Dan said.

"Oh no!" exclaimed Laura, who along with her husband thought he was struck by a car, for they did not know where he lived and each thought he might have begun his walk home on the side of the road that fed the Bituminous Brewpub's parking lot.

"What happened?" Jim asked Dan pointedly.

"Officer says he was shot, says a shot was heard by some customers leaving and also by some entering."

"Shot by who, surly not a mugging of a penniless unemployed coal miner? Did they catch the fellow?" asked Jim.

"No" Dan said, "The shot came from the fields across the road, over past Big John's home. Big John was standing by the stone foundation of the brewpub, away from the front on the side. Probably had the urge or stopping for a smoke before heading home. They think it was a stray shot from a night hunter, it's coyote season all year round around here."

"Terrible" Laura said.

"A terrible accident" added Dan, "Police are still taking statements. Two have gone over to the house to tell his wife. It'll be extra hard on her, two kids in high school, one ready for college next year. That stops that." As word got around the brewpub the demeanor of the evening had changed from happy to sad for many of the diners knew Big Jim personally and almost all recognized him by sight. Laura stood looking out the front window at the police cars when an officer escorted a middle aged woman onto the porch. The woman had her two children with her, a boy and a girl, and all three were crying. The three of the immediate family watched from the brewpubs porch as the stretcher carrying the body of their loved one was loaded onto the ambulance. Laura now also watching from the porch gave her condolences to the grieving new widow. She looked across the road to the two story frame house the family lived in. With a police car in front flashing its lights, it was on the side of a hill about a hundred feet from the edge of the road. Some lights were on including the front porch light and beyond it appeared nothing but darkness making it impossible to see if a field or forest was there, but with certainty no other homes with so many lights on could be made out in that darkness at the edge of town.

Laura watched and listened as the police told the shocked widow what they knew, which was little, before leaving her and her two children in the company of some friends. In time Laura felt she wanted to offer her condolences even though she did not know Big John's wife at all. She went to their table and introduced herself "Mrs. Rizzo, I just want to offer my condolences to you and your family. I'm Laura Verraten. You don't know me, I'm a visitor to the area. I just feel so bad for you."

"Thank you so much. My name is Jessica. I really appreciate your concern. These are our two children, Jim and Ashley." All three had red eyes from crying.

Laura shook hands with the two siblings. "So sorry about your Dad." The two forced a smile, sniffed, wiped their eyes and nodded. Trying to get their minds a little off the tragedy she asked "Are you in high school or graduated already."

"I'm a senior and my brothers a junior" Ashley answered.

"Ahh, and do you like school or just glad to get out at graduation?" Laura continued.

"I like it a lot, especially computer class" Jim said.

"I like school a lot and wanted to be a teacher, maybe a guidance consular someday" said Ashley.

"What do you mean wanted?" Laura quickly said then thought of something.

"I don't see how either of us can go on to college now since Dad's gone. We just won't have the money" responded Ashley who teared up.

"Oh, I see. I'm so sorry. There are grants and scholarships you know, maybe you can get one" Laura encouraged.

"Maybe, maybe not" Ashley said, "It's all up in the air now. I don't know much about scholarships. I don't think our guidance consular does neither."

"Yea, all up in the air, time will tell. Mom will need help with the home expenses, we'll have to work after high school graduation." her brother added.

"Well, I'm from Pittsburgh and my husband and I know a lot of people at the Universities there" Laura said. Jessica Rizzo stood up and looked at her two teenagers.

"Let's go home now kids. We have a lot of phone calls to make." The two teens stood and followed their mother to the door of the Bituminous Brewpub.

Laura had a thought and approached Mrs. Rizzo, "Do you mind if I stop by your home tomorrow afternoon. I would like to talk with your kids about college some more, I do have some serious connections in Pittsburgh."

"I wouldn't mind at all. We're going to need all the help we can get if they're ever to graduate college." With that the mother and her two fatherless children left to return home. Laura reentered the brewpub.

She found Jim sitting at the bar where she had left him. "Jim" she said "I feel so bad for this family. First, the husband loses his job then he is accidently killed. He had two kids almost ready for college."

"And..." Jim said.

"And now it seems they might not be able to go. They're already talking of going to work after graduation to help their mother."

"Hmmm. I see. Laura, life's tough and I'm sure in West Virginia life's tougher than most places. What they really need is to move up and out, or at least out, the economy here is dying, has been for a long time."

"I know. And I'm supposed to be writing a travel article on Wild, Wonderful West Virginia. Not so wonderful here in Teays Valley."

"But it is. It truly is wonderful. Just not an economic strongpoint. Nature is wonderful here, the forests are wonderful, the streams are wonderful. The seclusion is wonderful. Not everywhere has to be booming with industry and technology."

"Are you having another?" Laura asked her husband.

"I don't think so. Not unless you want one."

"Not tonight, not after this. I'm ready to go back to the hotel" she said. The couple settled their tab and left the Bituminous Brewpub. On the way back Laura brought up the song by Jimmy Dean, 'Big Bad John'. "It's so damn depressing, this whole coal mining business. They even make heroes out of guys killed in mine accidents, guys like Big Bad John."

"Big Bad John? Who's he?" asked her husband.

"Probably fictional, just a guy in a song that sacrificed his life so his fellow miners might get out of a cave in. But that's the mentality down here."

"Who sang that? Never heard that one" Jim said.

"Let me think. Old song. Sixties I think. Dean something or other, yeah Jimmy Dean, like the sausage. Easy to remember. I wonder if it's the same fellow?"

"Jimmy Dean, could be. Interesting. I'll have to check when we get to the hotel" Jim concluded yet his mind drifted on as he drove.

At the hotel in Charleston Laura turned in early; it had been a long exhausting day for her. Jim took the room's ice bucket and went down to the ice machine, returned, got a scotch and a diet coke out of the mini bar, pulled up a chair, plugged in his laptop on the desk, connected, poured his scotch and soda into an ice filled plastic cup then began. Jimmy Dean, he learned, did indeed sing that hit song of 1961 and did indeed go onto market a brand of pork sausage under his name. They were one and the same. That was interesting, but not surprising, considering Newman's Own salad dressing line. Laura had quickly fallen asleep; he would tell her tomorrow of the match of singer turned sausage maker. After putting his ear buds in he then called up the song Big Bad John:

Every mornin' at the mine you could see him arrive
He stood six foot six and weighed 245
Kinda broad at the shoulder and narrow at the hip
And everybody knew you didn't give no lip to Big John

Nobody seemed to know where John called home
Just drifted into town and stayed all alone
He didn't say much he kinda quiet and shy
And if you spoke at all you just said hi to Big John

Somebody said he came from New Orleans
Where he got in a fight over a Cajun Queen
And a crashin' blow from a huge right hand
Sent a Louisiana fellow to the Promised Land, Big John

Then came the day at the bottom of the mine
When a timber cracked and men started cryin'

Miners were prayin' and hearts beat fast
Everybody thought that they'd breath their last cept John

Through the dust and the smoke of this man made hell
Walked a giant of a man that the miners knew well
Grabbed a saggin' timber and gave out with a groan
Like a giant oak tree he just stood there alone, Big John

And with all of his strength he have a mighty shove
Then a miner yelled out there's a light up above
And twenty men Scrambled from a would be grave
Now there's only one left down there to save, Big John

With jacks and timbers they started back down
Then came that rumble way down in the ground
And the smoke and gas belched out of the mine
Everybody knew it way the end of the line for Big John

Now they never reopened that worthless pit
They just placed a marbled stand in front of it
These few words are written on that stand
At the bottom of this mine lies a big, big man Big John

Jim played it over again, then again. He had a thought based on the some stanzas of the hit song, a thought based on one man helping another in a time of greatest need, a thought of friendship and great sacrifice.

And with all of his strength he have a mighty shove
Then a miner yelled out there's a light up above
And twenty men Scrambled from a would be grave
Now there's only one left down there to save, Big John

With jacks and timbers they started back down
Then came that rumble way down in the ground
And the smoke and gas belched out of the mine
Everybody knew it way the end of the line for Big John

Another visit to the minibar then once more he sat down and got to work. First on his agenda was to hack into the police and newspaper records for details regarding the hit and run death of Gary Falconi. He now was deeply involved and knew he would be up until the wee hours of the morning searching for proof that he hoped would prove that his working theory was wrong. As unlikely as his hunch was to be correct he could not let it go untested.

The next morning at breakfast Laura inquired "Not so bright and bushy tailed this morning are you? By the numbers of those tiny scotch bottles you left lying around I see you were into the minibar as I slept."

"I guess I forgot to hide the empties under some scrap paper in the bin" he admitted, "But then I'd have to get to the checkout receipt before you."

"I'll drive home today, you can nap if you want. But first we have to go back to the Teays Valley, I have an appointment to talk to Mrs. Rizzo about her two kids and college. I might be able to help them find scholarships or some grants back home" Laura said.

"Good. I was going to suggest a visit myself. By the way, you know that sausage Jimmy Dean in our stores, that was the same man who sang Big Bad John. I listened to it last night" Jim volunteered.

"Oh really. I'll have to listen to it sometime" Laura commented. Jim just smiled as he drank his fourth cup of black coffee and finished his breakfast of eggs, ham, fried potatoes and toast. She added "What were you doing last night? When did you go to sleep?"

"About four, just working out a thought to completion. I'll tell you about it later I still need to do a bit on it" her husband said. Laura knew at times like this his thought could be anything about anything; if it was important she would hear about it sometime. After checkout they traveled westward down the Interstate and arrived at the Teays Valley by late morning. They parked at the home of the deceased coal miner and Laura knocked on the door while Jim stood on the porch a few feet away. The door opened and welcomed them in, however Jim had a different object in mind and asked Mrs. Rizzo if he could walk outside behind her home and into the fields and hillside beyond where the shot must have come from. She had no objections. Jim added that he would be back in a while.

Laura sat at the dining room table with Mrs. Rizzo and over a cup of coffee she said "Jessica, I know a lot of wealthy people in Pittsburgh and I think some of them might be up to establishing a college fund for your two children. Ashley thinks she might like to be a teacher and maybe guidance consular someday and Jim likes his class in computers. My husband is also named Jim and he is a specialist in computer security. He could talk with your Jim someday and maybe pull some strings. He was consulting at the State Capitol over in Charleston this week, that's why we are down here."

"That sounds very compassionate and helpful, but the truth is I doubt they can attend college now as I don't think we can even afford to stay this house. A college fund would help but there are a lot of other expenses that tuition in college I have heard" the widow replied. Ashley Rizzo then came downstairs and seeing Laura and her mother at the table joined the two women.

Laura asked "Ashley, do you know where you might want to go to college?"

"West Virginia University at Morgantown I had been thinking, my first choice" she replied.

"Do you know the cost of tuition there?" Laura asked.

"About $8,000 a year."

"Any idea of room and board?"

"I've heard around ten or eleven thousand a year."

Laura said "And books will be another thousand a year, so you need about $20,000 at least a year and that will increase every year unfortunately. So it will come to between $80,000 and $90,000 most probably. Your brother will need that amount also, so were looking at close to $200,000. That's a lot of money to raise."

"It sure is" added Jessica Rizzo "It sure is."

Looking at Ashley, Laura said "Do you have the grades to get admitted?"

"I think so, for sure. Almost an A average."

"And any extras like volunteer work or significant hobbies?" Laura inquired of the 12th grade girl.

"I've volunteered at the lunch counter in the hospital last summer and I've volunteered at the old folks home on pottery projects."

"Good. What was a pottery project? How did that work?" Laura understood lunch counter work but what was this pottery volunteer work she wondered.

"We have a pottery kiln in the basement, was my grandma's. At the home I had whoever wanted finish and decorate pottery pieces and I fired them in our basement and took them back to the home for them" the young girl explained, "I can show it to you if you want."

"I would like to see it." The two went down to the basement where Ashley explained the process of finishing delicate green ware into a sturdy glazed finished piece of pottery. Beside the open kiln was a window open a few inches which Ashley closed.

"Dad must have forgot to close it" she said tearing up, "Don't want any critters getting into our basement."

While all this was going on Jim was out in the fields in back of the house. The slowly rising fields extended for a quarter mile to the edge of a forest. He failed to see any human footprints although he did spot an assortment of critter tracks going here and there. He traversed the field from left to right in a sweeping motion and focusing on certain areas where a missed shot might have ended going in the direction of the Bituminous Brewpub but not a shell casing was found. Some of the fields had an overgrowth of weeds and some animal trails but he saw no evidence of human trespass in weed or grasses. He discovered that a stray shot had very few areas it could have been fired from and hit the particular location on the side of the brewpub where Big John had been hit. He searched those limited areas again and found no evidence at all of a hunter's tracks. He then headed back to the house of the new widow.

Entering her backyard he noticed the home was not aligned parallel with the Bituminous Brewpub, but at an angle where one side had an exposure to the brewpub and on the other one could not see the brewpub at all. He walked along the side that had an exposure to the brewpub across the road, he noticed two windows; one was closed, very closed as it looked painted shut over and over many times but the other, although also closed, had some scrapings into fresh wood and some scrapings of old layers of paint on the ground outside. He looked across the road and could easily see where Big John had been shot. He came to the front steps, went up, knocked and entered when Ashley answered. He joined them for a cup of late morning coffee at the table.

"Find anything interesting in the fields?" asked Laura.

"Yes and no, or I might say, no and yes" he replied to her as Ashley and her mom were retrieving a fresh pot of coffee and some cookies. "How about you? How's the college discussion going?"

"Very well I think. Ashley ought to be able to get into the University of West Virginia if I can find her enough financial aid. She has the grades, the ambition and the extras like her volunteer work and her hobby."

"Her hobby. What is that?" Jim asked as Ashley entered with the cookies and her mother followed behind with the pot.

"Just ask her" Laura said knowingly.

"Well Ashley" Jim said as he took a cookie from the plate, "Laura says you have a special hobby that will help in your college admission. What is it?"

"Ok. So I had this hobby of pottery making since I was a kid. We have my Grandma's old kiln and I finish green ware and glaze it and fire it in the basement. When I volunteered at the old folks home I worked with some of the people who wanted and took their pieces here and fired them. Do you want to see the kiln?" the young girl asked.

Being polite and inquisitive Jim answered affirmatively and the two headed into the basement. There he saw her pottery setup. Homemade shelves to hold glazes and pieces waiting to be cleaned or fired, brushes and sponges and Exacto knives for trimming and a box of little cones. "What are those for?" Jim asked.

"Those cones are what turns the kiln off at the right temperature, they sag at the temperature you want then the handle of a switch falls and the electric is turned off. They have different cones for different temperatures, so you have to know which one to use depending on your glaze" the youth answered proudly.

"I didn't know that. So it's a mechanical switch not a timer" Jim answered and the girl beamed with pride. "How long have you been doing pottery?" he inquired.

"Right, A mechanical switch I guess you can call it. I never used an electric timer."

"And how long have you been doing pottery?"

"Oh, since grade school."

Jim looked around. "Can I open the window a bit and look outside?"

"Sure. They both were painted shut but my Dad had started to work to free them up. He got this one done. I don't know how far it opens but you can try it if you want. We closed it a little while ago to keep any critters out."

Jim went over and with some difficulty moved the window up about two inches, all he could manage doing. He looked through the low opening and could see the spot again where the girl's father had been found dead with a bullet through his chest. He closed the window and said nothing to remind the girl of her loss. He looked at the kiln. The top was opened away from the window and parallel to it. It was about three feet in its octagonal diameter and about four feet deep. "That's a large kiln" he said.

"Yea, my Grandma was really into it, used to make bases for lamps and stuff for holidays. I think she sold some of it to her friends and at church sales."

Jim spotted a kiln manual and said "Ah, there's the manual for it. Do you mind if I sit at your workbench here and read through it while you go upstairs. I'd like to learn something about kilns; I might get one someday" Jim lied.

"Ok. That's fine. Here's a book about glazes too you can look at" Ashley replied after retrieving the book from a shelf then heading upstairs to rejoin her mother and Laura.

"I'll be up in a little while" Jim said and began reading the manual. Now free he put the kiln manual down and followed the kiln's 220 Volt electric line and saw it was plugged into a wall timer modified for a 220 line. The timer was plugged into the 220 outlet that serviced the heavy electrical needs of the kiln. Obviously Ashley did not know about it. Was it to be a surprise for the girl he pondered?

Next Jim examined the kiln itself following up on his hunch. He saw that it was raised up on a couple cinder blocks and essentially its top was at the same height of the windowsill a foot away. Again he opened the window the few inches and went to the kiln. When he looked at eye level atop the kiln's octagon opening, he saw not only the brewpub across the road but where the father of the family had been shot. He then looked down inside it and saw a metal bottom but firebrick sides. The sides had groves inside them for the electrical resistance wiring that would glow almost white hot to fire up the kiln. He went back to the manual and looked at the kiln diagram. There was firebrick on all sides and surprisingly on the bottom also, yet this one had a metal bottom. He looked at the bottom again and saw it did not appear to be a perfect cut of high temperature tungsten steel but was rather irregular as if barely liquid once. He saw how it seemed to have been higher on one side than the other. Looking around the basement he found Big John's workbench and located a level that he took back to the pottery area. Placing the level on the kiln he found it was not level but off by a half an inch. The lower side contained more of the metal than the higher side which showed some firebrick bottom in places. The appearance of the metal reminded him of barely melted lava that cooled before becoming perfectly flat and smooth. He replaced the level, closed the window and went upstairs. He had seen enough.

Ashley was in her bedroom getting something for Laura so Jim took the opportunity of her absence to tell Mrs. Rizzo to remove and discard the 220 V modified electric timer her husband had been trying to perfect, that it was a danger to Ashley and also to get someone in to remove the spilled metal in the kiln before Ashley used it again as her husband must have been trying to melt some metal for a project and spilled some. Mrs. Rizzo asked Jim to dispose of the timer for her. Jim said he would dig out the metal for her and dispose of it along with the timer.

After a while Jim and Laura left for lunch at the Bituminous Brewpub; Jim had the home modified timer that he would dispose of when he arrived back in Pittsburgh. The brewpub was fairly busy as they walked in. Laura was looking for a seat in the dining room but Jim said he wanted to sit at the bar again, so the couple walked past the dance floor, tables, miner's antique hardhats and old coal mining pictures then took a seat at the end of the bar where they had sat a night earlier. Jim smiled when he the same bartender from their visit on Friday evening; Dan approached them with the lunch menu in hand. "Back again?" Dan asked rhetorically while handing them the menus. "Will you be having a pint with your lunch?" he inquired.

"Dan, good to see you again. Yes we will. They've got you working two shifts here I see" commented Jim hoping to establish a connection with the bartender by remembering his name and recognizing that he had finished evening duty and was back again behind the bar right after he had awoken.

"Oh, I do double duty over the weekend, get my forty hours in over just three days. Not bad to have four days a week off. Sometimes I get some extra work or just go fishing" Dan replied waiting for their beer order.

"Laura, a beer for you or just tea?" Jim asked his wife.

"I think I'll have the Carbide Light, interesting pun" she said.

Dan smiled and responded "Glad you got it. Lot of people not from coal country don't. And you?" Jim ordered the 16 Tons IPA. "One of our best. Very popular and a new keg from a fresh batch, best of both worlds" Dan remarked.

While Dan was pouring the beers the couple looked over the menu. "How was your burger last night? Recommend it?" Jim asked his wife.

"I do."

"Then that's for me, with bacon on it. What about you?" Jim replied.

"I think I'll go with the bowl of chili with the side salad" Laura commented.

Dan returned with the two pints and took their order when Jim asked him if there was any news about the death of Big John Rizzo the previous evening. "Be right back" Dan said as he took their order back to the kitchen. Upon his return Dan indicated that he had heard nothing more directly from the police but heard a rumor that they were going to try and match the bullet that killed Big John to a hunter's rifle and another rumor that they considered it an accident as the hunter may not even have known he had killed a man with a stray shot. Jim now had the opening he had come into the Bituminous Brewpub for, and the bar was not crowded.

"Dan, so all three drinking buddies are gone. Do you know much about them other than they worked in the mines and were laid off?" Jim inquired.

"I know a little about them. They all worked together in the same crew, trusted each other, never had an accident. Gary, Tony and John were like brothers although not related to the best of my knowledge. Gary Falconi was the first to go, accidently killed by a hit and run while jogging. Police never found the car or driver and that was about nine, ten months ago. Gary ran the continuous miner, that's a machine that chews into the coal seam with large metal teeth and then had a catch conveyer that transports the coal to a second conveyer to ultimately reach the outside into a rail car. Anthony

Calabrase, Tony, was the crews roofer. His job was to install roof supports as the continuous miner ate farther and farther into the coal seam. Skilled work as Tony had to judge where and how to support the roof, sometimes with a temporary jack pole and sometimes drilling a roof anchor up several feet into stable rock. The crew's lives depended on his expertise. He died at the hands of a mugger, shot, over in Charleston a few months after Gary was hit on the road. John Rizzo, who everyone called Big John, ran the rock dust machine, set the water sprays and did the wiring for lighting. This was also a safety measure for the continuous miner that made a lot of coal dust. A water mist settled some of it down and the lime dust he blew out his machine also helped clean the air."

"They trusted each other" commented Jim.

"Very much so. Their lives depended on each other" added the bartender.

"You said they were very much like brothers. How long did they know each other?"

"From what I learned about them, they were in the same class in elementary school and graduated high school together. They were in cub scouts together too. Before they started at the mine Gary was a part time volunteer coach for track and field events at the high school. Tony worked for a while at an auto body shop but that closed down, John did a stint in the military, trained as a sniper. They used to go hunting together and John always brought back a deer or whatever they were after even if the others didn't. They were best man at each other's weddings but I forget which was which" Dan concluded.

"Quite a strong relationship then" said Jim.

"Very strong. Rare around these parts outside of kin" added Dan as a server brought out two lunches from the kitchen. The young woman brought the burger and chili over and Dan motioned the chili and salad went to Laura. "So why are you so interested in the three?" the bartender asked.

"Just wondering about a few things. How sad it must be to lose two lifelong friends as he did" Jim explained.

"Probably why he started drinking whiskey after the car hit Gary. He was in here with his wife the time Gary was killed. After that day he and Tony added whiskey to their Friday nights. Sad." Dan saw another customer and walked over to serve him.

"I'll be glad when we get home. This area is too depressing for me" Laura said while eating her salad.

"I know what you mean."

"How's that 16 Ton beer?" she asked her husband.

"Actually quite impressive for an IPA. Not so bitter it's hard to drink. Want a sip?" Laura took a taste.

"That's not bad. You can have another if you want. I'll drive for a couple hours. Why are you so interested in Big John anyway? I can see through your vague answer even if Dan can't."

"In time, Laura, in time."

The couple finished their lunch while Jim had a second 16 Ton IPA. As Laura shut the door and buckled her seatbelt behind the steering wheel of the Toyota Highlander Hybrid she turned to her husband and said "I hope I don't have to play a guessing game about your, shall we say, interrogation of Dan, on the way home."

"Laura, Laura, Laura. Just tying up some loose ends, that's all. Come on, let's get going. I have things to do this evening. I'll tell you more once we're on I-79 past Charleston."

The Highlander left the Bituminous Brewpub's parking lot and headed out of the Teays Valley. There they followed the Kanawha River on the old river road back to Charleston and then back to I-79 heading north to Pittsburgh, Pa. Laura was driving while Jim slept off his 32 tons of 7% ABV IPA. About an hour past Charleston Jim awoke from his nap. "Are we home yet?" he joked. Laura smiled.

" No. We just past Sutton" she said.

"Ok. Next place with a restroom pull over and I'll drive. A coffee for you?" he asked his wife.

"No. Maybe a diet pop though" she said as a travel center appeared on the left side of the Interstate. "Speak of the devil."

"Whaat luuck" Jim added in a drawl as Laura took the exit.

The Highlander left the parking lot with Jim and his dark roast coffee in a cup holder and Laura opening her diet root beer. As soon as they were back on the Interstate Laura said "So fess up now. What was all that interrogation of the bartender all about?"

"Just loose ends and confirming what happened back there" her husband said saying nothing specific.

"What loose ends? You mean about Big John Rizzo accident?"

"No."

"No?"

"Big John had no accident?" Jim said, "I can tell you about it now but I didn't want to bother you unless I knew for sure" he said.

"He was murdered?" Laura seemed shocked.

"In a way. He was murdered and was a murderer twice over."

"You've got a heap of 'splaining to do Mister" she demanded taking a sip of pop as they drove past countless acres of rarely broken forest.

"And 'splain I will. By the way, you won't need to try and set up a college education fund for those kids. Big John already did that. You see he had taken out a life insurance policy on himself about a year ago. It was for $750,000, enough to send each of his kids to college for four years and enough for his wife to get a fresh start. I found that out last night by hacking into life insurance databases on the computer while you were sleeping. You know what they say 'Follow the money'. So I found that and it got me thinking about his friends Gary and Tony. Sure enough, each one had taken out large policies, enough to take care of their family's needs as well. Their size seemed to reflect colleges for any kids and also to take care of their wives for quite a while."

"Interesting, but not proof of anything sinister."

"By itself no. And you see that was a part of their plan. They had not taken out the policies when they were first laid off, but only when they would have known they would not be going back to work in the mines. The minimum wage jobs they could get when unemployment ran out, if they could get a minimum wage job with thousands upon thousands of unemployed after them, would be far, far short of their needs as fathers and husbands. So they had to wait. They knew it would not look good if they each bought a large policy simultaneously or even a short time apart. They waited several months from each other, and then had to wait some more until they could carry out their pact."

"Jim, this does seem sort of nefarious. I hope you have an airtight case and not just mere speculation about a coincidence of three friends' deaths" Laura pressed.

"As you will see, I do. Open that coffee now please. It ought to be cool enough to drink now" Jim asked then continued. "You see, Laura, a lot of things just didn't add up. Each on their own was innocent of the other, trivial if you will, but under that appearance there was linkage. If you think of it there must be a motive, an opportunity and a means in murders. I think you will agree that extreme financial distress is a motive to gain money?" he said looking at Laura and waiting for a response while sipping the java.

"OK. I agree. Each of the three friends had financial needs that could not be met. I agree that an insurance policy could help their families but not themselves. After all, they didn't take out a policy on a fourth person with all three as beneficiaries, then kill him. That's a surefire way to go to prison. But they did have the need for money" Laura concluded.

"Fine, they were careful enough not to tie their policies together as beneficiaries of each other in any way. Each policy appears unrelated to any other, by date or by beneficiary. So we have motive. Now for opportunity" Jim said while putting his coffee back down. "Few murderers have ever had as much opportunity as these three friends for usually the murdered person is a victim and not an accomplice to murder. I looked at the local police records; they're usually some of the easiest sites to hack as I've told you before. The first was the case of Gary Falconi, hit by a car while jogging. Hit and run suspect never caught, no leads. He was out on a side road after dark. A road with not much traffic and no potential witnesses. Interviews found he had recently taken up jogging just a month earlier. Could have been his inexperience or part of his plan that put him there after dark. Coroner report was he was hit at high speed and died instantly. Blood alcohol level at 0.18%.

Wife reported he was drinking at home, unusual for him, and he said he needed a late evening run to burn off some stress. Now remember his friend Tony had experience working at an auto body shop before the three started at the mine together. I think Gary knew his time was up and according to plan he was to be at a certain spot on the road at a certain time while Gary would be speeding along so Gary's family would collect on his policy. I think Tony killed a willing Gary as a favor in a death pact. Then, Tony drove home and put his auto body repair skills to work on his car to fix and repaint all evidence of the violent impact" and with that Jim reached again for his coffee.

"Possible. Coincidental. Hypothetical. Does not rule out a true accident by a hit and run driver" Laura commented. "What about Tony Calabrese? Are you going to tell me Big John mugged him in Charleston and killed him there?"

"Exactly. After the car was repaired, and I am sure he paid scarce cash way out of town at different locations for whatever parts and supplies he needed. He set himself up on a street in Charleston where Big John would kill him, take his wallet and make it look as a mugging. But Laura, remember, muggers are usually drug addicts who just want money for a fix. They are not a typical killer although they threaten death a lot. Police report on this one shows no self defense wounds or evidence of struggle on the hands or arms. Appears to me Tony just took the bullet to the back of the head in cooperation. The street Tony was on had no logical reason he should have been there other than it was dark and somewhat out of the busy area in downtown Charleston. Police could find no witnesses and recorded his wife said he had no reason to be there. The area is known for back alley gambling but he was not known in his home town as a gambler and confidential sources said he was not in any den."

Laura commented "Well, if both those are true then there were two assisted suicides. But then there was no one left to assist Big John. So your theory falls flat unless he paid a hunter to shoot him. That would put his family in jeopardy of blackmail to share the insurance payout. But then it would be an admission of murder if the hunter disclosed what he had done."

"True. Big John would not have taken the chance on hiring his own assassin. That much is clear to me. He was a skilled marksman himself. He had trained as a sniper in the military. Laura, he shot himself."

"What?" Laura exclaimed with not a little surprise. "Wait a minute. Just wait until they find that hunter and match the bullet ballistic to the rifle."

"They can never do that" Jim responded with confidence.

"Why the hell not?"

"Because I have the rifle here in the car, or what's left of it."

"What the hell! You've got some more 'splaining to do Sir."

"I know. You see Laura, we have established motive for all three, opportunity for all three and method for two. In the case of the method of Big John's death remember that he was drinking unusually heavy on Friday night at the Bituminous Brewpub. Remember also that he was looking at his watch a lot for someone just sitting and getting loaded. At a particular time he got up and went outside and did not go home but stood at a certain spot where he was hit by a bullet, a bullet timed to arrive at a precise moment that he would be there. When I was at the Rizzo house yesterday I searched and searched the fields and found what I had expected."

"Which was?"

"Which was absolutely nothing. Not a human footprint in the still soft ground from the rain a few days ago, not a spent shell casing anywhere at all of any type. There was no coyote hunter in those fields Friday evening. When I came back to the house I noticed a partly open window in the basement. I went over. It had once been painted shut but had been cut open recently. Some of the penknife cuttings of the paint still lay on top of grass underneath it. The window wood looked rather freshly whittled. I looked over the road again from the vantage of that window and saw the exact spot where Big Jim was shot. I knew I had to get down into the basement somehow so when I went in the house the opportunity presented itself to me when you brought up the girl's pottery hobby. I jumped on that of course, and accompanied Ashley went into the basement and saw her kiln right by that window. I opened the window a little, about two inches was all I could, enough to get a gun barrel out and sighted with a perfect view of the brewpub."

"Interesting."

"Yes. But then I wondered what happened to the rifle? Was his wife his accomplice? I saw the kiln was up on blocks and level with the window. But why? I examined the kiln which was located very near the window, perhaps a foot or two away. It had metal piled up inside on its floor in a cooled down puddle. Strange I thought as I saw in the manual it should have a firebrick bottom like the sides and top which was open. I looked above it and saw a small bent nail attached to a wooden beam under the first floor. Only a nail, a new one bent to hold a string, a new one with no rust on it. So why would it be there?"

"Hmmm. I think I see where you may be going with this. Then what?"

"Well, that bend was the key and it had a residue of a lubricant on it. Big John, remember, was a trained sniper. He had used the laser sight on the rifle to precisely target where the bullet would go and he timed the shot by using a string attached to the trigger that ran up and over the bent nail and into a block of ice he had prepared. You see, Laura, he could make any size or shape ice block he wanted and freeze it with a length of the twine inside it. It would then melt at a measurable, predictable rate and drip on the floor leaving nothing but a damp concrete circle which would dry up in a day or two. I saw the dampness still on the floor by the drain next to the kiln and I doubt it's there now. When the ice melted and slowly dripped the tension on the string got less and less. He had connected the string on the trigger to pull the opposite way the trigger would move when fired, a counter check in a way, but when the ice had melted far enough the string would not be able to hold back the spring pushing on the trigger like a finger. Then the rifle would fire. I am sure he tried it many times without a bullet in the gun to get the timing right."

"Go on. There are still some loose ends in your theory."

"Well, he probably couldn't get the the timing down to a second or two but he could get it down to a few minutes either way. All he had to do was place himself where the bullet would go to when the gun fired and wait for the ice to melt. He probably had it down to a five minute window. That is why he was checking his watch so often Friday evening when we were eating dinner."

"But what happened to the gun then?"

"The rifle would have had its stock sawed off and been delicately balanced on the edge of the kiln next to the window with its muzzle outside. The recoil of the firing would have kicked it backward where it hit the open kiln top then and fell into the kiln. He probably secured it in place with some wax, just enough but not so much that the recoil could not break it free. Once inside the kiln, the electric timer would turn the kiln on at a predetermined time and melt the gunmetal into a puddle. The laser sight would be nothing but a bit of additional metal and a little melted glass puddle on the surface. Then the timer would shut the kiln off. Ashley didn't notice the dampness on the floor or the residual warmth of the kiln. In the final analysis, Big John shot himself but made it look like a hunting accident. Everything I learned from our bartender today reinforced the dedication each man had for the other and their families."

"That is some theory."

"Not theory. Fact. Nothing else fits and accounts for all the facts, taken together, of the three friends' deaths. As Sherlock once said in the Sign of Four 'When you have eliminated the impossible, whatever remains, however improbable, must be the truth.' I have eliminated the fictitious hunter. I have given a logical connection for each death. I have shown motive, opportunity and means for each; however improbable, it is what happened."

"I don't know."

"And your theory is?"

"I don't know."

"You will not need to do the fundraising. Insurance policies will take care of each family's needs on that and give the wives a fresh start. The police will never find a ballistic match but they will keep looking until another case comes their way. Then they will chalk this one up to 'accidental'. There is nothing to be found of interest in that basement, save for the loosened window and a few wood and paint shavings. The water has evaporated, the wax burnt up, the melted gunmetal in my trunk along with the bent nail and the electric timer. There is hardly a trace there to connect the dots as if anyone was looking for them, which they are not."

"If your right then your obstructing justice."

"A crackpot theory of mine is obstructing justice, hardly so. Police are not looking for anything in our trunk, only a hunter and his rifle. I have neither. But I do have justice on my side. That coal industry cares little about their miners, never did, never will. Black lung. Mine accidents. Failed safety inspections bribed away. I think it justice some families in Teays Valley will be helped by what we saw this weekend and by what I did. They've suffered enough injustice."

END

The Maibock Medium Mystery

#9 from the Series

A Brewpub Mystery

by

Fredric G. Bender

All rights reserved: no part of this publication may be reproduced or transmitted by any means without the prior permission of the author.

The Maibock Medium Mystery is a work of fiction. Any resemblance to actual persons, living or dead, is purely coincidental. Any resemblance to actual brewpubs, breweries or bars is purely coincidental.

Maibock

In 1617 German master brewer Elias Pichler of Einbeck was hired in Munich to improve the quality of local brews. That he did. It is thought "bock" to be a form of "-beck" or perhaps a takeoff on his 'Oanpock' beer. In any case dark, malty, minimally hopped Bock beer became associated with religious holidays of winter and spring, almost as a liquid bread. In the 1800's Hofbräuhaus began offering a paler version on May Day holiday, May1st, hence Maibock.

Malt Bill: Pilsner, Munich, and Vienna

Yeast: Bottom fermenting lager yeast

Hops: Noble German, Tetnang, Hellertau, Hersbrucher

Adjuncts: None allowed

IBU (International Bitterness Units): 23-35

ABV (Alcohol By Volume): 6.3% - 7.4%

SRM (Standard Reference Method Color): around 6-11

Taste: Rich with European Pilsner malts, Vienna especially. Moderate to low hop flavor, some hop bitterness unlike other bocks. Some toasty notes but no caramelization. flavor no fruity esters.

Carbonation: Large, creamy persistent white head

Variation: Stoudt's Blond Double Maibock: Medium amber, caramel, baked bread, floral hops overlay of malt with notes of earth and honey.

The Maibock Medium Mystery

Driving back to their hotel in Mystic, Connecticut Jim and Laura Verraten discussed the home they had just toured in Newport, Rhode Island. To say it was a "home" was technically accurate when completed in 1901 as far as a place where one lived was concerned, but it was a large summer home at 60,000 square feet and a ballroom that could hold 400 guests. Now it had become one of the many old museum mansions to tour in the area. "Well, I would" said Laura.

"Not me. I would ramble around in there like a pea in a shoe box. No, a pea in a shoe store full of shoe boxes" Jim replied.

"I could see myself spending the summer months in it, hosting parties and enjoying the seacoast. I'm sure Sarah enjoyed her time in it" she said.

"After the Breakers and that Marble House, I've seen enough of the Gilded Age. Any more you go. I'll stay in the hotel and work."

"Well, it is true somewhat, seen one you've seen them all, and we've seen three already" Laura concluded.

The couple had been traveling in the area for almost a week while Laura gathered material for a travel article she was writing. Jim had joined her on the trip but mostly stayed in the hotel room working online with several clients on cyber security issues. Jim said "It was really nice for your company to send you up here in May. Really great weather so far and lots to do. I hope you mention the Mystic Half Marathon that we saw. Lots of runners back in Pittsburgh."

"Already in Mr. Obvious, as is the Newport Oyster Festival we went to."

"Ummm, oysters" Jim said and smiled remembering the salty, savory experience, "Nothing quite like them."

"Ugh. I don't think so. Definitely not raw, but they were good in the oyster pie" Laura added.

"Before my first oyster I was a mere child, or something like that so and so said?" Jim erroneously quoted.

"I think you are trying to say "when I was fifteen eating oysters the child was defeated and the woman won."

"Yea, that's it."

"Anne Sexton" stated Laura, "Get to know your authors before trying to quote them in public, especially up here."

"I captured the essence anyway" Jim defended adding "Are you sure she was writing about oysters?"

"Well . . . yes you did, in a way, but rather just keep your mouth shut and look illiterate than open it and confirm the fact" Laura teased, "And I do think she was talking about oysters. . . but come to think about it, I'm not sure." She looked at Jim behind the wheel. "Hmmmmmm" she said.

"Hmmm" said Jim with a wink. "Laura, Laura, Laura. We are all ignorant just on different subjects. Will Rodgers" Jim responded with a correct quote. Smiling, he added "I'm a cyber security expert, not a literature professor" in a statement mimicking Dr. McCoy of Star Trek fame.

"Ok. Just leave the writing to me while you fix systems. I'm glad we took the coast road back today; it was a nice drive" Laura mentioned as they entered the Mystic area.

"Me too. I get tired of driving on interstates. This must have been one of the first roads in the area back when most people would have traveled by boat up and down the coast here. Odd though how this Mystic is not really a town but made up of two towns on the opposite sides of the river. A little like Budapest."

"That is odd. I'd love to get to Budapest someday" she hinted.

Jim turned into The Furled Mizzen B&B, their cozy home for the past week. "Time for some work" he said. The couple got out and looked momentarily at Mystic Harbor and all the yachts and sailboats in their slips knowing that they could appreciate the scenery again a few hours. Upstairs in their bedroom Jim was soon checking emails while Laura was compiling and organizing notes on what they had seen earlier in the day. "Looking like I might have to give a seminar out west in a month, new client wants a dog and pony. Keep your schedule flexible."

"Will do" replied Laura quietly without turning while organizing her report. The TV was tuned to soft music.

Earlier in the day, around noon, a plane had landed at the TF Green Airport in Warwick, Rhode Island. It was about an hour drive from Mystic. The plane carried one Mrs. Seduta, Mrs. Florence Seduta flown in to the northeast from the west side of Chicago. She rented a car for the drive to Mystic, Ct. Now around suppertime she arrived at her hotel.

Laura closed her laptop and looked at her husband still working. "I'm getting hungry, how about you?" she asked.

"In the middle of something. How about a half hour?"

"OK, then I have time for a shower."

The couple had eaten at most of the brewpubs and many of the numerous restaurants from New London to Newport. On Laura's radar was a relatively new brewpub in Mystic, The Bowsprit Brewpub. She had met one of the owners, a Bonnie McCarthy, at the Craft Beer Festival. As she showered, she thought they ought to go there for dinner; it was nearby and within walking distance. They would not have to drive back to their B&B and they both preferred a brewpub to a regular restaurant even if the establishment offered more beer selection that a brewpub would serving only what they made. They had visited many brewpubs in their life together and found each one different, each having its own special character. The more she thought about it, the more the facility a few blocks away appealed so she said loudly from the shower "I've got an idea." Hearing no reply, she turned off the water and began to towel down "Hey out there. I've got an idea where to eat tonight."

"Where?"

"A few blocks away, The Bowsprit Brewpub. I met one of the owners and promised to visit before we left town."

"An owner? You didn't tell me that. Where did you meet her?"

"At that beer fest a few days ago. I met a lot of people there, forgot to mention it to you I suppose."

"The Bowsprit, I'll look it up." Jim quickly found the website and wrote down the address. It was owned by Bonnie McCarthy and her cousin Joan Bezeik and founded two years ago. It looked interesting, its nautical theme evident in the online photos. Won first place at the beer festival this year. "Hey, it won first place at that festival."

"Wow, I didn't know that. They hadn't been judged when I was there."

"We can judge them personally tonight. Good choice."

In early evening the couple left The Furled Mizzen B&B, walked up to Route 1 and then west across the Mystic River bridge into the Historic District. Ten minutes later they stood outside The Bowsprit Brewpub. "Easy to see how the pub got its name" Jim said staring at the bowsprit that served as a mounting from which the name of the established hung. Attached to both the wall and also to the bowsprit was a life sized figure of a buxom woman in a low cut 18th century dress; she was holding a sheaf of barley in one hand and several vines of hops in the other.

Laura saw Jim looking at the figurehead. "At least she's not topless like so many others we've seen at museums" she commented.

"No, she isn't" Jim continued "but this is new, probably made just for the pub. They would have had to consider public viewing out on the street in today's world. This ain't exactly the whaling days in a seaport. But I like the theme, bringing beer to the New World."

"I'm hungry. That walk woke up my appetite; and thirsty too."

"Me too. Think your owner will be here?"

"Let's go in and see."

The spacious interior was busy, so busy that there was a small line to the reception desk. Looking around Laura saw a rich nautical décor. The building, once a large warehouse, had been remodeled to appear as the interior of an old wooden ship. Replacing square double hung windows between large upright beams were now round portholes. A round mast of over a foot in diameter rose in the middle of the room and through a hole into the second floor; a second mast of about the same size was toward the rear of the dining room. Past it Laura caught sight of the bar. "Jim, bar or table tonight?" she said looking at her husband.

He looked back with raised eyebrows without speaking. The maître d' asked Laura "Two for dinner, would you like a table in fifteen minutes or immediate seating at the bar?"

"The bar please" she responded.

"The bar is open seating. Enjoy."

The couple walked toward the mast in the middle of the room; in the ceiling before it was cut an opening between joists of about three by five feet containing what appeared to be an antique teak wood grating held together by old brass hardware. Above it seemed the sky, or at least a spot lit painting of an azure blue sky, with several cumulus clouds added for realism. The effect was one to complete the impression or illusion of being inside an old sailing ship. Decorating the walls were several whaling harpoons, antique or reproductions undetermined at a glance, several scrimshaw pieces again of undetermined origin, several sailing ships models, an old sextant, and pottery decorated with nautical designs. Past the second mast was another wooden grate fitted into the ceiling and again with a painting of a sky and clouds. Referring to the faux skylight Jim remarked "Nice touch" and then spotted two adjoining seats at the bar.

"Hi, I be Abby and who be you?" the bartendress inquired.

Laura smiled and replied, "The Verratens, Laura and Jim. And I'm Laura" she quipped.

Abby smiled "Just drinks or food too, will the Verratens be having?"

"How about beers now and food later" Jim interrupted the two women.

Abby produced a draft listing. "Just updated yesterday. We only offer what we make here."

"Just what we like."

The list was neither extensive nor gimmicky, but had solid choices typical of New England as well as a more traditional seasonal offering. The couple pondered the list for a few minutes before discussing it. Beer decision time, they knew from experience, could be one of the most difficult of the day if the taps had many selections.

BOWSPRIT

On Tap Now

Crazy Lazy Hazy IPA – Smooth and creamy, cloudy oats and tropical mangos merge, a Haze Head favorite. $7

Juice on the Loose IPA – Who let the juice out? Mosaic, Galaxy and Citra hops added at flame out. A tropical punch of a beer. Notes of orange, banana, cherry, peach passionfruit. $7

Libertine Double IPA – Hop centric flavor, hop centric aroma with a balance of bitterness and sweet, biscuit malts. $6

Great White Whale Triple IPA – Below the head, within the glass unseen lurks more hops, more pilsner malt, more flavors, more mouthfeel, and more alcohol. Thar she blows. $7

Double IPA Squared Rig – Double the gravity, double the color, double the flavor of our Libertine Double IPA, our Double Squared sits low in the water. Heave to. $8

Nantucket Sleigh Ride Pilsner – A noble hops crafted beer, but the most melancholy excitement ever held in a glass. $6

Beelzebub Stout – One warm spark from Hades in the heart of Artic crystal malts, fit for the Devil himself. $7

----------Seasonal this month----------

Maibock, traditional Munich style brewed with Tetnang and Hellertau Hops in a rich blend of Pilsner and Vienna malts. $6

Jim studied the intriguing list, somewhat odd descriptions. "How can a pint be melancholy?" he asked Laura.

"Poetic license. I believe some are taken from Moby Dick, never read Melville's classic?" she asked.

Silence.

"Hmmm? Usually required reading at school" she pushed.

"I did read the Cliff Notes. That book was way to long."

Laura smiled and looked back at the beer list. "We've had so many of these New England IPAs on this trip, I think I'll stick to a traditional and see how well they do it."

"Great idea. I'm IPAed out too. Two Maibocks then. Right?"

"Right."

Abby returned and took their beer order for two pints of Maibock. Returning a few minutes later she placed them on beer mats and placed two menus on the bar counter. "Back in a few minutes. Take your time."

129

"Cheers" both said as they clinked the glasses together. Each opened a menu to see what was available.

"How about we start with sharing a Crows Nest and half a dozen Albatross Wings, you pick the sauce" Jim queried.

"Fine, I think the Hawaiian pineapple-coconut sauce."

Abby took the appetizer order. "How is the Maibock?" she asked.

"Excellent" Laura replied.

"I'll second that, and have a second" added Jim looking at his half-gone pint. Abby smiled and left to put the order in. "I'm glad we picked the Maibock, if anything just to reaffirm all beers are not Hazy or Fruity IPAs" he added.

"Those fruity beers are good though; I think they have a place. But they do dominate up here. Might be worth another trip sometime if my editor thinks it's worth an article about New England breweries."

"I think it would make for a good travel article. Maybe combine it with a fall foliage trip, two birds with one stone."

"Heh, we'd be called 'leaf peepers' by the locals" Laura said.

"Leaf peepers! Where did you hear of that?"

"Oh, just talking around. Picked up a lot of local jargon. Lot of quaint expressions up here, and I don't think they're just for show."

"Well, it is a touristy area" Jim commented before finishing his Maibock. A few minutes later a fresh pint and the appetizers arrived.

"Are you ready to place a dinner order?" asked Abby.

"Not quite, after these." Abby smiled and walked away. Jim looked at the chicken wings; if not the largest he had seen in his life, then tied for it. They were whole wings and Jim knew the routine by heart. He would cut the drum and flat apart then cut off the tip from the flat. His wife would get the flats and he the drums.

Laura commented "This sauce is great, very Pacific. Fits the pub."

"That it does. These large wings might be from spent hens, big old birds they were" Jim said eying the Crows Nest. It was a large appetizer and might have been enough for a meal for one by itself. A dozen shrimp sautéed in garlic butter and topped with bacon bits and chopped scallions lay on a mix of spinach and arugula leaves surrounded at the edge by an alternating pattern of a dozen clams and a dozen mussels with chopped parsley and lemon slices garnishing the dish. Jim picked up a shrimp by its tail. "Very good, Laura, you'll like these" he said eating the tail along with the shrimp meat. While they finished their appetizers, Jim noticed an older lady sit at a table by herself. She was dressed somewhat oddly in a long pinstripe dress, almost floor length and with sleeves to her wrists, with a large black belt around her waist. On the belt was an ivory colored cameo of a girl on a black onyx background surrounded by silver. Odd dress, he thought. Laura began to eat some of the shrimp, but not the tails which she discarded along with the shells of the clams and mussels.

"I don't see why you eat those things" she commented referring to the shrimp tails.

"Because they're good" her husband replied "Can't get them like this back in Pittsburgh."

Abby came back for their dinner order. Laura ordered first "Planked shad with the fried roe, cranberry relish and boiled red potatoes." Then Jim ordered a steamed double cheeseburger with sautéed onion. "Another steamer?" his wife asked rhetorically before ordering her second pint. Looking into the bar mirror, she caught a view of the older woman with the cameo. She had been joined by two other women, one of which Laura recognized. It was Bonnie McCarthy, co-owner of the Bowsprit Brewpub, she assumed the other was the other co-owner, Bonnie's cousin Joan something or other. The three were talking while the older woman worked on her meal between sentences.

"Something interesting?" Jim asked.

"No, not really. Just spotted one of the owners I met at the beer competition. Maybe we can get a tour of the brewery here after dinner. I'd like to touch base with her anyway and congratulate her on winning Best Brewpub, Best Hazy IPA and Best Juicy IPA."

"Quite a hat trick."

"Quite. It will put them on the map, for sure." As the couple finished their dinner, she noticed when the cameo wearing old lady had left with Joan. When Bonnie McCarthy was walking past the bar Laura turned towards her "Hi Bonnie. Congratulations on taking the three top prizes."

Bonnie McCarthy stopped and replied "Thank you . . . Laura, isn't it? The travel writer?"

"Yes, we met at the Beer Fest. You really have a great place here and very busy too."

"Well, business has really picked up since we won. And we're in talks for distribution of our beers. Investors are lining up" Bonnie smiled.

"Congratulations again. You must be very happy. I'll have to make a special mention of the Bowsprit in my article. This is my husband Jim. Do you think we could get someone to give us a quick tour of the brewery?"

Jim shook hands with Bonnie. "Pleased to meet you. We're kind of brewpub hobbyists but your pub here fits right into my wife's assignment."

"Jim, I'm pleased to meet you too. I can give you two the brewery tour, I'd like to say I'm off duty now but an owner is never really off duty. My cousin and I are so busy after winning at the Festival, so much to do. Tell you two what. I'll be back in about twenty minutes and then we'll do the tour" she concluded.

"Great" concluded Laura. When Bonnie left, she said "You have time for another Maibock if you like."

Jim motioned to Abby. When she arrived, he handed her his credit card and added "One more Maibock please." Laura glanced at the entrance, there was still a line for a table. Twenty five minutes later, the tab and tip settled, Bonnie was back and the three left the bar for the brewery in the back. Opening the door to it the three stopped for a minute.

"As you can see, we need more space" Bonnie commented as they entered. The brewery was of a decent size for a beginning brewpub Jim thought. Bonnie continued "We sized it at a four barrel capacity and have ten fermentation tanks in the cellar. But we are at our limit here and desperately need to expand. We have orders we can't fill yet and no space for a bottling line." Jim looked around at the pallets of grain and shelving containing assorted hop varieties near the loading dock. "I'd like to introduce you to Paul, our master brewer" she said as they walked over to a desk at the side of the brewery.

"Paul, this is Jim and Laura Verraten from Pittsburgh. Laura is a travel writer and Jim has an interest in breweries."

Paul rose and put out his hand "Pleased to meet you."

"Nice meeting you Paul" Laura added as she extended her hand.

"Good to meet you too" responded Jim as he shook Paul's hand.

"Paul is on overtime tonight, can't make it as fast as we sell it" Bonnie said and smiled.

"Rather be too busy than not busy enough" Paul added.

"So, what are you making tonight, Paul?" Jim asked.

"Leviathan Lager, one of our rotating standards" he told Jim then added "Come with me, I'll show you around."

The two women were left at the desk, Bonnie sat at the desk chair and Laura on a chair beside it. "Going to expand then?" Laura inquired.

"We need to. But difficult to agree on what to do, my cousin and I. Don't put this in your article but Joan and I are looking at two different directions. One funded more slowly and conservatively with internal growth; in the other Joan wants to bring in investors and go big right away."

"Oh. Was that a potential investor I saw you with out in the dining room?"

"Oh no. That was Joan Bezeik, my cousin, and the old lady was Mrs. Seduta, my birthday present. Let me explain. Tomorrow is my birthday and Joan has hired a medium, you know, a psychic medium for a séance for me. Ought to be fun."

Laura smiled "A séance. Wow Bonnie. That's interesting. Just fun or are you a believer in spirits?"

"I'm open minded about it all. We used to have a Ouija board when kids. A lot of fun. Mostly goofy girl stuff but on occasion some very mysterious happenings too. We played with the Tarot Cards too but hard to figure out how to really read them. We never tried a séance but always wanted to."

"Interesting, are there a lot of spiritualists in Connecticut?"

"Yes. All over New England actually. Remember the Salem Witch trials, some people have not moved on all that much in the last few centuries."

Across the room Jim and Paul were having a technical discussion by the brew kettle; it centered on the production of the juicy type IPAs. "So, then the hops you use are not selected for their alpha acid content alone?" Jim inquired.

"No, not at all. Most of the hop varieties we use have a moderate to higher acid content so we have to be careful to minimize their extraction. We do a late hopping at flameout on some, a dry hopping on others and on some a combination of the two."

"I see."

"It's no secret, generally speaking but the details are."

"High oils hops then. Citra, Amarillo, Mosaic . . . " Jim said referring to the labels he saw in the storage area.

"Yep, and Galaxy and El Dorado among a few others. Mosaic with its tropicals, pine, berry, earthy notes and Citra adds more orange, lemon and grapefruit. Those are the two main workhorses. The others are accents like El Dorado adds noes of cherry, peach and mango."

"The combinations must be endless" Jim said.

"Like the deepest sea" Paul added, "That's why I like brewing here. It's a never ending exploration in the brew kettle. Makes me feel like rounding the Strait of Magellan back in the day. Who knows what we'll find in our foamy sea of malt?" Paul said.

"Very well put" Jim added, "And you sell the results of your voyage here in Mystic. Like the old whalers returning home."

Over at the desk Bonnie and Laura continued. "I trust that what I've told you is confidential regarding our finances and difficulties we are having seeking an equitable decision."

"They are" Laura assured sensing that Bonnie may have felt that she said too much about her cousin Joan. The two obviously did not agree on the future of the Bowsprit and there seemed to be an aggressive hostility on the part of Joan towards Bonnie.

"Joan was always somewhat greedy, always trying to act above her lot in life" Bonnie commented, trusting Laura and feeling she had a friend to confide in. "We're both from the same overall family, same class of people. We're not even distantly related to the ones who built the mansions over at Newport. Joan always looked with envy at them, tried to be like them, expected to be treated like them. As if she was different than her cousins."

"I understand."

"I just want to keep the Bowsprit as it is and slowly expand here and not sell out to investors who want to take it into the big time elsewhere in some large ware house operation. We're making a lot of money here but it seems not enough for Joan. I guess it's going to come down to who is going to buy out who?"

"And at what price" added Laura.

"Exactly. Joan thinks she has control but it's an even split, she just assumes she's in control. Keeps getting outsiders involved without my knowledge, doing things behind my back. But she isn't the one managing and running the Bowsprit, I am. I solve all the problems as they come up, she just sits back and takes half the profits. My idea would be to expand slowly, buy the building and lot next door and expand with profits. She wants to either sell it all out to investors for a big payday or get a huge loan and move it to Hartford or Providence, a huge gamble I'm not willing to take. Mystic is good for us, very touristy and a proven location. I'm afraid I spoke too much and bore you with my troubles" Bonnie said.

"Not at all. Sometimes you just need to let it out to someone not involved. Don't worry. My article will focus on the touristy sites around here, not the problems of the owners" Laura added giving Bonnie her business card.

The time had come for a round at the bar. Bonnie, Laura, Jim and Paul sat down. Jim and Paul asked Abby to provide a sampling of all on tap while Bonnie and Laura had a pint of Maibock. Laura asked Bonnie "Was that a Maibock I saw Mrs. Seduta having earlier?"

"I believe it was. Yes, it was. Not everyone is a fan of the New England styles, but with the locals they dominate" Bonnie continued.

"Heh, a medium, the Maibock Medium then. The Mysterious Maibock Medium who can talk to the spirits" Laura added. As Jim and Paul sipped their flights and discussed the fine points of hop flavors, the two women conversed about how the Bowsprit was founded on not much more than a shoestring. She learned Bonnie had always been the stable guiding force behind it and Joan had talked her way in as co-owner when Bonnie got into a very tight spot and needed cash. Soon it was time to leave; Bonnie and Paul still had work to do.

As the couple went outside it was dark yet the pub was still going strong with later night drinkers after the kitchen had closed. Jim and Laura walked over to the Bascule Bridge over the Mystic River. Standing near the Western side, looking at the lights of the harbor, seeing glows emanating from the cabins of sailboats the couple paused to enjoy the sight of the crescent moon arising. On some of the sailboats people sat around socializing over drinks; on others there might just be a rare individual simply sitting and enjoying the calm, windless evening; regardless all their ships reflected perfectly on the wave less harbor mirror.

At night the small iron truss drawbridge with its tiny two story wooden framed, light gray shingle clad exterior had its first story lights on; the battleship gray iron trusses, the two large counterweights and the pair of circular gears with connecting rods to the movable span itself were lit mostly by the street lighting onshore and yellowish gleam escaping from the windows of the town's buildings nearby. They walked away from the control building and overhead ironwork out onto the span; there the view was much more open and more masted ships could be seen in the distance. As flat as the harbor was, it must have been a slack tide although if high or low they could not figure out but the farther away they gazed, the more trouble they had distinguishing the source of various points of light from that reflected; it was almost that they were inside a kaleidoscope or even some sort of mystic snow globe with static points of light instead of swirling snowflakes. Beneath the still water, unknown to them, was a leviathan of planning to claim another victim.

"I could retire here, or somewhere like here" Laura said.

"So could I. But with global warming who knows what this will be like when we are ready. Might be under by then" Jim said.

"True. Probably get bored with the views after a few weeks anyway" Laura said sadly and with more than a hint of sour grapes. They crossed the small river and returned to the Furled Mizzen B&B for the night.

The B&B offered two choices for breakfast: Option 1 was fishcakes, baked beans and eggs while Option 2 was the four hour corned beef hash with a soft boiled egg on top. Both options came with a Johnnycake and choice of coffee or tea.

Since Laura had enough research on Newport and surrounding areas such as the Connecticut Trolley Museum, the Railroad Museums of New England and Danbury, the many Gilded Age mansions of Newport, the Florence Grisworld Museum of Art in

Old Lyme, a great many other attractions, restaurants and brewpubs, after breakfast they then walked over to the Thompson Exhibition building and there they purchased entrance tickets to visit the Mystic Seaport Museum. It was a blue sky day as they entered the reconstructed seaport. Along the river itself were an array of vessels including the large seaworthy Charles W Morgan, an old whaler capable of either the Drake passage or the Strait of Magellan around Cape Horn. Other vessels were an assortment of small oyster boats and a collection of harbor workboats. They learned the seaport village was assembled from historic structures relocated to the museum from around the coastal areas of New England. They went inside several old residences but also several industries including a rope making building a thousand feet long and a sail making building with its stove for heat suspended four feet off the floor below to allow greater uninterrupted work area. All in all, it was quite an experience – except for one thing. Most of these activities and the livelihood of the people involved the cruel death of whales by the tens of thousands. It was not their meat for food but their fat for energy that the whalers were after to sell for use by the public in the form of rendered whale oil for lamp light as had been before the invention of kerosene in the 1840s. The discovery of crude oil in Titusville, Pa. in 1859 and the subsequent production of massive amounts of kerosene from it in time switched the nation over thereby saving the lives of countless whales. Both Laura and Jim found the seaport museum interesting but sad in its own way. The whaling industry entered classic Americana literature through the story of Moby Dick by Herman Melville in 1851. Laura brought the book up again to remind Jim that there were many references to it at the Bowsprit Brewpub. "So I've heard" he responded with a laugh, "But seriously, you're the reader here. Although I did enjoy Melville's book The Confidence Man much better."

"Probably because you actually read it. Those Cliff Notes steal an education from the kids" Laura criticized.

"I don't think so, they allow many to graduate who might not otherwise."

"Not at their full potential."

"Maybe not, but graduate anyway. Not everyone holds literature so dear as you, my Dear Laura."

"I can tell. Say, I'm hungry. What time is it?"

"Lunchtime" Jim responded without looking at his watch.

The couple left the seaport and headed over to a snack shop. Jim ordered a New York System Weiner and a Moxie. The hot dog was about four inches long and topped with mustard, onion, celery salt and ground beef sauce. Laura was having a fluffernutter sandwich and a chocolate frappe when her phone rang. "Hello, Laura speaking."

"Laura, this is Bonnie. How are you?"

"Fine thanks. What's up?"

"You know that séance tonight, my birthday séance my cousin set up for me?"

"Yes."

"Well, I'd like to invite you as my guest if you're open tonight, you see my cousin Joan backed out this morning."

Laura paused a few seconds "Let me check with Jim."

"Jim, Bonnie invited me to her séance tonight. Do you have any other plans on your mind for the evening?"

"No, not really. Go ahead, I'll just hang out at the Bowsprit."

"Good then. Bonnie, I'll be glad to make it if you don't mind a skeptic. What time?"

"It's set for 8. Maybe start around 7:30ish."

"Good, see you then. Where?"

"The Bowsprit, we have the function room reserved."

Goodbyes were exchanged. Jim smiled and said to his wife as she put her phone away "A séance? You're really going. Thought you were above that kind of stuff."

"I am, really. But it ought to be fun. Never been to one before and besides I like Bonnie." The couple finished their touring of the seaport museum in the afternoon and went into the gift shop. "See anything?" Laura asked.

"Not really, just impulse buys. Need any family gifts?" he asked. That gave Laura an idea and she bought a board book for her young nephew and a mermaid dress up toy for his sister. The couple then headed over to the Bowsprit for a cold one, each having a pint of Maibock, before returning to the Furled Mizzen B&B for some online time and relaxation. Soon it was time for dinner and they decided it best to eat again at the Bowsprit as they would then be sure of being on time for the séance and also that there were a few more items on the menu that had caught their eye the previous evening. By daylight the drawbridge did not seem quite so mystical, unlike the night before. It was just past five thirty when they arrived at the eastern edge of the Mystic river so had to wait for a while until the drawbridge raised and lowered its span, a regular occurrence at forty minutes past the hour during daylight. Standing there they watched the single span, hinged on the other side, rise up to an almost vertical position. Five single mast sailboats and several motor yachts passed by producing ripples and small wakes that interacted randomly making the surface quite different from the mirror stillness of the night before when they stopped on the bridge to take in the harbor view. Jim looked closely at the water's height. He had found that the tide usually varied little at high and low, between one and two feet. "Laura" he said "I think the tide is out. You can see some shells now on the piers. Only down about a foot or foot and a half. Remember the Bay of Fundy we went to last year?"

"I do. There was a whole waterfall that reversed course. Really something."

When the drawbridge lowered and the pedestrian walk reopened the two crossed and went over to the Bowsprit. They took seats at the bar and Abbey came over. "Maibocks again?" she asked.

"To pints please. Wicked good."

"Hah" said Abby, "I see you picked up our lingo."

"Yes, we have, banged a few ueys, had a grinder. Can't say I appreciate the Moxie though" Jim mentioned. Abby handed them two dinner menus and went for the Maibocks. "What looks good tonight?" he asked Laura.

"I think the Ishmael's Clam Chowder and Starboard Tack Lobster Roll on Anadama bread. And you?"

"I just have to try Ahab's Double Burger with some onion rings on the side" Jim said, "Any appetizers tonight?"

"How about Fathomless Fried Clams?" Laura suggested.

"Done." Abby returned with the Maibocks and took the food order.

During their meal Jim mentioned Melville's novel 'The Confidence Man' again. "You know that book is where the modern term 'Con Man' came from. If you look, you can see them all over our society today, not just the criminal element, but in all fields from medicines to health supplements to politics to financial advisors and more."

"I suppose you include faith healers and spiritualists in your list too?"

"I do. But not magicians. A magician is a known fooler. Everybody knows he is not really disappearing someone or cutting his associate in half or making coins appear out of thin air. But that he is so good at hiding what he is really doing is why he is admired at his art. Everyone knows it's not real; in a real con man they think it is real."

"Interesting analysis."

Jim smiled feeling he had made his point, next he would have to convince Laura that what she was about to witness at the séance would not be real, at the very most innocent entertaining magic, at the worst a money making con job. "Take the séance this evening. For it to be real there has to be a suspension of reality as you and I know it. Thus, there has to be the regular life of the one we're in, an afterlife of the spirit world where spirits wander about and a final resting place where they find everlasting peace. The spirit itself is therefore a remnant of a conscious mind, a soul of the Christians, the Ka of the old Egyptians or some other such personality essence. In their wanderings these spirits can be urged to communicate with the living like us, usually in very obscure ways such as movement of a tile on an Ouija board, tapping on a table or swinging of a pendant. And, of course, a spiritual medium to encourage the spirit and translate the messaging."

"That makes sense, matches what I know of it. But it will be fun to see one for entertainment if not enlightenment" Laura said.

"Yes, as long as what you are seeing is taken as serious as a prediction of Punxsutawney Phil on Groundhog's Day, and even he uses handlers to translate what he says into English, kinda hog mediums" Jim added, "You know, they say Phil is always right but sometimes his handlers translate incorrectly."

Laura smiled. A few minutes later she spotted Mrs. Seduta as the maître d' slowly escorted her over to a table. The fat old woman, bent over and slowly helping herself along with her silver knobbed cane, was striking in her appearance, more so than the previous evening, and looked terribly out of place in the Bowsprit except for the fact that she was the evening's entertainment for a select few. The turn of the century full burgundy dress reached the floor and flowed outward obviously supported by several petticoats underneath. Her black waistband was fastened by the same cameo as last evening and formed the tucked border between her blue long sleeved blouse and dress. Over the blouse she wore a 3/4 sleeved jacket made of the same dark burgundy material as the dress. Even sitting nothing could be discerned of her shoes for the dress covered all. It appeared she was not just an overweight woman, but on the robustly obese side although it was difficult to see any specific body contour. On her head was a large hat, a very large hat known by students of the period as a Victorian touring hat. It was black wool with black accents on top of silk, feathers and even black faux flowers. Around her neck she wore a pendant of deep red garnet, a stone of 1" diameter at the top faceted on 10 sides down to a point about 3" down. At ½" from the top was a grooved ring of tarnished silver with points of attachment at opposite sides of its circumference. The silver chain worn around the neck was long and contained five garnet beads on each side. The clasp at the back of the neck was large and attached to it was a single 4" strand of silver chain with a ring at the end used to hold the pendant when it would swing freely. Obviously, the pendant could and might be used to 'con'jure up a spirit. On the medium's fingers were several large rings set with cabochon stones; one was a star in a black mineral and the other a nice moonstone. Two bracelets of assorted cabs hung from her wrists, one on each. Laura turned to Jim and commented "Well, there she is in all her glory, decked out for the evening. This ought to be a real treat tonight."

"Like when Phil's handlers wear tuxes and top hats?"

"Perzackly. Don't remind me. I was so sleepy that night on Gobblers Knob I fell asleep standing up" Laura said.

"I know. I was there holding you up."

The maître d' had gone to alert Bonnie that Mrs. Seduta had arrived and by the time she arrived at the table, the medium was enjoying her Maibock and salad.

"How was the Ahab burger?" Laura asked looking at the few remaining bits.

"Actually, a tad too much for me but I got it in."

"So I see."

"The combination of ground filet, diced bacon and minced lobster was much better than I expected though." Before they knew it, it was seven thirty. Laura had had only one Maibock and Jim two. Bonnie came over "Hi Laura, Jim, glad you could make it" she said to Laura "Are you finished here?"

"Yes. Time yet?"

"Time to meet the group." As Laura and Bonnie left, Jim was finishing his onion rings and ordered another Maibock. Bonnie showed Laura the way to the function room then returned for the other guests at their table who she knew very well. Soon all returned to the room the séance was to be held in. "Bonnie, I'd like you to meet some friends of mine. Judith, Beth and Emma. Beth's my cousin, but I don't hold that against her" she joked.

"Yea, I'm a cousin. I'm obligated to be here" Beth joked in return.

"Emma and I came for the free meal" joked Judith. Bonnie thought this didn't seem like hard core spiritualists, just friends out together for a fun evening.

"I'm the new girl on the block" Laura said "I'm from Pittsburgh, you know the Steelers hometown."

"We do. We've handled them before" said Beth jokingly.

"Now, now girls. Put those claws back in. I'll go get our medium for the evening and we can begin" said Bonnie. Momentarily, she returned with Mrs. Seduta moving slowly behind her. "Girls, I want to introduce you to Mrs. Seduta, our medium for the session tonight."

"Séance, not session, if you please" Mrs. Seduta said taking control of the room as she put her satchel down onto the table, "The spirits must know this is a séance for them as well as you and we're not here to play bridge." She looked around. Everything seemed organized as she had requested, or ordered. The table was neither too large nor too small to hold the six attendees. Name tags were in place in front of chairs and Mrs. Seduta inspected every one in turn as she slowly made her way around the table leaning heavily on her cane. Returning to her seat at the head of the table she said "Please take your seats." The four guests sat down at the chairs indicated by their nametags, arraigned according to the instructions of the medium herself. At the opposite end to the medium was the nametag of Bonnie McCarthy, the birthday girl. "Please Bonnie, close the door then take your seat at this time" the medium slowly spoke. All except the medium herself were finally seated, the door closed and all instinctively knew to remain quiet. Mrs. Seduta then took off her hat and placed it upside down on the table. She then reached into her satchel and removed a short wide candle and placed it into the center of her upturned hat and then placed on either side of it an additional candle, each shorter still. She struck a match, lit the candles then went over to the switch and turned out the lights. Returning to her seat she took a circular wooden disc from her satchel. It was of black ebony wood and had the word 'Yes' lettered in gold into it where the N and S would be on a compass; the word 'No' was where East and West would be indicated. The two 'Yes' were opposite each other on the disc as were the two 'No', lettered in silver. Mrs. Seduta then removed the garnet pendant from around her neck and held it by the chain over the center of the ebony circle. Slowly at first it began to move. "Is anyone here who is not alive? Has anyone gathered here with us?" she asked. Within a minute the garnet stone began to pick up speed. Laura looked for movement in the woman's hands inducing it to oscillate but could see none. Yet the deep red garnet, the color of dried blood, began vacillating between the two edges marked 'Yes'. "Then Welcome" the old overweight woman said and then remarked "We are glad you are here with us. Do you wish us any harm tonight?" The pendant swung between the two No spots of the disc. "A No. Thank you. We are honored in your presence. Are you a man?" The spirit answered with a Yes on the ebony wood. "A man eh. Do any of us know you?" Slowly the garnet turned to reflect No. "Did you live here in Mystic?" the blood colored stone answered Yes. "Are you familiar with the cards of Tarot?" Again, Yes was the answer which Mrs. Seduta repeated. "May I sit?" The pendant answered Yes.

The medium sat down, placed her satchel on the floor and removed from it a large deck of Tarot Cards. "Fellow sitters, we will now turn to the Tarot Cards. Most spirits prefer them to communicate with. Unite your hands in harmony and channel your energy to him whose presence we have contacted to learn why he is here tonight." The five women sitters held hands in a U shape with the medium at the open end. Putting the garnet stone back around her neck, she took the cards from the card box and placed the empty box into the hat with the candles. She shuffled the cards then turned the first over. It was Justice. "Justice, the card of balance, of empathy, of fairness. What may this mean ladies?" She turned the second card over. It was the Wheel of Fortune. "Ladies, we now see change, we all will find ourselves changing in time and occupying all spaces on the Wheel of Fortune." The third card was the Hanged Man. "Oh, we did not know. We are sorry for you as you await your final judgement but feel your innocence for the crime for which you were hung." The two lower candles began to flicker. The next card was the Moon. "The Moon is tranquility. Now ladies. He is signaling us to all hold hands together, for we need to relax in a circle and I will then enter a trance so that he may speak directly to us all. Please look at the candles residing in the home of my hat."

The group of six now formed a hexagon of linked hands, somehow beginning to pulsate by gentle squeezing. Then one of the candles to the side of the center one went out, its thin wisp of smoke lasting but a few seconds. The medium went silent. Less than a minute later the second side candle grew faint and went out. "He . . . he is . . . is here. Here now" the medium stated with difficulty before putting her head on the table, then lifting it up again she spoke with a different voice "Call me Johnathon. I seek understanding not retribution." The center candle dimmed. "I wish only, only . . . "and the last candle went out. The room was now in total darkness. "I wish only to cease my wanderings." Then from around the table in the darkness it seemed to continued "I spoke out against one." Then farther away "One who committed sin against the Almighty." Then again from a different location "But he was powerful. I was not." The spirit seemed to circle the table repeatedly. Laura felt Mrs. Seduta's hand pulse with rhythmic squeezes as the spirit explained slowly how he had been framed in the distant past by elders of the town for a crime he did not commit. Johnathon stressed that he was innocent and he sought help in leaving the spirit world that had entrapped him. In time the voice returned to the area of Mrs. Seduta and Laura felt a tug on her hand as the medium seemed to wake up. All was quiet. No one dare say a word. Minutes passed.

"Laura. Laura" the medium said softly. "Laura, he is gone. Laura, turn on the lights." Laura released the hand of the medium and went over to the door and flipped the light switch. She saw the women in the room were still holding hands. "Laura, please Laura. I need some water" the medium said. Seeing a pitcher of water on a sideboard and some glasses Laura brought a glass of water over to Mrs. Seduta. The medium looked up and released Beth's hand, took the glass and sipped from it. Then spoke in a clear voice "Ladies, Johnathon is gone. The connection to the spirit world is closed. The séance is over" and with that she rested her head face down on the table. The women, somewhat surprised at the abrupt ending, released each other's hand and looked at each other wondering what to do. They saw that not only was Mrs. Seduta's head resting face down on the table, so was that of Bonnie, the birthday girl, and that her hands had not moved. Emma shook Bonnie's hand. Nothing. She looked at Judith across from her. Judith saw that Bonnie was not responding.

"Bonnie" Judith said also shaking Bonnie's hand "Bonnie, wake up." Stillness.

Assuming Bonnie had passed out from fright or emotion Emma said "Bonnie, it's over. Wake up" while shaking her limp hand. Bonnie remained still. The two women continued to shake her hand, then confused raised her head. In horror they saw blood emanating from between her lips and a small pool of blood had formed on the table where her mouth had been. Bonnie's eyes were open, motionless; she did not appear to be breathing. Emma cried out "Oh no!"

Judith rose abruptly and then saw a circle of blood in the back of Bonnie's blouse that had oozed downward toward her waist. Horrified she cried out "I think she's dead!" before collapsing back into her chair.

Emma ran over to the door, "I'm going for help." The other women were either crying or screaming in panic. Out in the pub, sitting at the bar watching a baseball game sat Jim. He saw out of the corner of his eye the door of the function room open and a woman emerge. He thought he might not get to watch the end of the game, in its 6th inning, as he expected Laura to be out soon. But to his surprise the woman ran over to the bar and said "We need help in there, please, someone go in and help." She then remembered her cell phone and immediately dialed 911.

Jim went to her and asked "What's the matter?"

"Someone's dead, please go help."

Jim, somewhat in disbelief, made his way to the function room. Must be a mistake, he thought, some trick by the medium for the entertainment of the group. When he arrived, he saw his wife trying to comfort one of the women. Confused, he saw Mrs. Seduta with her head down on the table and Bonnie with her head down at the other end. He went to

Laura and said "What happened? What's going on here?"

"Jim, go check on Bonnie. She might be dead." Her husband immediately did so and saw a slit in the back of her blouse at the center of the fresh bloodstain, and returned a few minutes later.

"Come over here" he said, walking towards a corner of the room and taking out his cell phone. Laura followed. "She is dead. Looks like she has been stabbed in the back. I'll call 911, I think one of the guests is doing that but just to be sure. Just try to calm down the other guests and not move or touch anything until the police get here."

"Will do" Laura replied with a tear in her eye for Bonnie. Mrs. Seduta looked up and just stared into space.

The police took charge of the situation as soon as they arrived. The women were all escorted out of the function room and into the brewery office to give their statements to an officer one by one. All agreed that everyone was holding hands from when the candles flickered out until the lights were turned back on. They listed the order of their seating starting with the medium, then Laura, then Judith, then Bonnie, then Emma, then Beth then back to the medium. It would have been impossible for anyone to have broken the chain of hands and plunge a knife in the back of Bonnie although either of the two women next to her theoretically might have released Bonnie's hand, killed her, then took her hand again. But then where was the knife? For anyone to get up in the darkness and move to kill Bonnie would require the person on either side of her to let her hands go. Accomplices? Motive? Again, where would the knife be?

Mrs. Seduta was the last as she walked down the hall to the office in her hunched over slow manner. In her interview she said that she had heard that once in a great while a spirit would lie about not doing harm, that there was some danger in contacting the spirit world but it was very slight. She had never encountered a hostile spirit herself and did not know any other medium who ever did. By and large the spirits were harmless, drifting entities.

The police searched all the purses as well as the function room itself. They searched the satchel laying open on the floor. They looked for secrete compartments everywhere in it as well as in the room. A police matron patted down all the women. Nothing was found. As this was occurring Bonnie McCarthy was pronounced dead at the scene and was being removed inside a body bag on a gurney and headed to the morgue. Jim approached the officer in charge. "I'd like to introduce myself, Jim Verraten" he said, "Your staff interviewed my wife Laura already, she was a replacement guest at the séance."

"I see" said the officer "What do you mean 'a replacement'?"

"There was a cancellation, a cousin was unable to attend and Laura was invited this afternoon" and with that Jim explained the reason Laura and he were in New England. He also gave his references to his contacts on the police force back in Pittsburgh and offered to help in any way he could with their investigation.

"We are capable of conducting our own investigation, but thanks for the offer" the Detective Cooper responded. That said, Jim found that Laura was free to go but that she would have to advise the police department when she was leaving the area.

The couple left the Bowsprit for the walk back to the B&B. They were silent until they reached the drawbridge. Laura stopped and stared at the harbor with tears flowing down her cheeks. "Jim" she began, "I have a feeling about this. There are some things I haven't bothered to mention to you about Bonnie and the Bowsprit. There was a lot going on between Bonnie and her cousin Joan, Joan Bezeik, I think was her name. Bonnie started the brewpub but Joan wormed her way into it bigtime."

"What do you mean by bigtime?" Jim asked.

"Half ownership. Bonnie was in need of cash and Joan gave her some to get over a production problem but for fifty percent ownership. It was either that or go out of business."

"I see."

"But that's not all. They were in a big disagreement about the future of the place. Bonnie wanted it to grow locally and more conservatively but Joan wanted to get other investors involved and go regional now. She was looking then at selling out her part in a while for tripling or more here investment and leaving Bonnie as a minority holder."

"Oh oh. Like a fish in a shark tank."

"Right, that's kinda how Bonnie described it too, but not in those words. She told Joan she would not sign the papers Joan had been working on with the investors."

"Go on. Anything else."

"It seems Bonnie was the founding brains behind the Bowsprit and enjoyed building the business. Spent almost all her waking hours there. Joan didn't put the time in much at all. Rarely in the place except to get a free meal with friends she was trying to impress as part owner. Bonnie said Joan was always spending money on a lifestyle above her means. You know the type, fancy clothes, expensive car, meals and vacations; that she felt she was better than everyone else and descended from the Mayflower pilgrims but could not prove it."

"A dilettante? Pretentious?"

"Yes, something like that. I have a bad feeling about her . . . and this tonight. You know Joan set this all up, got the medium and so forth, planned it for weeks, then the morning of the séance she cancelled due not feeling well. Blamed it on her stomach."

"Interesting. She had motive, but a lot of people have motive. Quite a jump you know from irresponsible lifestyle to murder. And Joan wasn't even at the séance to plunge the knife in."

"I know, but still."

"Let's get back. I'll look into it a little."

"I was hoping you'd say that" Laura concluded.

Back at the Furled Mizzen B&B Laura took a shower to relax before turning on the TV to get the evening out of her mind. Jim, wanting to assure Laura that she ought not worry about it, started to look into the situation on his computer; he did, however, remain somewhat intrigued. Jim thought that his wife's main concern was the cousin Joan, so he began there. Using his legal skills on computer searching as well as some less legal, hacking abilities, he researched what he could about Joan. First, he found that her ancestry could not derive from the Mayflower as he traced all her ancestors back to Europe and arriving in America in the late 1700's to late 1800's. The Mayflower had landed in 1620, so Joan could not possibly be descended from anyone on that ship no matter what she thought. So, he thought, Joan either did not know the truth of her ancestry or refused to divulge it and carried on a deception for status. That alone obviously was not illegal but did point to a personality that needed to be fed with respect if not actual praise.

Jim checked for Joan's medical records, there was no evidence of any stomach or intestinal troubles on record. On its own, it meant little. Jim hacked into Joan's financial records. It appeared she had inherited quite a bit of stock from her father, but as they were growth stocks, they paid no dividend. They had been sold off piecemeal over the years since his death without any apparent rhyme or reason. Her checking account and broker records indicated the very last had been sold immediately prior to Joan investing in the Bowsprit. As it were, except for the half ownership in the Bowsprit Brewpub, Joan was for the first time in her life broke and without any source of money; it appeared she had no job record what so ever and no formal education other than high school.

Searching for criminal history did turn up two police records on one Joan Bezeik. The first was from eight years ago and was for shoplifting; the second was of only three years ago when she was arrested for assault and battery during a heated argument. Jim thought for a few minutes. Was this just the tip of an iceberg that had eluded the police? Was this the true essence of Joan's character, lack of respect for others property and a tendency to use violence?

Jim thought further. All this could be nothing, nothing at all. It appeared Joan was no where near the Bowsprit when the murder occurred. In any case, the room had only the one door in and no windows. Although it was not a 'locked room' it was very close to it. There was no way, absent a hidden door or trap door in the floor or moveable wall panel that Joan or anyone else could have secretly entered the Bowsprit's function room without being seen by everyone at the bar, including Jim himself.

Next Jim decided to look into Mrs. Seduta, the medium who had been hired by Joan. She was an obese old woman who flew in from Chicago the day before to conduct a séance. Jim wondered why Joan would go to all that expense just for a birthday party, especially when she was, for all practical purposes, out of funds. Were there not mediums available locally that would at least save the travel expenses of a flight, rental car and hotel? He searched for them and there they were. All types of them, from members of formal churches to freelancers to 'party' mediums who did not seem to take it seriously. Why not just use one of them? He began to search the Chicago area for available mediums, he found some but not a Mrs. Seduta. He expanded his search to areas that would use the Chicago airport. There were none named Seduta. Finally, knowing Chicago was an airline hub, he conducted a lengthy search of each state. There was no Mrs. Seduta, medium for hire, anywhere to be found. Perhaps Seduta was just a stage name for an act after all? It was clear to him that the old medium had held hands with his wife during the entire séance up to the end. If any of the guests had knifed Bonnie in the back, she would have had to release two hands, one of which would have been Bonnie's if it had been Judith. The distance between the women was such that neither Judith nor Emma could have released Bonnie's hand, taken a knife from under the table or in a purse then reached around to stab Bonnie in the middle of her back. And if he was wrong, Jim wondered what became of the knife since the police had searched the guests and the room thoroughly. There was no murder weapon to be found anywhere, no hidden passages or trap doors. The more Jim thought about it while his wife slept, the more intrigued he became at the puzzle before him.

Somewhere after the late, late show and into that part of the nighttime programming that was more infomercial than entertainment he turned off the TV. He called up the airline reservation system on his computer and easily hacked into it, mere child's play for a cyber security expert like him. He did find the reservation for a Mrs. Florence Seduta. It was a morning flight from O'Hare Chicago to T F Green airport at Warwick near Providence, Rhode Island. Further searching showed a Mrs. F. Seduta had rented a car, a Toyota Camry, at the Warwick airport upon her arrival. It had been logged out with 6,372 miles on the odometer. Jim remembered seeing several of the popular cars in the parking lot of the Bowsprit when he and Laura had left some hours ago and surmised that the rental was one of them.

When Jim began a search for the name 'Seduta' or 'Florence Seduta' he came up empty. Apparently, it was not a common surname or even a surname at all. All he found was a reference that the word 'seduta' in Italian meant something akin to a meeting, a sitting or even a séance. His attention was now both fixed and focused. Seduta, what a perfect name for a medium, too perfect to be real; it must be a sort of stage name. But as none of the guests would ever get the joke, why bother, any name would do. There was something fishy here in Mystic, and it was not all in the bay. He decided that was about all he could do at the moment. He sent an email to the detective he had met earlier with all the information he had found. The police ought to be able to do what he had just done, but one never knew for sure, and how long they might take to do it going through official protocols.

His tip might save them time. He would talk with Laura in the morning after he had a couple hours sleep if he could stop his mind from continually turning and returning things over about the murder.

The sun arose to the east, on the other side of his bedroom window's view of Mystic Harbor. He woke up when he heard Laura getting out of bed. Outside the window he saw the night mist calmly in place in the deep, long shadows extending across the harbor; where the sun did strike the surface there were thin currents of mist beginning to slowly rise and dissipate into nothingness. Jim had a terrible thought flash through his mind, the murderer was probably still in Mystic but would disappear into thin air as sure as the mist would soon be gone. "Laura, get dressed. What time is it anyway?" Jim asked impatiently.

"Time to go back to sleep" Laura responded with a yawn coming back from the bathroom and heading to the bed.

"No seriously, get dressed. The sun's coming up. What time is it?"

Laura looked at the clock. "About a quarter past five. What's up?"

"We have to talk. I've been up most of the night. I need to ask you more about the séance and we don't have much time. Put on that coffee maker" he asked, "I'll fill you in."

In ten minutes the sun had burnt off more of the harbor mist and the aroma of coffee filled the room.

Laura was fully awake and Jim told his wife all that he had found out after she had gone to bed. There was the police record of Joan, her running out of money, her bringing in a medium at some expense when plenty of locals were available, the mysterious Mrs. Seduta who did not seem to exist anywhere under that name. How did it all fit together?

Laura shook her head "I don't know. The other women at the séance were all just regular married women, kids at home and longtime friends of Bonnie. I can't begin to imagine why any of them would wish her harm."

"Laura, let me ask you some questions about the séance. I want to close my eyes through this and be as if I am in that room with you."

"Ok."

"Ok, so you meet the women and enter the room. Then what, in detail?"

"Well, I was introduced to the other women by Bonnie. There was her cousin Beth and two friends Emma and Judith and we chatted for a minute or two while Bonnie went for the medium. When she returned with Mrs. Seduta the old woman just took over. She was into it right from the get go. She walked around the table inspecting it. She had us sit down at prearranged seats with our nametags on the table in front."

"Nametags, interesting. Not random seating then."

"No, not random, assigned. She had Bonnie close the door and sit down. Then she took her hat off and put it upside down on the table directly in front of her, about six or eight inches from the edge. Her satchel was on the table. She then reached into it and removed a short wide candle and placed it into the center of her upturned hat and then placed on either side of it an additional candle, each shorter still. She struck a match, lit the candles then went slowly, almost hobbling with her cane, over to the switch and turned out the lights. She took a black circular disc from her satchel with the words word 'Yes' and 'No' lettered in at the four opposite compass points. The Yes seemed in gold and the No in a silver or white paint. She took a fancy garnet pendant from around her neck and held it suspended by the chain over the center of the circle. It started moving, slowly 'Is anyone here who is not alive? Has anyone gathered here with us?' she said. The stone moved faster and I looked for hand movement but didn't see any. It started to swing back and forth between the two yes marks. She said 'Welcome' at that point. She said that we were glad the spirit was here and asked it if it wished to do any harm. The pendant then began to swing between the two No points. She used the pendant to answer her questions. She asked it if the spirit was a man, it was. Anyone that anyone knew was answered with a No. Did he ever live in Mystic was answered Yes. She asked if the spirit understood tarot cards and he indicated Yes. Finally, she asked if she could sit down and a Yes was indicated.

"Interesting. I feel as if I am there, keep going."

"Well, she sat down and then put her satchel on the floor. Then she took out a deck of Tarot cards from it. She said that the Tarot cards would guide us now. We had to all hold hands except for her. So we were kinda like a U shape with her at the gap and Bonnie at the bottom."

"What was the exact order?"

"Starting with me then came Judith then Bonnie then Emma then Beth then at the top of the U was Mrs. Seduta. We were focusing our energy toward her and the cards."

"OK, got it. Go on."

"She told us that spirits preferred Tarot cards to pendants. She put her necklace back on. She then took out the cards and began reading them."

"What did she do with the Tarot box?"

"Oh, she put that into her hat by the candles."

"Go on."

"Well, after she shuffled them she started to turn them over one by one. The first was Justice. I thought that's interesting, a spirit who has had some injustice done. She asked us what it might mean but it was a rhetorical question and no one answered but I'm sure we all had our thoughts prepared. Next was the Wheel of Fortune. That one I thought was comical as it reminded me of the game show but to her it represented change, always changing, time for change, something like that. The third card was the

Hanged Man. I was quite shocked. I could not see where this was going. Mrs. Seduta explained the spirit had been hung, an innocent man for a crime he did not commit, and was seeking Justice in the ever changing times before he could rest. But as she spoke the candles began to flicker and dim, especially the lower ones. The next card was the Moon indicating it was time to relax, to all hold hands including her for maximum spiritual energy, that she felt the spirit entering her soul. She wanted us to look at the candles as she entered a trance." Laura looked at her husband. It was hard to tell if he was still listening, in a hypnogogic state, or had just plain fallen asleep. She continued anyway without disturbing him.

"Then one of the candles went out. It had been dimming for a while. But then another went out in a similar manner by growing fainter then just going down to nothing. Not even a red hot wick tip. The medium said in a pausing voice that he was here now, entering her. She put her head down on the table. I was stunned just starring at the candle and the medium. In a minute or two she raised her head and spoke with a deep voice 'Call me Johnathon'. The center candle dimmed as Johnathon said he wanted only understanding not retribution. Then the last candle dimmed and went out as the other two had. It was spooky. We were in the dark. Johnathon continued saying that he wanted to stop his wanderings, the voice seemed to move around the room. I felt a cold draft on my arms. He explained how he spoke out against someone powerful who committed a sin against God. I felt the coldness on my lap and legs then. That voice seemed to circle the table repeatedly describing how he had been framed and hung. All the while I felt the medium's hand pulsate in her clasp of mine, like a gentle squeezing. In time Johnathon's voice softened and quieted; he seemed to be leaving the medium's body. Finally, it was quiet. I didn't know what to do. I'm sure no one else did either. Then I felt a tug on my hand. She was calling for me. She said Johnathon was gone. She wanted me to turn on the lights to the room. She asked me for some water which I gave her from a pitcher on the side of the room. She announced that the spirit had left and the séance was over. They all released each other's hands and looked around. I wondered what to do. Mrs. Seduta had laid her head down on the table again. We saw Bonnie's head also face down on the table. She was not moving. Emma shook Bonnie's hand. It didn't respond. Then Judith looked at Bonnie. Emma couldn't wake Bonnie. Judith tried too. Nothing. Then they raised her head and Judith saw blood out her mouth and her eyes open and unmoving. Then they saw the blood on Bonnie's back and screamed. Judith fell back onto her chair and Emma ran out of the room to get help."

"And that's when I saw her" remarked Jim, who obviously had not fallen asleep but was in deep concentration.

"I believe so, yes. Then you came in."

"That I did. But I will tell you now, I don't believe in spirits or the spirit world, but I don't know how she was murdered except by an unfound knife somehow. Some things we ought to clear up. You know when we have been to Vegas how we like magic shows and at home watching Penn and Teller Fool Us?"

"Um huh."

"A good magician easily fools us and neither of us are as sharp as Penn and Teller. Even they sometimes get fooled. Now when the medium came in, I refuse to call her Mrs. Seduta as there is no such person in any registry nationwide let alone Chicago. . . "

"I didn't know that" remarked Laura.

"True, Seduta is a stage name of sorts. It means gathering, meeting or even séance in Italian."

"Interesting."

"When she came in, she, like any magician, had set up the room to control perceptions, from her elaborate dress, to the seating arrangement, to the lights out. Then she takes off the pendant necklace and pulls out the circular board and waves the pendant over the board. Possibly minute hand gestures even though in the candlelight you saw none, or perhaps small magnets concealed in her palms. Palming is one of the oldest tricks. By a variety of ways then she could get the pendant to swing the way she wanted, the way to point out the answer out she wanted. Look at her whole performance as a magic act, not a spiritual contact."

"That makes sense."

"She prepared the candles. But why in the center of her upturned hat? Why not out in the open? What was the real purpose of the hat? I think I know. She sat down and removed the satchel from the table and withdrew a deck of Tarot cards, and like any good magician, that is what she wanted you to think. The candlelight not only set the mood but the lower light level made it easier to do sleight of hand. She apparently removed the cards from the Tarot box and shuffled them."

"What do you mean by apparently?"

"I doubt the cards were ever in the package box. There was something else in it that had to be placed into the hat in secrete. The Tarot reading was just misdirection. Any skilled magician can make whatever card appear whenever they want. The cards were probably hidden in her clothing and just seemed to be taken out of their box. They would have been in the order she wanted and her false shuffling did not mix that order up but left the deck stacked just the way she wanted."

"I can get that, but what about the empty box."

"The box was not empty. It was full of a suffocating gas. But there had to be enough of it to extinguish the candle flames. A block of dry ice would do the trick. As the dry ice turned to the gas carbon dioxide it would be heavier than air, it is anyway, but the intense cold of it would make it much, much heavier. So as it sublimed away as the magician spoke about spirits the suffocating gas would collect in the hat replacing the oxygen containing air and then putting out the lowest candles first and the tallest one last, as long as it was below the brim of the hat. Was it?"

"It was."

"And that later when the last candle went out, smothered by the cold carbon dioxide gas, you felt a cold draft on your arm then body then legs."

"I did."

"The cold gas, heavier than air was overflowing the brim and in total darkness was flowing over the table, your arm noticed it, and it seeped by gravity onto you're lap and down your legs. That was the coldness that you felt. The darkness it created was needed for the murder to occur. Everyone was holding hands including the magician who could not therefore be suspected of plunging the knife into Bonnie's back. I just don't know who did. Joan had a financial motive but was not in the room or pub. And I don't know where the murder weapon went to."

"Financial motive?"

"Joan was broke, her last inherited money invested in the Bowsprit. She had a small police record of theft and assault and battery. She enjoyed a lifestyle above her means and could see a big payoff by selling the Bowsprit to investors."

"I know she didn't give a damn about the business, Bonnie said so, it was all about a big payday. They even had life insurance policies in each other's names just in case" Laura added.

"I see. Complimentary life insurance policies in case a partner dies, probably the survivor inherits the business and the life insurance pays off any debts. It would appear that now Joan will be the new sole proprietor of the Bowsprit, someone with no experience brewing, someone that doesn't know how to run a pub, someone that doesn't want the pub. I wonder how long until she sells it off and pockets a windfall. What time is it?"

"Six thirty. I think we can get breakfast now" Laura concluded.

"Good. Get ready while I send an email off to Detective Cooper" Jim responded reaching for the detective's card. Laura dressed for the day and saw that her husband was still in his pajamas.

"Not ready yet? Thought you were doing a quick email?" she complained.

"Took longer than I thought, you go ahead. Order me a fishcake, soft eggs, couple johnny cakes with maple syrup and some coffee. I'll be along shortly, just thought of something I need to check."

Laura saw where this was going. Now in the universe of measurements the word shortly had many meanings and she had experienced a variety of them. Just as time is relative so was Jim's 'shortly'. It ranged from a minute to a couple hours, so when she placed her husband's order at the breakfast table, she warned them not to make it until they saw the whites of his eyes. As she was finishing her meal and sipping on her second cup of English Breakfast tea she was joined by her husband.

"Not bad, forty minutes. Find anything?"

"That I did. That I did" his coffee arrived. "You know those sites with all the searchable old newspapers, well I searched for the name Seduta, got some hits" he said sipping his java. "Actually quite interesting, quite disturbing. Seems as the name Seduta has come up over the last five years all over the country, but usually associated with a death in some way. There are some where the murderer was found guilty at trial and some where there was an accident and others unsolved. Too coincidental. There aren't any in which no one died. All the hits involved a death."

"Well that would not make the newspapers. Séance held, no one died" Laura reinforced.

"True. But there are almost a dozen séances where someone did die. Hardly a coincidence" he remarked as his breakfast arrived. "I sent the links to Detective Cooper, his morning just got busier."

"I see and I agree. Reminds me of the old law that rotten fish cannot be sold inside the town, they must be sold in another town" Laura hinted between the lines.

"Yes, yes. You know there was a Murder Inc in America back in the Al Capone days. The hitmen would be New York based and go out on assignment all around the country, quickly in and quickly out. The ones who wanted it done would be sure to have solid alibis" Jim said as he finished his breakfast. "Let's go over to the Seaport Museum, our tickets are good for reentry. We can think a bit there. We have a lot of loose ends but no way to tie them all together."

At the museum they chose a lone bench overlooking the Mystic river. "What you are suggesting, if you are suggesting it, is that Mrs. Seduta was a hit woman and then who hired her, Joan Bezeik?"

"Well" said Jim "Who else?"

Laura just looked into the river, neither really observing the mist had mostly cleared nor that the ships were moving about. "I can't see how that feeble old woman could murder anyone. She never left her chair."

"Apparently so. But why would she travel around the country, or to here, using her stage name, clever as it is? Why not just be introduced to the group as Mrs. Seduta?"

"But if she truly is a hitwoman, why would she use the same name to repeatedly travel on?" Laura queried.

"Who knows. Overconfidence? Less trouble than having to get new identities each time? Hard to say" replied Jim. The mist is almost gone, and I'm sure soon she will be too."

At a dead end in the conversation Laura suggested "Let's go up to the bookstore. I might get something for my Dad's birthday." Jim followed her into the shop. The large, spacious building was crammed full of books, lithographs, magazines, journals, stationary, reading and writing accessories, such as pens, lights and magnifiers decorated with Mystic Seaport Museum logo on them. It was not quite a tourist trap as there was a very large selection of books for all ages and tastes including a rare book room. Laura went in thinking a first edition of Moby Dick might be a great gift. After seeing the price, deciding it wasn't, she left.

The two kept looking around. "I just loved Moby Dick, for the story anyway" She said to her husband as she picked up an illustrated copy and flipped through it. Inside was a scene of whale hunting on the high seas. The small whaleboat, powered by oars was out on the waves with a man, Queequeg, at its pointed bow throwing a harpoon into the whale. The whaler, a large three mast ship was off in the distance. It had discharged the whaleboat and was awaiting the kill for processing into valuable whale oil. Laura starred at the illustration, a mere black and white etching that stirred something inside her. She looked around the room. There were lithographs and prints of a similar nature. It was a standard operation back then, she remembered. On her deck the large whaler carried several thin fast, whaleboats loaded with rope and harpoons. Then at the call of 'Thar she blows' the small whaleboats were released onto the high seas to make the kill while the whaler awaited their return dragging a dead whale behind. A wounded whale could drag the small whaleboat for miles at quite some speed giving name to the phrase 'Nantucket Sleigh Ride' before it lost enough blood to finally die. It was dangerous work.

"Jim" she said "Look around, look here. See how the whaler doesn't participate directly in the kill. See how she just sits back and waits for it to be done.

Somehow Seduta did it through someone else, she was the whaler. She had someone else do it, a whaleboat, an accomplice, a Queequeg."

Jim looked at the images of the small whaleboats and the harpooner who stood at the ready. Dangerous work to be sure, but potentially rewarding. "Laura, I think you might be onto something here. She must have had some kind of partner" he said as he began to gaze into space.

"Can I help you?" asked the clerk.

"Oh, Oh no. Just thinking" Jim replied. His eyes resumed looking at the books in front of him and he saw a copy of 'The Confidence Man' also by Herman Melville. He picked it up and thumbed through it. He had read it long ago but now much of the detail was coming back to him as he scanned the pages quickly. "Laura, I think your Dad might enjoy this one by Melville, and you might too."

"The Confidence Man?" she asked.

"The Confidence Man!" was Jim's firm reply.

Laura purchased the book at her husband's suggestion and the two returned to their bench overlooking the Mystic River. "I need to call Cooper. Give me a minute." He dialed the detective's number and went through the small talk quickly. He learned that Bonnie had been knifed in the back with an atypical weapon about an inch wide. The knife was very thin and easily passed sideways between her third and fourth ribs on her left side, just above her heart. He learned from the overnight autopsy that the knife did not end in a simple point making a narrowing slit in the body. It seemed the entrance wound was much smaller than the slashing carnage within the body, around the heart and aorta. It was presumed it had a razor sharp flattened end on it much like some harpoons designed to bleed the animal to death but without the movable hinge of a harpoon that prevented retreat from the inside. Apparently by wiggling it around sideways Bonnies aorta had been completely severed and she would have passed to unconsciousness in seconds and died shortly after, within minutes. The internal damage was over three inches wide indicating a right and left wiggling of the knife pivoting at the entrance wound. "Thanks for that information, Detective. Now we need some information that your men can gather. By the way, is Mrs. Seduta guarded I hope."

"That she is. She is in her hotel room and told not to leave town until we allow. She's already threatening to call a lawyer and doesn't want to miss her plane" Detective Cooper indicated.

"Good. Don't let her out of that hotel room. I need you to find something out. I need to know how many miles on her rental car and what is the level of the gas tank. You probably will need a search warrant, but if I'm correct, you might have the murderer within your grasp already."

The detective indicated that a search warrant for the car would not be a problem and he would let Jim know the results as soon as possible. Turning to

Laura he said "I think your reference to the whaling boat is the answer." Who was that Queequeg anyway?"

"In the story he was the harpooner on the whaleboat."

"Then we have to find our Queequeg. I think he has returned to his whaler. Where else on the high seas to go?"

"By that you mean Mrs. Seduta?" Laura asked.

"I do."

At the bench Jim paged more thoroughly through The Confidence Man. "You ought to read this before you give it to your Dad" Jim said. "Takes place aboard a steamboat on the Mississippi. No one is who he seems to be. But I don't want to give the book away. But consider Mrs. whatever her name is. She is a con to be sure if one does not believe in spirits and you know I don't. She conceals her role as a magician so well that her audience does not even know they are witnessing simple tricks that a beginning magician with cards or a science teacher with dry ice and a candle might do. I am beginning to doubt that she is even a woman, how do we know she is a woman? By her introduction to the group and the dress she wears and no mustache or beard."

"But Queequeg?" Laura said accepting much of what Jim asserted. Just then the cell phone went off and Jim answered.

"Hello. . . Yes, I see. . . Well that didn't take long. . . A very small town. . .Let me write this down." "I need your pen a minute" he said to his wife and opening the back flap of The Confidence Man he wrote down the number 6,553. Back on the phone with Detective Cooper he asked "And the gas gauge? . . . I suspected so. I'll call you back in a few minutes. . . Bye." Turning to his wife he said "I think we're hot on the trail of your Queequeg. I need a little time on the computer. They ought to have Wi-fi at the restaurant there."

Inside enjoying a later morning coffee Laura took the book she bought for her dad and began to read while Jim plodded away with a double expresso. On a spreadsheet he had typed in the 6,553. The box below he put 6,372, then subtracted one from the other to get 181. The larger number was the mileage from the odometer of the Toyota Camry now; the smaller number was the mileage when Mrs. Seduta checked the car out. That 181 was the number of miles that Mrs. Seduta had put on the car, yet the distance between Warwick, RI and Mystic, CT was but a mere 44 miles. Where had she driven to log on an extra 137 miles, almost three times the requited distance. Certainly not a missed turn. And that explained why the fuel gauge showed about half a tank instead of slightly off full. "She drove an extra 137 miles, used up almost half a tank of gas. That needle shouldn't have moved much off full in the 44 miles to get here" he said to his wife.

Laura looked up from the book. "So where did she go?" Jim just shook his head negatively. "Another airport to pick someone up?" she asked.

"Let me check some distances." Jim began to check mileages from Warwick to various points and then onto Mystic. Aside from small towns there were two interesting possibilities. "It's hard to say, but either Logan Airport in Boston or Bradley Airport over in Hartford are likely candidates if they didn't want to be on the same plane together or even arrive at the same airport. A good con man covers his tracks as much as a magician deceives and obscures. Both those fit the mileage driven. The half tank remaining fits too. That's a 15 gallon tank so she used six to eight gallons at 25-30 miles a gallon, dropping the needle halfway."

"She was busy" Laura grimly added.

"Very. I have to call Cooper" Jim concluded. In the phone call he described his travel analysis to the Detective. Cooper agreed and concluded that she may have picked up an accomplice at either airport before arriving at Mystic for the séance. He indicated that he would ask the local police at each for security camera footage of the pickup areas. The Detective said he would put several plain close men as backup to the officer in the hotel lobby in case she decided to make a run.

"She may not run as an old woman" Jim said and the detective agreed. Cooper told Jim that one of his men had already taken the room across the hall at her hotel and they would be watching her second floor window from the parking lot. "Good. Talk to you later" Jim said as he hung up.

"Hah, that was an understatement" Laura commented, "She may not run as an old woman because she may not be an old woman. He or she may not be fat, not be old if your book here has anything to say about it."

"Interesting analysis. . . She may not be fat." Both Jim and Laura came upon the same thought at the same time. Laura spoke first.

"Let's think outside the box. We could be dealing with a thin person who under a large, old fashioned dress hides a shorter partner under it somehow and wraps him and herself with padding to look like an obese woman. You've seen these fat suits in movies and remember Weird Al's video I'm fat?" she asked.

"I'm fat, I do indeed, one of his best. If done right the ruse would avoid the police finding a knife during a pat down search. I wonder if the police can get any surveillance tapes of Seduta arriving at the Warwick airport and picking up her rental car? I'll give Cooper a call." Jim got ahold of detective Cooper and asked him to look at the Warwick Airport tapes and try and spot Seduta. He explained how she might have the accomplice with her in the hotel now trying to think of a way to get out of the mess. They agreed the only way to resolve the suspicion was to have Mrs. Seduta subjected to a strip search in her room and to thoroughly search the room. That would require a search warrant and the Warwick tapes might just get them one if she appeared significantly thinner. For now, all Jim and Laura could do in their unofficial capacity as consultants was to sit at the Mystic Seaport Museum and wait it out. Laura returned to reading and Jim to getting caught up on incoming emails.

Laura was downing the last of her Raspberry tea and scone with clotted cream while Jim sipped the second of his Italian roast double expressos finishing an email to his corporate office when his cell phone went off. It was Detective Cooper calling. "Jim Verraten here" he said. "Yes, yes I am sitting down. . . That is great news. . . A what? . . . Yes we are. . . Yes. . . What time?. . . We'll be there, 8 PM. . . See you then."

"What is the great news?" Laura asked.

"They caught. . . what's his name you gave him. . . Queequeg."

"The accomplice. You mean they have him?" Laura asked.

"That they do and we are having dinner tonight at eight with Cooper. He will explain it all then."

Laura sat back, smiled and thought at least they caught the murderer but it would not bring Bonnie back to life only give her justice. In a while the couple headed back to their B&B to freshen up for dinner up at a restaurant in Olde Mystic Village. Since the weather was ideal and they wanted the exercise, they decided to walk rather than take their car to the eatery. Arriving a little before eight they checked in with the maître d'. The reservation was in order but

Detective Cooper had not yet arrived so they decided to wait in the bar. "Look Jim, they have Maibock on tap" Laura spotted. They each ordered a pint and Laura asked the bartender if it was the Bowsprit's Maibock.

"Yes it is" he answered, "We've got just one half barrel left and I doubt any more coming. Have you heard about the Bowsprit. Closed today. The owner was murdered."

"Yes, we heard" Laura answered avoiding the subject. Halfway through their Maibock pints Detective Cooper approached them at the bar.

"Hello Jim, Laura. Sorry for the lateness. Unavoidable" he said.

"No problem Mr. Cooper" Laura responded.

"Call me Mike or I won't buy you dinner tonight" he responded in turn.

"Ok Mike, let me buy you a pint" she offered.

"No can do. Against department policy, can't accept gifts. But I'll get one at the table since I'm treating tonight." The three diners with two half pints in hand went to their table. Soon another pint of Maibock arrived, the dinner order was placed and the discussion turned to the murder. "We owe you a big debt, both of you. Without your help they both might have gotten away on the next flights out." Laura and Jim just listened. "We looked at the Warwick airport tapes and saw a rather thin woman with a large suitcase emerge from the luggage pickup. Turns out that was where he kept all the padding."

"He?" they both said almost simultaneously.

"Yes he! We also saw the rental car at Bradley airport near Hartford picking up the accomplice. License plates are a giveaway. We obtained the search warrant and entered Mrs. Seduta's room. She was sitting nervously on the bed. We had several women officers conduct the strip search while we waited just outside the door. That's when they discovered Mrs. Seduta was not a woman at all. She was not obese either, not that old and her padding designed to hide a very short man, one of the little people, under her long dress. On each leg was attached a small platform or step about a half a foot above the ground and these were attached to metal rods, braces, that fastened into her special metal reinforced shoes. The small accomplice could then be hidden from view by the old fashioned floor length dress covering her shoes and all the padding she wore concealed him from a pat down. At the séance table then, he would have needed time to unfasten himself and in the dark, when the last candle went out, leave his hiding place and walk quietly around the room speaking as Johnathon, the spirit. At the right time he then plunged the knife accurately between the ribs of Bonnie and probably muffled any sound she might make with his hand or cloth. His shortness did not deter from his experienced deadliness as he plunged the thin knife horizontally between Bonnies ribs and then wiggled it back and forth sideways to sever as much and more as was needed to cause a quick bleed out into the body cavity. Then it was back to the leg braces on the medium who ended the session when she knew all was done."

Jim and Laura just looked with their mouths slightly agape.

Detective Cooper continued "I see you are as stunned as we were. When the matrons did the search, they uncovered not just a little person hiding between the legs but also later that Mrs. Seduta was not a woman, although I must add that he had given up that pretext before any visual confirmation of the fact was done. That came later."

"What about the knife?" Jim asked.

"Find it?" Laura added.

"Yes we did, hidden in a cloth with blood stains inside some of the padding where it would have been undetectable in a pat down. These were not just a couple amateurs, but hired pros."

"And hired by who? Joan the cousin" queried Laura.

"That's what the medium is saying. The accomplice says he doesn't know. We've just taken Joan into custody and she is denying everything. Seduta has given us her real name as Castaferio, living in New York. Says her accomplice was only supposed to rough Bonnie up and scare her into signing the contract Joan wanted. I don't think so, but I'll let the District Attorney get to the bottom of it all. Seems this Castaferio is known to do some enforcing for the mob and says Joan Bezeik was referred to him by an associate when she approached him looking for someone to do some work."

After the dinner they sat discussing the events of the last two days and the topic turned to the Bowsprit itself. "What do you think will happen to it now that Bonnie's gone?" Laura asked.

"The court will appoint a trustee to hire a manager to run it while the murder charges are decided. Then if Joan is found guilty, it will probably be sold off and all proceeds go into Bonnie's estate. If Joan is innocent, and I don't see how that is going to happen with Castaferio testifying against her, then it would all probably end up owned by Joan. You know, a hit man doesn't just go around killing people. Someone calls them to do it, so Joan will probably serve a long term in the pen. We can thank you both for getting involved and playing a big role in helping us solve this so quickly. And I think some of those other Mrs. Seduta unsolved incidents in the papers will be looked at again when we notify the other officials. Thanks again for that."

"Don't just thank us" Laura said "Thank Herman Melville. It was his Moby Dick with the whaler, whaleboats and Queequeg that showed the way."

"And his Confidence Man with the many ruses, deceits and false appearances that showed how it might have been done" added Jim.

END

Horror in the Hop Yard

10 from the Series

A Brewpub Mystery

by

Fredric G. Bender

All rights reserved: no part of this publication may be reproduced or transmitted by any means without the prior permission of the author.

Horror in the Hop Yard is a work of fiction. Any resemblance to actual persons, living or dead, is purely coincidental. Any resemblance to actual brewpubs, breweries or bars is purely coincidental.

Northwest Black IPA

A variation of the American IPA style first commercially produced around 1990 in Vermont but popularized in the Pacific Northwest and Southern California of the US starting in the early-mid 2000s. This style is sometimes known as Cascadian Dark Ale (CDA), mainly in the Pacific Northwest.

Malt Bill: Debittered, not burnt, roast malts for color and flavor.

Yeast: Top fermenting

Hops: Cascade, Citra, Centennial, Mosaic, Simcoe

Adjuncts: None

IBU (International Bitterness Units): 50-90

ABV (Alcohol By Volume): 5.5% to 9.0%

SRM (Standard Reference Method Color): 25-40 Very Dark Red-Brown to Black

Taste: A moderate to high hop forward aroma, often with a citrusy, resinous, and/or piney character. If dry hopped, can have floral, herbal, or grassy aroma. Very low to moderate dark malt aroma and taste. Slight caramel acceptable. A dry to slightly dry finish should predominate.

Carbonation: Medium carbonation up to a bit of creaminess may be present in an off white to tan head.

Variations: Chocolate, coffee, caramel or toast flavors.

Horror in the Hop Yard

A shriek followed by a long, deep scream came from between the ripe hop bines, seemingly a few rows over from Olivia Morales and interrupting her from putting any more mature Cascade hop flowers into her basket; then shortly after the first came another, louder scream, one of unmitigated terror causing Olivia to look in its direction then climb down the ladder that she was on. Was it a rattlesnake sighting? Was her friend being accosted? She walked down the row of twenty foot tall bines in the hop yard to their end, turned and quickly walked the pathway toward the source of the screaming woman. At the end of the hop yard the pathway entered a field just beginning to be cultivated with the recent planting of the Mosaic hop variety and within the young plants stood a young woman, her friend Kumiko Chang, looking down at the ground a few feet away with her hands on her cheeks. Her ladder was empty at the Cascade hop bine Kumiko had been picking. As Olivia quickly ran over to her friend, she saw what Kumiko was staring at and screaming. She embraced her friend and said "Kumi, it's OK. I'm here. What happened?"

Kumiko pointed at a bloody corpse. "I don't know" she said, her body shaking as she turned away into the comfort of Olivia who looked over the shoulder of her friend. What she saw was absolutely horrifying. There lay an eyeless face upwards to the sky, a body, probably of a young man for no gray hair was seen, with red blood in splattered, dripped patches all over his yellow shirt and on his trousers. Blood lay in coagulated pools on the ground near him. His bloody shirt appeared torn or cut in the neck area and right shoulder area. But that was not the worst. As well as missing his eyes, the right half of the face was gone and the entire nose was missing; the skin, cartilage and facial muscle were gone leaving a jagged pattern from the forehead to the nasal area slightly past where his nose would have been then to the scalp past the missing ear. The remaining hair was intact yet bloody. The jawbone and teeth were fully exposed. The removal of flesh continued down the right side of the neck exposing the vertebra and down the shoulder into the upper arm. The clavicle, joint and humerus were all defleshed and the blood stained yellow shirt ripped and shredded in the area. Flies were swarming above and on the corpse as the warmth of the sun that morning gave them the energy to seek a fresh kill following the fresh scent of death unrecognizable to people yet.

"Kumi, let's go. We have to get back to the farmhouse and have them call the police. We have to find Jane and take her back before she stumbles on this too." Kumiko nodded her head in agreement and the two friends began a retreat from the horror in the hop yard.

****

The Previous Day

The sky was deep blue, a Persian blue, where it could be seen from Interstate 90 above the deep emerald green fir and hemlock trees of the Snoqualmie Pass of the Cascade mountain range of Washington State. The rental car of Jim and Laura Verraten could use gas and Jim could use a break. "What say we make a pit stop?" he said to his wife.

"Fine with me" Laura responded, "They must have gas stations along here somewhere."

"They do. There are some people living up here for the skiing, maybe even all year for the recreational opportunities. I think there's one in about two miles according to the sign we passed a while back." A few minutes later they turned off the Interstate and into a gas station. Jim got out into the clear, crisp mountain air and filled the rental up while Laura went inside. Even in a small town like this the refreshing beauty of Nature could not remain hidden from him; there was just too much of it and all of civilization appeared to recede into a small anthill of population. If Bigfoot was anywhere he was here hiding out somewhere he mused and smiled. He pulled the rental over to the curb and went inside for the restroom. Laura was looking over the available snacks. Shortly he joined her and they decided to stay away from the packaged sweets, probably stale with little turnover up here in the mountains, but instead grabbed an apple for each and a stick of peppered jerky for Jim. To this was added a couple coffees and they were off on the road again for Yakima. "Keep your eyes open for a Bigfoot sighting" he said with a smile. Jim had finished a three day cyber security conference in Seattle and had spent a day with aerospace engineers on the nitty gritty of protecting their computers from malicious software and attempts at intellectual property theft. As usual, Laura had joined her husband and wrote a travel article on what to do when visiting the Seattle area. She had ventured as far as Mt Saint Helens, over three hours away for her work and was amazed at how fast the devastation was restoring itself after the 1980 eruption. Now Jim's work was done for the week, but not for Laura. There were always interesting places to include in her travel articles and this weekend would be no exception. She had booked a room for Friday and Saturday night at the 484 Farmhouse Brewpub. She felt it was a modern day equivalent of a Dude ranch. It was a place where one could help make beer, see various hops growing or even spot some two row barley. They even taught a small class on how to turn barley into barley malt of various types. That was the clincher. Although the brewery there used more barley ingredients than they could grow by themselves, they did have acreage enough to grow all the hops needed for their own use with a large surplus to sell.

"Wow, the vegetation really changes on this side of the mountains" Laura said as they emerged into the Yakima Valley, "That must be the rain shadow effect at work. Most of the water drops off as soon as the Pacific winds hit the Cascades."

"Yea, but they are really great with agriculture. Maybe they use well water irrigation?" replied Jim.

"Maybe."

"I'm curious why a brewpub has 'Have A Great Big Baked Potato' on their website" Jim said.

"Me too. And also what that 484 means. Kinda cryptic if you ask me" Laura added. They soon entered the dusty town of Yakima with its railyard and block after block of one and two story buildings. A few lights and they were on the south side of town leaving it behind. Laura got out the directions to the 484 Farmhouse Brewpub, they had several more miles to go as they drove past field after irrigated field of all types of agriculture produce. "Turn left in a mile" she navigated. After a while on the rural road she said "There ought to be a gravel road up ahead. Go slow, don't miss it." On the gravel road the chips bounced from the tires to the metal underbody of the rental causing quite a ruckus inside. This reduced their speed considerably and after another turnoff by a stone marker with 484 chiseled into it they went up a driveway with acreage of hops and barley beside. "Good" said Laura, "I think we made it."

Stopping in an area labeled 'Guest Parking' in front of a family farmhouse with 'Office' painted on one door and 'Bar' on another. The 484 Farmhouse Brewpub also served as a small B&B of sorts for it had a single story wing added to its south side that contained the bar, dining room and attached guest suites. They entered the office not really expecting to see anyone at the desk doubting it had enough overnighters to warrant a full time clerk. Their suspicion was confirmed when they saw a button and above it a sign: Visitors Please Ring Buzzer. And so they did and about five minutes later a young woman arrived at the front desk. "Hi, I'm Heather. Welcome to the 484. Do you have a reservation?" she asked.

"We do" Laura replied "For two nights under the name Verraten."

A minute later it was up on Heather's screen. "Yes, here it is. You must be Laura and Jim from Pittsburgh" the owner's daughter said looking up from the screen.

"That's right."

"OK. We have you for the From Grain to Malt class tomorrow afternoon, the Northwest Hop class this evening and the hop picking event for anytime Friday and Saturday with an award given out at dinner Saturday night. Annnd, let's see now . . . your room is the Amarillo suite. That will be four doors down on the right down the veranda when you leave the office through the bar. Continental breakfast is available from 6 to 9:30 with cooked eggs and meats available from 7 to 8:30. Lunch from 11:30 to 1:30 and dinner from 6 to 9 with the bar open noon until midnight if anyone is up that late. Your food and drinks are included with your stay. Just ring the bell there if Ryan is not tending the bar. He's always either there or prepping in the kitchen. If you can't find anyone, then you can feel free to self serve at the bar. My mother and several of us do the most of the cooking and are usually around the kitchen, if out of sight. My brother Eric and my Dad do the classes, brewing and farming. So, here is your key. Just register here" said Heather Sanders, daughter of the owners, moving the registry book toward Laura.

"Thank you. Do you have Wy-Fi out here?"

"Certainly, from your room or the barroom."

"I see you have other guests this weekend, from back East like us, one from Charlottesville, Virginia and one from Orangeberg, South Carolina. So business is good then?" commented Laura as she signed and looked at the other bookings, one from Illinois and three from Oregon.

"Yes, it is. We get a lot of hop heads from all over the States and our share of tourists and day trippers out of Seattle, Vancouver and Portland. What brings you out from Pennsylvania? Just hops?"

"Business in Seattle and some side trips this past week. Going back Sunday night on a red eye" Jim interjected, "But were fans of brewing and have never been to a hop field before."

"I can tell you haven't. Around here we call them hop yards. And we have lots to pick this time of year. Nothing better than the smell of fresh picked Cascade before they're dried, and fresh they make the best beer. You'll see in the hop class Eric runs."

"Looking forward to it" Jim said.

"Looking forward to dinner too" added Laura. The pair left the office and went through the barroom to the veranda in the back of the homestead. There they turned right and walked to their Amarillo suite named after a hop variety discovered in the Yakima Valley. The suite was spacious with a queen bed and separate sitting area with a TV. The window at the rear looked over a flower garden and beyond row after row of tall hop bines about twice their height or more. Looking out the window Laura commented "This is a beautiful place. I'm glad I found out about it. Really got some from all over this weekend. I saw registrations from South Carolina, from Virginia, from Illinois and from Oregon. Then there's us from Pennsylvania."

"Yea, from what she said that seems rather rare, but exceptions make the rule." Jim responded as he set up to check the Wy-Fi connection, "When you're ready let's go for a small beer and a big walk or preferably a small walk and a big beer."

"Small walk, big beer."

The Verratens left their suite and walking towards the sun along to the end of the wing noticed all the suites were named after Northwest hop varieties; there was Cascade, Mosaic, Simcoe, Citra, Centennial, Chinook and their room, the Amarillo. The wing was a later addition to the farmhouse and served as rooms for guests on its southern side. They could not tell its age but it did not look like it was built as brewpubs had gained popularity. They thought the rooms were probably remodeled farm workers quarters out of the past. At the end of the building they went a few steps off the veranda with its Adirondack chairs near each suite and onto a path leading to the hop yards; there they picked a couple ripe ones, rubbed them between their palms and smelled the aromas released at their late summer peak. "Wow" remarked Laura.

"Even just one flower packs a punch" added Jim. Their curiosity satisfied they made the way back to the farmstead using a different pathway and saw the patio. The spacious patio was conveniently set with tables and chairs surrounding a fire pit with wood and kindling beside it. From it a set of steps lead up to the shade of the veranda and doors into the barroom and dining room also presumably later additions to the farmhouse. There was no dividing wall between the two rooms which were simply two areas of one large room, the bar being the smaller of the two. There was a couple enjoying their pints and a group of three girls enjoying their pitcher. The walls contained an eclectic mix of hop related pictures and drawings interspersed with photos of old trains and locomotives and an old railroad map from Minneapolis to Seattle with branches along the route. Behind the bar was an old advertising rectangular poster with a red border and yellow fill. In the upper left corner of the fill was a circular yin yang logo done in red and black with the words Northern Pacific set around it. But what really stood out was the massive brown baked potato, split open at the still steaming top with an embedded spoon aside a generous pat of melting butter. The considerable potato had a single line of large white letters in quotes "Great Big Baked Potato" superimposed on it; in the space below the giant potato was printed in smaller letters *'The kind served on all dining cars of the Northern Pacific Railway'*; it was an interesting piece of memorabilia that Jim knew he would have to find out about over a beer. He knew that back in the day before airplane travel it was rail travel that carried people from coast to coast in days not hours and he and Laura had done earlier in the week. He also knew that each railroad had special meals and menus that usually featured the foods of the area they ran their trains through. Putting two and two together, he thought that these large potatoes would be a regional specialty that the Northern Pacific Railway had once featured, but what he could not tell from the antique poster was how large that potato might have been.

They looked above the taps and saw on a chalk board a listing of the currently available beers.

Northern 484 Beers

Northwest Black IPA - Coal black at 7.7% ABV

Northern Pacific Pilsner – Simcoe and Chinook hops at 4.9% ABV

North Coast Limited – Our Porter at 5.1% ABV

484 * – Our biggest malt and biggest hops at 6.2% ABV

Great Big Baked Potato ** - Our mild flavor lite at 4.2% ABV

The Three C's IPA - Cascade, Centennial and Citra hops at 6.7% ABV

James Hill Double IPA - at 8.2% ABV

P&S 1905 - West Coast style hazy fruity at 5.5% ABV

Most pints at $ 6.00

48 ounce pitchers at $20

* 484 at $7.00 / $24 a pitcher

** Great Big Baked Potato at $5 / $16 a pitcher

Jim was intrigued. It was an odd mix of beer naming and there was that baked potato again. What was that, he thought, beer made from potatoes? He and Laura took a seat at the bar and rang the bell. Momentarily the bartender wearing a yellow shirt and blue jeans entered from what appeared to be the kitchen door and wiping his hands on the bar towel he asked "What can I get for you?"

"A pint of Northwest Black IPA for me and Laura, what are you having?"

"What exactly is the Great Big Baked Potato beer?" she asked the bartender.

"It's a lite beer made with about half russet potatoes in the grain bill. Lightly hopped with Mosaic grown here. Do you want a taste to make up your mind?" the bartender responded.

"Sounds interesting. I'll give a pint a try. I'm sure it will be fine" Laura responded declining the sample.

"Hard to find a beer this girl doesn't enjoy" Jim added looking at the bartender. When the pints arrived, Jim said "By the way, do you have a minute?"

"Sure. What's up? My name's Ryan."

"I'm Jim and I'm puzzled about a couple things here. Like what is that Great Big Baked Potato thing all about and the 484 in the name of the place here? Is that the address?"

"That's easy. Afraid you were going to ask me about differences in hops. That Great Big Baked Potato was a slogan used by the Northern Pacific Railway back in the day. They featured it in their dining cars and were known for it. Supposed to be over 2 pounds each. I don't think hardly anyone could finish it" Ryan explained.

"That's more than my wife and I could eat together" Jim said, "I never saw a potato that big."

Ryan continued "I have but not in the stores. Just at competitions at the fairs out here. By the way, how's the potato beer" Ryan asked looking at Laura.

"Actually, quite refreshing. Just enough flavor and bitterness so it's not like a glass of ice water, but as refreshing as an oasis in the Sahara. Very sessionable"

Ryan smiled "The 484 is also from the Railroad. The owners are into the Northern Pacific Railroad's history as you see in their beer names. It used to run through the Yakima Valley. It was merged into the Burlington Northern and all the stock bought up years ago. I think they even owned some back then. The 484 is a type of locomotive, there's a photo of one over there on the wall." The Verratens both glanced over at it. Ryan continued "The 484 refers to the wheels of the loco. You see the 2 small wheels then the 4 large wheels then another 2 wheels. So that's on each side double what you see and add them up and you get 484; locos where known by their wheel arrangement back then says Mr. Sanders. He says the Northern Pacific developed this special type of engine, first to use it so it was nicknamed a

'Northern'. Mr. Sanders says that they can be found in some museums around the country, but I've never seen one; he has. Don't ask him about it though unless you have an hour to spare."

"Interesting. I'll remember that. Thanks for the warning. What about the other beer names?" Jim asked.

"Well, the Black IPA is common out here, the Northern Pacific Pils just named after his favorite subject, the North Coast Limited named after a passenger route, the 484 and Potato you know, the Three C's after the hops, the James Hill after the founder of the Northern Pacific and the P and S 1905 after the year the Portland and Seattle Railway of James Hill started. If there was a way Mr. Sanders could travel back in time a hundred years or more, he would."

"That explains a lot" Jim said.

"That's about all I can explain about it. Had to learn it to work here" Ryan answered.

"We appreciate it. How long have you worked here?" added Laura.

"About 3 years."

"Do you work with the hop plants?" she inquired.

"No. Mr. Sanders has Jorge and Miguel for farm work. I just work here in the kitchen and bar and a little in the brewery building. Mr. Sanders has some cabins we hired help live in a couple yards over."

"Well, this is one for our book of memories. The Great Big Baked Potato beer, and she liked it. Thanks for the history lesson" Jim smiled.

"No problem, see you at the hop tasting class then in about two hours" the bartender concluded.

"We ought to go over to the table with the 3 girls and their near empty pitcher, buy them another one and fill up our time" Laura suggested.

"If they're like us and bought the weekend package deal then their food and drinks are included" Jim reminded his wife.

"True. Even so they might like some company."

"Well, you go on over and introduce yourself and buy them a pitcher if they need it. I'm going to the room for an hour to catch up on emails."

"Hello girls, mind if I join you" Laura asked.

"We don't mind. We enjoy company. Where are you from?" one asked.

Sitting down at the table Laura responded "Back East. Pittsburgh, Pennsylvania. I'm Laura Verraten my husband's Jim, and were on vacation this weekend."

"I'm Olivia Morales" said the black haired girl with dark eyes.

"And I'm Kumiko Chang, just call me Kumi" said another girl with dark hair.

"Bondel, Jane Bondel" the blonde haired girl smiled.

"Don't mind Jane, she always gives her name like that. Watches way too many 007 movies" Kumi said.

Laura smiled and laughed a bit. "And how do you like your martinis, Miss Bondel?"

The four refreshed their drinks, a pitcher of potato beer for the table; they were on the weekend package deal like Laura. It turned out the three were college friends from the University of Washington in Seattle and would be graduating next year. Olivia was a marketing major, Jane was in computer science and Kumi was going to be a teacher of math. "We just spent a week in Seattle. My husband is a computer security expert Jane, you might want to drain his brain a little this weekend. He just finished a 3 day cyber security seminar there. Might be a field you'd like to consider specializing in."

"That'd be great. I'd like to talk to someone with real world experience, not just professors, for career advice" Jane responded.

"So what did we miss in Seattle? I did get to the Space Needle, the Aquarium and even Mt. Saint Helens" Laura intoned.

"Pike Place Market, watch the throwing of the fish" said one.

"Chihuly Garden and Glass" said another.

"Museum of Pop Culture and Seattle Art Museum" said the third.

"Pacific Science Center" "Ballard locks" "Great Wheel" "Underground Tour" "Museum of Flight" "The Arboretum" "Sky View Observatory" they all said one after the other.

"OK OK I get it. I missed a few spots. But I did like the arboretum and the underground tour. I write travelogues for a magazine so I covered some restaurants and brewpubs too. You girls really know your city" Laura complimented them on their rapid fire enumeration of highlights.

"Well, we all lived there our whole lives" replied Jane.

"And we were just getting started" added Kumi.

"I wish I had another week in Seattle and you to show me around, but we're flying out Sunday night." The conversation continued about the subject at hand and Laura took mental notes for her article that included some things not easily found by the general public. In a while Laura saw her husband reappear and holding up an empty pitcher motioned for him to come over to their table with a fresh one. Arriving with a new pitcher of Great Big Baked Potato and a pint of 484 for himself he squeezed in next to Laura and was introduced. Before long Jane was asking him all kinds of questions about the computer security field he was involved in while the others carried on their own conversations. The other guests arrived for the hop class and Ryan served them the pints of their choice. It seemed no one was paying so Laura assumed the package rate was de rigueur at the 484. Laura then saw Ryan in his yellow shirt setting up a table, presumably for the hop tasting, with seven small pitchers of about twenty ounces or so and a large pack of small plastic cups holding around an ounce for sampling. On a card in front of each pitcher was a name of a hop variety: Cascade, Simcoe, Citra, Centennial, Mosaic, Chinook and Amarillo. Names familiar to her from the suite names. Her interest was piqued. Then Ryan brought out small plastic bags containing the various hops and put a bag near each nametag. Finally, another young man appeared.

Ringing the bell on the bar a few times to get the attention of all the guests and then, when all were looking at him, he began "Hello and welcome to the hop class. I'm Eric Sanders, son of my dad Robert who is responsible for the Northern Pacific theme of our farmhouse brewpub. I will be your guide this evening into the wonderful complexities of all the Northwest hop varieties we grow here in the yards. We don't just grow them for our own use but we are a commercial grower too so you've probably tasted our hops in many of the beers that you've drank around the States, but just didn't know it. For those especially interested I can give you a list of brewpubs and breweries around that we sell direct, but we also sell wholesale. Now just give me a minute to count heads and see if we're all here."

Eric continued "Perfect. Eleven hop heads all present and accounted for. Now we'll do our class over at the table where Ryan, your bartender here, has finished setting up chairs for everyone. Let's move over there now and you can bring along your beer if you want or get a fresh one. This will be hop tasting primarily although at the end we will taste some beers and see if you can pick out the hop type in it." Eric moved over to behind the long hop table as the guests, some with beers and some without, sat in a single row of chairs in front of the table. Eric continued "First a little about our family's farm and hop yards. My great grandfather George Sanders bought the undeveloped acreage from the Northern Pacific Railway Company back before the turn of the century, 1900's that is" he said with a smile. "It was a great place for a cattle farm then with grasses over six feet tall, but over time the orchard business was more profitable. Then hops were found to grow especially well in the Pacific Northwest climate and especially so here in the Yakima Valley when irrigation was put in. So over time our family planted more and more hops as demand in America kept growing and growing. Our old orchards were given over to hop yards as the trees lost productivity. Now we grow mostly commercial hops and some barley for our own use and some vegetables for use here such as cabbage, carrots and the potatoes in the Great Big Baked Potato Beer. Any questions so far?"

"Why does your dad like that railroad so much? Did he work on it?" someone asked.

"He worked for the railroad for a while when he was young but the farm needed him more and railroad work was very hard for low pay. I think he spent like 3 or 4 years as a railroad man. But he knows that without the Great Northern of those days and earlier back into the 1890's we would not have a farm here today. Has to be a way to efficiently move product and produce out of the valley to where it's needed. You could say the railroad created the farm you are in."

"Any other questions? No? OK then, as I said I'm Eric Sanders from Yakima Valley. Can each of you introduce yourselves and where you hail from. You'll all be together this weekend so let's do a meet and greet." As Laura was at the end of the row of chairs, she began by introducing both herself and Jim to the others and giving their hometown. All the others followed in turn and the tasting class in essence then started.

"Ryan has set us up all the hops varieties that we grow here. They are some of the oldest and most common types the Northwest is known for. But there are others and more are constantly being developed much like apple and grape varieties are, some become hits and others don't make it. We don't do any experimental work here or try to develop hybrids, this is a working hop yard for the successful ones that get used all over. What I will do for the tasting is put a standard weight of each hop type in the pitcher then add moderately hot water. This brings out the flavor and aroma. They have to sit in the hot water for a few minutes then I'll put the pitchers in an ice water bath to cool them down. While they do I'll explain about each one's history and use. Then I'll put some in each of your little tasting sample glasses. Ok, here we go."

Eric took the pre weighed hop samples from the plastic bags and put them in the pitchers making sure they all matched the names correctly. Then he took the near boiling water and filled each pitcher to a uniform level. "Now you may be wondering why use so hot a water. Well there are many ways to add hops to beer. They can be added to the boiling hot wort for an hour, a half hour, fifteen or five minutes or at lower temperatures even in a way called dry hopping and even double or triple dry hopping. Each of these techniques will make a different beer even with the same hop. Here at this time of year, we use freshly picked whole hop flowers. But they can lose flavor in time once picked. That's were hop pellets come in. We send our hops to a facility that grinds and extrudes them into hop pellets and those are sealed in a vacuum packed bag for use in commercial breweries all over the Nation. Oxygen is the enemy of flavor you know. They also vacuum pack our whole hop flowers for some customers. But back to the hops themselves and the temperature and times of steeping. Hops have two basic components. The first are Alpha acids for bittering. This is why some hops were developed to have a high acid content and those are the ones put in boiling wort for a long time to extract all the acids and add bitterness to the beer. But in doing so most of the volatile aromatics and flavors boil away leaving only the bitter acids. Therefore, often a second hop addition is used at shorter times and lower temperatures, sometimes called dry hopping, to get the aromatics and flavor out and not lose them. The Alpha acid in these aromatic hops are low often at half or less of the acid levels use acid hops. The industry has developed dual purpose hops with moderate acid and flavor and aroma, but brewer purists will use more than one hop variety in their beers and especially the brewpub craft beer types."

Ryan entered the room with 7 labeled pitchers on a tray and set them up on the table. "Thank You Ryan" said Eric. "Ryan has brought us some samples that used the same weight as in these fresh pitchers I just made, but they were kept near boiling for an hour to extract the maximum Alpha acid content and are now cooled down. The ones I've started here might be representative of the short or dry hopping technique for aroma and flavor, so now into the ice bath they go. Now let's start on the long boil ones we did this afternoon."

Eric had each person take a sample of Chinook extract. "Notice the bitterness on your tongue. Chinook is around 14% Alpha acid. Now try the Simcoe" he said placing the pitcher of Simcoe out for his guests. "I can tell by the expressions on some of your faces that it has bitterness too. It is also around 14%. Now let's rinse our mouth out with a cracker and water" he said as he put out a box of white crackers.

"Is this the amount they put in beer?" asked Olivia.

"Approximately. That depends on the brewer and what he is after in IBU, that's International Bitterness Units. Remember you're tasting these extracts in plain water, malt would cover some of the bitterness as would other hop or yeast flavors. But the level I use in my hop class could be considered typical in beer. Now let's taste the Cascade" he said placing that pitcher out.

"I don't get much bitterness at all" Kumi said.

"No, not at all. Very mild" added Jane,

"That's because Cascade has only around 5% Alpha acids, a third of the previous two. It's used mostly for flavor and aroma although those are lost on the long boil. Now taste the others, I'll arrange them in order of bitterness for you." Eric arranged the 7 hop varieties of the long boil and the tasters sampled each again and again rinsing with water and sometimes eating a cracker.

"So why not just use the most bitter hop first, get what you want then add the flavor one later. Why so many high Alpha ones?" asked Jane.

"Good question. The bitterness can vary not just in intensity but taste profile, and there are some other components that come along. Except for the Amarillo the hops we grow are called dual use, for bitterness and aromatics and flavoring. The Amarillo is just for flavor and aroma. There are some we don't grow that are called bittering hops, for the acid only. Now each hop type has a yield per acre to consider as that affects the cost and in different regions and seasons that Alpha can vary a bit. It gets complicated. Some brewers want to use just one hop, so a dual use is perfect for them, add some at the long boil for acid and some later at dry hopping for aroma. Speaking of aroma are we ready to move on now to the dry hop simulation?" the three friends and the Verratens nodded yes as the others looked on.

"Now here it gets more interesting" remarked Eric as he put out the new pitcher of Amarillo next to the one they had just tasted. "Take a little of the long boil and compare it to Amarillo that had a dry hop method."

"They're very different" remarked Laura "The dry one has so much more flavor, very citrusy, and much less acid bite."

"Hard to believe they are from the same type hop" said Jane.

"And what citrus? Anyone?" Eric inquired of the group.

"Orange?" replied Olivia.

"Very good" said Eric, "Amarillo is noted for its very high orange citrus notes. "Now compare it with Citra."

"This Citra has orange too but also grapefruit and lime I think" said Kumi.

"I think you are right. Citra is very popular right now for all the tropical notes in its profile. It's a new variety from 2008 and derived from East Kent Golding, Tettnang, Hellertau, Brewers Gold and Mittelfruh varieties. Yields about 1500 pounds per acre, about average for a dual use hop. Try the Simcoe next."

"Very different. Earthy or musty. Pine maybe. None of that in the long boil, or maybe a little" said Jane.

"Good" replied Eric to the fast learners. "Simcoe is used for piney and earthy flavors and it has decent acid too. It yields around a ton per acre if the season is good. Now I want you to continue tasting all the varieties, compare them to their long boil pitchers and to each other while I tell you some details of each. And please ask any questions you have." The hop class continued tasting and comparing while listening to the story of how each was developed and why. Of the couples at the other end, the two men did most of the tasting and asked a few questions. It was the three college friends and the Verratens who kept Eric busy answering their queries. Eric concluded his class by stressing that there was no really right way to hop a beer, that it was an art as much as a science and that although some styles used traditional hop recipes there were variations and the craft brewers were an experimental lot. He described the movement much like the French Impressionist movement using colors in unusual ways to get effects not seen before. The range of hop flavors was like an artist's palette he said, "Each beer is a painting created by the artistry of the brewer. Some beers use 3, 4, 5 or even more hop varieties throughout the process."

The hop class now over the guests were encouraged to mix with others as dinner was served country style. Laura and Jim sat with the two couples from back east, Brett and Nicole Greene from Orangeburg, South Carolina and Kevin and Kimberly Lucas from Charlottesville, Virginia. Courtney Greene sat at the table with the 3 college friends along with Mackenzie Peterson of Springfield, Illinois. The meal menu was a tossed salad, fried chicken, a creamed green beans and mushroom dish, and of course a Great Big Baked Potato. Dessert was fresh apple pie.

"That was an interesting lesson about hops, don't you think?" Laura asked the group to start a conversation.

"Well, I certainly learned something" replied Brett Green passing the salad dressing.

"It was a complicated tasting" added Kevin Lucas as he buttered his roll. No one else responded. Laura sensed a dead end of interest.

"So Kimberly, where do you hail from?" Laura asked.

"Charlottesville, Virginia, and you?"

"Pittsburgh Pennsylvania" she responded, "We've never been to Charlottesville. Someday though. Read that Monticello is worth a visit."

"Yes, yes it is."

"Home of Thomas Jefferson. How much time do you think to see it?" Laura asked Kimberly.

"About an hour, nice house" Kimberly responded.

"What else is worth a visit there?" she pursued.

"Oh, the usual stuff, museums, art shops, restaurants" Kimberly answered.

"Brewpubs?"

"Certainly."

"Any to recommend?"

"They're all good" Kimberly answered and her husband nodded his head in agreement.

Laura remembered something she had seen a story on involving Charlottesville and the Russian Czar's daughter. "Let me ask you, what about that lost daughter of the killed Czar of Russia, Anastasia."

Mrs. Lucas just looked at her a moment then said "Russia? I don't know about that."

The group was now served the main course as platters of fried chicken, vegetables and a great big, but not two pound, baked potato were brought out and passed around. "You know Brett", who was on the overweight size and about six foot tall, "I don't think I could eat a real Great Big Baked Potato at one meal, unless maybe it was the only thing served. It weighed a minimum of 2 pounds, you know" said Jim.

"Neither do I, and I can put down a half dozen ears of fresh corn or more" Brett replied.

"What about two pounds of Gold Rice" Laura interjected.

Brett just smiled and shook his head negatively as he put a chicken breast on his plate. "So where are you from, Brett?" Jim inquired.

"Orangeburg, South Carolina. Not far from the coast" he replied.

"Great for Low Country cuisine then" Jim remarked remembering their visit to Charleston, South Carolina a while back.

"Right. Low country foods. Great stuff" replied Brett.

"Ever go to the Gullah Girl Brewpub in Charleston?" Laura inquired of Nicole Greene.

"Never. We'll put it on the list. Was it good?" Nicole replied.

"Really good. Try the Carolina Gold Ale or have you had it already somewhere" Laura added.

"Never had it. Must be good for you to remember it" Nicole said back.

"It really is. Any favorite Low Country dish?" Laura asked.

"Well, they're all so good it's hard to pick one. Probably one of the steak ones" Nicole answered.

"Definitely steak" added Brett.

"Tell us about Pittsburgh" Nicole asked Laura, "We ought to go over, err, up there someday." Laura filled them in about all touristy things Pittsburgh, from the Carnegie Museum of Natural History to a ride on the incline and everything in between. After dinner, around 10 PM the group broke up and most went off to their hop named suites. Laura rejoined the three girls and together with Jim stayed for a pitcher or two after everyone else had left. As usual, Jim sat there glued to his latest device and his latest app but as it was in the middle of the night back East, and a Friday at that, there were not many emails to reply to so he filled his time searching Laura's reference to Charlottesville and the Czar of Russia and read of a most interesting historical fraud that had only relatively recently been solved by DNA. Done with that, and with the four women busy in girl talk boring to him, he relaxed just doing nothing but enjoying a pint of The Three C's IPA and tried to pick out the different hop contributions of each to the pint. Failing to determine that on the first pint, he went to the bar for Ryan to draw him another.

"Ryan, I must say that the combination of Cascade, Centennial and Citra in this beer is difficult to separate."

"Like mixing paint I suppose, once mixed who can say, I can't, especially when there are three in there" the bartender responded.

"So you've been here three years, somewhat in the middle of nowhere. Like it being so rural" Jim asked the bartender.

"Peaceful out here once you settle in, kinda like where I grew up in a way. I live in a cabin a few hundred yards off. Free rent and food is part of my pay."

"No taxes on that perk" hinted Jim.

"Hush hush" winked Ryan with his finger to his lips.

"Are you from the Valley here or Washington?" Jim asked to make conversation.

"No. I'm from Iowa. Came out to Washington two years before I started here. Used to work in Seattle, bars and coffee shops basically. Don't like the city living much."

"Well, it's nice here this time of year. Very pleasant. Bad winters here?" he asked Ryan.

"Not really. More or less like where I grew up."

In time the girls and his wife had finished their last pitcher and left him alone nursing his nightcap pint sitting at the bar; when they left Jim decided on a refill pint and to sit in an out of the way location to enjoy the refreshing breeze from an open window. Without the light pollution of cities, he could see outside the dark, moonless night sky with the stars gleaming and shimmering brightly beyond the veranda outside. He decided to sit out there in the darkness of the veranda to catch a little more of the slight breeze and observe the stars in all their glory as he rarely had an opportunity to do so at home in the city. The only light was from the stars and a few small low safety lights on the veranda to see where one was walking. These were scattered about the pathway now and then over to the patio but their light was minimal.

There on the veranda, folded deeply in an Adirondack chair the first thing he saw was the Milky Way reaching across the sky, the second was the momentary flash of a meteor and the third was a young woman walking past the suites and turning into the barroom. She did not see him in the darkened corner. It was guest Mackenzie Peterson from the hop tasting class, a late night drinker he assumed, and he looked back at the cloudless Heavens to catch another meteor.

At some point the barroom light was turned out and he was alone in the dark, so he thought. He had forgot the late night imbiber had not left the barroom yet and he was trying to decide if he should just go and tap himself another Three C's IPA or simply go to bed, but it was so peaceful out on the veranda and the stars seemed so alive above the Yakima Valley he lacked the motivation to make that decision. Down the walkway toward the suites he saw light from a room spill out when the door opened. A couple from one room emerged and went over and gently tapped on the door of the other couple. The larger overweight man, Brett Greene, answered and let them in thereby returning the veranda to shadowy darkness. Odd Jim thought, they didn't appear to know each other at dinner, maybe they are secret swingers hooking up? After all this remote spot would be a perfect place not to get caught. He finally decided on another pint but before he could raise himself up out of the Adirondack for a second nightcap, the pub door opened and Mackenzie Peterson and Ryan walked hand in hand down the steps and once off the veranda they stopped and starlight was enough for him to see them kiss before they continued hand in hand to the pathway that lead into the hop yards where they disappeared into the darkness. Interesting, Jim thought, this 484

Farmhouse Brewpub must be more than what it openly advertised. But on second thought, maybe not. Instead of imagining things that were probably not there with the customers, he went to the bar and tapped himself another pint of Three C's IPA and returned to the Adirondack chair to look at imaginary constellations above.

Partway through the second 'final' nightcap he saw the door of a suite open and five people leave it, walk away toward the end of the veranda, go down the steps and enter the same pathway to the hop yard where Mackenzie and Ryan had gone. Odd, he thought, but perhaps they liked looking at the night sky away from the city lights too. Perhaps not. In any case none of his business. He looked up at the sky again to the constellations he admired so in all their glory. Cygnus, the Swan, that he had been following in its flight westward was now mostly over the veranda and he could only see its tail containing the bright star Deneb, one of the brightest in the entire sky. From where he sat Deneb would shortly pass over the veranda roof blocking his view of it, so he decided when it did he would finish the last of his pint and retire to his Amarillo suite to bed. It was sometime around eleven, certainly no later than 11:30 he thought.

"So when did you get to bed last night? It was after midnight and you were still out!" Laura asked he husband at 7:30 AM while drying off after her morning shower.

Opening his eyes he said "Are you sure? Past 12? Thought it was around much earlier than that."

"Hungover?"

"Not really. Don't think so. But a couple coffees would be great. Basically, just looking at the stars for an hour or two. You ought to join me tonight. A real treat. What time is breakfast served anyhow?"

"Right now, if you want any meat or eggs, otherwise just sweet rolls, coffee and tea" Laura responded.

"OK. Give me a minute to shave and I'll join you there."

In the dining room was an assortment of cut fruits, melons and baked goods. An urn of coffee and one of hot water for tea was on the side table. The three college girlfriends were finishing their breakfast as the Verratens entered and exchanged pleasantries. They appeared to be the only ones having a breakfast. When Heather Sanders came over Laura ordered a slice of ham and two eggs, scrambled. Jim went for the sausage links and three eggs sunny side up. The college girls left for the hop yard and with a cheerful 'See you later' went out to the veranda and pathway. When Heather returned with their orders Jim asked her how they were to know how to pick the hops and which were ready for harvest.

"My brother Eric is out in the yard or the barn. He'll give you baskets, your tags and directions. Would you like anything else from the kitchen?" she asked.

"No. We're good. Anxious to get a-pickin" Jim replied. The couple finished their morning meal then went to the veranda looking for Eric. Not seeing him they thought he might be over in the barn but before they began to walk over to it they saw the three college friends coming up the pathway out of the hop yard in a rush. Thinking one may have been hurt somehow or been scared by a snake or something they waited on the landing to see what was the matter. As they got closer, they both could see they were really upset, tears streaming down their faces and when they saw Laura they changed from a fast walk to a run to her.

"Laura. Help!" cried out Olivia. Kumi just held out her arms and collapsed into Laura's arms. Olivia began to sob.

Jane remarked "They told me that they found a dead body out there, I didn't see it but I think both of them did."

"A body?" Laura repeated, "A person? Not an animal?"

Jane nodded up and down then shook her head left to right, "A person, they wouldn't let me go see. They said it was horribly mutilated." Jim came over.

"What's going on?" he asked, seeing the girls so unsettled.

Laura responded "They found a body out in the hop yard, say it's mutilated."

"We better go see. Where is it?" Jim asked.

"I'll show you" Olivia volunteered, "Jane, you wait here with Kumi. I'll be right back." With Olivia in the lead and Jim and Laura second and third, the three walked down the path to the hop yard. The path curved around following the terrain and soon they were down a slight hill into an acreage that could not be seen from the veranda three hundred yards away. They turned off the path and into the rows of bines. At the end of the row they heard a humming or buzzing. Olivia pointed to the fly covered body in the open yard beyond. Laura stayed with Olivia while Jim went farther into the freshly planted yard of Mosaics stepping over a puddle of blood as he got closer. There he saw the horror that had driven the girls from their weekend activity. It would have been visable from Kumi's ladder in the fully grown bines. The body was probably that of a young man, he thought, although jeans were certainly not definitive of that. He stared at it for details. The hair color and length were that of the bartender, Ryan, as was the bloody yellow shirt. The eyes were gone, the right side of the face was gone exposing bones of the jaw and skull. The body lay slightly to one side so that the part of the face that still contained flesh lay mostly grass side down obscuring detail. The flesh had also been stripped from the shoulder, upper arm and most of the neck. The yellow shirt was ripped, torn and blood stained and blood was all over the ground. As he had not seen Ryan this morning, he thought it was possibly or probably the bartender.

He looked over at Laura and said "Laura, you may not want to see this, pretty gruesome stuff."

"Olivia, can you wait back at the end of the row while I go over to Jim?"

"I'm OK to walk back to the house" she replied.

"Ok then. I'll see you back there" Laura said as she went over to Jim. The body had not yet started to swell or decompose and the eggs the flies were laying had not yet turned into the maggots in 24 hours, yet the scene took Laura a few minutes to comprehend and then compose herself standing beside her husband who was taking cell phone pictures of the corpse. "What the Sam Hell has happened?" she remarked.

"Don't know. We have to get the police out here. Look over there." He had spotted something. Walking over he saw a black raven feather and a little farther away what appeared to be a hand rolled marijuana cigarette. He took pictures of both, leaving them untouched. "Laura, let's walk around the area a little before we go back to the house."

"Over here, look" Laura called out. She had spotted a Kirkcaldy #3 golf ball about twenty feet from the body.

"And here" Jim replied looking at a hunting arrow point into the ground. Within a few minutes they had located an empty shotgun shell and a brass compass and had taken pictures of all. Coming back to the corpse they saw one of those miniature liquor bottles, a common brand of vodka, laying under the left side of the face next to the ground, the cap was off and the contents appeared gone. A picture was taken.

Looking farther afield for a few more minutes they found nothing so quickly rejoined the path back to the farmhouse.

Upon reaching the veranda they saw the 3 girls sitting around a table, somewhat more composed than they had left them. Laura asked them "Do the owners know yet?" They all shook their heads no. "Well, we have to find them and tell them to call the police" she continued. "Jim and I will do that, just stay here or go to your room. Don't go back down into the hop yard" she concluded and the girls nodded acceptance.

The Verratens concluded that the owners would either be in the kitchen, in the barn or working the hop yards, the kitchen was closest so they tried it first. Entering it through the door to the bar room they saw Mrs. Alice Sanders working on a Waldorf salad for lunch. "Mrs. Sanders?" Jim asked the older woman half assured it was the mother of Eric and Heather whom they had already met.

"Yes?" she said as she looked up while continuing on peeling the apples.

"Mrs. Sanders, I'm afraid we have some bad news for you" he got right into it, "One of the guests discovered a dead body of a person out in that new Mosaic hop yard this morning. Someone has to call the police. Do you want me to?" he concluded.

"Dead body? Are you sure?" she said putting down her peeler on the table.

"Yes, we're sure. We saw it too" Laura spoke out.

"Oh No! What happened? Accident? I've got to call my husband, it's not him is it?"

"We don't think so. It might be Ryan. See if you can reach Mr. Sanders on the phone."

Mrs. Sanders took out her cell phone and called her husband. To her relief he answered and she told him what the Verratens had just told her. They all agreed to meet on the veranda at the steps to the path. When they arrived, the girls were still there, sitting in the Adirondacks, and Jim took the owners down to the newly planted Mosaic yard. Mr. and Mrs. Sanders and Jim walked back to the house and from there Bob called the police. "Probably take them fifteen or twenty minutes to get here" the owner indicated. On the veranda he tole the Verratens and the three girls "You can stay here on the veranda, at the house barroom or in your room, but no hop picking or wandering about until the police say so." The 3 college friends went to their rooms as the owners went to alert the other guests who, skipping breakfast, had not been out of their rooms yet.

Laura and Jim retired to the Amarillo Suite and made a pot of coffee. "Laura, something I didn't tell you about last night, after you went to bed."

"Oh? What is that?"

"Well, I didn't think anything much about it at the time. I was sitting on the veranda star gazing in the dark and listening to the coyotes in the distance while finishing my beer. A girl went into the barroom, not one of your friends, one of the other two staying here. I think it was Mackenzie, pretty sure it was her, long hair and tall. The bar lights went out. I saw one of the couples leave their room and enter the other couple's room, I think it was Brett who opened the door to them. They had their suite light on and it spilled out until they closed it with the two couples inside. After a while the girl at the bar went with Ryan down the veranda steps to the path to the hop yard. They stopped and kissed then went hand in hand down the path into the darkness. Then I went in for another nightcap and when drinking it and watching Cygnus the door opened and five people walked out and then down the path to the hop yard. A couple minutes later Deneb passed out of view, I finished my beer and went to bed."

"Deneb?"

"Deneb is the tail of the constellation Cygnus, I think about the one of the top 25 brightest stars in the sky. But I was surprised by all the late night activity here. Hanky panky is none of my business, but now I wonder; they were all headed to where the body was found."

"That's very suspicious activity" Laura added and sat back to think. The coffee was ready and Jim served. Laura continued "Last night at the hop class the only real interest seemed to be you and I and my three girlfriends. The others went through the motions but didn't really seem to have much enthusiasm for it."

"I remember that, and I agree."

"Then" Laura continued "at diner afterwards they didn't seem that interested to carry on a conversation and when I was asking about their home towns I got only very vague answers out of them. Kimberly said only an hour to take in Thomas Jefferson's estate and I know it's much, much more than that, and she could not name anything specific to do in Charlottesville other than 'the usual stuff, museums, art shops, restaurants' and when I asked for a brewpub recommendation all I got back was that they were all good."

"Right. And she didn't know about that Anastasia and the Czar of Russia" Jim added.

"Right. If they're really from Charlottesville then they certainly would have known of the old woman living there for decades trying to pass herself off as the long lost daughter of the killed Royal Family of Russia. It was National mystery and news for a long time. And their Southern accent sounds phony."

"I remember Brett passed on the comment about eating two pounds of Carolina Gold rice, wouldn't you think anyone who lives in the old Rice Kingdom would pick up on that reference?" Jim said.

"If they were true locals, I would think so. And they never heard of the Gullah Girl Brewpub in Charleston either. Look up Orangeburg, South Carolina" Laura asked. Jim called it up on his phone.

"OK. Done" he said.

"How do you spell Orangeburg" Laura asked.

"O-r-a-n-g-e-b-u-r-g" Jim replied.

"They're not from there" Laura authoritatively spoke out, "I remember how they spelled Orangeburg when they signed the register, they spelled 'burg' with an e, you know 'berg'. You don't misspell your own home town."

"Hmmm" was Jim's only response.

"And that Nicole and Brett are so phony too, I was shocked when they put a steak as their fav low country dish. Steak's not even a low country dish at all. And that pretend accent. And they made a mistake saying they would like to come 'over' to visit Pittsburgh. Did you notice when they caught it and said 'up'."

"No, I didn't, but if you say so" Jim responded.

"Something is fishy in Denmark. . . "Laura suggested.

". . . and it doesn't smell so good here" Jim concluded, "So where does that leave us? What do we think we have?"

"Two couples from who knows where, hiding where they are from; two couples and a girl out late last night going off to the hop yards where a dead body, probably the bartender Ryan, was found this morning; two couples who appear to have no interest in brewpubs or brewing except for their being at a farmhouse brewpub off the beaten track" Laura concluded.

"But why? That is the question. What links them together other than hiding their real hometowns and trying to hide their lack of interest in brewing? What brings them to the 484?" Jim rhetorically queried, "Maybe I can find out something." With that comment Jim set up his laptop, reconnected to Wy-Fi and began.

First on his mind was to trace the cars. "Laura, will you go out to the guest parking spaces and pretend to get something from our car. Get the license plates of the other guest's cars and report back please. I've got to call up some of my old hacks."

Within fifteen minutes Laura had returned with the license numbers, all from the State of Washington, and Jim began searching them. Three were from car rental agencies and a fourth was registered to a Blondel, Jane Blondel from Redmond, Washington, over near Seattle so along with Olivia and Kimi most probably just three college friends out for a weekend. Hacking into the rental car registrations he saw that Brett and Nicole Green were from Armstrong, Iowa; ten minutes later he found that Kevin and Kimberly Lucas were from Cedar Rapids, Iowa and finally that Mackenzie Peterson was from Fairfax, Iowa. "Laura, do you remember where the girl Mackenzie Peterson registered from?"

Laura thought a minute then responded "Ummm. . . Lincoln has something to do . . . Ah, Springfield, Illinois."

"Interesting. Well she's from Fairfax, Iowa according to her driver's license, the Greens are from Armstrong, Iowa and the Lucas are from Cedar Rapids, Iowa. All three rental cars are rented by someone out of Iowa" Jim concluded.

"That didn't take much time and that explains those phony accents too. They're Midwesterners not Southerners" Laura remarked "Now the hard part for you. What do they have in common, why are they here? Did they kill Ryan or was it some accidental death and a coincidence?"

"Let's look closely at the pics I took of the body, or I'll look if you don't want to" Jim said as he transferred the pictures from his phone over to his laptop.

"I'm OK with looking."

With the pictures in his laptop, Jim called up the first one. Although a lot of flesh and muscle was removed there was none laying around on the ground, but there were some pools of blood here and there around the mutilated corpse, more blood than would have been found if a dead body was stripped of some flesh like the corpse was. They both agreed that the quantity of blood in the various pools at various distances might indicate that the throat was cut and blood spurted out while the deceased was still alive; that would indicate murder. If a wolf had attacked the body ought to show defensive wounds on the arms and hands and neither believed a wolf would go after an adult human. Perhaps if rabid but perhaps not. Neither would coyotes attack an adult, but either wolves or coyotes might be opportunistic scavengers enough to use a food source they had stumbled upon.

"What about the eyes, Jim, they're gone."

"Birds. Probably from that raven feather I saw near the body. Bird scavengers go for the easiest pieces to pluck out first."

"Ugh."

"Well, don't knock eyeballs if you haven't tried them. I saw on late night TV some cultures around the world like them and Andrew Zimmern ate them." Jim loaded a close up of the mutilated neck, then he zoomed in on the edges that remained, the border between the stripped and intact flesh. Laura pulled up a chair and joined him in the examination. "Look here. I think this may be the end of a cut mark." Laura looked closely. The cut in the skin was smooth, not jagged. It ran horizontally and seemed to go deeper into the skin layers as one looked to the border where the flash had been removed. Much like a ravine climbing in a formation of layered rocks, the gash seemed to climb through layers of skin tissue. It was deepest nearest where the neck had been defleshed, here the fatty hypodermis, dermis and epidermis all had been cut through. Then several millimeters away the hypodermis was intact and the slice only went through the tougher dermis and epidermis, then finally, again a few millimeters away, only the uppermost epidermis was cut into.

"This looks like a sharp knife slicing along and finally here coming up and out of cutting the neck. It's not a plunge mark" Laura analyzed in her amateur photo autopsy.

"I agree. I have seen similar effects when you have me cut up skin on pork loins from the store. The upper skin much tougher and harder to get through than what's underneath. It looks like whatever did this took the easy meat after the throat was cut. Look at the chew marks at the edge, all up and down, rough jagged. Then there are these remaining slice marks running from where the tissue was gone into and then out of the skin a half inch later on this left side of the neck. On the right side, the flesh is entirely gone, so nothing can be determined" Jim added.

"Right. There is so much missing flesh on that side of the body. And there's no evidence of anything ritual, like piles of cut off flesh laid out in a pattern with candles. Does seem like scavenger activity" Laura concluded.

"I totally agree" Jim agreed with Laura's diagnosis, "So, it seems what we probably have here is a murder by throat cutting of the carotid arteries and jugular veins followed by scavenging by animals."

"That was the easy part. Lucky for us that the animals didn't eat all that neck skin off" she said.

"Right. By the looks of chewing and tearing I bet there will be tooth marks on some of the bones too" Jim guessed.

"Now" continued Laura, "Who did this last night? Do you think you can find out anything more searching the computer? Like what are those Iowans all doing out here the weekend of a death?"

"Well Laura, don't jump to conclusions. There are other people on the hop farm here. A couple workers live on it and there is the whole Sanders family too. But I agree, the Iowans seem very suspicious, but you know, they might be up to something other than murder. They might be up to swapping partners or swinging and that single girl from Iowa might be a party to it. The 484 might be a secret swinger hideaway."

"Swingers!? Come on now. Why do you suspect that?" Laura asked.

"Well, last night on the veranda, when I saw them going to visit each other in their rooms and also they don't seem interested in beer or hops at all" Jim replied.

"That's nothing. They wouldn't have to travel this far to hook up in confidence. Lot of swinger clubs around the Midwest if one seeks them out. Most hotels are anonymous in a certain sense" Laura replied.

"True enough. But if one of them is prominent in politics or something sensitive, maybe a minister back home, they might have to travel out of their area. I'll look into it. Give me some time. Go have a beer and see how the girls are doing." Laura knew at times like this her husband did his best work when left alone with his computer. She knocked on their room and all four then went down to the shady veranda and shared a self-served pitcher. In time the police arrived and then the coroner. The four went inside to avoid seeing anything of the body being removed; they all thought it was for the best. Laura did not mention anything that she and her husband had been discussing. The other guests came out of their rooms around noon to the dining room, probably expecting a lunch to be served, and when they saw the police they seemed surprised – more or less – causing Laura to wonder if it was an act like their cover story and poor Southern accents. Alice Sanders approached the Iowans and filled them in on what was going on and then told Laura and her friends that lunch would be delayed about an hour but she would bring out some small snacks in the meantime.

Laura saw who she thought to be a detective talking to the owners out on the patio then go into the office. She knew it would only be a matter of time until he got around to getting statements from everyone. The light snacks of cheese and crackers over, the lunch was a simple one of hamburgers and hotdogs prepared by Alice and her mother and while all the guests were in the dining room the detective told them that he would be getting all their statements later in the day and, since they were all booked for the night, they were not to leave the hop farm Sunday until checking with him on the phone. After lunch, Laura took a hamburg and a hot dog back to the Amarillo suite for her husband.

Jim smiled when his wife walked in with the food. "Glad you remembered me" he said. "I have some interesting information, but more work to do."

"Ok, bring me up to date."

"Well, first of all I was looking into the background of the deceased, Ryan Woods. I got his last name and social security number from the 484's computer, a very easy hack. They're not very protective of their info here. And guess what?"

"I've no idea" replied Laura without venturing a guess.

"Ryan was from Iowa. Went to Iowa State and the University of Iowa too. Never graduated from either. Belonged to Kappa Phi Lambda fraternity."

"What! Iowa?"

"Yepper, Iowa."

"This is way too coincidental now" Laura remarked.

"Right. They are all connected somehow, have to be. Thanks for the food. How are your friends?" he asked.

"Resilient I would say. Talking about picking hops after the coroner leaves with the body. I'll probably join them in the yards. They cancelled the malting class today. Hop picking contest instead. Think I'll wear my 'Don't Worry, Be Hoppy' tank top I brought along. It'll be hot out there."

"Great. That's the right thing to do for your friends. I didn't think they would still have the grain class. I'm surprised we didn't have to go out for lunch somewhere. Well, enjoy yourself as much as you can while I try and crack this nut."

Throughout the afternoon Jim continued searching and hacking into the background of Ryan Woods. Most of his effort yielded nothing. Ryan Woods was a below average student and did not graduate. But finally he found something that caught his attention like a bolt of lightning on a blue sky day. While at his first school, Iowa State, and a Kappa Phi Lambda frat member he was investigated in the hazing death of a Freshman pledge Michael Greene. The record of the investigation was in the Iowa State computer and was picked up by the local newspapers. The death of the pledge was caused by alcohol poisoning and attributed to the pledge being required to chug down a pint of vodka, a six pack of beer and a pint of bourbon all within a half hour. Ryan Woods was the pledge master in charge of the hazing. Newspapers indicated Michael Greene was the only son of Brett and Nicole Greene. A fact Jim confirmed at the State's birth registry. Although it was never proven in the inquest that Ryan Woods had forced Michael Greene physically to drink that much that fast, there was testimony that he set the pledge rules and was at the drinking event the night of the death and had refused to allow anyone to call 911 after Michael had passed out. His comments were that he would sleep it off and just have a bad hangover in the morning.

So finally there was a connection, and possibly one that might motivate a parent to murder. It was after that semester that Ryan Woods transferred out of Iowa State over to the University of Iowa. Jim easily achieved access to the computers of the University of Iowa.

Jim found that Ryan Woods had attended only two semesters at his second university and again with below average grades including some failures. To Jim's amazement he saw that again Ryan Woods was implicated in another death of a pledge trying to join Kappa Phi Lambda at the University of Iowa. This time the youth's name was Carl Lucas. Archived online local newspapers from the Lucas's hometown of Cedar Rapids showed that he was the only child of Kevin and Kimberly Lucas and that he was engaged to his high school sweetheart Makenzie Peterson also of Cedar Rapids School District who lived in the small town of Fairfax. The circumstances of the pledge's death were eerily consistent with that of Michael Greene, that of pressured overconsumption of hard liquor in a short period during a hazing ritual. The cause of death was identical – alcohol poisoning. In both cases the investigators at the schools learned that all the pledges drank the same quantity of alcohol, but the two boys that died pledging under the supervision of Ryan Woods had been the lowest weight of each group.

This was certainly interesting and potentially provided a motive for murder for all of the guests at the 484 from Iowa. Combined with the actions of the various guests he saw Friday night while sitting in the dark on the veranda, it pointed to only one thing. It was time to go see Laura.

As expected Jim found Laura out in a hop yard far away from the site where Kumiko found the mutilated corpse. The three college friends were in the same row as her, all four picking away. "Laura, how's it going."

"Good, I wouldn't want to have to do this for a living but it is quite relaxing for an afternoon, terrific aroma out here as you pick" she replied.

"Talk to the detective yet?" he inquired of her.

"No, not yet. Except for Kumi, the detective talked to her about finding the body and to the owners here. Then he got called away to something or other. Told us he would be back tomorrow morning by noon for our statements and that no one was to leave Sunday until they cleared it with him. Find out anything?"

"Yes. Lots. Fill you in after I pick some. I need a break. Where's the baskets?"

The next hour was filled picking several bushels of ripe Cascade hops. The Iowans were seldom seen. "I think it's time for Happy Hour" Jim begged with a smile after looking at his watch and rubbing his sore back.

Laura whistled. "Quitting time" she yelled to her friends. They looked at her. "Anyone for pitchers yet? On me."

"How about in half hour?" Olivia responded.

"See you in the bar then" Laura responded as she came off her ladder and put her basket of Cascade flowers onto the wagon. At the bar the Verratens thought there would be no bartender now. They were correct and again since it was an all inclusive weekend, Jim acted as bartender tapping a pint of North Pacific Pilsner for himself while asking Laura of her preference that late afternoon. She responded "Tater". The barroom was empty. Jim sat at a table facing the door and Laura faced him at his direction with her back to the veranda door. "What did you find out this afternoon?" she asked him bluntly.

Jim finished a long sip of North Pacific beer and, keeping his eyes watching the doors to the kitchen, the veranda and the office he said "Laura, I think we have six murderers here with us. In fact, I'm sure of it." Laura looked on silently. Jim told how each couple at the 484 had a son who died from alcohol poisoning while being hazed at Kappa Phi Lambda fraternity while Ryan Woods, at each school, was pledge master and present and personally encouraging or even mandating the drinking the night the deaths occurred. He told her of the single young woman staying alone who was the high school fiancé of one of the pledges who died.

"Sometimes you amaze me. It's kinda scary so much of our lives is out there on the net."

"Indeed. One just has to know where to look and how to hack in. But a lot is just sitting there, like the newspaper accounts" her husband replied, "Put all of it together, Laura. The fact I saw the fiancé of a pledge whose death Ryan was implicated in walking hand in hand into the hop yard with Ryan; and add to that the night he was murdered the couples who lost their sons followed the fiancé shortly after along with a daughter. It just seems both compelling and conclusive, undeniably so."

"They will deny they were out there in the hop yard. You know that. You don't know exactly what time it was when you saw them, you didn't even know what time you came to bed. Some witness." Laura remarked.

Jim thought a while. "Well, I'll just have to look at my clock."

"Clock? You don't usually wear a watch. What are you talking about? Your cell phone? You didn't tell me you looked at it" Laura asked.

"Laura, Laura, Laura. I can tell you precisely when I came to bed, but I can't do it until tonight."

"Argh. What the Sam Hell are you talking about?" she remarked in a sense of bafflement.

"Cygnus, Laura, Cygnus. The brightest star in the constellation of the Swan. I came to bed as soon as it passed out of my sight. Tonight we can sit on the veranda exactly where I was sitting last night, exactly so, and we can look at the time when it passes over the veranda roof. It will be accurate to within a minute or two." This plan was agreed upon. For with this more precise time that Jim would have seen the Iowans depart their rooms and head for the hop yards

Laura felt it might convince them that they were caught. "Change the subject now" Jim said when he saw the three friends up on the veranda making their way to the bar door and a cold one after a hot day picking. He got up and went over to the bar as they entered. "Girls" he said "What can I get for you?" Jim poured the pints as requested then sat down at the table with his wife and her three friends. After a second round the conversation turned to the corpse. Kumiko relayed to them what the detective's interview involved. She indicated that he was mostly interested if she thought he was dead when she first saw the body; did anyone come to her when she screamed or did she leave the scene alone; if anything had been moved or disturbed; if she saw or heard any animals around in the bushes or in the distance. She said he seemed to focus on the fact there was so much tissue removed from the corpse and mentioned that there had been a lone wolf sighting recently and it was common for a wolf to go after the face and throat. The detective also told her that sometimes a pack of coyotes would take over a fresh kill from a lone wolf. They might happen on a dead body, say a heart attack victim for example, and scavenge it. But overall, he said it was rare for a wolf to attack a human.

"Well Kumi, animal predation is part of Nature. Sometimes difficult to accept especially when you see it" Laura said trying to keep the girls innocent of the crime they believed was committed. Robert Sanders, owner, walked into the barroom, saw the group having a beer and asked if he could join them. The table was now a little crowded with six people and their pints. Mr. Sanders apologized for the event that ruined the malting class as the conversation turned to the death.

"Mr. Sanders, have there been wolves or coyotes around Yakima Valley recently?" Jim inquired.

"Wolves? It's hard to say. Not really. I guess you would have to ask the game commission. I think a lone wolf was spotted in the valley this summer, but not a pack. They come in from Canada sometimes. There might be some packs up near the border now that I think of it. But we have cougars here in the State, they could do that. And a few grizzlies too. But they stay in the mountains and if it was a grizzly there would be much more damage than that. I've seen what they can do to a cow. Huge claw marks from paw swipes, totally different from a wolf or coyote or cougar kill. I've seen those too on sheep, deer and elk. I think the game commission is sending someone out Monday to put some night cameras up. At least that's what the detective said."

"Well that's good" said Laura.

"If only Ryan hadn't been out on the path alone. He lived out of one of the cabins we built for the hired help along with Jorge and Miguel. I hope I don't have to move those cabins, used to never have any wildlife trouble except the occasional rattler and I keep them out of my fields as much as possible. Haven't seen one in a couple years."

"Are the police going to notify Ryan's next of kin?" Laura asked.

"Yes. I gave them all the information I had about him, social security and all that. They said they would take care of tracking down his kin" Mr. Sanders replied then continued, "Well there fixin' tonight's dinner now, I'll go and lend a hand. Steak night tonight and oh, a Great Big Baked Potato too. We just love them out here."

"I see that" replied Jim as he glanced at the old advertisement on the wall. With the owner back in the kitchen Jim asked the girls who they thought would win the hop picking award to be given out before dinner.

"It might be Laura, but maybe not. She's a fast picker but wasn't out as long as us. I think maybe Olivia" Jane Bondel responded.

"Hard to say" replied Olivia "but it will be one of us four, that's for sure."

"Yea, the others staying here only picked for a little while and when I saw them picking, they were very slow. And you Jim, you spent so much time in your room" commented Kumi who seemed back to normal after her morning's experience.

"Computer work for business, a little emergency" he stated, "Always something comes up on the weekend it seems."

The Greene couple and their daughter came and sat at a table. Obviously they did not seem to realize that it was more or less self serve from now on. Jim assumed the role and tapped their pints of choice.

While behind the bar Kevin and Kimberly Lucas came in and Jim again inquired what they wanted. While tapping their pints he asked what they thought of the death on the property.

"Heard it was some sort of animal attack, a wolf pack or mountain lion or something. A shame." Kevin said while his wife took her beer to a table.

"That's what I heard too" the volunteer bartender replied, "They got something wandering around this valley, that's for sure." Kevin smiled and joined his wife at a table next to the Greenes. He could overhear them talking about wolves and coyotes and thought he could discern a hint of a smile emanating from the corner of their lips. Perhaps they would open up more after a few more beers or make a slip; he decided they probably would not and to leave the bartending to someone else. It was time for a shower and a break in his Amarillo suite.

"Laura, I'm heading back to the room for a shower and some TV time."

"OK. I'll be along shortly" his wife indicated.

While in the shower, and unbeknownst to him, his wife had decided to stay for another potato pint and see if she might pull anything out of the other guests, so she excused herself from the three girls and pulled up a chair between the table of the Greene and Lucas families. "Mind if I join you?" The two families were a little surprised but welcomed her.

"We were just discussing the tragic event last night" Nicole started, "We think it was a wolf pack."

"Or something like that. I never saw a real life coyote but they can take down a deer I think" added Brett.

"I think they have wildcats or mountain lions out here. I think in California they have been known to attack joggers and hikers" said Kimberly.

Laura nodded in agreement. So that's their story and their sticking to it while wondering what it would have been had not an accidental animal scavenged the corpse. She added "They might be able to ID the type of animal by saliva DNA or teeth marks on bone." All nodded in agreement. The conversation turned to lighter subjects of sports standings and Laura saw no use in staying, so after finishing her beer remarked that she would see them later for dinner. "Hope y'all like great big baked potatoes, the owner does" she said excusing herself from the tables with a little Southern drawl thrown in. She just couldn't resist. Time for a shower, in more ways than one.

The time for dinner had come. Jim was dressed in jeans and a T-shirt he had bought for the weekend. It read 'Hoptimist: One who believes everything is better with a craft beer' and included a large drawing of a hop flower. Laura wore jeans and a green polo shirt. As they entered the dining room, they saw that the tables were arranged for a family style dinner again. It was the owner's thing. Son Eric Sander's appeared to be the bartender for the evening passing out pints to all who wished one. Eric's father came out and stood behind the bar with three manila envelopes. He began. "If I could have your attention, I will begin. I am sorry to have cancelled the malting class this afternoon but with everything going on this morning I just could not get it organized. I am glad you arose to the challenge of the hop picking contest Eric dreamed up. I will now award the prizes based on the weight of the hops you picked. The envelope please, Eric." Eric handed him an envelope with a large number 3 on it. "I hold in my hand the winner of third place." He ripped it open. "And the winner is . . . Jane Bondel." He handed Jane a printed certificate of achievement downloaded and printed by Eric.

"That's Bondel, Jane Bondel to all my fans out there" she responded with a big smile getting into the moment quickly as she took the certificate.

"And now for second place, the envelope please. And the winner is . . . Kumiko Chang. Good job Kumiko."

Kumi smiled and jokingly said "I owe it all to my quick fingers, balance on the ladder and years of study."

"Now finally for first place, the envelope please. . . and the winner is . . . Olivia Morales!" the girl came up and accepted her certificate of achievement.

"Hard work always pays off. I've always dreamed of this" she chided.

While clapping Laura whispered to her husband "I thought I might get third maybe."

"Hard to compete with motivated college kids" he replied.

At dinner the potato was indeed greater and bigger than the night before. Few finished it. The exception being Jane who did but went light on her steak. After dinner, some headed off to their suites rather early and some lingered on. Jim told Eric he would stay up a while yet and serve anyone who wanted a night cap. Jim had discovered he enjoyed being bartender on occasion but certainly not full time. There was no sense for Eric to have to stay late after the rough day he must have had. He thanked Jim for the relief and in a while only Jim was left in the bar. No one seemed to be returning so he turned off the light and went to his chair of the night before on the veranda where he phoned his wife. "All clear on the veranda, and it's a clear night." She joined him there as he sat in the identical Adirondack as the night before, seemingly no one had moved it from the previous night. All was set. When Laura arrived and brought up another chair, Jim showed Cygnus and Deneb in its tail to her and the two watched as the Swan slowly flew over the heavens. The night was so clear, several flashing meteors were seen appearing mid sky and burning out in seconds and also some satellites that traveled from one horizon to the other in less than a minute never varying in brightness. Jim explained that the stars rise about four minutes earlier each night so they must therefore adjust their time accordingly. When Deneb disappeared behind the veranda roof, Jim said "Now. What time is it?"

"12:39" Laura responded. They now had the time within four minutes, say 12:43, of when Jim left the veranda for bed. It would have been around twenty or thirty minutes earlier, say between 12:15 to 12:35, when Ryan went to the hop field hand in hand with the girl Mackenzie followed shortly later when the other vacationing families went down the same path. They had all they needed for Sunday morning.

Back in the Amarillo suite they lay in bed in the darkness discussing the coming morning's light and what they would do when it arrived. Yes, it was wrong the families and fiancé had killed Ryan Woods. Yes, it was true Ryan Woods had essentially avoided significant, if any, punishment for his actions as pledge master of Kappa Phi Lambda. Yes, it was true that he was directly responsible for ending the lives of two sons of two families, in one of which he was an only child. Yes, the families had some justification for their criminal act and had already suffered much more from the death of their sons than a conviction for premeditated murder that a jury trial might add. Yes, it was true that even if guilty they might get a very light sentence, especially as they were no threat to the general public. Yes, it could be that a jury would ignore the factual evidence and nullify it by deciding the killing was justifiable in their judgement and vote 'Not Guilty' or if one believed so then it would result in a hung jury. Yes, it was true that although all six guests were involved, it might be impossible to determine who actually slit the throat of Ryan Woods in the hop yard late one night and who was simply there to witness a form of justice being applied.

In time they came to a conclusion.

Sunday morning's minimal Continental breakfast was appreciated by the Verratens who had been overfed on large baked potatoes the previous night. They would not be ordering from the kitchen at all. Croissants with butter and jam, assorted donuts and sticky buns along with coffee and teas were just perfect. They arrived at shortly after six and sat where they could keep an eye on the office desk for anyone checking out and through the window into the parking lot in case anyone was leaving without breakfast. This was mostly unnecessary, they thought, as the detective had warned them to be available for statements by Sunday noon and any guest not there might raise some suspicion in his mind. Their concern was unjustified as both the Greene and Lucas family arrived within five minutes of each other followed ten minutes later by Mackenzie Peterson. It was around eight when their breakfasts were over and they retired to their suites to wait on the detective's arrival.

Not knowing how much time they would have before he arrived, the Verratens walked down the veranda where Jim knocked on the door of the Centennial suite. Mr. Green answered. "Brett, sorry to bother you. May Laura and I come in for a moment. There's been a new development about the body found yesterday morning."

Brett Greene opened the door "Sure. What's new? We're waiting to give our statement when he arrives. Is he not coming?" he said with a puzzled look on his face. Nicole and Courtney Greene were sitting on the sofa watching television. "Please have a seat" he said motioning to a couple of chairs at a small, round table by the door. Brett sat on the edge of the bed.

The Verratens took seats and Jim began "Well Brett, it's not about the detective's schedule. It's about something Laura and I have been thinking about all this weekend. You see, you're not really from Orangeburg or berg, South Carolina as your registration here indicates. You live in Armstrong, Iowa. I have your street address and phone number in my pocket if you want me to show them to you." The three Greenes looked at the Verratens like they had seen the proverbial ghost. They were stunned and said nothing.

A moment later Laura continued "We also know that Kevin and Kimberly Lucas are not from Charlottesville, Virginia but from Cedar Rapids, Iowa and that you two families have good reason to know each other."

"I believe you should call Kevin and have them join us here now before it's too late, I really do" Jim suggested.

"Oh, and tell them to pick up Mackenzie Peterson from Fairfax, Iowa on the way over. You know as well as I do that she's not from Springfield, Illinois. Make sure they bring her along" Laura insisted seeing

255

Courtney's jaw quivering a little and her eyes open in shock.

"Yes, please do as Laura says. It's time we all had a meeting together."

Brett Greene called Kevin Lucas on his phone while his wife put her arm around their daughter's shoulder and turned off the television. "Kevin, Brett here. Can you come on over now with Kim? Yes, now, right now. . . Important. . . Get her out of the shower right away. And get Mackenzie on the way. Make sure she comes. Give her a call first. OK. See you in a couple." Brett turned to Jim "Can you tell me what this is all about? You have my interest."

Laura went over to the window to observe the veranda to where the other suites opened. Jim answered "I could, but I don't want to have to repeat myself two or three times. Patience for a few minutes more, then all will be clear."

Kevin did not like that remark and clenched his teeth. "So what if we're all from Iowa" he admitted.

"Patience."

Laura said "Mackenzie just left her room and entered the Lucas suite." A couple minutes later the three were on their way to the Centennial suite "Going to get crowded in her in a minute. They're on the way." Laura opened the door and stood outside it while Mackenzie, Kevin and Kimberly entered. "Please find a seat" she insisted. When inside she stayed standing near the door and Jim gave up his seat to stand near her. Between the beds, the couch and the two chairs all had found a seat.

"What's this all about" demanded Kevin Lucas.

"It's about time you come clean. You and Kimberly are not from Charlottesville, you come from Cedar Rapids, Iowa and you Mackenzie are not from Illinois but Fairfax, Iowa and all six of you know each other well, in fact very, very well."

"How do you think you know all this? It's not true" Kimberly said.

Laura answered "I thought your Southern accents were not quite correct, a bit southern – yes – but somehow just not right, too put on, and by the way, Nicole, Orangeburg is spelled with a 'u' not a 'e' as you did on the register here, anyone from Orangeburg would have known how to spell the name of their hometown. None of you knew any real details pertaining to your false hometowns, anyone really from Charlottesville, Kimberly, would have known of the famous imposter Anna Anderson living there pretending to be the long lost missing daughter of Czar Nicolas II of Russia, last of the Imperial family and possibly not killed at the time of the Communist Revolution. It was National news for a long time. She died in 1984 and was later proved by DNA not to be related to the Czar at all. Great copy. It was all over the news when you would have been living there. And everybody gave very vague answers to brew pubs in the area, points of interest and so on. I just felt that you were not telling the truth and asked my husband to look into it especially when he saw you from the veranda."

"Let's not get too far ahead of ourselves, Laura" Jim said then he continued. "I have a friend who can find things out at motor vehicle registrations around the States, that's how we know your real addresses. From your driver's licenses at the car rental agency. But let me tell you to what Laura and I saw Saturday morning in the hop yard after Kumi and the girls returned from hop picking and were so upset. We went to see the corpse. I took a lot of pictures, close up as well as from distance. We saw the six 'clues' too not far from the corpse."

"Wait a minute" interrupted Brett "If you think we had anything to do with that. . ."

"You'll have a say shortly" Jim authoritatively interrupted back "Patience please. When I got back to my room, I had the pictures on my laptop and blew them up. As you know most of the flesh was scavenged off certain areas of the body, but I was able to see in the blowups along a skin line the distinct marks of a sharp knife. A knife does not cut like an animal chewing, you must know. Maybe not. There was not much of the cut left but I have it clearly in pictures that any coroner would identify. By the way, they are forwarded to my worksite for safekeeping. Those cuts and the blood on the ground that spurted out of a cut artery indicated strongly, if not conclusively, that Ryan Woods was murdered before being scavenged later that night in the hop yard. And you know what else I found?" Jim asked rhetorically.

"I found that Ryan Woods was from Iowa too, and lived in the same high school district as you Mackenzie." Mackenzie began to cry. "Now none of you were interested much in hops or beer this weekend. That much a blind man could see."

"A lot of coincidence, a lot of bull shit" Kevin stated, "we have a little hobby that we cannot practice near home, so we take vacations from time to time to do our thing. Ryan? I didn't know he was from Iowa. Interesting coincidence, a chance in 50 I'd say."

"I think not. And if you are referring to a little hobby of swinging, I hope you have other vacation records to back up that claim and I don't think you do. But as the saying goes 'But wait, there's more.' I happened to be sitting in the dark on the veranda Friday night taking in the stars. I saw Mackenzie enter the bar when only Ryan was there. I saw the bar lights turned out. Then I saw you Kevin and Kimberly too go over to Brett's room. I observed Mackenzie and Ryan walk hand in hand from the bar down the pathway leading to where Ryan was found in the hop yard. I saw then a bit later at around twelve twenty, give or take a little, the five of you leave Brett's room here and make your way down that same pathway. You did not come back and I went to bed at forty-three minutes past midnight."

"Busybodies, you're both busybodies. That's all you two are, poking into other people's business" Nicole said angrily, "Look how you're upsetting my daughter. Get out!"

"What you've said are lies. Are you blocking us from leaving now, standing near the door?" Kimberly added, "That's kidnapping where I come from."

"You are free to go if you want" Laura replied calling her bluff.

"If you want the consequences of leaving" Jim added.

The six settled down. "What's the point of all this anyway?" Brett inquired.

"The point is that I found out Ryan Woods was responsible for the tragic deaths of each of your sons and Mackenzie's fiancé, a high school sweetheart" Jim answered to the shocked group upsetting them more. "You see, I am quite good at finding things out on the internet, quite good. Ryan was the pledge master of Kappa Psi Lambda fraternity and as you know oversaw the hazing when your sons died of acute alcohol poisoning." The six listening were stunned. "Mr. and Mrs. Greene your son died pledging at Iowa State and Mr. and Mrs. Lucas your son Carl, an only child, died pledging at the University of Iowa to where Ryan Woods had transferred after the investigation. I am truly sorry for your loss, each of you. But as a group you all have motive and opportunity, only the means is missing, a small knife or razor blade perhaps. You know as well as we do that the six of you conspired and actually killed Ryan Woods Friday night in the hop yard where his scavenged remains were found by Kumi the next morning."

Silence.

"By the way, the six red herrings that you scattered around down there to act somehow as distractive clues were about as convincing as your Southern accents and fictitious hometowns."

Kimberly Lucas began to cry. "You know, I lost two babies in miscarriages. Carl was our only child and I could not have any more. That Woods is as bad as they come. He destroyed two families and hurt an innocent girl badly. He deserved to die. I'm glad I slit his throat; I'd gladly do it again."

"Be quiet Kim, he can't prove anything. The police suspect an animal attack or it might have been those two farm hands had an altercation with the bartender here" her husband said.

"I think I heard their voices arguing with Ryan when we were out for a stroll Friday about midnight looking at the bright stars" added Brett quickly trying to save the situation.

"Jorge Rojas and Miguel Santana were away in town Friday night" Laura said.

"But when did they come back? Can they prove their whereabouts?" countered Brett.

Jim countered firmly "If you try and blame this on the hired help, we will spill all the beans immediately to the detective in our statement to him shortly."

"What is this then? Extortion? Blackmail? How much for your silence then you two?"

"Mrs. Lucas, I cannot begin to feel your grief at the loss of your only child, but we are not interested in blackmail money" Laura said to her.

"I don't know what your plan was, really. Without the luck of the animal scavenging the body after you left it there, you know the police would have found the neck cut through and started a murder investigation, false clues or not, they may have zeroed in on you here in this room in time" Jim added.

Brett went on "We took a chance to get justice and revenge for our sons, plain and simple. Risky for us - Yes. If they were looking for a murderer then we might just appear as swingers and that was our story if they found out as you did that we were all from Iowa. If they connected Woods to us like you did, then we would take our chances with a jury to either go not guilty or to get a light sentence. But now it looks like it will be blamed on an animal attack. We will not try and blame it on the farm workers. You have our word on that now. We just think we were justified in doing what we did."

"Then so be it. All Laura and I wanted was to get at the truth and have your admission of guilt. We both think you have suffered more already than any jail sentence and will suffer more for years to come. Neither of us want any innocent person to go to jail for this and we do not want you to be put behind bars either. So as long as you never implicate anyone else, we will not tell the detective later this morning what all we have discovered. He knows that we both went down the path and looked at the body briefly, that's all Kumi knows and would have told him. It seems he might have decided it was an animal attack already. But we will not lie for you if he suspects you."

Laura added "If you decide to come clean with him and plead guilty, I don't think you would spend much time in jail, especially if none of you admit actual guilt, it would be hard to separate the one who slit the throat from the mere accomplices."

"I didn't slit his throat; I was going to but then I just could not. I was the lure to get him into the field" admitted Mackenzie.

"I just wanted to see the justice done" said Courtney in tears.

"And where is the knife that was used? The murder weapon" Jim asked.

"I'll tell you. I had bought a flint knife at a county fair. After we killed him it was a simple matter to break the flint up into pieces with rocks laying around then scatter the flint pieces all over. It would just become part of the background gravel. We all were going to hold him and cut, but some of us just couldn't and who did and who didn't remains our secret. We all brought a false clue to throw police off track. We had all decided that we would accept jail in the end if we got caught" Brett concluded.

"The flint knife was actually a smart idea, but those clues point to someone trying to cover something up. Very suspicious. As much as I dislike what you've done here, I don't think at this point you will be implicated. Your clues may be overlooked by the local police. The knife marks may have been chewed off if an animal came back before the police arrived. Don't know. In any case we don't know how observant their coroner is here in Yakima anyway. I had to blow up the images to make it out. I'd say you have a very good chance of getting away with it and you're not really going after anyone else, are you?"

"No, it was the pledge master from everything we found out at the inquest. Not the other frat members."

"What about bloody clothes? They have no common laundry here. What did you do with them? Bury them in a field?" Jim inquired.

"We all took off our clothes when we did it. Took showers when we got back" Kevin responded.

"Interesting. Then I would say we part ways. I'll check back from time to time on the computer about this Ryan Woods found dead in Yakima Valley and we'll only get involved if we see that someone innocent is being prosecuted for his murder. I don't like what you did, but I understand it. I don't know what I would do facing a similar situation and hope I never have to find out" Jim concluded.

Brett offered to shake his hand. "No thanks, got blood on it" Jim said as he and Laura left the room for their Amarillo suite.

While packing up to go Laura said "I think we did the right thing."

"I think so too."

At their interview with the detective, they indicated that they had gone to the hop yard briefly after being told of the discovery, saw the mutilated corpse and returned to comfort the girls and make sure the police were called and owners told. The detective remarked that the coroner indicated an animal attack although of what type he was not sure. He said they could leave anytime they wanted to get their plane out of Seattle back home. He was going to interview the others next and unless they had something important to add, they would be able to leave soon after. Laura sat with the three girls for lunch. Kumi commented that she did enjoy her weekend even after she discovered the horror in the hop yard.

END

The Banker and the Berliner Weisse

#11 From the Series

A Brewpub Mystery

by

Fredric G. Bender

All rights reserved: no part of this publication may be reproduced or transmitted by any means without the prior permission of the author.

The Banker and the Berliner Weiss is a work of fiction. Any resemblance to actual persons, living or dead, is purely coincidental. Any resemblance to actual brewpubs, breweries or bars is purely coincidental.

Berliner Weisse

In the class of sour ales, the wheat based Berliner Weisse was considered the Champagne of the North by Napoleon's troops. Probably derived from a similar beer in Hamburg, it was popularized in Berlin by Dr J S Elsholz. It's a small beer served in a large goblet, fishbowl or chalice glass with clean lactic sourness.

Malt Bill: 50%+ wheat, lightly toasted Pilsner malt

Yeast: Top fermenting, Brettanomyces, lactobacillus,

Hops: Low level of low alpha acid Noble hops

Adjuncts: Raspberry or Woodruff syrup when served

IBU (International Bitterness Units): 3-8

ABV (Alcohol By Volume): 2.8% to 3.8%

SRM (Standard Reference Method Color): 2-3 Very pale straw yellow.

Taste: No hop bitterness. Clean lactic sour. Some malty or bready presence. Very dry finish.

Carbonation: Very high, always effervescent. Large, white head with poor retention.

Variations: Berliner Weisse is a protected name in Germany, only 2 breweries make it in Berlin. American Berliner Weisse are "style" beers and can vary with lower that 50% wheat and ABV as low as 1% and up to 5%. Fruit syrup can be added in the bottling process instead of at the tap.

The Banker and
The Berliner Weisse

Sunday in their hotel room in downtown Columbus, Ohio after their three hour drive from Pittsburgh, Jim and Laura Verraten were thinking of dinner. As usual, Jim had picked up the lobby brochures while Laura did the check-in routine, now he sat on the bed looking at the restaurant choices while Laura put the clothes from the luggage into the drawers for their week long stay. Spotting several brewpubs around town, he thought they would be able to visit more than one, perhaps all, before leaving for home in the Southside of Pittsburgh, Pa on Friday. It would be a busy week for him for on his schedule was a series of meetings at the Ohio State Capital regarding a proposal for increased cyber security in their various computer systems. They were fearing a computer hostage situation whereby a ransom would be demanded to unlock their system. Jim needed no preparation that evening; what was already in his presentation had already been fine tuned.

As he scanned the brewpubs around the city, there were several that caught his eye down in what was referred to as the German Village, about a mile or two from their hotel. All seemed excellent, yet one interested him more than the others. The write-up said:

Albrecht Durer Brewpub and Art Gallery

Reinheitsgebot German Beer

Traditional German Foods

Selected art of Albrecht Durer available

Now this was a first. "Laura, they have a brewpub that appears to sell art. Interested?"

"What kind of art."

"Art of someone named Durer, Albrecht Durer. Ever hear of him?"

"No. What kind of art does he do?"

"I'll check." Within less than a minute, he had an answer as Laura came over and sat next to him on the bed. "Seems he doesn't do art anymore, he died in 1528. Here, look at this. Here he is."

What they first saw were several self portraits of Durer, a young man in his twenties. Looking further they saw a wide variety of themes done in paint, as engravings on metal and also as woodcuts. It seemed the brewpub was named after Germany's greatest painter of the Northern Renaissance. "This is quite a find for us. Should be interesting. I can't wait to go, how about tonight?" Laura said.

"Tonight it is then. It does look interesting and I'm both hungry and thirsty after that drive" Jim replied.

"You're always thirsty."

"And hungry. Here, put the address in and let's go."

It was not far to the Durer Brewpub, close enough they could have walked if they wanted a small hike. As they passed over I-&70/71 a large sign on a building proclaimed the Brewery District. It referred back to the many German breweries once located here in the 1800's, most of which did not survive Prohibition. They turned left then right onto South Pearl Street, the border between the Brewery District and the German Village. They turned left again then at South 3rd Street made a right. It was not far until they spotted the Albrecht Durer brewpub on their right. "Don't stop yet, Jim" Laura intoned, "Drive around a little. This is a neat area."

The area had a plethora of small thin, two story homes. Based on the type of cars around, they looked that they would be very pricey; Laura confirmed on her iPad the area was heavily gentrified. "What did you find out?" Jim asked.

"Well, we can have a fine meal here tonight but don't plan on moving in. We'll be in Southside Flats for a while yet." Laura looked up and out the window "Hey, there's the Book Nook, says 'Willkommen', what a nice garden patio for browsers. That's going into my travel article this week."

"You'll be back" Jim said in his Terminator voice as he went up and down a few more streets. "Seen enough?" he asked.

"Seen enough. Time for a beer."

Although there was some street parking, the couple pulled their Toyota Highlander into the Albrecht Durer Brewpub's parking lot in the rear off an alleyway. They then walked past the loading dock and steps up into the small brewery to arrive at the customer entrance facing the street. Jim thought that there might have been an earlier building, now gone, on the lot that now was for parking; a few old bricks lay scattered around what appeared to be the foundations of old walls sticking up a little here and there. At the front by 3rd Street, they walked a small pathway between the brewpub and a 10 foot wide garden planted with tall hedges in its back row and shorter flowers toward the front providing a pleasant view to passersby.

The building itself was of red brick with the lintels above the door and windows of stone with fancy detail carvings, aged somewhat over more than a hundred years, but not yet eroded away. The building that proclaimed itself the Albrecht Durer Brewpub and Gallery was an old two story commercial one on a corner lot. It was narrow, but long, running halfway down on the side street to an alley dividing the block. Jim thought the front, with a door and window, was about 50 feet wide and the side with windows only, no door, perhaps 150 feet long. It was just two limestone steps up to stoop. The old wooden door with a glass window opened easily enough and before they knew it, they were standing inside by the hostess station.

"Welcome to the Albrecht Durer. Do you have a reservation?"

"We do not, do we need one?" Laura asked noticing the brewpub's tables were quite busy.

"No. I can take your name and call you when a table opens up."

"Can we just go to the bar?" asked Jim.

"Yes, you can."

"And can we eat at the bar too?" asked Laura.

"There is a bar menu, not as extensive as at a table."

"Well, just get us when a table opens up, but we might just stay at the bar anyway if the food looks good" Laura concluded.

"That will be just fine. I'll let you know. The bar is seat yourself and it's in the next room down" the hostess concluded.

The couple made their way through the dining room through a doorway that lead into the bar room. It too was quite busy, there was an assortment of single seats available but only a few where the two could sit together; they chose the closest one. Jim took the seat next to a middle age man and Laura sat next to a younger girl probably in her twenties sitting with a guy who appeared to be her boyfriend. Settled in they spotted the taps on the counter and the beer list behind them on the back bar.

Albrecht Durer Brewpub
Biereliste

Berliner Weisse - wheat based sour 3.3% ABV

---- Raspberry or Woodruff syrup added ----

Munich Helles - light lager 5.0% ABV

Munich Dunkel - dark lager 5.3% ABV

Kolsch - style of Cologne, Germany 5% ABV

Albrecht's Altbier – old beer style 5.5% ABV

Durer's Doppelbock - extra dark 9.8% ABV

Schwarzbier - roasted black, yet smooth 4.8% ABV

Marzen - elegant and malty 6.2% ABV

They both looked the list over then Laura said to her husband "I don't remember ever having woodruff in a beer, do you?"

"No. I only remember having it in May Wine. I think I will try it here in the Berliner. How about you?"

"I think I'll have the Berliner too but with the raspberry I know I'll like. But I'd like to taste yours."

"Then that sounds like a plan" Jim said as the bartender came over; she was dressed in a traditional German costume, a dirndl.

"Hi. You two decided on a beer yet?" she started.

"We have" Laura replied. "Two Berliner Weisse, one with raspberry and one woodruff."

"And would you like to see our bar menu?"

"I think we would" she added.

The couple watched as two glass goblets resembling fishbowls on a thick short stem were filled with the beer from the tap. Then a squirt of red raspberry syrup was added to one and the green woodruff syrup to another. Since the syrup was rather dense compared to the beer it settled to the bottom of the glass, more or less. The bartender added a swizzle stick to each and brought them over to the Verratens saying "You can stir them up if you want, but many don't. The syrups will mix in on their own as you tip the glass to drink. Each sip will be a little sweeter than the last. I'll be right back with your bar menu."

Laura smiled. "I'm not swizzling, fo' shizzle my dizzle." Jim chuckled and put his swizzle stick on the beer mat also. This was observed by the slight turn of the head of the man sitting to his right who smiled and reached for his glass. It was also a goblet of greenish Berliner Weisse, half finished and greener on the bottom than the top.

The man took his goblet and held it over towards the Verratens saying "Prost."

Jim and Laura responded by raising their goblets with a 'Prost' of their own. The bar menu was placed in front of them. "I'll give you some time to decide" said the barmaid in the sky blue dress.

After looking the menu over, the Verratens decided to eat at the bar. They ordered a large soft pretzel with beer cheese dip, the Nuernberger sandwich of three little sausages on a bun for each, some cucumber salad for Laura and potato salad for Jim and a dish of pickled herring and onion in white wine sauce to split. They would decide on a dessert after they ate.

After ordering they sipped their Berliners and Jim saw the bartender bring another goblet with woodruff over to the man next to him. He asked the man "Are you new to the woodruff Berliner like me? It's quite refreshing."

"Oh no. Certainly not. It is my favorite when I am at home in Berlin. I'm from Germany" he said with a slight accent.

"You are far from home then. My name's Jim Verraten. Nice to meet you."

"Well Jim, I am Kurt Vogel. Also good to meet you. Do you live in Columbus?"

"No. We are from Pittsburgh Pennsylvania, about 3 hours away. I'm here for business this week."

"I know of Pittsburgh. I am also here for business this week. I only arrived this afternoon. What business are you in?"

"Computer technology. I specialize in computer security. Like prevention from hackers, you know."

"Certainly. A locksmith who can pick locks just as well, I'm sure. Our company takes computer security very seriously. But I am not in that group. I am in financials and deal with commercial loans. I work for Prussia Bank, a private bank out of Berlin."

"And you have customers over here in Ohio, or a branch" Jim asked.

"Not a branch. Just a large customer I call on."

"That's interesting" Jim said.

"Yes, it is. Actually. I invested some of my own into this brewpub. Too small for Prussia Bank to get involved in. That's why you can get the Nuernberger sausages here, I made sure of that. I am originally from Nuernberg."

"That is interesting. I wish I had enough money to buy into a brewpub" Jim said as their meal arrived.

As their beers were about halfway finished, Laura sipped the woodruff Berliner Weisse.

"Not bad. Not bad at all. I think I will get one" she said, "And Kurt, that explains the name of this brewpub and the art for sale also."

Kurt said "Yes it does. Not many know of Albrecht Durer here in America. Are you an artist by chance?"

"No. But we sometimes like to research the brewpubs we visit" Laura responded.

"If you ever visit Germany, you would enjoy a day in Nuernberg. It was once an Imperial City of the Holy Roman Empire and they have a very old castle there to see. It was rebuilt after the war in its old style, not modern like Frankfurt did."

"We ought to plan a trip to Europe. Laura and I have never been there" Jim said.

"The Albrecht Durer house is a museum now. It was where he lived." Kurt added.

"What about Nazi remnants, anything to see? I know Nuernberg was an important center for Hitler and the Nazis" Jim said knowing he may have said something non-PC, "I hope I've not said anything inappropriate."

"No, you have not. It is a common question of American tourists of the recent generations. The war was long ago. There are a lot of buildings and remnants and such all over Germany and elsewhere in Europe, but you have to search them out. Germany has a policy since the war of not glorifying or marking them with signs or directions. We wish to put the mistakes of our past behind us and not boost them up for tourism or worse. Many of them that survived hold prosperous modern businesses now and no sign of those years. Nuernberg has the Nazi party grounds and plazas where rallies were held. But you must search for them on your own as the routes are not marked. But they still exist."

Kurt continued "You know there is a saying of our generations, we sons and grandsons of the war veterans, that if you meet a Westerner and the war comes up, just say your father fought against the Russians, but if you meet a Russian then just say he fought against the English and Americans."

Jim smiled. "Makes sense. Here in America, we still have to watch ourselves a bit when we travel to certain parts of our South. We had a Civil War you know and 150 years later the wounds have not yet fully healed."

"I know a little of your Civil War" Kurt replied, " There are some groups of reenactors in Germany who dress up like them. They want to remember that there were a lot of German immigrants who fought in that war, mostly for your President Lincoln."

The bartender came and brought the food and two more Berliner Weisse beers, both woodruffs. As they ate, Laura began a conversation with the couple sitting next to her. Jim enjoyed his Nuernberg sausage sandwich. The sausages resembled the popular breakfast sausage finger links in size and shape that are so popular all over the country, but the spicing was different. This little sandwich had three on a smallish, firm bun. He asked Kurt "These resemble our breakfast sausages but the flavor is different. Do you think ours came from yours in the past?"

"A good question. I've had yours and can tell the difference. But they are so similar overall and so many Germans immigrated to the States that I think it likely they adapted the Nuernberger sausage to American tastes. Like the Italian's mortadella turned into bologna here."

"And like most of our pizza" Jim added. "You sound like you have an interesting job. Do you travel all over the world or just to the States?"

"Mostly the States, but Russia, Italy a little and the Caribbean too."

Jim turned to the bartender who was clearing their used plates, she asked "Will you be having dessert tonight? We have apple strudel, Linzertorte and Black Forest cake available. I 'll be right back" she said taking the plates away.

"Laura, they have apple strudel, Linzertorte and Black Forest cake tonight. Interested?"

Laura thought a moment. "A piece of the cake" she responded. When the bartender returned Jim ordered the Black Forest cake and a piece of strudel for himself.

Returning to his banker acquaintance Jim explained how his job took him all over the country and how interesting it was. Kurt felt much the same way about his position in Prussia Bank. When dessert was finished the two men decided on a Doppelbock for a nightcap. When Kurt was leaving, he asked Jim for a business card. "It's not for our company" he stated "We have a great cyber security team in place. But I'm going to leave it in the art gallery with instructions to give to you a print of your choice upon showing Jenny your matching business card. My gift to you and your wife and hoping you will visit my hometown someday and tour the Durer house."

"Thank you. Thank you very much. I really appreciate this. We were going to look for something in there later this week. Maybe we'll meet again some evening."

"It could be but normally I have a schedule that includes working evenings." The two shook hands and Kurt left the bar while Jim waited for Laura to wrap up her conversation with the couple next to her who was joined now by the barmaid. They seemed in deep conversation, all four of them, to the point that the dirndl clad barmaid did not notice Jim's empty glass. Jim made eye contact with her and asked for another Doppelbock and the bill. As he sipped his beer, Laura, the bartender and the couple wrapped up their conversation. It was time to go.

The next day, Monday, the couple split up after breakfast at the hotel. Jim was off to his meeting at the Ohio State Capitol, a short walk away, while Laura would take the car and do some touring for her travel article. Jim was going to initially meet with the cyber security team of the Capitol's Information Technology group before other scheduled meetings. The system he would propose to them would need approval at several levels within the Ohio State Government and he would have to work his way through them all in the coming week.

While he was working, Laura would be visiting the Central Ohio Fire Museum and the Ohio Craft Museum in the morning. After lunch she looked forward to the Jubilee Museum. The day was productive for both of them, all seemed going well for Jim while Laura was taking notes and making files on whatever she visited. At around 4 o'clock she received a message from her husband that he would be heading back to the hotel in a half an hour.

Together again, they faced a hard decision. Columbus had so many brewpubs they would not be able to visit them all by Friday. After some discussion they settled on one that did not itself serve food but had an interesting food truck scheduled for Monday evening – the Asian Fusion Taco Truck. It was off to the suburb of East Beechwold, a fifteen minute drive away. Although the brewpub was nice and produced a standard compliment of beers from Pils to Stout with IPAs in between, it was the tacos that really caught their interest. They were essentially a standard large taco shell filled with any of six fillings topped off with shredded lettuce, diced tomato and some queso fresco. The six Asian fillings were: Szechuan Triple Delight, General Tso's Chicken, Hunan Beef, Kung Pao Shrimp, Moo Goo Gai Pan and Chop Suey.

Enjoying several beers, the Verratens did manage to try all the six different Asian tacos, then went back for seconds of the ones they preferred. Jim knew he had a very busy day Tuesday, starting at 9 AM; after their meal they headed back to the hotel.

On Tuesday morning they split up with the same plan, Jim would call Laura when his day was over and they would meet again in the hotel room. Her first stop would be the Center of Science and Industry, just across the Scioto River from where Jim would be meeting at the Ohio Statehouse, then if time allowed and depending on her interest of the COSI, she would visit the National Veterans Memorial and Museum in the afternoon, a short walk away.

Laura entered the Dinosaur Gallery at the COSI first. Although she had seen several dinosaur exhibits at various Natural History museums before, no two were ever alike. There was always something new to learn about these amazing animals and their untimely end 65 million years ago. While reading about the difficulties of being a large, heavy animal her phone rang, she saw it was Jim calling. Had plans changed? Would there by a dinner with business associates tonight instead of a brewpub?

"Jim, what's up?"

"Did you read any online news yet?" he asked.

"No. Just the USA Today newspaper we got at the hotel."

"OK. You remember the man we met at the Albrecht Durer Sunday evening?"

"Yes. He said we could have a free print. Why?"

"Well, someone here said that a body was found this morning in the parking lot of the Albrecht Durer. Police are working on the identification now, but it appears to be an older man."

"Could be anyone then" Laura responded.

"Could be. Lot of the people here talking about it. Usually a very safe part of town. I'll let you know if I hear anything else. How's your morning going?"

"Very cool. Great museum. I'm back with a T Rex now."

Jim smiled "You get to do all the interesting stuff while I plod on. See ya. Got to go."

"Bye bye."

The morning went well for Jim and Laura both. Laura made notes about COSI that she could use in articles for various age groups, parents with kids in tow to seniors. Jim had a lunch of deli sandwiches at the Statehouse during which he learned from a new friend that the city police had learned the identity of the dead man found at the Albrecht Durer. They would be releasing the name at a press conference at 3 o'clock. Jim texted the new information to Laura.

Laura was in the National Veterans Museum when her phone rang at 3:45, it was Jim again.

"Did they have the presser yet?" she asked.

"Yea, slight delay. It's on the local news now. Couple of TV's around here. People talking about it. It was the German man I was sitting next to Sunday night, Kurt Vogel. He had his head bashed in and wallet stolen. I think we might be going together to the police station sometime this week to say what we saw Sunday night."

"Which was nothing" Laura replied.

"Exactly. But every little piece fills out their puzzle. That we spend some time with him Sunday evening meant he wasn't elsewhere. But they could get that from the barmaid also. I feel bad, he seemed to be a really nice guy."

"We ought to go down there again tonight" talk to the barmaid, maybe get our print. Did they say if it was a mugging?"

"No. Just his wallet gone, people are saying a mugging gone wrong."

"That's interesting."

"Your guess as good as mine" Jim responded, "See you back at the hotel then. Same time as yesterday. These fellows like to leave the office on time."

As their rental car crossed over the Interstate and into the German Village, the Verratens wondered if the Albrecht Durer brewpub would even be open.

"Maybe we should have called first" Laura intoned reaching for her cell phone.

"Don't bother, we're almost there." A few minutes later they pulled into the parking lot behind the brewpub. It appeared open with plenty of cars except where the police tape had sealed off a few spaces around a rental car, presumably where the body of Kurt Vogel had been found. Leaving their car, they looked past the tape and looked around in a 360. The death had occurred in a rather obscured corner of the lot. There did not appear any windows from neighboring buildings that would have provided a view. Neither did the brewpub have any windows looking toward the spot. As they walked through the parking lot, Jim saw that something seemed different, but he could not tell what. It wasn't just different customer's cars but something else he could not lay his finger on.

Inside the brewpub they went directly to the art gallery, all the better to decide on a piece of Albrecht Durer before imbibing. The brewpub was in a very large old building with a lot of capacious rooms, so space was not an issue for displaying the works.

"Hello" said the salesperson Jenny "May I help you?"

"Actually, you just might" said Jim reaching for his business card. "A few days ago, I met someone at the bar who said to show you my business card for a free print" he said while holding the card out to her to take.

Jenny did not seem surprised but saddened. "That would have been Kurt. He was always doing that. I believe I have your card that he signed over in my file." She started over to her desk. Laura noticed her demeanor had changed and her eyes seemed glassy. Laura went over.

"Hi. I'm Laura. We met Mr. Vogel Sunday evening. We saw on the news he may have been killed in the parking lot out back. Is it true?"

"I'm Jenny, excuse me for tearing up" she said as she used a tissue to wipe her eyes. "Yes, Yes, yes it is true. Herr Vogel was killed sometime last night. He was found by the brewer this morning."

"I'm sorry to hear that confirmation" said Jim, "He really seemed like a nice man."

"He was, always friendly and smiling. Always giving out free prints. Ah, here it is. They match. I guess this will be the last time I get one of these now that he's gone."

"Maybe the other owner will continue the tradition on in his memory" Laura mentioned hopefully.

"I doubt that very much" Jenny replied strictly, "He'll probably close down the art galley here and even change the name of the place entirely. I imagine it will become the Lugner Brewpub or something like that."

"Lugner?" Laura said inquisitively.

"Yea, that's the name of the other partner, Max Lugner."

"Also from Germany?" Laura asked.

"Oh no. He's American, old German family from Columbus."

Jim asked "So he is not a fan of Durer?"

"No, not in the least. He's just in it for the money. He's big around these parts. A developer. The Durer part was all Kurt's idea, he was always so proud of his hometown, Nuremburg you know."

Jim nodded "We know."

"Why don't you two look around for something to take back to . . . "

"To Pittsburgh." Laura added, "Thanks we'll do just that."

"Kurt would want you to. He was like that. Pick out something to remember him by" Jenny said.

The couple began to look around. Most of the works were either of a religious nature or portraits of individuals including several self portraits. A few were neither. An intriguing one was a watercolor scene from the countryside looking at Nuremburg in 1497. Some others were simple animal studies. The woodcuts and engravings were highly detailed yet the subject matter was not that interesting to the Verratens. Finally, they settled on the brown rabbit.

Entitled Young Hare or Feldhase, a watercolor with the AD 1502 monogram on it.

While Jenny wrapped the Giclee print for Laura, Jim snuck off to the bar to find two seats. There he ordered a Berliner Weisse with woodruff in memory of his now dead acquaintance. The barmaid was the same girl as was there on Sunday evening but in a different dirndl. The bar was not as crowded as before, maybe Tuesdays were slower than Sundays or maybe it was the news that kept some customers away. In any case, Jim introduced himself. "Good to see you again. My name's Jim, I didn't catch your name Sunday."

With time to talk, the barmaid replied "Good to see you again, Jim. I'm Amanda. Weren't you here with your wife Sunday?"

"Yes, she's in the art gallery. Probably talking. We just picked out a piece, the brown rabbit."

"Oh, that's one of my favorites. I liked the little mouse or rat too, reminds me of Mickey a little with the big ears. That and the owl would make a great pair, the always seeing owl hunting his supper and the watchful mouse trying to avoid becoming it."

"Didn't think of that. But makes sense."

"Did Kurt give you a free print?"

"Yes. We heard the news today and thought we would come over to express our condolences, he seemed a nice guy. Did he treat the staff right?"

"Yes, all of us. I don't know what's going to happen now. The other partner has a bad reputation. We all liked working for Kurt, we don't know anyone who likes working for Lugner. Time will tell. Did you two come in just for drinks or are you going to have something to eat?"

"Probably eat here at the bar again, we'll see what the boss says. Have the police said anything about motive or questioned anyone here."

"Nothing. Seems he was killed after hours, none of us was around. I think they did talk to our brewer who discovered the body when he came to work in the morning."

"By the way, do you think I could see the brewery itself, kinda a hobby of mine? I travel all over and always like to see the various setups."

"I can arrange that with Jake, that's his name; Jake puts in 13 hour shifts three days a week. He does brew tours for groups sometimes. I'll go see when he has time this evening." Jim looked at the clock behind the bar and thought 'Laura's been in there a while. My beer is over half gone. Probably lost track of time and is just talking. Hope Amanda gets back soon before my glass is empty. I'm starting to get hungry. I wonder who will get here first, Laura or Amanda?' With his glass now empty Amanda returned from the brewery. "You're lucky. Jake can show you around now. I'll watch for your wife to come out of the gallery. What is her name?"

"Laura. She'll be looking for me here at the bar."

"OK. Now you go to the end of the bar, turn left, go down the hallway past the restrooms on the right and there is a door marked brewery. Just go right in and Jake will be there at his desk in the corner. He knows so much about beers."

With that sendoff Jim proceeded as directed and entered the brewery. It was roomy, unlike some he had visited which were shoehorned into undersized spaces. To his right was a regular doorway onto a loading dock which also had large old sliding doors on cast iron rollers to accept deliveries of pallets of malted grains and hops. Inside was the malt bill storage area with oversized ceilings. The area had once been a ware house or factory of some sort, clearly industrial in nature. Over in the corner was the brewery office, of sorts, which was simply a space reserved for a few desks and chairs with computers, some filing cabinets and stacks of papers, probably records of production runs and invoices. He saw Jake and waived. Jake got up and came over. "You must be Jim" he said.

"Yes, and you are Jake. I appreciate your taking time to show me around, especially after this morning."

"Thanks. But life has to go on. As soon as the Albrecht Durer gets back to normal the better for all of us employees. Sad thing though."

The tour began at the loading dock and progressed into the next room, the mash room. The equipment was sized for a 9 barrel system, next to the mash tank was the lautering tank and then the brew kettle where hops were added. Then there was another interior brick wall with a doorway through it, stainless steel pipes made their way from the brew kettle to the filtering tank. Jake explained that they use whole hop flowers as a liner in the filter tank to add extra hop flavor and serve as an extra filter for spent hops and trubs. Next in line were several double walled fermentation tanks where the yeast could do its job under temperature controlled conditions. Finally, in the aging room, the fermented beer was matured in the cold as the entire room was insulated and refrigerated. Filled barrels were labeled and stacked in half of the room ready for the bar.

"This is quite an impressive setup you have here Jack."

"Thanks. We do have the room to spread out. We were thinking of a bottling line next year. But who knows now?"

"Yes, very sad news. What do you think will happen now?" Jim asked.

"Don't know. Maybe a name change. I don't know if Lugner will buy the Vogel estate out or if we will get another partner. We could be managed for growth or just used as a mortgageable cash cow until everything is pulled out and we go bankrupt. That would fit Lugner's style."

"Really?" Jim said as they walked back to the loading dock.

"Really. Lugner is into big stuff. Here in Columbus and a lot of Ohio. An empire builder. I just don't see where the brewpub fits, just too small. It was Herr Vogel's idea anyway" Jack said. Jim thought a moment, Kurt Vogel was Lugner's banker, maybe the brewpub was a twist of the arm by the banker.

At the desk by the loading dock door Jim thanked Jack for the tour as Jack returned to his paperwork. Out of the corner of his eye he saw a can of paint and a brush on top of it next to the door. "That's going to get knocked over. Let me move it somewhere safe for you." Moving the gray paint can over to an out of the way spot he noticed the uncleaned brush was still somewhat soft and tacky. He wondered why the brush had not been cleaned since its recent use.

Laura spotted her husband as he approached the bar from the hallway. "Enjoy your tour? Took you long enough" she asked.

"That I did. Went over the Berliner Weisse recipe in some detail. It's an interesting brew."

Amanda returned. Laura was having the Woodruff Berliner. Jim ordered the Raspberry flavored one. "I could drink these all day long at three percent" he told his wife.

"I'm sure you could."

Amanda returned with the Raspberry Berliner. "Would you like to see a menu?" she asked the boss.

"Yes. I think we will" Laura replied. When the barmaid went for the menus Laura whispered to her husband "Something's up. Still waters run deep here."

"Here you go" Amanda said, "I recommend the beef Rouladen tonight with potato pancakes. I'll give you some time to decide."

"Tough decision tonight" Jim pondered.

"Very." Finally, Laura said "I'm ready, how about you?" With that Jim motioned to Amanda and their orders were placed. Laura continued whispering "I got an earful after you left the art gallery, then another from Amanda while waiting for you to return from your tour."

Jim nodded and whispered back "About what? Kurt?"

Laura replied "That and more. I'll fill you in at the hotel. Stick to your Berliners tonight. Work to do."

The starters to share arrived. The pickled herring in sour cream again and some Munich Radish spirals topped with chives and vinegar. The two were opposites and went well together. For dinner both had the Rouladen, Laura chose the potato pancakes and Jim went with the large potato dumpling. Dessert was cherry soup served cold with sour cream. Before they left Laura had the email of both barmaid Amanda and art gallery clerk Jenny.

Out in the parking lot Jim stopped short of their car. He turned and studied the outside of the building with his attention focused mainly on the loading dock area. Now he remembered what it was that was bothering him. He walked over closer to the building and saw an area above the door and over to the left that had new gray paint on it. He could tell it was newly painted because it had no dirty grime or bits of moss or lichen that the older wooden trim had on it. There were four small holes in the wood forming a square about four inches corner to corner with a half inch hole in the middle. The smaller outer holes appeared to stop part way into the old wooden beam, but the center hole went in deep, perhaps to the other side? "What are you looking at?" Laura asked.

"Tell you later. Still thinking it out" Jim answered.

In the car Laura said "I want to see something" and directed him to a large casino on the east side of town just inside the 270 beltway. Approaching it they saw the name in lights – The Lugner Casino and Track. It was large, very large. They circled around the parking lot. Although not as large as the very biggest of the ones in Las Vegas, it would have fit in well there in the downtown or near the Strip. "I wanted to show you this, no need to park. Let's keep going" she said. Before they left the parking lot, they spotted a tall building called the Lugner Hotel and Resort. It had a connecting walkway over to the casino and greyhound racetrack. Laura then directed Jim over to the Lugner Mall, a three level shopping mall, then past a strip mall named Lugner's at Ardmore. Finally, as they were in the downtown, they saw the Lugner Capitol City Hotel, an older building that had been obviously upgraded.

"Seems Lugner is into everything" Jim remarked passing the Lugner Hotel.

"That he is" added Laura.

Back in their room early, it was time for Laura to continue to fill Jim in with what she had learned from Amanda and Jenny. "Jim, I don't think Kurt is going to get a proper investigation on his murder. Max Lugner has the city tied up, more or less according to the women at the pub. He's like Teflon. A girl at the brewpub quit six months ago when her charges of sexual harassment were dropped by the police, and she was not the first. A lot of these girls stick together and know each other from similar situations. Jenny said women at his hotels and casino have been molested and filed charges only to have no action taken and they themselves questioned as if they were guilty, and sometimes charges filed against them!"

"That must be fairly common though, murder is not. What has that got to do with Kurt's death?" Jim asked.

"I don't know. It's just his character. He is a louse. They say he lies his way out of everything. Doesn't pay his contractors what he owes them, tells them to sue him and most of them cannot afford the litigation against his army of lawyers. He ruined several of the women's reputation that he molested with his lawyers, and now he's got everyone afraid."

"Still, I don't see the connection with murder. And I don't see why Lugner would do a deal with a banker on the brewpub. First of all, it is a very small business, almost insignificant compared to his little empire in Columbus. Second, it's named after Durer, it's not the Lugner Brewpub. Odd" Jim added.

"Yea. Very odd. Doesn't seem to match his personality. There are lots of banks in Columbus and in the States, virtually unlimited money to borrow. Why is he in business with a German banker who works for Prussia Bank and has a brewpub named after a hometown hero?"

"Why indeed. I thought about that myself. But in today's world maybe banks want to spread their investments globally?" Jim added.

"Amanda told me that Jack's usual brewing schedule is 13 hours a day on Tuesday, Wednesday and Friday. He was not there on Monday and it was Tuesday morning when they found the body in the lot. Both women work Mondays and although Jenny saw both Kurt and Max around the pub that day, Jenny spent most of her time in the art gallery and didn't see much outside it. She said the men seemed a little cold to each other, not like usual. Amanda saw and heard more. She said both Lugner and Vogel spent most of their time at the brewery office. She left at midnight and the two were still meeting when she punched her timeclock in the hallway at midnight. That was unusual. She has worked at the Durer for several years and the two never met that late into the night."

"Did she tell this to the police?"

"No. They did not interview her, even when she asked them if they needed to talk with her."

"Well, that's interesting" Jim said.

"Yea. Really. Like they never really investigated the women's sexual harassment charges" Laura tied the two to each other. "By the way, what were you looking at so intently in the pub parking lot?"

"Something. Something I've been trying to remember. You know Sunday evening when we first parked, then got out and walked towards the Durer."

"Go on, I remember" Laura responded.

"What do you remember about the parking lot? Did you feel safe there, I mean if you were alone?" Jim asked.

"Yea. I guess I would. Well lit at night. Secure" Laura responded, "Not some dark, dirty place where a creeper might hide."

"Hmmm. Subliminal. So your overall impression, your intuition, then was that of safety, of confidence" Jim asked.

"Yes it was" Laura responded.

"I think we men are not as perceptive as you women in such things. Few tall, strong men worry much or pay much attention to a parking lot going into or out of a pub."

"We women do. I liked that there was a CCTV camera pointing at the lot" she said as a forgotten image came to mind.

"Yes! That's it! CCTV. I remember it now. That's what I was trying to remember. Just walked by it then, hardly noticed it, but now I remember. It was up over the door of the loading dock" Jim added.

Laura closed her eyes and thought in silence, her eyes moving around as if looking. "Agreed. It was up over the door pointing at the parking lot. Jim, it would have caught the murder!" she declared.

"Yes, it would have. But it's not there now. It's been removed" Jim murmured, "And I found a can of gray paint with an unwashed brush, still not dried out, on the inside of that loading dock door. The place where it was has just been freshly painted over!"

Laura spoke next. "I think you better see what you can find on the computer tonight. That Lugner just moved up a peg. But why would he kill his banker?"

"And why was he his banker. The two must be connected somehow. I'll see what I can dig up. I've got a meeting tomorrow so I can't pull an all nighter. Best get to work now, fill you in tomorrow."

Jim Verraten, a cyber security expert, or locksmith as Herr Vogel commented, could hack his way into almost any site be it a motor vehicle division or a bank, yet he started out with a simple search for properties owned by one Max Lugner, suspect. Before Laura went to bed, he had informed her that Lugner owned a Casino over in Cincinnati, Lugner's Riverfront Casino; one in Cleveland, Lugner's Lakeview Casino; and one in Toledo, Lugner's Paradise with a Lugner branded Hotel at each. He also owned several other Lugner hotels around the state as well as over in Indianapolis, Indiana. His holdings included several malls he appeared to have developed. Laura was amazed. 'What was he doing messing around with a simple brewpub?' she thought while going to sleep as Jim worked at the desk.

That night Jim got deeper and deeper into both Lugner and Prussia Bank. Lugner had been developing his properties since a young man 30 years earlier essentially continuing the family business his father started. The Lugner family had settled in Columbus as did many, many German immigrants and Max Lugner's father was the first in the family to make a small fortune in the building business by constructing many of the 1950's neighborhoods in the baby boom years following the Second World War. The elder Lugner was not able to serve in the war, but got his start with military contracts for housing that the federal Government furnished to armament factory workers. After the war, he bought back those rental units for pennies on the dollar as war surplus and from there kept on building. His obituary in 1979 and estate probation records showed his only child Max had inherited all with virtually no debt.

At this point, Max assumed full control of the family business and, from what Jim could tell in the public records of property transactions, he instituted a sell off of many of the properties and mortgaged the remaining ones as much as possible. Flush with cash, Max had begun a building and spending spree that could easily be followed in the newspaper archives. They all carried the Lugner brand prominently in their name and began with strip malls, shopping malls, apartment complexes, condos, then progressed to hotels and finally, when Ohio legalized gaming, into casinos themselves. On the face of it all, it appeared that Max Lugner was a very successful businessman, but Jim had also noticed the disappearance of many of the businesses over time. He decided to check court records for bankruptcies. What he found explained a lot.

Max Lugner had started with his inheritance and some experience working for his father in the business. His father was what is termed a conservative businessman, that is he used borrowed money sparingly; the son Max was anything but. After selling off most of the hard assets he inherited he put the money to work in image building as well as property building. Image building was expensive and included a private jet, penthouse condo in an apartment building named the Lugner Haven, an assortment of luxury cars including two Rolls Royce and a very large yacht on Lake Erie based at his lakeside vacation home near Cleveland. Achieved newspapers online more or less documented his high living jet set lifestyle. Now it was time to search deeper, time to go beyond what was in the public domain.

Although Lugner lived the life of a wealthy playboy developer, some bankruptcy court records had showed all might not be well in paradise. Jim searched the various banks who were listed in the creditors of the bankruptcy proceedings, digging into their private records of the properties in question. After hacking into several properties and bank records, Jim saw a pattern. It seemed Max Lugner would make a deal with a seller on a property to develop giving a bond in exchange for the land or building, not cash. Then as owner, Max would approach a bank for a development loan. Once completed and leased out or sold if condos, he would pay off the building loan by taking out a first mortgage much as a homeowner would after a builder's construction loan. One of his corporations would take over management of the property for a hefty fee. But then a while later at a different bank, he would take out a second and at another even a third loan until he had removed as much cash as possible from the property leaving it with debt in excess of its value. This was much more than if he had simply sold the finished property and paid off the loans and bonds. In time the property's income could not pay the interest on the loans and defaulted sticking the banks and original seller while Max went onto another project. All this without putting in any of his own cash. Nothing was ever done in his personal name, just corporations which he could form at will and dissolve into bankruptcy just as easily.

It was midnight, but Jim's blood was up. He decided to continue working a few hours longer, 2 or 3 hours of sleep would be enough to get him through the next day. He wondered how Max Lugner could have ended up with such a current empire by sticking the banks.

Within an hour of hacking into a particular banks records of meetings of its Board of Directors and levels below, he learned that Lugner had been blackballed at the bank; absolutely no new loans would be allowed to him either personally or to any corporation he owned significant shares in. At a second bank the story was the same. Hacking into the financial records of this second phase of building projects, sans the usual banks, Jim observed Max had discovered the use of junk bonds.

These bonds were developed in the 1980's and originally issued with very high interest rates and very low grading. Traditionally, corporations tried to always issue Grade A bonds as these were seen as very safe and carried a lower interest rate because of the corporation backing them. The other Grades were B, C and D. The Grade A might fall into one of the lower grades if the company which issued it faced a reverse or serious trouble. Grade D meant Default when a company could not pay the interest on the bond at all. Grades B and C did not sell at "par" value – the original value of $1,000 each - but lower upon resale from one investor to another if the company appeared to be getting into trouble.

Junk bonds were invented to be issued originally at a low grade such as a B- or mostly in the C range. Where a A grade or AAA grade might pay interest of 5%, a low B or C grade might pay 15% plus. Obviously, greed of the investor allowed many to ignore the shady background of the issuing company. Rather than investing it was approaching gambling.

Jim saw that a second major round of projects was carried forward with these junk bonds, the price however was that the high interest rate often meant little if anything left over for profits. But on paper, and in the newspapers and media it looked like a growing business empire with a high flying magnate on top. As each property was held by a different corporation Max Lugner had set up and controlled, if one could not keep payments up Max simply defaulted and worked out a refinancing deal with the junk bond holders.

It was during this period when the name Prussia bank began to appear in the financial records, but at 3 AM Jim needed sleep before his morning presentations. Prussia Bank would have to wait until tomorrow evening.

Wednesday morning Laura knew her husband had been working late into the night and would appreciate a fresh pot of coffee and room service breakfast. "How did it go last night. When did you get to bed?" she asked.

"I was a good boy. No minibar and about 3, more or less. Five hours sober sleep, not bad. I'm fresh as a daisy."

"I don't know if I'd go that far. What did you find out?"

"That I have more work to do this evening too. Seems our Mr. Lugner has had his share of financial problems, to say the least. Doesn't seem to be the successful developer he likes to project" Jim replied taking a sip of java. Jim then went over the basics of what he had found out.

"Don't most developers use a lot of leverage?" Laura suggested.

"I'm no expert on developer finances, so I don't really know. They get financing somewhere, but not as much like this guy who stiffed a lot of his backers. I was just getting to the Prussia Bank connection at 3, that's my focus this evening after an early dinner, say back here by 8. What's on your agenda today?" he asked.

"Franklin Park Conservatory and Botanical Gardens. And I might give Amanda and Jenny a ring. I think they know more than they are saying. I'm sort of surprised they said so much already about Lugner, he seems to be a vindictive type. I'm sure they're afraid of him if something they say gets out and around to him. I have to gain their confidence, and I think I know how" she told her husband.

The couple parted at 9 and went their separate ways, Jim to his meetings at the State Capitol where he would be showing the cyber security plan he had developed and reviewed favorably by IT to the IS staff. If they liked it and thought it workable, he would be one step closer to his goal of a meeting with the Ohio Attorney General, Treasurer and Governor. Laura had checked the weather and knew it would be sunny all morning with a chance of rain in the afternoon. A morning at the Botanical Garden would be great and around 11 she would call Amanda and Jenny.

The Franklin Park Conservatory had a lunch garden, a convenient out of the way place to invite Amanda over for lunch. "Ok Laura, I'll see you at noon, I live about a mile away." A little surprised at how easy it was to get Amanda to join her for lunch, Laura thought the barmaid might sense something and was eager to meet in private away from the brewpub.

"This is a wonderful resource for Columbus" Laura said while the two women looked at the lunch menu.

"It is. We used to come here on school field trips. Takes me back a little. I guess you see a lot in your travels Laura."

"Yes, I have. I've had a lot of experiences. Once in Charleston, South Carolina at the Gullah Girl brewpub there was a murder of the cook. Police had arrested a special ed boy. Jim and I got involved with the DA when we thought he was innocent, that the evidence didn't fit. I even went undercover."

"Are you undercover now?"

"No. Not at all. It's just that we have been involved in solving different murders we have stumbled upon. Sometimes we uncover things the police don't."

"That's interesting" Amanda said.

"Yea, and what is interesting about Kurt Vogel is that I don't think the local police will catch the real killer, it'll be put down to a mugging gone wrong. They didn't even interview you and take your statement, did they?" Laura inquired.

"No, they didn't. You have to understand they know Max is part owner of the Durer and they don't want to find anything that might connect him to it or embarrass him. An unsolved mugging is a safe outcome" Amanda said.

"Yes, I can see that. A safe outcome but I don't think a true or just outcome and I think you agree with me."

"I do."

"So then tell me what you saw or heard Monday evening at the Durer. What you tell me will never have your name associated with it if you don't want it to" Laura said.

"OK. I've been working there almost two years now. I first met Kurt Vogel a month after I started at the bar. He was there most every evening that week which I thought strange. I would have thought a German in Columbus would have liked to try American restaurants. Then I saw Max Lugner was joining him most evenings during the week. I didn't connect it at first but on later visits I did. Lugner and Kurt would meet in the brewery office for long hours whenever the brewer was not working, and sometimes they would meet in the art gallery when he was. They would just hang up a sign 'Closed' on the gallery door. Sometimes they would just sit and talk at an out of the way table. I always wondered why he would meet Max at the Durer instead of at his regular office, wherever that was."

"That's interesting. I wonder why too" Laura agreed.

Amanda continued "This went on about every three or four months. It was none of my business so I didn't pay much attention to it. But this week was different. Tuesday evening when I was going to the restroom, I heard them arguing in the brewery office. They were loud. I know I shouldn't eavesdrop, but I couldn't resist they were so loud. I thought of interrupting them and telling them they could be heard in the hallway if any customers were using the restrooms, but thought it not my place to do so."

"Did you hear what they were arguing about?" Laura inquired.

"A little here and there. It was about money. I couldn't catch all the words but Max was the one really upset. He was using the word bankrupt a lot along with loan. Kurt kept saying a decision had been made, that there was nothing he would do. I heard what I think was a fist slamming onto the desk in anger, you know, like when you're really trying to empathize a point. I think it was Max's fist because it slammed down only when he was talking. He was using the word ruin off and on then. I decided for sure not to go in there with them in that state. What was it to me if a customer heard them? They ought to be more discreet. So I just left and went back behind the bar."

"And the police don't know of this argument?"

"They never asked me."

"Amanda, you've been very helpful. These things are like a jigsaw puzzle, every piece adds to the picture."

"Just so you know, I'll tell it to the police if they ever ask me. But I'm not going knocking at their door."

"I'll remember that" Laura said as they finished lunch at the Conservatory.

As threatening dark clouds moved overhead Laura's visit to the Botanical Garden was over and she was looking at the Conservatory flowers under its glass roof. She had a lot of information for Jim now and wondered if Jenny had anything else to contribute. A text caught Jenny at home, work at the gallery didn't begin until 5, so she agreed to meet Laura at a coffee shop near her apartment on the north side of town at 3 o'clock.

As the two women sat down at an out of the way table, Laura with a cappuccino and Jenny with her latte, Laura felt that with Jenny agreeing to a coffee she might be signaling she had more to say. She began by telling her the story of their visit to Carmel-By-The-Sea in California and how they assisted the police in solving a murder, and that she and Jim were looking into the murder of the German banker.

"Are you working with the police now?" Jenny inquired.

"No. We don't feel we can trust the police in Columbus, maybe not even the State Police. It's just that we are both wondering if justice will be done, or if it will be whitewashed over. If Max Lugner was involved somehow, that might be a possibility knowing his influence here in Columbus" Laura replied, "So we're freelancing, as you might say."

"I see. I agree with you that if Max was involved somehow, his name will be kept out of it. Of all the women who went to the police about sexual abuse, not one charge was filed, not a word in the press. He has a lot of power under the table."

"Jenny, I'm wondering if there is anything more that you can tell me other than what you said at the art gallery about all the sexual harassments. Anything you say is in strictest confidence, your name will never come out unless you wish it to. Did you ever overhear any conversation between the two men?"

"Well, I know a little more but I don't think it's worth anything."

"Every little piece fills in the jigsaw puzzle, even if it's off in the corner" Laura remarked.

"Whenever they used the gallery to meet in, they put up that closed sign, and I was told to go work elsewhere, like helping serve or something for a while. But one time they didn't tell me to go, I think they forgot about me or maybe didn't care. I was unpacking a shipment of prints in my little corner work area where I frame and price them. It's out of the way. They were sitting over at the sales desk on the other side of the shop. This happened a couple times. I didn't follow the conversation, but I could hear it. It was all financial stuff that I don't understand, I guess banker and client talk. But I was surprised that Russia was mentioned. At first, I thought Kurt said Prussia, for I knew he worked for Prussia Bank; but then I heard several times he was saying Russia and Russians. He was also mentioning Sicilians and a couple other countries."

"That's very interesting, Jenny."

"They were talking big money, not just a million or two, but tens of millions, like sixty, eighty million at a time."

"That's really big money."

"Yea, it is. But there were several of these. Tens of millions for each deal, I never added it up but I bet it was three or four hundred million I heard about one night. I didn't understand why they were using the gallery for this type discussion; I know they couldn't talk openly at the bar or restaurant, but why not back at one of Max's regular offices somewhere. I figured they just liked our food at the brewpub."

"Did they ever argue, like over money or anything?"

"No. Never. Mind you I only overheard them a couple times and it was always the same. Something financial about some project or other and the big money needed to get it done. They were always quite friendly and seemed to like one another" Jenny concluded.

"Jenny, you've been very helpful. I don't know where Jim and I are going with this death of Herr Vogel yet, but I'll keep you posted."

The two women finished their coffees and talked a little more about Kurt Vogel and his love of his hometown of Nuremburg. "Jenny, I'm just curious, do you sell many prints from your gallery?"

"You'd be surprised. We do. Some like you pick one of the natural animal or plant subjects, but others go for the religious themes. We get some church people in here all the time from all over. And some like the portraits. Usually if they are buying one, they are buying several."

"That's very interesting and good to hear. This is the first time we had ever heard of Albrecht Durer" Laura concluded.

Jenny then went to her sales job at the Albrecht Durer while Laura waited at the coffee shop for Jim's call since he would be finishing up for the day soon.

Jim's call came at around 5 and Laura drove over to the Ohio Capitol building to pick him up. They decided on the Malz Biergarten over in Olde Town East., a brewpub housed in an old fire engine house. There they enjoyed a meal of schnitzels, rotkohl and kaesespaetzle along with Kolsch and Dunkel beers to wash it down. Although it had outside seating, all the customers were inside due to the still sprinkling sky. It was a lovely place and they wished they could have spent more time there, yet after what Laura told Jim about her conversations with Amanda and Jenny, both knew Jim had much work to do that evening and sobriety would be key to getting it done successfully. They were back at the hotel by seven, Laura settled down with a book while Jim opened up his laptop.

At this point, they both felt the key to the murder lay in the heated argument between the banker and his client in the brewery office. Jim began where he left off the night before, finance, but now he had new information. There appeared to be some sort of Eastern European connection, primarily Russia but intriguingly a Sicilian one also. In his mind the only real connection to Sicily would be Mafia money. In the early evening, Jim saw a pattern appear in Lugner's earlier properties, those where he had used traditional bank financing. It seemed that after taking as much cash out of the property in the form of additional mortgage loans stacked on top of each other, he would increase his companies management fees for running the property. Within a few years defaults occurred and bankruptcy followed.

"Dracula?" said Laura, "Did you just mutter Dracula?"

"I suppose I did. Lugner just bled the properties dry into his own pockets. He was not so much of a property developer as a con man. That's why when the banks go onto his scams, he had to turn to junk bonds. No bank would touch him." Jim continued on his research. Around the time Laura was going to bed, Jim cracked the Prussia Bank cyber security system. He thought the system not very secure, probably created by the IT department staff and not professionals like himself. Kurt had not realized just how weak it was; the door was now open. The German language did not bother Jim, there were plenty of easily accessible on-line translator programs he could plug into to read the various documents he was now seeing in Kurt Vogel's files. He started with the oldest ones and by 2 in the morning had worked his way up to the present time. What he learned was both surprising and predictable in an oxymoronic way. An hour later, his work concluded, he got some sleep before Thursday's meetings.

Again on Thursday morning, Laura had called for room service breakfast letting Jim sleep as long as possible although she did make fresh coffee in case he awoke before breakfast coffee was delivered. When it arrived, Laura woke her husband up, anxious to hear what he had to say about last night computer sleuthing.

"Laura, you know what money laundering is, don't you?" he asked his wife.

"You mean like when some of your pocket change goes through the washing machine at home and comes out looking like new? Or do you mean like when money from illegal activities comes back on the books looking like legal profits?" she replied to his disparaging question.

"No offense intended. I'm just waking the little gray cells up, buying time."

"Well, OK then. Here's your coffee for that" Laura added.

"It's all clear now" Jim said "Lugner was up to his old tricks again. Prussia Bank wasn't loaning him any money for quite a while, all they were doing was acting as a conduit and Kurt, as nice a guy as he was, was the point man for the bank."

"So where was the money coming from, tens and tens of millions?" she asked.

"Primarily Russians, the oligarchs. But some from the Sicilian mob, probably drug profits, and a little from some others. This was all dirty money in one way or another that needed cleaned up. Say if a crook had 25 million he needed to launder, he would go to Prussia Bank and they would hold it in a separate account not co-mingling it with other bank assets, then find a purpose for it like with Lugner for example. If the investment went belly up, that was a chance the crooks took. But they used the money to buy condos and other Lugner properties that Lugner built and paid far more than the going rate for them with no questions asked, then in time they could sell the properties even at a loss, and the remaining money was laundered and free to use above board and suspicion here in our country. Just a cost of doing business."

"Interesting."

"That it is, for example one property was a Lugner built strip mall probably worth 15 million on the open market. Lugner got 20 million for it, and it kept the Lugner name and Lugner managed the property for a hefty fee. A few years later the property could be sold for whatever and the crook's money was cleaned. He didn't have to lift a finger for the service Lugner provided."

"Well, that seems to be somewhat foolproof. Doesn't answer what went wrong, why Kurt was killed" Laura remarked.

"It was a great scam; everyone was happy until Prussia Bank came under investigation in Europe. You see Laura, America was not the only laundromat in the world. Prussia Bank was stopping all such activity globally and that was what Kurt's orders were on this trip, to tell Max Lugner there would be no more financial deals of this nature and that Prussia Bank itself would not loan any money to him."

"Whoa! That would hurt" Laura exclaimed.

"A world of hurt. Lugner was so leveraged, in so deep in debt over his head that he relied on a steady stream of money laundering to get cash to keep his casinos afloat. Without that extra cash inflow, his empire would collapse as one then another business succumbed to bankruptcy, casinos included" Jim forecast.

"And I thought casinos were very profitable" Laura remarked.

"They have that potential, but they do have operating expenses for staff and utilities. What is left over goes to pay off any interest or loans they have, if there aren't any, then the remainder is pure profit."

"And in Lugner's casinos?"

"In his casinos the leftovers can't even pay the interest let alone pay down principal. There is no remainder for profits. True to form, Lugner has taken all the equity out already leaving a mountain of debt. He may have spent it, or stashed it away, but he saw it would only be a matter of time until his reputation was, should I say, kaput."

"And his empire finished with no chance of a reboot either" Laura mentioned.

"And possible jail time. Money laundering is a felony here you know" Jim added.

"Wow. No empire, possible jail time."

"Probable jail time, I think. What I saw last night would be more than enough to convict; Lugner knew where the money was coming from."

"But killing Kurt would not solve anything."

"It would not. It was a decision way above Kurt's pay grade. Lugner just lost it Monday night. As they say, he killed the messenger."

"What are we going to do now? He might get away with it here in Columbus" Laura said in reference to Lugner's apparent control over city politics including the police and the DA's office.

"The video. If we can find the CCTV recording, if it still exists, it can send him away on murder charges. If I remember correctly, the brewer has today off. Give Amanda a call, see if she's working tonight. See if Thursday is Jack's day off. If so, we'll see her at seven."

After breakfast the two went their separate ways, Jim to his meetings at the State Capitol and Laura to see some art, the Columbus Art Museum and the Pizzuti Collection. Around noon, she got ahold of Amanda and told her they would see her at the bar at seven, and she did make sure Jack was not working in the brewery. With an hour extra to fill, Laura drove into Germantown to the quaint Book Nook with its Willkommen banner and inviting garden. Room after enticing room awaited perusal and knowing she had not the time for really taking it all in, she did spot a new series called the Brewpub Mysteries that looked interesting before returning to the hotel to await her husband. There she was reading the first in the series, A Poisonous Pilsner when he arrived from work.

"How did your day go? Think you have them sewn up?" Laura asked her husband on the drive down to the Albrecht Durer brewpub.

"I feel good about it. I did get a meeting with the Governor, Attorney General and Secretary of Finance tomorrow morning along with the head of IT and IS departments. I don't expect a decision, but the meeting tomorrow was the goal of the week" Jim proudly relayed.

When they arrived around seven at the brewpub parking lot, they noticed the police tape had been removed and Kurt's rental car removed. Things had gone back to normal quickly. Inside they met Amanda at the bar.

"Good to see you both again, becoming regulars here" Amanda quipped.

"Regulars for the week, it's back to Pittsburgh soon" Laura replied.

"So what's up with Jack? Why did you need to know if he was working today?" the barmaid asked.

"First two Berliner Weiss please, make mine with woodruff. Thirsty after a long day" Jim requested.

"And mine the same" said Laura.

Amanda returned with the two goblets with the green syrup on the bottom. "There you go, no swizzle sticks, you guys are pros now."

Jim took a sip. "Ah, that's good. About Jack, he really is a great brewer. But I'm here tonight to see if I can find some evidence to nail down the murderer."

"Jack? Do you mean Jack had something to do with it?" the barmaid asked with surprise.

"Oh, No no no. Not at all. Let me explain. There was a CCTV camera outside facing the parking lot for guest security. It was there on Sunday evening when we first came here, but it's gone now. It was mounted above the door at the loading dock. Do you know where the monitor was? Who was supposed to watch the parking lot?" Jim asked.

"Well actually I was, not that I did it a lot. Things get busy here at the bar. There was a small monitor down here on the shelf, but it's gone now. Come around and I'll show you where it was."

Jim walked around the bar and looked where Amanda was pointing. It was a small space under the bar that customers could not see. "I would glance down at it once in a while, not very often though, more after dark when the place was emptying out. But then there would be several people leaving so not much danger for anyone."

"Kurt was murdered well after you left at midnight; I'm not implying anything. I just needed to know the setup" Jim replied sensing Amanda might have felt a little guilty, but after all she was the bartender not the security staff which was non-existent. "I would like to go into the brewery if it's OK with you. A CCTV security system is more than a camera and a monitor. I'd like to do what the police should have done, see if any recording of the murder exists."

"By all means, there's no lock on the brewery door. You'll be alone in there."

"Great" Jim said "But first I need something to eat. Lunch at that Capitol building's cafeteria leaves much to be desired. What's good tonight?"

"I can get you the Sauerbraten Special off the dining room menu."

"Sold, two of those then" Laura quickly responded. "We both love Sauerbraten."

After dinner Jim got the all clear from Amanda and entered the brewery where he first went over to the door. There he saw the hole did indeed traverse all the way through the wood, presumably for the video cable. A foot in was a coupler where the camera would have been attached to the security system. He followed the cable where it went behind shelving stacked with hops and dried yeasts. It came out the other side of the shelving and went through another hole and into the bar, presumably for the monitor below the bar. He knew the camera and the monitor were adjuncts, not the heart of the system. He started removing hops and yeast packets from the shelving and saw what he knew must be somewhere – a junction forming a three way connection. One ran to the camera, one to the monitor and one headed straight down. Emptying shelf by shelf he reached the computer that was the systems heart. It was near the floor and plugged into an outlet. He saw the manufacturer and model number and got out his iPad.

Now he looked up the owner's manual and carefully read it. Gone were the days of a continuous VHS tape recording and then recording over the week's events caught on camera every few seconds. Now the data would be of much higher resolution and stored on a hard drive indefinitely.

Getting the password was relatively simple for Jim and took ten minutes; now inside he found the file for Tuesday and began a fast forward through it. It didn't take long. At around 1:30 in the morning the camera caught two men apparently coming out under the CCTV and walking over to the parking lot. The one walking quickly in the lead Jim recognized as Kurt Vogel, the other he did not recognize but suspected it was Max Lugner. Vogel was constantly turning to Lugner who was just steps behind, they seemed to be shouting at each other or more than just polite conversation anyway. As Vogel moved towards his car and was taking the keys out from his pocket, Lugner spotted a loose brick nearby an old wall's remains, picked it up and went over to Vogel as he had turned to open the car door. Lugner raised the brick and used it to hit Vogel in the head. Vogel immediately fell to the ground where he was stuck in the head repeatedly by the brick.

Lugner then stopped, paused a few minutes looking at the body on the ground, looked around and seeing nobody took the wallet out of Vogel's pocket then went back toward the loading dock with the brick in one hand and the wallet in the other. As he neared the door he looked up at the CCTV and stopped momentarily, then went inside. The last image was a short time later when the camera caught Lugner's face and hands as he reached up to the camera then went back inside. A minute later the recording stopped. There was no more recorded at all after that, close to 2 AM.

Now Jim used the port on the security system's computer to link onto the adapter for his iPad and downloaded what he had just watched. After disconnecting, he restacked all the hop and yeasts that he had moved.

Back at the bar Laura and Amanda awaited his return. Finally, he appeared out of the hallway and sat down at the end away from other customers, Laura moved over next to him. "Anything?" she asked her husband.

"Everything" he responded. "Got it right here" he said holding out his iPad. "Just one last thing, I need a positive ID. Amanda?"

The barmaid looked at him. "Amanda, I need you to identify someone on this video from your security system. It captured the murder. It's not pleasant to watch and I can stop it when you want. What do you say?"

"I say I'll do it, and you don't have to stop it."

With that Jim played the recording in real time starting when the two men were first seen on camera. "I know it's hard to ID someone from the back, but he turns around in a few minutes." Amanda first identified Kurt Vogel, then when the second man went to grab a brick, she identified him as Max Lugner. She confirmed that with a 'definitely Max' as he walked back to the steps after the murder and looked up at the camera.

The three looked at each other. The unspoken question in all three minds was 'What to do now?'

Amanda spoke first "He'll never get a fair trial in this town. Even with that evidence and they're not even looking for it. Vogel's rental car was towed away and the police tape removed. Mugging gone bad is all I hear."

Laura was next. "Even if we give a copy to the police, they might just file it away or consider it unusable due to lack of custody concerns, meaning it might be doctored."

"But" Jim began "If I get it to the news media anonymously, their hands will be tied if it gets airtime. I can send it to the local TV stations and a National chain or two. Lugner might have some local influence but not in New York City."

The three agreed that sending copies to the news media would be the way to go. Dropping the local news rooms idea, they decided on a Nationwide newspaper out of New York due to the Prussia Bank connection. A murder of a German banker in Columbus who was involved in money laundering would be just the type of story they would jump on. Then the local police would have to act with so many eyes looking at them.

So it was decided. There would be no mention of Amanda or Jenny when Jim would contact a reporter in New York on Friday afternoon.

"I guess I ought to start looking for a new job. I can't see the Durer surviving what's coming" Amanda said.

"You could do that, but think for a minute. When the finances of Lugner collapse he's going to be looking for all the cash he can get for defense attorneys and bankruptcy lawyers. The Durer is expendable, a source of little cash to keep him going. I am sure he would accept a reasonable offer if he still has any equity in it, but if the Durer goes under then the banks take control. Banks don't want hard assets on their hands to manage, not even Prussia Bank, they want some cash out and go onto the next deal. Now Vogel's half will end up in his estate, again whoever that is in Germany will probably not want it and would rather cash out. I believe it could be bought very cheaply. You see if the Durer just closes and goes under, neither the Bank nor Vogel's estate gets anything at all. An employee buyout gives them something" Jim concluded.

"I don't have that kind of money" Amanda replied.

"You don't have to. Local banks have money and need to keep it invested" Jim responded. "Now from what I have seen and what you've told me, the Durer essentially runs itself. The brewery by Jack, the chef in the kitchen, you at the bar, Jenny in the gallery does the ordering of prints not just sales, and so on. You don't even have a full time manager. You guys handle it all."

"Yes, we do, more or less."

"Then you ought to talk with the others and see if they're interested in doing a leveraged buyout. When, not if, the Durer goes under it will be for sale – cheap. If you all have an employee buyout proposal in place and approach Prussia Bank and the Vogel estate quickly, I think you have a real chance to become co-owners of the place, free and clear of Lugner's debts and Vogel's estate. I think due to the nature of what is going to happen to Lugner, other investors or buyers will be scared off this hot potato here. All you have to show a bank is that you all, as a team, have been and can run Durer's profitably. That ought to get you the financing. I can get you the names and emails of who you need to talk to without any trouble, and you will need a local lawyer to put your proposal together officially" Jim concluded.

"What do you think Amanda?" asked Laura, "Interested at all?"

"This is so quick. I think so. I can talk to the others."

"But wait until the story breaks. It ought to be in the media in a few days" Jim added.

"Of course."

On Friday as the Verratens were driving back to Pittsburgh, Laura asked Jim how his meetings with the Governor went. "Very well. As well as can be expected. Now it's not about what we can do technically for them but pricing, so Bob will have to get involved. But the door is open for negotiations now after this week."

"And the leak to the press?"

"All done too before we left Columbus. As they used to say, I dropped a dime on Lugner."

"You know Jim, I was hoping for a quiet week just doing our jobs. We rarely seem to get one."

"Coincidence, I am sure of that" he said driving East on I-70.

On Sunday afternoon, Laura received a phone call from Amanda. The story had broken on the news Saturday evening in Columbus. She said the noon news Sunday continued to add detail and the police had revisited the Durer and had found the CCTV system and taken its computer away while news media recorded the event. And at the press conference the Chief of Police remarked that the case had moved from a simple mugging death to a homicide. Amanda quoted the Chief's response to reporters' questions.

"Is it true that Max Lugner is a suspect?" asked one reporter.

"I am not at liberty to respond to that. We have an ongoing investigation now and I cannot comment on it."

"Is it true that it is Max Lugner in the tape we saw. It looks like him."

"No comment on that. We have an ongoing investigation now and I cannot comment on it."

Amanda also commented that the police were talking to all the employees of the Albrecht Durer regarding Lugner and Vogel and she had already told them about the ongoing argument in the brewery between the two men when she punched out on the time clock late Monday evening.

"Jim, it seems to be just a matter of time before an arrest is made" Laura said to her husband behind the wheel.

"Yes, it does. They work fast when the heat's on. Did Amanda say anything about looking into an employee buyout?" Jim asked.

"She said that now that it was out in the open she would start putting a few feelers out on Monday and see if there was any interest at all" responded Laura.

"Well, that's good. They may have to move fast when an arrest is made. Their future will depend on it" he said reaching for his coffee after his third little white donut.

On Tuesday morning, one week after Herr Vogel's body had been discovered, that arrest was made. Max Lugner was taken into custody and charged with the murder of Kurt Vogel.

END

The Patsy and the Porter

#12 From the Series

A Brewpub Mystery

by

Fredric G. Bender

All rights reserved: no part of this publication may be reproduced or transmitted by any means without the prior permission of the author.

The Patsy and the Porter is a work of fiction. Any resemblance to actual persons, living or dead, is purely coincidental. Any resemblance to actual brewpubs, breweries or bars is purely coincidental.

Porter

Originating in England around 1722, porter evolved from 'Entire' a blend of equal parts beer, ale and strong beer mixed at the pub upon order. This precursor to stout is said to have been favored by porters and other physical laborers, evolving into the stout style of today.

Malt Bill: English types: Pale, Brown, and Chocolate

Yeast: Bottom or top fermenting

Hops: East Kent Goldings, Fuggles, Williamette

Adjuncts: Treacle, sugar, molasses; moderate carbonate hard water

IBU (International Bitterness Units): 18-35

ABV (Alcohol By Volume): 4.0% to 5.5+%

SRM (Standard Reference Method Color): 20-30 Light to dark brown

Taste: Moderate to low hop flavor, mild hop bitterness; mild to restrained moderate roast malt; medium light to medium body

Carbonation: Medium low to medium high, off white to tan head

Variations: Robust styles, often with a ruby or garnet highlight, come close to stouts but lack strong roasted barley component. Influenced by Russian Imperial Stouts, Baltic Styles are strongest in alcohol and stone fruit flavors. Pastry Porters are gaining in popularity.

The Patsy and the Porter

On a bench at the train station platform, Jim and Laura Verraten sat waiting sipping their Chocolate and Peanut Butter Pastry Porters in 16 ounce red plastic cups. They were not far from Branson, Missouri in the very small town of Galena Junction awaiting boarding time on the Ozark Mountains Scenic Railroad. The old logging railroad was part of a growing business, Porters Pub and Brewery and its ticket office was inside the brewpub. Porters Pub specialized in Porter beers and railway style foods from the golden age of steam. Its logo featured a Porter from those times.

The Verratens, on a long weekend holiday, after a week's work in Branson, had just enjoyed a breakfast featuring items taken from the old Harvey House menus of a hundred years ago. Laura had the tenderloin of trout, potatoes, toast and coffee while Jim had the corned beef hash with fried egg, toast and coffee. Now waiting for the train in the summer morning's coolness and shade, they had started with the Pastry Porter. They knew others would be available all along the trip.

The couple had booked well in advance for this ride which always sold out this time of year. It was the Murder Mystery trip – Death of a Spy. They looked forward to a fun Whodunit full of suspense and intrigue. During the day long ride, they would be served a simple lunch and a dinner upon the return at the Porters Pub. The train's club car would have all the Porters available along with an assortment of other beers and soft drinks. With their plastic cups almost finished they downed the balance as they saw the smoke of the steam engine above the buildings as it approached the station. A small crowd was assembling, some had just finished their breakfast at the brewpub, others came directly from the parking lot across the street.

"Well Laura, here's our list of usual suspects."

She replied "Yea, but hard to see who the spy is. Wonder if it will be obvious, like wearing a fedora hat and raincoat?"

"Surly you joke, Mrs. Verraten. You've solved enough real cases, this one ought to be a slam dunk for you."

"Well Inspector, this one is not real. It's written to deceive and probably has an ex machina ending. We'll never figure it out. Any guy in a fedora is definitely not the spy, just a red herring" she forecast.

"Hmm. That could be true but then again a good writer might hide the spy inside the obvious red herring" Jim added.

Laura shook her head in agreement. "He could, couldn't he? Anyone with a fedora could just be a guy who likes period trains and dresses up a little when he rides them. But then again, a writer could play on that. A spy who knows better could dress up like that on this ride on a vintage train. Incognito like. Hiding in the obvious."

Jim added "Then this may not be as easy to solve as we think."

"Depends on the writer, my dear, on the writer."

"Yes, it does. And that's just trying to figure out who the spy is. The real puzzle will be who killed him as I assume he is going to get it."

"Agreed! That's the real challenge. Could be anyone. We don't know how many shills or decoys are taking part. Let's see. We have a spy, a killer of the spy and a couple others, say perhaps four or five in the troupe mixed in with 75 paid guests like us" Laura guessed.

"Sounds a reasonable assumption" Jim concurred as the steam engine passed the station and slowed to a stop with its club car first and passenger car second followed by a red caboose; all lined up along the platform. The engineer rang the bell and let out a whistle of steam. The engine was an Atlantic type, a 4-4-2, meaning it had 4 unpowered small wheels up front on a trolly to carry some weight, 4 large driving wheels in the middle and at the back two small unpowered wheels on a trail to again simply carry weight. It was originally powered by coal but had been converted to cleaner oil, per modern green regulations, to turn the water into steam. As steam engines went it was of medium size historically speaking.

The passenger car door opened and out walked a young black man in a sharp looking porter's uniform. The two inch bell collared jacket had six brass buttons stamped 'Pullman' in a centered vertical row from just below the neck to the waist. Each sleeve had two buttons on the cuff and a small embroidered design on the wrist. The navy blue jacket had flapless pockets on the left breast, the right hip and the interior of the right breast, all reinforced with a heavy seam. The trousers of the same color as the jacket had five pockets and a small leather reinforcement at the bottom instead of a cuff. The fly closed with blue buttons. He wore polished black leather shoes. His matching cap had a stiff, vertical crown and a black visor. The side of the cap had silver colored buttons with an off white cord strap connecting them than ran over the visor where it met the crown. A silver plate with the word Pullman over the word Porter fit the front of the cap. All in all, he looked as if he just stepped out of some long gone past.

He turned and before coming down the steps to the platform, paused, smiled and said loudly "Hello all. I am James, your porter, your conductor, and your bartender for this trip, and a trip it will be. That I guarantee you. I'll be coming down to collect your tickets. When I do you are free to come on up and enter the second car, the car to my right and your left, and take any seat you like, two to a seat on each side of the aisle. Once we get going, I'll be in the club car to serve you drinks. So now, without anything more to say, down I come. Tickets please."

The boarders moved toward the steps and held out their tickets for James to take. Each then climbed up the steps and turned left into the car finding a seat they preferred; although there was little difference between them one was marked 'Reserved'. It was at the front to the right as they entered the car and its seat had been reversed to face toward the rear seats. It had a new plywood box of some sort behind it. The Verratens chose a seat in the middle of the car with Laura at the window and Jim on the aisle then watched as the guests arrived. To their amazement they saw a middle aged man enter with a Fedora hat on his head and a 30 something woman on his arm choosing a seat towards the rear. Then shortly after, a younger man, bald, with a black patch over his right eye came aboard with a twenty something girl with a streaked blonde French bob hairstyle. A bit later entered an older man in a black Bowler hat with pencil mustache carrying a black umbrella traveling with, presumably, his wife in in a salt and pepper pixie haircut carrying a large brown leather purse.

Usually, old steam train rides involved a lot of family outings with kids; this one was different. It was restricted to those 18 and older due to the nature of the mystery. Included with the passengers were several other couples of various ages and groups of friends as well as a few singles. When James had collected all the tickets and verified all that had arrived, he came aboard himself and faced them all in their seats. "I see you all have found seats to your liking. Remember the seats are reversable so you can turn them around and talk with your neighbors. The restrooms are at the rear of each car. We're ready to go then. I'll go and notify the engineer of that and then I'll be in the club car just ahead if anyone would like a refreshing drink or small snack once we are underway. But before I go, it is my pleasure to introduce you to the co-owner of The Porter's Pub brewpub and of this ride. He will be your host for the trip." At that point out of the club car walked a man. "Ladies and gentlemen, Mr. Al Bjarus."

"Thank you James, for that wonderful introduction" Al said while shaking hands with James as he left for the club car. "When Matt Nekaltas and I started the restaurant Porter's Pub some years ago in an old railroad station I don't think either of us thought it would grow into the brewpub and excursion train ride that it is today. But here we are thanks to people such as yourself. Once we are underway feel free to leave your seats and spend some time mixing in the club car, it can seat about half of you but the scenery out the window is the same as here. And yes, you can bring your drink in here. Now to make you all into amateur sleuths and help get to know your fellow travelers, here are some sticky labels and Sharpies I hope you'll use. It makes it easier to remember the names of everyone, for you never know who will do the nasty deed. You can lie about your background or tell the truth, it's up to you." A steam whistle blew once, then a few seconds later two shorter bursts. Steam from the boiler entered the driving cylinder and forced the piston backward. The engine slowly started to move taking up any slack in the couplers with a slight jerk. "I feel we are beginning our trip" the host said as he walked down the center aisle passing out labels and stickers to those that wanted, all did.

Soon a slow second, third and then fourth push of steam in the two cylinders were visibly causing the brewpub to apparently move away; soon the pace had increased and the exhaust of spent steam was not a puff followed by another, but grew onto a seemingly continuous stream as they left the town behind. The host continued from the front of the car "You're a very sociable group, everyone took a label. Your challenge then is two fold. See if you can identify who is the spy on the trip and then, once the nasty deed is done, see if you can identify whodunit. Neither will be easy. Does the spy hide in the open in plain sight or deep undercover? Is his assassin a man or woman, working for our government or a foreign one. In the club car is a register of our guests today, James your porter has it. Is he trustworthy? If you want to venture an official guess, he will write it down in the register. Anyone who guesses correctly will win a prize. Remember there are two categories, spy and assassin. We're moving smoothly now; we're off and into the countryside. Watch it pass by, listen to the rapid sound of steam exhausting when its job is done and see its spent clouds swirl down past the engine and the cars. The club car is now open so feel free to move about. I'll be around to answer any questions."

At the window Laura saw the train picking up speed and the flow of spent steam moving backward. At the aisle Jim saw the guests put their named stickers on their shirts and wondering what to do with the paper backing. Soon Al was traveling the aisle with a small waste bucket for them. Some of the guests had begun to talk with the others across from them, others now got up and went into the club car. Jim was talking to Ralph across from him. The two men decided to go to the club car and their wives declined to join them, preferring to sit next to each other. Laura explained their being on a weekend holiday away from work while Becky told of a side trip while on a vacation to Branson, Missouri. Each asked certain questions that might discover an inconsistency in their story. To Laura it seemed that if Becky was indeed a spy or assassin, she would not be asking such questions to her as she would already know how the mystery would end. Then again, remembering her earlier discussion with Jim, she thought 'What a perfect disguise, trying to find out if I am in on it, how is one ever to ferret out this one?'

When Jim and Ralph entered the club car, they both noticed that James, behind the bar now, had changed into his white linen jacket. It had five silver buttons vertically arranged down the front ending about an inch above the jacket's bottom below the waist. The neck was open slightly exposing a white shirt and black bowtie. On each shoulder was a dark blue epaulette with gold initials PPRR embroidered on it. His blue porter jacket and cap hung on the wood paneled wall at the end of the bar.

The bar itself was ten feet long. It ran parallel to the side of the car. Past the bar, on each side of the club car were tables for four on the right and tables for six on the left with the aisle between. Jim and Ralph stopped at the bar. On the wall behind was the drink list.

****

Porters Pub offerings

by the pint at $5

2 ounce Flight of porters $4

Classic English Porter

Robust 1435 Porter

Baltic Black Porter

Chocolate Peanut Butter Pastry Porter

Pub Pilsner

Pub IPA

Soft Drinks $2

Bottled water $2

Snacks $1

****

The two men stopped and looked at the offerings. All was included with their ticket on the Murder Mystery trip. "Just had the pastry porter, it was excellent if you like a sweet one" Jim recommended before ordering the Classic English.

"What's the 1435 about?" Ralph asked James.

"1435 is the width of standard gauge track in millimeters" answered James. Ralph thought a minute then ordered the Pastry Porter. The two men moved to the front of the car, where the tables were. They saw a table for four with only two men, Gary and Nate, sitting at it and were welcomed to sit with them. Jim had decided to tell the truth about his occupation, a cyber security expert programmer which to some might suggest a form of spy work, hence less correct answers for the drawing if anyone named him. Ralph was a bus driver, Gary an insurance salesman and Nate an office manager for a car dealership. Each said where they were from and how and why they decided on the mystery trip. Although they did not say so, Jim thought Gary and Nate were traveling together since they sat together in the passenger coach. He would rule them out as either spy or assassin, but then again, he second guessed himself. A spy or assassin might take a willing or unwitting accomplish along for cover. This was going to be difficult. Did the writer of the mystery pen it deep, convoluted and tricky or simple at face value?

"You know fellows, this game we are part of is rather tricky. Now I could eliminate the three of you based on what I now know about you, but that would be a simple face value look at it. Either of you may be under deep cover, as I might be to you, how do you think we can get to the bottom?" Jim said to them. The three men pondered the question.

"I think we have to look for a simple answer. It might not be exactly face value but not far from it. Look at us and the others. I doubt there are any professional detectives or police here" said Gary.

"I agree. The writer would be writing for the average person, make some obvious clues. Why would he make this mystery so hard no one ever solved it" Ralph commented.

"Sounds logical" Jim added.

"Right. We have to look for real clues here somewhere. There are about 70 or 80 people on this train Nate remarked and only two are the ones we are after. We can't interview everyone, we can't use a lie detector. We just have to assume almost everyone is innocent and not fret about it" Nate remarked to the other three men.

Back in the passenger coach some had flopped their backrest over and faced the other way. This made it easy for four people to face each other and socialize, which Laura was doing. Next to Laura was Ralph's wife Becky, across from them were two college age girls, Sarah and Vicky.

"Is this your first old train ride?" Laura asked the two seniors.

"Since a kid, yes. It sounded more fun than just an ordinary train ride" answered Vicky.

"Are you with the other young women over there?" Becky inquired while pointing to four others also facing each other.

"We are, those are our sorority sisters. First time for all of us" Sarah responded, "But what about you two? Tell us where you're from and what you do."

"I write articles on travel for a local magazine in Pittsburgh, Pennsylvania. I travel around the country with my husband Jim who's up in the club car having a beer no doubt" Laura replied.

"And I work as a waitress at a restaurant" Becky said, "My husband Ralph and I are taking a vacation in Branson. Were from Kentucky. He's up with Laura's Jim in the drinking car."

"So, you're a writer then Laura. Maybe you wrote this mystery. Maybe you're the spy or the assassin?" said Sarah.

"Maybe the cow would not have become hamburger had she not tried to cross the road" Laura responded, "I wouldn't exactly say writing travel articles about places to see and local attractions to visit exactly qualifies me to be termed a writer."

"I would. Right now, you're my number one suspect for the assassin" she concluded bluntly.

"Sarah, let's move on. We have a lot more people to meet. And our sisters are doing nothing but talking to each other. We must uphold the honor of our sorority and solve this case" Vicky suggested.

When the two girls had left, Laura remarked to Becky "I think we can rule out all those six sorority sisters." Becky agreed and the two decided to move onto the club car for a while.

"I think I'll have the Porter Flight" Laura told James. "And you can have the Pastry Porter sample, I had a pint of it earlier. See if you like it" she told Becky. Flight in hand the two women spotted their husbands but decided not to join them as there was work to do.

"Excuse me ladies" Becky said to two women sitting at a table for four, "Do you mind if we join you?"

"Not at all. Please have a seat."

The two women introduced themselves after sitting down, then the other two followed.

"I'm Emily from Fayetteville. I work for Tyson Foods in accounting."

"I'm Ashley from Fayetteville too. I'm a bean counter also. Have you had any luck with the mystery yet?"

Becky replied "Not yet. We ruled out those six college girls hanging out together. They're sorority sisters."

"That's a start. We won't have to talk with them. I can't see how a group of six young girls could be part of the plot" said Ashley.

"That's what we think. This chocolate peanut butter porter is good. Think I'll get a pint. Be right back."

Emily and Ashley were having coffee and danish. When Becky returned the four women agreed to form a pack and share their information as the ride progressed. They would work as a team of two pairs, divide up the guests, and keep in touch with each other. A few tables away Jim and Ralph sat.

"Excuse me for a minute. There's my husband. Gonna touch base" Laura said.

"Tell mine too we've got a plan" Becky replied.

Laura approached the table where Jim and Ralph were talking. "Excuse me boys, can I borrow my husband back for a minute?" and in saying that took his elbow and led him to a quiet spot. "Becky and I are a team now and we just teamed up with the other two women at our table. We're going to share information as we get it. Cross check each other too. Becky wants you to tell Ralph. I think you and Ralph ought to become a team also. With three teams working together we might be able to narrow the field of suspects down quite rapidly."

"Always the optimist, aren't you? Well, any plan is better than no plan. Agreed. Just remember people can lie."

"I know that. But why would an assassin travel with a companion? Don't they usually work alone?"

"Did John Wilkes Booth work alone?"

"See your point. And a spy may be traveling with a cover or his manager" Laura added.

"Right. If that's the case I don't see how we can figure this out. But we can make a list of priorities, those would be any people traveling alone and those in some sort of costume. And if we cross check stories any that are inconsistent."

"OK, let's get to work. We both need to talk with the couple in the Bowler hat, the Fedora and the eye patch guy. Get some detail we might be able to trip one up on. Like how long they've been married. Stuff like that." With that last comment by Laura, the couple went back to their nascent teams to get to work.

Rejoining the woman's table Laura told Becky that Jim would inform Ralph of the plan.

"So now we are six" Ashley spoke and smiled.

"Did we all notice the three couples dressed in suspicious clothing?" Laura asked. All at her table nodded in agreement. "We need to talk with them as separate teams, get some details that we could catch them up on. Like where are they from? Married? How long? Maiden name? Why are they dressed up?"

"How did they hear of the mystery train ride?" Emily added.

"Have they done other murder mystery parties? Which ones?" Becky added.

"Where did they meet?" Ashley added.

"Just follow your instinct when talking with them. Don't be obvious. Wait a while before one team is finished and another approaches, and best is if they approach you. Make yourselves available if they seem to be trying to talk with people. Now let's split up into pairs and get to work. Cheers!" Laura concluded raising up a 2 ounce Baltic Black Porter.

Becky and Laura went back into the coach car with Becky nursing her Pastry Porter. There they saw two older men sitting together and talking. "May we join you?" Becky asked. The fellows nodded and smiled. They introduced themselves as Nick and Nate, two history teachers off on a holiday. They expressed that they were more into the train ride than the mystery and it was the particular engine, the Mogul, that was their primary reason for attending although they picked the mystery ride just out of curiosity. Both were steam buffs and were trying to ride on as many different engines as they could, documenting each one with photos. They didn't have any particular questions for the women, so Laura and Becky moved on.

The man in the black Bowler hat and woman entered the club car, purchased two porters and some pretzels then took a seat. Jim saw an opportunity. "Care to join me in the interview, Ralph?" The two excused themselves, got up and approached the table of opportunity.

"Why yes, you certainly can" the man in the Bowler responded, "After all, this is a socializing event, isn't it?"

The man was Mark and his friend was Nancy. The two were traveling companions, Mark was divorced and Nancy was a widow. They had met at a Meet and Greet pre-play event at the theater. They viewed these mystery themed parties as a sort of a play that they could be part of. The Bowler hat was simply a costume prop he always wore to them. Jim and Ralph told their backgrounds to Mark and Nancy. Then Jim inquired as innocently as he could about what other mystery parties they had attended, nothing like putting someone on the spot. Mark quickly listed several and then Nancy added a few more. It seemed they were either telling the truth or had rehearsed their part well. 'Damn' Jim thought 'How could one ever get at the truth. A little later he and Ralph excused themselves and moved on. They sat down in the passenger car and were soon joined by Julia and Austin, both middle aged and both very inquisitive. Jim aroused their suspicion due to his job, a cyber security expert. Regardless if it was true or not, they suggested that anything to do with keeping spies from breaking into computers, was a great clue. It would be only a small leap for them to believe his work extended to assassinating cyber spies. Satisfied they had discovered something very important they removed themselves and began their search for the spy.

Outside the passing view was subtly changing. As town had given way to outskirts, outskirts had been left behind for planted fields of corn, soy and other crops, the fields were now giving way toward hilly pasture, with some wooded areas where the slope was steeper. Steam passed rapidly from the locomotive past the club car and then past the passenger car. Jim estimated its speed around 30 miles an hour, certainly not its original maximum but still fast enough to prevent stopping quickly. A whistle rang out two hundred yards before every road crossing and then, a hundred yards closer, it sounded continuously from that point on until it cleared the intersection accompanied by the constant clanging of its bell. The shrill voice of the locomotive and thumping of its chest warned all of its arrival.

Laura and Becky jumped on an opportunity to sit with the bald man with a black eyepatch over his right eye. They learned his name was Tyler and his twenty something tattooed girlfriend with punk hair tinged pink was Taylor. Becky asked "Tyler and Taylor. Come on now. Is that your real names?" To her surprise they each pulled out their driver's license and showed it was.

"We get that a lot" Taylor said smiling.

"You know Tyler, being bald with an eyepatch is very suspicious if I may say so" remarked Laura.

"So is being a writer" he responded, "Great cover story."

"Do you think his eyepatch is for real or just a prop?" asked Taylor.

"Real" said both women. Tyler just smiled.

"Want to see him without the patch? Brave enough?"

"Sure" Laura answered. She had seen much worse than a missing eye at a hop field once.

"You got guts girl" Taylor said, "Go ahead and gross them out Ty." Becky looked away. Tyler looked at Laura and his hand came up to his face, slowly. He took hold of the patch then without warning it came off in a flash. Both Tyler and Taylor began to laugh as Tyler stared at Laura with both his eyes before putting the patch back on. Taylor said "It's a little game we play sometimes. Usually, we don't get anyone who wants a peek. You got balls, Laura."

"Interesting hobby" Laura said.

The two women decided they had seen enough to rule Tyler and Taylor out as suspects in the drama. Walking back to the club car they said to each other that the personality of the couple suggested they were more interested in being a little rebellious, anti-social and shocking rather than having the discipline to pull off a scripted part in the mystery. It was all fun and games to them, it seemed. At the bar Becky said to James "You do get a variety of guests on the mystery ride. More than normal I suppose."

"Your right on that Ma'am. It seems to bring them out. Anything I can get for you two?"

"How about two coffees, plain. That OK with you Laura."

The ladies took their coffees to a table. Most of the tables were humming with conversations. It was the same in the passenger car where most seats were turned to face each other. "I wonder when the murder will take place?" Becky said to her new friend.

"Hard to say" I would think around lunch time. They need to give the guests time to try and work it out on the way back. If it happens before lunch then the meal will distract attention away. Maybe right after lunch then is my guess."

"Look over there. Seems Ralph and Jim are talking to the man in the Fedora" Becky said pointing to a table on the other side of the aisle, up towards the front. The two women enjoyed their coffee break, talking to another two women who had asked to join them. It seemed to go nowhere interesting as far as the mystery was concerned. They were sisters on an outing. In time they went their way, looking for more suspects to talk with.

"Seems the boys are alone now. Let's join them and exchange notes" Laura suggested.

"Hey guys. Any luck? What did the Fedora have to say?" Laura asked as the two women sat down with their husbands.

"That was Tony and Crystal. Said he always wears a Fedora, just likes them and didn't think it would raise an eyebrow here. Seemed honest enough" Ralph answered.

"Either that or a good cover story. We talked to the man in the Bowler too. Think you did also. Let's exchange notes" Jim said.

The four of them discussed all that they had found out, especially comparing notes on those where both the men and women teams had each interviewed the same persons. Try as they might again and again, they could not discover any inconsistencies in what they had been told. Everyone seemed legit, everyone rather commonplace, more or less, the only exception being Tyler and Taylor. They felt they were getting nowhere.

"Did anyone spot anything that might be a physical clue?" There was silence. Looking out the window for either inspiration or out of disinterest, the four saw the pastureland had given way now to woodland and they were chugging along by the side of a stream in a rather narrow valley. Jim looked at his watch, it would be 45 minutes before lunch at the turn around. He decided to get up and walk around both cars looking for clues. "Be back shortly" he said.

Jim slowly walked around the club car, looking for something, anything, that might be a clue. There were no paintings, no pictures that might have a clue in them. The restroom was standard. At the bar he carefully looked at the labels, nothing of interest. He opened the door between the cars and went outside onto the connecting way between the two cars. There was a safety railing in place. One would have to have suicide in mind to fall off. He saw the car to car connector of the air pressure safety brake. Its pressurized air kept the brakes in the off position allowing the wheels to roll. If the engineer wanted to stop the train, he would turn a valve and let the air pressure in the line drop. This allowed the spring loaded brakes to clamp down on the wheels. 'Thanks George Westinghouse' he thought. He saw another pipe connector in place but did not recognize its purpose. A man was coming out of the passenger car, so he took advantage of the open door and entered where they had just left.

Inside the passenger car he saw the host, Al, sitting and talking with some guests. He also saw a modification to the car where two rows of seats had been removed and a new temporary plywood framework installed. This was just ahead of the seat labeled reserved that faced backward. The MC stood up and walked up the aisle toward him. Jim spoke first. "It's Al, isn't it?"

"Yes, Al Bjarus."

"I'm just wondering about that plywood in the corner. Seems you're doing a little remodeling?"

"We are. That's going to be for a small steam calliope we bought. We're at the end of its restoration. It ought to do well in here, not too loud. We toned it down somewhat."

"Interesting."

"Going to face it outside so most of the sound goes out the windows with the steam exhaust it releases. It ought to be a real treat. Now we just have to find a player."

"Just a piano player? Similar enough?" Jim asked.

"So we've been told. Maybe another month or two. You'll have to come back and hear it."

"I just might." Jim lied. He had heard calliope music before. It was not one of his favorite instruments. Jim continued his walk down to the end of the car looking for any clue along the way. He found none. He did see a few guests alone in their own world, simply looking out the window as the scenery went by. Hard to say if they were traveling with someone who was away at the time. In any case they did not seem very sociable so he did not approach them to talk.

Returning to the club car he sat with his wife and the couple they had teamed up with. Wouldn't it be funny, he thought, if one of them was either the spy or the assassin? He, like the singles he saw in the other car, began to simply look out the window. Soon a steam whistle blew three loud blasts. James said "We are going to enter a tunnel. For your safety, please take a seat as it will get dark in here and we don't want anyone falling." The host addressed the passengers in the other car with the same message. A few minutes later the train had slowed down and entered the tunnel. It quickly turned dim inside the cars, but when they came to the curve the remaining light from the entrance vanished completely. Neither the tunnel interior nor the cars themselves were lit. For less than a minute it was completely dark, then at the end of the curve as they straightened out, light from the exit portal started to return the cars to various levels of dimness until finally they burst into the light again.

The guests looked around, most expecting to see a faux dead spy somewhere. There was none. "That was interesting" Laura said to Jim.

"Very" he answered.

"It's probably where the murder will take place on the return trip" she continued.

"I totally agree. Its too close to lunchtime for it to have happened now. Would shift the attention from murder to lunch then back again after reboarding. Too complicated."

"I think your right. I would never have thought of that. I'm ready for lunch, hope not too much longer." Ralph added as his stomach growled.

"I told you too eat a breakfast and not just have coffee" Becky said.

"Wasn't hungry then, am now."

The Mogul chugged on through the hills on the valley floor. Now and then an old dilapidated building was seen next to the tracks with a dirt road leading away into the forest. One even had the remains of a narrow gauge railroad going from it along with a few other collapsing buildings and sheds. "See that Laura? An old logging terminal. All these trees we see are second growth. The whole area has been cut once, probably a hundred years or more ago. You don't see any forest giants."

Fifteen minutes later they arrived at the place for lunch. The engine slowed down and creeped past some switches. Jim could tell that the switches and the rails beyond them were recently used. The tops of the iron rails had no rust, only the sides. Unused rails he had seen had a rusty surface that matched the sides. The engine stopped. Al got out and went over to a switch where he manually turned a large lever. The engine slowly moved backward and at the switch the cars rolled off the main track onto the side track. Al was way ahead of the moving cars and threw a second switch onto which the cars moved onto and the entire train went in reverse for a hundred yards past it. Then it stopped.

"Ladies and gents, we have arrived for our lunch picnic. Please carefully exit the cars the way you came in" James said loudly and clearly in both cars. The guests did as told and found themselves in a clearing in the forest. There were picnic tables set up all around, some under trees at the edge and most out in the open with sunlight on them. Near the caboose were picnic tables set in a line. James and Al went into the caboose and began to carry the lunch down and place it on the table. When finished they had the engineer ring the Mogul's bell and James announced "Lunchtime. Form a line on each side please."

Lunch was a simple picnic. There was potato salad and Cole slaw. There was fried chicken and a couple trays of sliced lunchmeats: ham, salami and turkey breast. There was a relish tray. There was a large basket of buns and a tray of lettuce, tomato and cheese. James had growlers of all the Porters Pub beers out with plastic cups stacked beside them. Two liter bottles of various sodas were out. All in all it was a nice spread on a nice day. "What if it was raining?" Jim asked James.

"Look at that pavilion down the line. See it?"

Jim nodded.

"We just back down next to it and everyone's under roof."

"How long do the tracks go back past the pavilion?" Jim asked.

"They used to go on to the next town. The roadbed is still there but the tracks are long gone. They put these in a few years ago when they decided to add the train. The tracks go on another hundred feet past the pavilion, that's all."

Jim joined Laura in the picnic buffet line. When finished eating he saw the host standing by the food line while James poured out of the growlers. He approached Al. "I'm wondering Al, why is this turnaround here at all? Did you guys build it?"

"No, it was here already. We repaired it and got it working again. It originally wasn't a turnaround, it was a junction. See the rail line used to go on and on in the direction we have been traveling, on up to the next town about 30 miles away. It stops now about a mile ahead where a bridge was washed out. The part we've backed onto now used to go on another 25 miles or so to another town. They each went on from there. This was the junction so a train coming from any direction could go to either town ahead. They all had to obey scheduling rule so not to run into each other. They had logging trains and passenger ones and freight too. There used to be a couple pull off sidings to allow one coming from the opposite direction to pass by."

"Something like air traffic controllers managing planes today then" Jim said.

"Yes, I think so. All very coordinated and controlled. It's why we have time zones now. Railroads started that. You have to all agree when the 9:35 is coming through."

Jim spotted train fans Nick and Nate talking to the engineer by the Mogul and decided to join in. When he arrived both fans were taking pictures of each other next to the engine. "Hi. I'm Jim" he said to the engineer.

"And I'm Casey. Any questions today?"

"A few. Since you're converted to oil from coal, you don't need a fireman to shovel. So why do you have one?"

"Easy answer. The law. It's not a union thing like it was once, but a safety issue. What if I have a heart attack or stroke up there" Casey said pointing to the engineer's cabin, "There would be no one to control or stop the train. My engineer is actually a fully certified second engineer for backup in an emergency."

"I should have known that. Co pilots in airplanes today. OK. What is the steam pressure inside the boiler of the engine?"

"About 160 psi. That's about eleven times standard air pressure of fourteen and a half. But that 160 isn't constant, it varies somewhat depending on what load we are pulling and how fast we're going. But for us it is usually within a few pounds of that. Our load is always what you see here and our speed is low, so it's easy to keep it around 160."

"Is that considered high pressure for steam engines?"

"No. Not at all. We could run a little higher, but its and old engine so we don't and we don't need more pressure. Some larger engines ran at double and even triple what we do. But the Mogul was never designed to be what they call a high pressure engine."

"It's still hard for me to imaging this one, a Mogul, that's its name right, pulling a long load of heavy logs. After all, our pressure cooker at home goes up to 30 psi, that's about one fifth of your engine. It couldn't pull one fifth of what your engine can? Somewhat puzzling."

"Let me demystify it a little. The Mogul is the name of this class of engine, not an individual name. Now that 30 PSI means pounds per square inch as I think you know. So our 160 psi means the same. Now look over here." The two men walked up to the front of the engine. "Look at this. It's the drive cylinder, the real engine of the engine. Everything up top just makes steam at pressure, this cylinder and the piston inside put that steam to work. There's one just like it on the other side too. Ours is 18 inches in diameter. But if you calculate the surface area of the piston inside, you get 254 square inches and each square inch gets the same 160 pounds pushing against it. That's a total of about 37,000 pounds of force on it, and the same for the other one so we have close to 75,000 pounds of force here. And I did remember to take away the air pressure that the steam pushes away. Now look at the length of the piston, 25 inches. Those 75,000 pounds of force work for 25 inches of length, before having to start over again. As long as the steam keeps coming it's putting out that force consistently on each filling of the cylinder and a rotation of the wheel. Now lastly, you would have to do some more calculations to get at the torque and horsepower being applied to the driving wheels. That depends on gearing just like cars, except we don't change gears, just have one and it's determined by where on the wheel the push rod out of the cylinder is attached, that means how far from the center. Closer to the center, more power; farther out near the rim, more top speed. These moguls were built for low speed power, essentially freight and heavy loads so you see the pushrod attached closer to the axle."

"Fascinating, just fascinating. I didn't know there was so much to it."

"There's that and more" Casey smiled, "lot of top notch engineering went into steam engines back in the day."

"I can certainly appreciate that."

"This baby here can easily spin its wheels from a dead stop, even when building up speed up to about 10 or 15 miles an hour, and that's with a light load like now. I have to be careful on the throttle. You ought try and start one on a railroad sim."

Jim smiled. "I think I will. You get a lot of train fans like those two?" he said motioning to Nick and Nate looking out of the engineer's window while the fireman below took their picture.

"That we do, usually older gentlemen."

"What I like about these engines is that you can actually see how it all works, all the linkages, the steam exiting the piston, the smoke coming out the stack. Its very visual, very sensual. It looks powerful. I can feel the heat of the boiler standing here with you. I can hear it chugging along. The modern diesels or electric engines on railroads, all you see is the moving wheels. They go as if by magic. Kind of boring" Jim said.

"Some rail fans like them."

"Well, nice talking with you. Thanks for all the information."

"Glad to help." With that the engineer started walking to the switch just ahead of the engine and then the one a little farther away that would direct the train to head back to Porters Pub. The entire turnaround used only three switches. It was like the capital letter Y, with a line across the top. The bottom was where they were now after backing in. The line at the top was the line they had arrived on, they could then choose either way, right or left, to proceed.

Back at the picnic tables he sat down and took a sip of his wife's porter. "Decent. Which one is this?"

"The classic English" she answered.

James, now dressed in his blue porter's uniform went around the tables announcing a fifteen minute warning to begin reboarding. Guests were told the club car would be closed until after the tunnel and they could reboard with a drink in hand if they wanted. He and Al then began putting the food back into the caboose leaving the growlers for last. They then came around with large plastic trash bags. Some guests were already back inside, others were moving toward the cars. When James reentered the club car he changed again into his white jacket. Host Al reminded everyone the club car was closed until after the tunnel.

Laura said to the others at her table "I think it means the murder will take place in the tunnel." They all agreed. After a head count to make sure no one was left behind, the locomotive started its slow start, the 75,000 pounds of steam doing its job slowly at first. Before long the train was moving at a healthy clip. All the seats had been turned around facing forward by Al and James. There were a few empty seats and a few that had only one sitting in it. Jim enjoyed sipping on a Baltic Porter he brought aboard and telling Laura all he had learned about steam pressures and how deceptively powerful it was. Fifteen minutes later the whistle blew three loud blasts. The tunnel was ahead shortly and the train slowed down again. There was not much talking after lunch in the can, but now there was none. It seemed everyone expected something to happen in the tunnel's darkness. They entered. It grew dim. At the curve the wheels screeched and shuttered against the rails as darkness enveloped the train. It was now or never. But how? Strangulation, a knife, a gun? All were possibilities just as poison had been earlier on. Now was not the time nor place for poison. It had to be quick. Now! A flash, a gunshot! The game was afoot! The darkness started to subside as they rounded the curve and then dimness gave way to full sunlight. Who was shot? Who was the spy? Everyone looked around. The shot seemed to have come from the front of the car. All seemed well, all except for the man in the reserved seat facing the guests. His head was slumped over, his eyes closed. Both Laura and Jim recognized him as one of the single middle aged men on the trip. 'Well that figures' thought Laura. His body slumped forward.

The host came out of the club car. He glanced at the body slumped over. "Seems now we know who our spy was. Now it's up to you to try solve the case. The club car is now open" he said as he turned and went back.

"Wow. I guess that means no extra clues." Becky said to Laura across the aisle. It took a few minutes before some of the guests got up and began to move around. Jim thought the assassin would not be among them, but would remain seated for a while longer. Some had gathered around the spy, peering and wondering.

"Look at that" one said.

"Realistic" said another.

"Is he breathing?" said the first. Blood appeared dripping out through matted hair.

"Probably a little tube of red paint in there somewhere."

The first shook his arm. "We know you're supposed to be dead, but could you just give me a wink or squeeze my hand?" the first said taking his hand in hers. Nothing. She reached down and shook him. Again nothing. She parted his bloody hair and saw a hole into his skull. "I think he's dead" she screamed in shock. "Really dead. He's got a hole in his head."

Laura and Jim looked on wondering if this was part of the mystery play, hopefully it was. But when a few more guests confirmed the hole in the skull, Jim got up and had to see for himself. To his dismay, it was true. There was a hole in his skull still seeping blood. He checked for a pulse. None. "Laura, come here" he yelled out. "Please , everyone back to their seats" he said. "Is there a doctor or medical professional aboard?" None came forward.

"What's happened? Is he really dead?" Laura asked Jim quietly.

"I'm afraid so."

"Is there anyone here who is a policeman?" Laura asked. None came forward. But a single girl, about 20, did come forward.

"Are you sure he's dead?" she asked Laura.

"Yes. Positive. No pulse and a hole in his head. That gun was loaded for real."

"Then I'm guilty. I pulled the trigger. The gun is in my purse here" she said handing her purse to Laura.

"So you're the assassin then?"

"Yes, I have been all summer" she said beginning to cry.

"And you name is?" Laura asked.

"K Kayla T T Trimble" the girl stuttered then began to collapse. Laura caught her and walked her over to a seat, put her down and sat next to her. Jim saw what had happened. He dashed into the club car.

"Al, I'm sorry to tell you that your spy had been shot. For real. He's really dead. You better come out quick and take control." Al Bjarus quickly hurried out. "James, is there a blanket or something we can drape over the body?" Jim asked the porter

"Just this jacket" he replied taking off his white linen coat and changing into his blue uniform thinking it was better to show some level of authority.

Al had entered the passenger car and examined the body briefly before addressing the guests. "Ladies and Gents, it seems we have unfortunately had an accident. This was not part of the script. I must close the club car for the remainder of the ride. James can get water for those who need it, but I ask you all to remain in this car and in your seats." He turned to Laura and Kayla Trimble, the assassin. He bent down and whispered to Laura. "I think it's best for Kayla to move up into the club car. Can you stay with her, make sure she's Ok until we get back." Laura nodded affirmatively.

James arrived wearing his blue Porter's uniform with his white coat in hand. He looked at the dead spy and said to his boss "We ought to cover him now, if you're sure."

"I'm sure. There's been an accident. Seems a real bullet was used instead of the blank." James looked at his boss momentarily then put his white jacket over the spy's body. Both men knew the dead spy was in reality one Matt Nekaltas, co-owner of the Porters Pub, brewery and train ride. He always played the spy. Now he was dead. Accidentally shot in the head.

Laura and Kayla entered the club car. As they walked past James, she noticed significant eye contact between the two. They moved past Jim and took a seat midway down the car. Kayla began to cry with large tears running down her cheeks. "What have I done? I just killed a man. I ruined my life? I just don't understand it."

"What don't you understand, Kayla?" asked Laura.

"I don't understand how I shot him. I always used a blank. I never aimed at his head" she said. Laura thought she was telling the truth and it would be hard to pull off the crying and level of grief as an act if not genuine. There certainly was a dead body in the other car, shot in the head. Someone had to do it and Kayla was in the only position to do it. The logic did not support her feeling about Kayla. "Are you OK here for a few minutes without me?" Laura asked.

"Yes."

Laura went over to Jim and told him her feelings about the girl. It had to be an accident of some sort. Jim listened attentively. "What would be her motive to kill him?" he asked, expecting no answer. "You stay here with her. I'll be back in a couple."

Jim entered the passenger car after passing James on the connector making his way back into the club car. He saw the body had the white linen jacket draped over it. He carefully looked at the back of the head. There were no singed hairs, no obvious gunpowder residue on the back of the shirt collar. He did notice several areas on the upholstery fabric of the seat rear that appeared to have some blackish areas that may be singed material or powder residue or just dirt. He could not tell any more by looking. Al Bjarus was sitting across from the body in the seat just occupied by Kayla. He just looked at Jim, shook his head and said "Tragedy." Jim nodded in agreement and went back into the club car. Al did not try and stop him since Laura was with the girl now.

James had now joined Laura and Kayla at the table. He was holding Kayla's hand and kept repeating "It's gonna be alright, Kay. You'll see."

"James, can I talk with you?"

James nodded a yes.

"Let's go up near the front, a little privacy" he said looking at Laura. "Some things I'd like to know." The two men sat at a table out of earshot of Laura and Kayla. Jim sat facing the door. He wanted to keep an eye open if anyone walked in. "James, I want you to know something. Laura and I have worked both officially and unofficially on solving several murders in the past. Laura does not believe Kayla killed the man on purpose. I don't know. But I'd like to get some more information if I could. I already have a few things to tell the police when we get back. You decided to join me here. That's a good sign. You could have clammed up."

"I'm not like that. I'm just shocked by it all. I don't know how a live round could have got in that gun" James said.

"We'll get to that in time. But first. Who is the dead man who played the part of the spy, do you know?"

"He is Matt Nekaltas, the co-owner of the business."

"And by the business, you mean . . ."

"Porters Pub, the restaurant, the brewpub's brewery and this train excursion."

"And Al is the co-owner. The only co-owner, do you know?"

"As far as I know the only one."

"How long have you worked for them?"

"Going on three summers now. It's my summer job. I'm at the university. So is Kayla. I got her the job here for the summer."

"Then it's Kayla's first year here."

"Yes."

"How do you know her?"

"We met at the Future Actors Club at the university. We're both English majors."

"I see. And are you two an item as they say?"

"We dated a few times and have an interest in each other. She's a very good friend. I feel terrible about all this, if I hadn't got her the job here. . ."

"But you did. What's past is written in stone. I'm sure your intentions were both professional and honest. Now what about the gun. What caliber is it. Do you know?"

"32 revolver. The blanks we use are half charge, just some noise and flash."

"Where is the gun kept usually?"

"Al keeps it. I don't know where."

"Who puts the blank in the gun?"

"I do. He gives the gun to me before the guests arrive. I load it and give it to Kayla who puts it in her purse and blends into the crowd."

"I see. So the gun goes from Al to you to Kayla. Only you three have access to it?"

"Right. As far as I know."

"Is or was there ever any incident between Kayla and Mr. Nekaltas? Did he ever assault her or make unwanted advances?"

"None that I'm aware of."

"If there was, do you think Kayla would have told you?"

"I think so. We're fairly close. Not a hundred percent sure though."

"How would you describe Kayla back at university?"

"Just a typical student. Nothing really outstanding about her."

"About the two partners, how do you think their relationship was? Generally speaking."

"I would say, from what I saw of them, not bad, not great. Sometimes they seemed to work together well, like on this mystery trip. Other times there were arguments. But I suppose that that's like all partners, even in marriages."

"Did you over hear what they argued about on those occasions you heard them?"

"Sometimes I caught a little of it. Never on the train though. Sometimes back at the Pub or when I got a fresh barrel out of the brewery. It was almost always about ownership. From what I gathered Al wanted to buy Matt out but Matt wanted too much money. Sometimes Matt just said he liked the business and would probably just hold onto it."

"But everything has a price, right?" Jim added.

"Something like that. I had the feeling Matt just wasn't going to sell out his half."

"How long had this been a subject of discussion."

"Off and on over the last two summers, I just work summers remember."

"I remember that. James, you've been very helpful."

"I just don't know how a live round got into that gun. I hate to say it, but only Kayla had access to it as far as I know" James added.

"I know. But it's a little complicated. You see, if she was in fact molested or whatever by Nekaltas that would be a very strong reaction, especially in public. Seems a bit out of character for her. A young undergraduate student with a lifetime ahead to go berserk, unless it brought up very bad memories of her past and she just snapped. Quite possible then she could have brought a live round with her today and switched it. The blank could have been disposed of anywhere on out trip. By the way, did you hear the gunshot?"

"No. I was in the club car and with the wheels screeching, I did not. I never do. It always takes place in the dark sharp curve of the tunnel where the wheels screech as they rub the side of the rails. Why?"

"Just wondering if it sounded like all the other times or was louder. That's all. Where was Al when the shot was fired."

"Not in here, not in the club car this trip. Probably back with the passengers. Sometimes he is here or there."

Thanks for the info. Keep this all between us and the police when you're asked. You know that there is some suspicion on you also. You may have put a live round in the gun without Kayla's knowledge" Jim concluded. James nodded in agreement and looked down at the floor. The two men separated, James going back to Laura and Kayla while Jim went forward into the other car and walked to the front. The car was all seated and mostly subdued. Those who were talking did it quietly.

Jim saw Al sitting by himself across from the body, also facing rearward. He sat down beside Al and looked over towards the body. The plywood enclosure for the calliope extended down the aisle then back toward the outside window at a right angle to the aisle. The seat was in the only position it could be due to the calliope project limiting its reversal for seating toward the front. "Al, I wonder what's going to happen to the girl."

"I don't know. The law around here is pretty strict on murder, even accidental ones. I would think at least manslaughter, maybe more?"

"What do you think? Accidental or intentional?" Jim asked.

"Hell if I know. Just that this was our last mystery trip because of that. That I know. Well just run the scenic ones from now on."

"I'm just wondering, if it wasn't an accident, then what would motivate a college girl to kill someone like that? Had to be something serious."

"All I know is she complained to me about Matt's unwanted advances, asked me to tell him to quit."

"Doesn't seem much of a motive for murder. Did you talk to Matt about it?"

"Certainly. Last thing we needed was a sexual harassment lawsuit against our company."

"And what did he say then?"

"Said it was none of my business and she was lying."

"Might be a motive then. How might an accident have happened though?"

"I don't know. When they dust the gun they'll find my prints on it, or they should, also James's prints and Kayla's prints too. There shouldn't be any others as far as I know. I guess they'll have us three as suspects in a way. Maybe Kayla was innocent and James put a live round in the gun."

"Why would he do that? Would he have any motive you know of?"

"None that I know of. But who can say?"

"Did you hear the gunshot?" Jim asked nonchalantly.

"Yea, seemed louder than normal."

That particular answer seemed a bit strange to Jim. Why didn't he just say 'Yea' and leave it at that? "You and Matt friends before Porters Pub?"

"Known each other a few years before, not real deep friends. Just had a common interest in beer and brewing so thought we could give it a try."

"More business partners than buddies?"

"I guess you could say that, but we did get closer working together."

"I know what you mean. Still, you must feel terrible" Jim said.

"I do. We weren't golfing buddies but we worked long weeks together. I think we respected each other's strengths."

"What were Matt's strengths?"

"On the brewing side. That guy could really make great beers. I mean, just look at our offering of

Porters. He came up with all those. And he had a knack at seasonals too."

"What are you going to do without him now. Brew them yourself?"

"Oh God No! There's no time for me to do that. I'll have to hire a brewer. He can use Matt's recipes. There all in the brew master recipe book. After a while brewing, I ended up on the business side of things. You'd be surprised how much needs to be done in an operation like this."

"So that was your strength then, the books and business decisions."

"I guess you could say that."

"I'm surprised you didn't offer to buy Matt out. Maybe there isn't enough profit in the business to do so. Sorry, I don't mean to pry."

"No, you're not prying. Never considered it. He did what he did very well, we were a good team. It will be hard to replace him. And there was enough here for both of us. We even had plans for expansion."

"Excuse me Al. I want to go get a water. I'll get some for your guests too." Jim got up and looked again where the body was. He looked at the plywood covering the calliope space again, then went into the club car.

"How about a cold water James?" he asked, then when James the Porter went to get it, he said quietly so only Laura would hear. "Al's sitting across from the body. I need to look closely without him in that car. How do we get him from there in here with you?"

James arrived with a bottle of cold spring water. Laura looked at it as Jim poured some water into his plastic cup as the cars bumped and swayed along the uneven track. An idea came to mind. "I'll be back in a few minutes with Al. Be ready to go fast. I'll stall him in here if he tries to go back." She then went to the bar and asked James for a bottle of water and a cup.

Jim saw what she was doing and said "Take some water back for the guests, I told Al I'd get some." Laura then handed the purse with the gun inside to her husband and made her way into through the passageway and handed out waters to any who wanted them until she only had only one left and her cup in hand. She walked back to Al.

"Mind if I join you, Al" she said as she started to twist the cap.

"Be my guest" Al said.

Although the cap was loose, she pretended it was not; still standing she fidgeted with it then got it off, then seeing a curve ahead, she slowly poured a cupful while standing and began to sit as the car rolled over the curve. She lost her balance and had to grab for the back of the seat. The water spilled over Al's shirt and pants as she tumbled down into the seat getting water all over herself too. "Oh. Sorry. Terribly sorry. Lost my balance" she said as the remaining water trickled out of the bottle onto Al's lap.

"Damnit!" a wet Al said. "Sorry, not your fault. This roadbed needs more work. Are you OK."

"I'm fine. Just wet. Any towels up in the club car?" she asked.

"Not sure. I think so. Let's go see. I don't like to leave Matt alone in here with everyone."

"You're soaked. We'll send my husband back in to watch over things. He's probably done with his water by now."

"Good. Let's go" Al agreed.

The two entered the club car together. Al barked out "James, any towels you have hidden around somewhere?"

Laura said to Jim "Jim, go keep watch over Matt for a while until we dry off some."

James brought over a couple hand towels and beer mats saying "This is all we have, a couple more beer mats but no big towels. Jim saw his opportunity and went into the passenger car.

The passengers were all seated, most by now had reversed their seats to avoid seeing the linen draped body. Jim worked quickly. First, he examined the screws that held the plywood to the frame underneath. They all had Phillips heads. Then he looked at the plywood behind Matt's head. Phillips also, except for a regular one in the center, directly across from where Matt's head would have been. Odd. As the cars jiggled and weaved along the

379

somewhat uneven rails, Jim noticed that particular screwhead had some play in it. He looked at the others, they were firm in their position. He looked back at the loose one. It moved a little side to side but it also flexed in and out. The head did not shrink down to a threaded stem like most screws did, at least not what Jim could see of it. It also seemed the size, approximately, of the bore of a 32 pistol, that is 32/100 of an inch.

Jim looked back at the passageway door. So far so good. Laura, please keep him occupied, he thought. His attention was now focused on looking for a crack or opening in the plywood where he could glimpse into the interior. Luckily it was not well fitted, certainly not the work of a craftsman, probably just an unskilled do it yourselfer. He discovered several opportunities to glimpse into sections of the boxlike structure. From the other side there was a window that let light in. Jim expected to just see a simple steam fitting ready to accept the calliope when it was installed. He did not see that. What he saw was a series of pipes and a reservoir in the middle. He also saw some interconnected steel rods, not unlike those on the engine running from the piston to the wheels, and they seemed to be attached to a small cylinder of sorts, maybe 3 or 4 inches in diameter. On their other side they seemed to be connected to a series of levers that lead up to the mysterious jiggling screw.

He had seen enough. He now walked out between the cars and down where the new steam line for the calliope was recently installed, he saw a valve. A single valve ought suffice, and that could had been in

380

the locomotive cabin for the engineer to operate or even in the car next to the calliope. Outside here, it was not especially secure, way too accessible. Beside the valve was a metal ring on a pull cord that went into the car alongside the steam pipe. He reentered the passenger car and took his seat across from the body. He thought.

In a while a somewhat still damp Al returned and sat next to him. "Thanks for keeping guard. I think it makes the guests feel more at ease if someone in authority is here with the body" Al said.

"I have no authority" Jim remarked.

"In a way you do. You and your wife Laura have been very helpful. The guests see that and they see you and I together. So they look at you and her with some control in my absence, I am sure of that."

"I see your point, Al, I think you're right. By the way, are you dried out yet?"

"Getting there. Dry enough anyway."

The locomotive chugged along mile after mile. Jim closed his eyes and the gentle sway of the car soon had him in a state of hypnagogia, that presleep condition noted for its enhancement of creativity and problem solving. His thoughts involved his computer and what he might find out if only he had access to it, but out in the forest there was not even a cell phone connection yet. So he just kept replaying the murder over and over in his head, each time with a little variation until they all muddled together. Out of his past a vision arrived in the mix. A vision of one of his summer jobs while in college. It startled him enough to open his eyes, then he closed them again and tried to remember the thoughts, tried to organize them. He may have drifted off to sleep, he was not sure. But when he awoke to the sound of Al talking on his cell phone, he looked out the window. The forest was replaced by hilly pastureland and the occasional plowed field that was level enough for tilling. His earlier confusion of the murder and his college job came into his mind. It was all clear now. All the pieces fit. "Goodbye" said Al.

"I must have dozed off" Jim said to Al. "Cell phone working again?"

"For about ten minutes now. I got ahold of the police. They'll meet us at the pub when we pull in. Excuse me now. I have to make an announcement." Al stood up and went to the other end of the car, there he turned, steadied himself and said loudly enough for all to hear. "Ladies and gentlemen, I have just made contact with the police who will be waiting at the station when we pull in. They will want to talk with each of you before you leave for home. We have a meeting room at the pub where you can sit and wait your turn. I don't think it will take long. When you exit the car, please use the door behind me and not the one you came in on. Probably the police will be using that one. I apologize to each and every one of you for the most unfortunate incident. I will call and order my staff at the pub to return all your ticket money while you wait for your interview with the police. Thank you so much for your attention." Al walked back and sat down next to Jim. The train rolled on.

As they neared the Porters Pub brewpub station Al asked Jim to stand in the aisle and see that no one tried to leave past the body. Al walked down the aisle and as the train slowly came to a stop, he made sure all the guests had safely exited reminding them to go to the meeting room and await their turn to talk with the police. Outside the car the Chief of Police, a detective and the coroner awaited with a several officers. When Al saw all the guests except for the Verratens had left, he helped the officers aboard and led them to the body, still covered by James's white linen jacket. "We haven't moved him. All I did was feel for a pulse in his neck and there was none. Thought it best to leave him here" Al told the officials.

They removed the blood stained jacket and felt for a pulse then confirmed the death. The coroner began taking pictures. "I'll be in the club car if you need me. Through here" Al said pointing the way.

As the coroner did his job the Chief asked Jim who he was. "Jim Verraten. I've been assisting the owner Mr. Bjarus along with my wife Laura over in the club car. She has been tending to Kayla who was the play assassin in this mess."

"Bjarus told me of her, the one who shot the victim. And there is a James involved somehow to?"

"Yes. He is their porter in the play they were staging. He's in the other car too."

"Good. I'll keep them all in there for a while yet, you and your wife too. My men will handle statements from the other guests. I assume you were just two guests who got involved somehow?"

"Correct. But I want you to know that both my wife and I have been involved in some other homicides a while ago. We have worked with the police before. I can give you several references of cases we were deeply involved in and helped get at the truth."

"Well that's interesting. What do you do for a living?"

"I'm a cyber security expert, software. My wife is a travel writer for a local magazine back home in Pittsburgh, Pennsylvania. We're on a holiday here."

"From what Bjarus told me over the phone it seems not too complicated. Most probably an accident, maybe a homicide. I'll have to wait on the coroner's report and witness statements before our detective Josh here and I decide on the charges."

"I think I can make your job easier than you think. Let me say something first when we move into the club car."

"I might give you ten minutes. But first I will require the list of police references before I do" the Chief said.

Jim borrowed a pen and paper from Josh, sat down in an empty seat and began writing down the names and phone numbers of several. There was the one in Charleston, South Carolina, the one over at Carmel,

California, one back in Pittsburgh and one up in Mystic, Connecticut. He handed the references to the Chief who sat down out of earshot and began calling as the coroner finished his work and the body was placed in a body bag to be carried outside to the waiting ambulance. Remaining inside the car were the Chief, Josh the Detective, Jim and another officer.

The Chief finally rose up and went over to Jim. "You checked out just fine, Jim. Got ahold of two of those jurisdictions. You seem a very perceptive fellow that comes up with a lot of information somehow. And that wife of yours going undercover is something, really something."

"Something special, I think" Jim added.

"Maybe you ought to tell me here what you have to say, instead of in the club car?"

"I think the club car is better. Trust me on that. In front of everyone. I am sure one of them is a cold blooded murderer and I will easily prove it. The reaction of the murderer might be of great value to you. It will come as a shock" Jim said.

"That's fine then. I see your point. No need for me to know a few minutes before. This is a little irregular but you've been right before and I'll take the chance you're right again. Let's go."

The four men entered the club car. Laura and Kayla were seated together at a table. Kayla began to cry again when she saw the uniforms. James was at another one next to it and Al was across the aisle at a third. The Chief and Detective Josh sat at another nearer the door they had entered and the officer stood at the other door. From his seat, the Chief said "I believe you all know Jim Verraten. He has asked for a few minutes to speak and I don't see why not. Go ahead Mr. Verraten."

Laura thought something was up. Might her husband have found out something without spending half the night on his computer hacking away?

"Before he starts, here is Kayla's purse. The gun she fired is inside it. It has not been opened since and I or Jim have had it in our possession since.

"Thank you. I believe the five of us in this car who were on the tragic ride know by now that the finger prints of Kayla, James and Al will all be found on the gun used this afternoon, thus they will not be definitive. There is speculation of accident or murder. Each has very different ramifications. Kayla, a university student, here plays the role of an assassin turned into an accidental killing. Her need for comfort from my wife Laura and her tears of grief would seem to indicate the accidental nature today. Yet, Kayla is in training to be an actor at the school. She may have motive for murder. It is said that she suffered unwanted sexual advances by the victim, perhaps grievous and frequent enough to motivate her to take his life."

Al began to nod his head affirmatively, saw Josh look at him, clenched his lips and gave one last nod after the two had made eye contact.

Jim continued "It has also been said that there have never been such advances. Now the porter James had access to the pistol before giving it to Kayla. James is the one who puts the half charge blank into the gun. If in fact he did and did not place a full live round in the chamber, he would be innocent. But what if he placed a live round in the chamber instead? What would be the motive for James killing Matt Nekaltas, co-owner of the business? James, a university student also, and also training to be an actor, might have any one of a large number of motives to turn Kayla into a patsy. It might be revenge for affection unanswered, there are those types of men aren't there? It might be a financial payment for getting rid of Matt. Such might be from an old flame or business rival or might have nothing to do with either. Some get caught up in computer sim games of death. Men's private lives can be full of shadows and who knows how many were in either James's or Matt's closet. Certainly, Josh here can look into student loan debt and see if that might be a motive that would make him susceptible to putting a live round in the 32. Maybe forensics will find his fingerprint or partial one on the spent round, or maybe even Kayla's. Maybe James had a big gambling problem. Some college students do. Who can say? Not I."

Jim paused a moment and looked around the room, then continued "It might be a simple mistake of bullets, but why would a live round be mixed into a box of blanks in the first place? No, I do not think it was a mistake. I think it was intentional. You will see what your coroner says after his autopsy, but I don't think he will find any powder residue in the hair surrounding the entrance wound. Yet, he will find a 32 slug inside the brain. And that bullet, I suspect, will match the ballistics for the 32 pistol in front of you here in this room, the same one Kayla fired a few hours ago."

Again, Al nodded affirmatively.

"I believe the powder residue can be found on the back fabric of the seat. Safety would be an issue and I highly doubt the blank 32 would have been aimed at the back of the head of a living person, instead it would be aimed into the back of the seat in a direction away from harm or injury."

Kayla looked up.

"How did the bullet fired from the 32 miss the upholstery and end up in the head of the victim. It was a puzzlement to me. A big one. I stood where Kayla stood. From her angle over in the aisle, she could not have aimed a perpendicular shot to the center of the back of Matt's head. Impossible. At most it would have entered on the side closer to his ear. Your coroner's photo's will show this or you could reconstruct it with the right sized mannequin. Then there is the shot. The guests in the passenger car certainly heard it, but had nothing to compare its loudness with. Someone did hear it and said it seemed much louder than usual."

Al again nodded in affirmation.

"Now remember, the train wheels were screeching as they rubbed against the curve in the tunnel where all goes dark for a while. It would be a simple test to reconstruct the event with different powder charges, and a live round as well, precisely at that curve in the tunnel. A forensic team ought to be able to document the various sound levels."

So far the Chief and Josh thought what Jim was saying would be a great help in their investigation, but it seemed to be leading somewhere, and where they knew not.

"Allow me to digress a moment. Kayla and James are doing this as summer jobs at university. Good for them. My first summer job was working at a Pittsburgh meat packing company. I really cleaned up there, so to speak. But I got a chance to observe the whole process, from live hogs coming in to packages of sausage and hot dogs going out. It was interesting how they dispatched the animal. They use a 22 caliber pistol blank. But they do not put it into a pistol, they put it in what's termed captive bolt gun. Firing a live round with a bullet would be too dangerous in a meat factory, and any lead fragments might end up in the meat as head meat and jowls are used in various products. The captive bolt is shaped like a long bolt with a big nut welded on the end. They place the gun on the skull and fire. The bottom of the bolt enters the pig's head about an inch or so but stops from going any farther by the wide nut at the top that can't fit through the short barrel. Then a spring automatically withdraws it from the skull. It makes for a safe, clean kill."

Jim continued "I had forgot all about my summer job until this afternoon when dozing a little. I had reentered the passenger car began to look around where the calliope would go. I saw the plywood which covered that area and that it was fastened to a frame by Phillips screws, and there was one regular screw also. It was at the part that would have been directly facing Matt's head. Unlike the Phillips, it jiggled around a bit as the train swayed. Why? I wondered. The construction of that plywood covering was amateurish. It has places it did not come together well so I was able to peer inside and as the other side was against a window, I had light enough to see. I saw a small piston, like a little brother to the large one on the engine itself. I thought of the 160 pounds of steam pressure and how it could be multiplied by the area of the piston in the expansion cylinder. The 3 or 4 inch cylinder I saw, could generate 1 or 2 thousands of pounds of force from that steam, and the steel levers attached to its piston could multiple and focus that force into a short distance of a few inches. Considering the diameter of a 32 slug, that's a tremendous magnification onto a slug a third of an inch in diameter. You see, it's all about pressures, areas, volumes and lengths with steam."

Jim paused to let that settle in, then began again "Now a captive bolt would certainly kill Matt, but when the autopsy was done there would be no bullet. That would not work for the killer. So there must have been a 32 bullet on the end of the fake screw. The screw and the bullet both recessed flush with the plywood to avoid notice. If that were the case, the forensics would have to do ballistics on the bullet and gun to get a match. That meant the gun would have had to fire that bullet previously into a soft substance to retrieve the slug undamaged. A large amount of feathers would work as would sponges, anything soft and giving and in quantity would work. It would be a relatively simple matter to retrieve the spent bullet, mount it to the captive bolt, then trigger the steam mechanism with an all or nothing quick release valve exactly when the gunshot was heard. If not heard, then when it was happening. After all, this little mystery play was a twice a week job that always occurred at the curve in the tunnel. Anytime within 5 or 10 seconds would work in that darkness and the hiss of the released steam would just blend in with the engines hissing steam and screeching wheels."

Jim paused momentarily again. Continuing he added "The 32 slug, now with the right ballistic profile to match the pistol, would be pushed into the head with bone crushing force, just like if fired from the pistol, and when the captive bolt automatically withdrew the slug would be left inside the brain where the coroner will retrieve it later today and find it matches the pistol in your possession, the one in which Kayla fired a blank a few hours ago. You see, James the porter could not have organized this. He had possession of the pistol only right before and after the mystery play. He had not the opportunity to fire a live round then retrieve the spent slug. He is innocent and caught in the middle."

Jim turned and looked at Kayla. "Kayla also is innocent. She is a mere unknowing patsy, as all patsies are. She has been set up to take the fall. She had no access to the pistol except during the performance, she lacks confirmable motive. All suggestions she had a motive, such as abuse, have come from the real murderer who has been trying to communicate her guilt with body language during the past quarter hour. No, it was not Kayla, neither accidentally nor intentionally. She was just the patsy the murderer had selected to take the blame. Whether the police would think it an accident or murder, whether the police would think the patsy acted alone or with the Porter, Al would not care. It is Al Bjarus who alone had motive of killing his business partner who was continuing to resist his pressure to sell out to Al. It is Al Bjarus alone who had access to the pistol away from the mystery play to get a fired slug into position at the head of a captive bolt. It is Al Bjarus who has left fingerprints all over the mechanical apparatus where the calliope would be installed. It is Al Bjarus whose prints you may find on the metal ring next to the steam valve between cars that triggers the instant steam release. That ring is the real trigger that fired the slug."

Silence. Jim sat down. Al Bjarus sat expressionless, motionless. He was in a state of shock from the impact of what he had just heard. He thought of making a run to the door but knew he would not be able to get past the other five men in the club car. His head spun with the impact of what had transpired. His carefully laid plan to become full owner of a growing business had just collapsed. He saw the detective and the Chief had finished whispering to each other. The Chief stood up and spoke. "Al Bjarus,

I am taking you into custody as a suspect in the murder of Matt Nekaltas. Officer, cuff him."

Laura felt vindicated in her belief in the innocence of Kayla. Kayla just looked on wide eyed in amazement and felt a great weight had been lifted from her. James just stared directly at his boss. Al Bjarus was taken from the club car into a waiting police car. Josh looked over the plywood box and Jim pointed out the steam valve and metal ring that operated what he was sure to be an all or nothing valve. Josh peered into the crack, saw the small piston and said "I'll get some tape and tape this whole area off. We don't want anyone touching anything until the boys from the crime lab dust it and take it apart. I see what you were saying about the dark marks on the upholstery now." Josh bent over to smell the area. "Smells burnt, like powder but the lab will document that, I'm sure. We owe you a lot for your observations. We would have spun our wheels on the Patsy and the Porter and I don't think we would have looked at Bjarus at all, I hate to admit. He would have had time to disassemble all the apparatus here and get away with murder."

Jim shook his head.

Josh continued "You'll have to testify in court, unless we get a guilty plea. But we do need you to give us a formal statement of what you just went over. You're a computer guy, eh?"

"A cyber security analyst."

"Well, you might consider getting a job as an investigator on a police department."

"I don't think so. I already miss my keyboard."

Laura, Kayla and James were outside waiting for Jim. "Laura, thanks for believing in me. I thought I had shot him" Kayla said.

"And thanks from me too. I don't know how I would have come out of all this." James said. "I just have to chalk this summer job up to experience."

"Sometimes that is all we can do, and sometimes that's enough" Laura concluded.

END

BONUS

The Verratens Call

A Brewpub Mystery

by

Fredric G. Bender

All rights reserved: no part of this publication may be reproduced or transmitted by any means without the prior permission of the author.

The Verratens Call is a work of fiction. Any resemblance to actual persons, living or dead, is purely coincidental. Any resemblance to actual brewpubs, breweries or bars is purely coincidental.

Beer

Beer is one of the oldest drinks humans ever produced, probably predating agriculture itself. Collections of wild grain placed in water to soften would have picked up wild yeast spores and fermented. The earliest archeologically provable beer is dated to 5,000 BC in Iran. 6,000 years ago Sumerians sipped beer through reed straws from a communal bowl, anyone like to share a pitcher and discuss it? A 3,900 year old poem to Ninkasi, goddess of beer, records the earliest recipe.

Malt Bill: Barley, Emmer wheat, Einkorn Wheat,

Yeast: Wild

Hops: What? Try cedar.

Adjuncts: Grapes, Honey

IBU (International Bitterness Units): Who knows

ABV (Alcohol By Volume): probably 3-6%

SRM (Standard Reference Method Color): Hard to say

Taste: Very bready as made from the practice of fermenting baked bread. Try blending some whole wheat bread with a growler then sip through a straw.

Carbonation: Some, rather warm and flat

Variations: Ninkasi as cup bearer brings joy and gladness, mixing beer, walking back and forth the keg on her hip making serving beer perfection.

The Verratens Call

The owner of the Dauphin Way Brewpub in Mobile, Alabama was in a celebratory mood. William Sanders with his wife Ava and their only child Carter were not only celebrating Carter's 22st birthday in the private dining room at the pub, but the opening of another tied pub for their beers and the reelection of Eva to the State House of Alabama.

"Cheers to Carter" his father toasted and held up a glass of Dauphin IPA.

"And many more" added his mother holding up a Dauphin Heritage Pilsner.

"Thank you" Carter said clicking his own glass of Irish Red to theirs.

"Someday son, when your get that law degree, we can build an empire, maybe not a big one, but a beer empire the likes of Alabama has never seen. The new place up in Huntsville, our 6th, ought to do well. By the time you are ready to join me here we ought be ready to begin opening in Georgia. Your mother has just told me before dinner that she received an email that the Alabama legislature will accept me next week as the head of the liaison committee between all the brewpubs in our State and the State regulators. There will be no pesky competitors hampering us anymore. That's a fine mother you have there, I couldn't have been accepted without her help behind the scenes."

Carter smiled. The future looked very rosy. With his mother in the State legislature running interference and blocking unfavorable legislation, it did seem his father's goal of a multistate chain of brewpubs would become a reality sooner rather than later. Carter's law degree was specializing in interstate commerce and his particular interest was Federal liquor laws and ways around them. That, coupled with his father's MBA and his mother's influence not only in the legislature but as a member of the state board of the church they attend allowed her great influence on a variety of issues. Being on the committee that regulated alcohol in the State, which still has several dry counties, and working through both church and state to open them up to beer while continuing to exclude wine and spirits has made her an important member of the family business's future.

The three were the only diners in the private dining room which was closed to others for the evening. After the salads and shrimp appetizers were finished, the waitress/bartender brought out three steak dinners. A 24 ounce T bone for the portly William Sanders, a 4 ounce filet for his wife Ava and a 16 ounce New York Strip for their son Carter. Life was better than good, it was great!

"At the rate of a new pub every three months, we ought to have finished up the expansion in Alabama in less than two years. I have a meeting Monday morning with some brewery specialists to come up with a design to triple our capacity. It'll include a bottling line. We have to increase production before we start selling to outlets outside our pubs" Mr. Sanders said.

"Have you finalized anything with the convenience stores yet?" Carter asked.

"Not yet. But several have basically agreed to carry Dauphin Way beers when we have the bottling line up and running" the father said.

"And I'm working on legislation to increase the alcohol level in beer sold in them" Carter's mother added.

Carter smiled, cut off another bite of steak, then said "What about getting some of those dry counties to go wet? Any movement on that?" Carter asked his mom.

"That's a tough nut to crack. But I think I've made a little progress. Very slow though and I can't promise anything yet" Ava responded.

"What's your current approach? I remember the last one hit a brick wall" Carter asked.

"Trying to get interest in a bill that would tie state financial support of private faith based schools tied to allowing low alcohol beer only to be sold there."

"That's a start if you can pull it off" the father said, "Just get it open a crack at first, then widen it later on."

The dinner was over and dessert was served. William and son Carter each lit up cigars after finishing their moon pie ala modes and Eva lit a cigarette when done with her raspberry gateau. The family always enjoyed a smoke to go with their after dinner coffee. Their conversation continued now revolving over Carter's newest girlfriend he met at the university.

The waitress entered the private dining room and waited to be recognized. Mr. Sanders turned and said "Yes? What is it?"

"Pardon my interruption but there are two young people, Jim and Laura, who say they are calling about something very important. Should I allow them in?"

"What is this important something?" asked Mr. Sanders.

"I don't know. They said it was confidential."

"Eva. Carter. You expecting anything tonight?" Each answered no. "Well, go ahead bring them in. I'm curious. This should be brief enough to send them on their way quickly" he laughed.

A few moments later the Verratens entered. "Mr. Sanders, William Sanders, I presume," said Jim.

"Yes, yes I am."

"I'm Jim and this is my wife Laura."

"We're just celebrating a birthday. May I get you something, a beer perhaps?"

"No, no thank you. Not tonight I'm afraid."

"Well then, what can I do for you?"

"A few hours ago, a young woman died at her home. A terrible tragedy."

"Sad, but what has this got to do with me?"

"Her name was Amelia Craft" Laura said.

"Is that name familiar to you Mr. Sanders" Jim asked.

"You don't have to answer anything to these two" Carter spoke out.

Looking at Carter, Jim said "And you are?"

"Carter Sanders"

"I see. I'll speak to you later. Mr. Sanders again, is that name at all familiar to you."

"Very vaguely."

"This is a picture of her" Laura said holding out her iPad for the father to see.

"She does look somewhat familiar. Amelia Craft you say. I believe she worked at one of my pubs, a bartender I believe."

"Worked?" Jim said.

"Yes. I had to fire her. Must be around a year ago. I have to check my payrolls. Why do you ask? I haven't seen her since then. I assure you of that."

"And why did you dismiss her?" Jim asked.

"Well, it's not any of your business. On what authority are you here asking these questions about a death I had nothing to do with."

"My wife and I have worked with the police many times. We are trying to clear up some loose ends surrounding Amelia Craft's unfortunate death."

"I see then. Well, I have nothing to hide. I believe I fired her for being a troublemaker and for some missing cash from the register."

"What kind of trouble was that" Jim asked.

"She was going around trying to get the other barmaids to hold out for more pay. Things like that."

"And the register money?" Jim asked.

"That, it turned out, was not her fault. It continued after I fired her until I fired another girl."

"I see."

"Did you ever give her a reference Mr. Sanders?" Laura asked.

"No. Why should I have. She was more trouble than she was worth the year she worked for me. One of those union types I suspect. This is my business and I don't want any damn union interfering with how I run it."

"Did you know what happened to her after you fired her?"

"No. And I don't care. I've told you everything about her employment with me. Now you are finished and can go."

"I'll say when I am finished Mr. Sanders. I still have business here. If you're as smart as I've heard you are, you'll cooperate. I'd hate to see some of what I've uncovered be in the newspapers this week" Jim said.

"Very well then. What have you uncovered when there is nothing to uncover?" Mr. Sanders patronizingly ssaid with a sigh.

"Oh, but there was. You see, I am heavily involved in cyber security. There is no password I cannot crack. No record I cannot access. The girl that died today, Amelia Craft, left a record as good as a diary, better in fact, in her email account. Better because that account included replies from others in most cases."

"I don't remember emailing her."

"No, I don't think you ever did."

"Then were done here tonight."

"As I said, I'll be the one who says when we are done, if you're smart."

"Go on then" Mr. Sanders agreed reluctantly.

Jim turned to his wife Laura and said "Perhaps you would like to speak with Mrs. Sanders now?"

"I do. I've been waiting." Laura turned to Mrs. Sanders and said "Mrs. Sanders, I've been looking at you record in the state legislature here in Alabama. I see your quite active."

"I am."

"The bills you sponsor or cosponsor have had quite a success rate."

"They have."

"They are an interesting mix. Many seem to focus on alcohol production and sales."

"They do."

"And that is not a conflict of interest to you?"

"Not at all. What I do is out in the open. People know my husband's business."

"I see. I assume that backroom trading in what they used to call the smoke filled rooms is not part of the public record."

"Never has been. Deals get made. Everybody knows that."

"I've seen not all of your bill's are with alcohol, a lot are about abortions."

"That's true. I have a deep faith and am very pro-life."

"Since Roe v Wade legal abortion was to be the law of the land. I see you've worked hard to reverse that in Alabama."

"I have, very hard. And I'm very proud of that."

"Your bills have made it all but impossible to get an abortion in Alabama. Bills restricting numbers of clinics, size of clinics, co-registrations with hospitals, zoning and so on."

"Laura my dear, abortion is legal in Alabama, the bills I worked to create and pass have just been rules for the safety of the mother and protecting the rights of the unborn."

"Yet they seem to result in the closure of most clinics in the state here."

Mrs. Sanders just smiled.

"Abortion may be theoretically legal here, but in practice it is virtually eliminated."

"Laura, I think you are a liberal. I fail to see your point. I am a faith based pro-life person and work hard for my beliefs. Bills I created, sponsored or cosponsored have been very successful in saving the lives of the unborn and I am very, very proud of that. If a girl gets pregnant before marriage, then she must do her duty to the unborn and bring it into the world."

"But what if she was raped? Even then?"

"Even then. That unborn is innocent. Punish the father on that if and when he is caught. A man like that is despicable, loathsome man who deserves nothing but an extensive jail sentence. Any family who brings up such an immoral man ought to be made public and shunned by the community. And any girl who lets herself get raped must suffer the consequence."

"Lets herself?" Laura asked.

"Yea. Lets herself" Mrs. Sanders repeated. "How many of the so called rape victims wore provocative clothing, how many got drunk at a party, how many went a little to far and things got out of control. They cry rape when they want an abortion. I see through that."

"That's all very interesting, Mrs. Sanders" Laura concluded looking back at Jim.

"I don't see what my legislative career or religious beliefs have to do with either of you. Where are you from anyway, you don't sound like it's Alabama?"

"I'll ask the questions Mrs. Sanders" Jim said sternly

"Carter, come here and see if you recognize this girl?" Jim said while Laura held out her iPad.

"No. No I don't. Who is she?" Carter asked.

"Carter, I am in no mood for your lies? Who is she?" Jim said forcefully.

"Now just you wait a minute. You have no call to disrespect my family as you are doing. I've had just about enough of your rudeness, from both of you" Mr. Sanders said.

Jim looked at William Sanders. "Mr. Sanders, I am merely stating facts. The lie of your son Carter has disrespected all of us gathered here, not I."

"How dare you!" added Mrs. Ava Sanders.

"Again Carter, have another look. Look closely this time. Do you recognize the girl this time?" Jim said.

"She looks a little familiar. I might have seen her around town. Maybe at my father's pubs somewhere, if that's the same picture you showed him a while ago" Cater said.

"It is. It is a picture of Amelia Craft. The girl who died recently. Did you know her well?" Jim asked Carter.

"No. Not at all."

"Then how do you explain this email?" Jim read from his iPad. "Carter, then that's a date. C U Friday at 8 Amelia."

"How did you get that email?" Carter asked.

"Simple. It was in her sent email box. Along with many others to you" Jim said.

"On what authority did you get access to her emails?" Carter asked.

"On my own. Remember I can hack into almost anything I want" Jim said.

"That's totally illegal. I ought to call the police right now and report you" Carter said.

"But you won't and you know why. So how well did you know the dead girl?" Jim asked.

"We had a couple of dates. You don't get to know someone well on a date or two."

"A couple usually means two. The email record shows more like every week for a few months."

"We were dating."

"Ah, now the truth emerges from hiding. And when did this relationship break off?" Jim asked.

"A while ago" Carter replied.

"Do I need to refresh your memory in front of your parents?" Jim said.

"We broke up two months ago" Carter replied.

"And what was the reason?"

"I don't think that is any of your business."

"We have made it our business" Jim replied. Carter did not reply. "The email record shows the relationship ended after one particular evening. That was the evening when you took the girl against her wishes when you were drinking heavily. I will spare your parents the details that Amelia emailed to her mother and a few girlfriends. It seems she was a virgin until then."

"I didn't know that."

"She claimed to her mother that she told you so."

"Mere hearsay at this point" Carter added.

"It may not be legal but it is damning. Did you know that Amelia and her family were preparing to file a rape charge against you?"

"I did not. That would be preposterous."

"Did you know the result of your action was a pregnancy?"

"Preposterous."

"You were told that by Amelia, we have that in an email she sent to you" Laura said.

"Damn your infusion into our private lives" Carter replied.

"In fact, Carter, Amelia wrote to you several times about it, and you always responded with the same thing. You denied it was rape and you told her to get an abortion."

"What!" Mrs. Sanders yelled. "It can't be so."

"Do you want to see the email?" Laura asked the mother.

"I do." After reading it the mother said "Carter, you were raised better than this. My own son. Suggesting a girl get an abortion."

"Not just any girl, Mrs. Sanders, the mother of your grandchild" Laura said.

"There is no proof of that" she said in denial.

"There will be soon. You see, Amelia Craft did indeed seek out an abortion, but could not find a clinic to go to. However, she did find what is called a 'back alley abortionist'. The procedure did not go well; this is how she died. She bled to death afterwards."

The entire family was silent in shock.

"I can tell you that Amelia's mother is working now with the police to have DNA done on the aborted fetus to support a lawsuit against Carter" Laura added.

"You cannot make a person testify against himself. I will never give a DNA sample" Carter said.

"You don't have to. We have a hair sample from your trip to the barber this morning. A haircut for your birthday no doubt."

"Carter, how could you put our business, your mother's career and your career in jeopardy like that" Mr. Sanders shouted.

"You two are always so prim and proper, sneaking around on this and that, twisting arms here and there, always concocting and conniving. Don't look at me like that. Mother, if you had never passed those abortion restrictions, Amelia would be alive now. It's all your fault" Carter said.

"Now Son, I want you to show respect for your mother. You are not permitted to talk to her like that" Mr. Sanders said.

"I'm not permitted? I'm not permitted! That's a damn joke. I'm not a little boy anymore. Mother, not me is responsible for her death. And yes, I knew her, I knew her well. I knew she could not get a job after you fired her. Your talking around town poisoned the well for her. No one wanted to take a chance on a petty thief" Carter said.

"She was not the thief. She didn't take money from the bar till. I fired the one that did" Mr. Sanders said.

"Yes. who knew that? Did you approach her, apologize and give her a reference then? Or just let the rumors persist. Was it too much trouble to set the record straight? Was it you just didn't want to appear wrong for once in your perfect life?" Carter said.

"That's enough Carter" the mother said. "I don't take any responsibility for the girl's death. She could have had the baby."

"Hard to accept Mom? Your perfect little boy spread some wild oats and got caught. What now? 'Punish the father if and when he is caught. That kind of man is despicable, loathsome. One who deserves nothing but an extensive jail term.' And Oh, before I forget 'Any family who brings up such an immoral man ought to be made public and shunned by the community.' So now what? Are you going to stand by your earlier words now that it is in our lap?" Carter pressed.

Mrs. Sanders broke down in tears as both men stared into the distance. Mr. Sanders turned to speak with Jim and Laura. They were not to be seen. He looked around the room. They were not there. He went outside and found out that they had left minutes earlier. He sat in a chair and slumped over. "Are you OK Mr. Sanders? Would you like a glass of water?" the barmaid asked.

END

The Verratens Call was not a murder mystery, or was it? It all depends on your point of view. The author suggests that if the reader was at all interested or intrigued by the story then they might especially enjoy the movie "An Inspector Calls" on Amazon Prime or any of the books of that title including a graphic novel, radio play and play version.

"An Inspector Calls" was written as a play by J B Priestley first published in 1947 in England. It has won the 1993 Laurence Olivier Award, the 1994 Drama Desk Award and the 1994 Tony Award; all for Best Revival of a Play.

Made in the USA
Columbia, SC
17 June 2021